the Dream Merchant Saga

BOOK ONE
the Magic Crystal

Written by
L.T. Suzuki
in collaboration with
Nia Suzuki-White

Book Cover, graphic design and layout:
Scott White
Shinobi Creative Services
www.shinobicreativeservices.com

Acknowledgements

A special thank you to my husband, Scott
for helping make this book a reality.

To my nephew, Tyler Nelson
for taking the time to proofread this story.

To Corbin Silverthorn of Silverthorn Press
for the use of his surname!

Dedications

This story is for all my
nieces & nephews, near and far!
Love, Lorna

To all my good friends and
the great teachers at
Coast Meridian Elementary School.
Thank you for keeping me inspired
and wanting to do my best!
With love & respect, Nia

Contents

Prologue

A hero, a villain, a curse and a quest: all the elements of a classic fairytale, right?

To be perfectly honest, this story is not your typical, run-of-the-mill fairytale. Most begin with *'once upon a time in a land far, far away...'* and usually ends with *'and they lived happily ever after'*, but if you dare read on, you will soon discover this neither begins nor necessarily ends in this manner.

Now, in this mystical world lives the most unusual assortment of Elves, Wizards, dragons and other strange and magical creatures, but this particular story revolves around one beautiful, young princess. And just like this tale, she is far from typical. Unfortunately for her, this adventure, or misadventure, depending upon your point of view, all begins at her royal residence of Pepperton Palace.

Like a magnificent jewel crowning a great hill overlooking this peaceful, bucolic kingdom, the palace rises above the tallest trees and certainly overshadows all other man-made structures. However, if you peer behind the imposing walls, glance beyond the grand gardens of meticulously pruned boxwood hedges to look within these stately halls and palatial chambers of the castle keep, a seemingly perfect existence belies a less-than-perfect life.

And as this is a tale about imperfect people living imperfect lives, dreaming of greater things that might make them perfect one day, let us begin this saga with Rose-alyn Beatrice Elizabeth Wilhemina Pepperton, or more simply, Princess Rose.

A Grand Plan

"Ooow! You are torturing me!"

These are the pained and angry words that echo across the fair lands of Fleetwood to break the tranquil dawn and accost early morning travellers near and far. No, it is not the anguished wails of a prisoner being lashed deep within a castle dungeon; it is merely Princess Rose being readied to meet the day.

Her shrill squeals of protest laced with an equal measure of indignation easily eclipsed the sounds of chattering teeth and the clattering of knees knocking together in fear as her personal attendants: Mildred, Alice and Evelyn endured the Princess' angry tirade.

Sadly, it had become a daily ritual for these three ladies to tolerate, as best they could, these unruly outbursts as they attempted to brush the Princess' flaxen tresses after a night of sleep.

"You useless fool!" scolded Rose, her alabaster complexion turning many shades of red as her perfect features grimaced. "You must be gentle with me. Being a princess, I am as delicate as a peach!"

"A *rotten* peach, I'd say!" Alice muttered beneath her breath as she readied a gown for her to wear.

"I am sorry, Princess Rose," apologized the youngest of the handmaidens. Poor Evelyn had the misfortune of drawing the short straw amongst her peers this morning and was relegated to the task of brushing the Princess' hair. "I am trying to be gentle."

"Well, not gentle enough!" snapped Rose; snatching the brush from Evelyn's trembling hands. "You are utterly useless! If you cannot handle this brush as you should, then surely you have it in you to hold this looking glass for me."

"Of course, my lady," responded Evelyn, shrinking beneath Rose's angry scowl and scathing tone as she attempted to hold the mirror steady while the Princess preened.

As the morning sun bathed the bedchamber in a warm, golden hue to wash the Princess in its glorious light, Rose admired her features: the flawless, porcelain skin; the dewy lips; the pert, little nose and the striking violet eyes accentuated by impeccably plucked and shaped brows.

"I look lovely!" declared Rose, smiling demurely at the reflection she so admired as Evelyn tried to hold the mirror just so.

Soliciting no words to confirm this declaration, Rose cleared her throat as she announced once again and a little louder, *"I look lovely!"*

"Ye- yes, you do, my lady," squeaked Evelyn.

"Then say it! Do not stammer like a complete ninny. State the obvious," ordered Rose, glaring at the three harried servants.

"You look lovely!" chimed the trio, smiling with forced affability as they cowed yet again to her demands.

"You are absolutely correct!" chirped Rose, sweeping the soft boar bristles through the golden strands that glimmered in the sun. "Mind you, I do not like this light. It makes my skin look sallow. Do something about this light, Gwendolyn."

"Evelyn, my lady." A timid voice whispered from behind the looking glass.

"What did you say?" snorted Rose, her nerves bristling with impatience.

"Evelyn, my lady. My name is Evelyn." She remained hidden behind the mirror, too nervous to correct the Princess to her face.

Rose scowled in annoyance as she snapped at the girl, "Gwendolyn, Evelyn, dolt, fool... I shall call you whatever I please! I am a princess, after all."

"Yes, my lady, however, if this light does not please you, then perhaps you should move away from the sun?" suggested Evelyn. Her slight frame seemed to shrink all the more under Rose's harsh words.

"The sun should move for *me!*" grunted the Princess, scrutinizing the pores on her cheeks that became more visible in this light. "It is unbecoming on my natural skin tone."

"I dare say, my lady, it gives your lovely complexion a warm, sun-kissed glow," offered Mildred, the oldest of the three servants. However, these kind words did little to pacify the Princess.

"Well, I do not like it! I am supposed to be the *fairest* in all the lands," pouted Rose, her feet stomping the floor like a spoiled child. "It makes me look like a lowly commoner who had spent too many days toiling in the fields under the brutal summer sun."

"Well, this should do wonders for you, my lady," offered Alice, holding up a silk and crinoline gown. It was adorned with dainty bows and encrusted with glistening crystal beads. "There is not one commoner I know of who owns a dress as lovely as this."

Rose's perfect nose wrinkled in disgust as her dainty, well-manicured hands that had never known a day of work waved off the gown. "That will simply not do!"

"But it is absolutely beautiful," insisted Alice, admiring the dress she had selected from Rose's extensive wardrobe.

"It is *old*."

"You have worn it only once, for your father's birthday gala but two months ago," reminded Alice.

"I know when that was. And if I've worn it once, then consider it old," reasoned Rose, pushing the gown away with certain disdain. "Find me something new to wear!"

"But all the gowns in your wardrobe have been worn at least once," responded Mildred, her hands rifling through the racks of fine dresses custom designed for every occasion imaginable. "And they are all in absolutely perfect condition!"

"That may be so, but I want some new gowns made for me."

"But that will take time," groaned Mildred, exasperated by this new order. "And the dressmaker, she is already busy creating the special gown for your sixteenth birthday celebration."

"*But, but, but!*" snapped Rose. "The only *butt* you will have to consider is my silk brocade slipper to your backside if you do not make it so! Now get me a new wardrobe! Do so now!"

"Yes, my lady," gulped Mildred, as she motioned for Evelyn and Alice to back away to the door. It was as though they were trying to escape from a frothing mad, pit bull terrier waiting to attack. "Right away, my lady."

"And be quick about it!" growled the Princess.

With frightening accuracy, Rose lobbed one of her shoes at the door just as it slammed shut behind the fleeing women. With such an accurate aim that comes with years of practice, the heel of this shoe added to the grouping of indentations marring the door.

Rose listened for a moment. She could hear her attendants as they rushed off, scurrying away down the corridor.

Alone with nothing more to comfort her than the grand opulence of her bedchamber, Rose slumped down on the plump, goose-down counterpane, leaning dejectedly against the gilded post of her elegant canopy bed. The Princess sulked, plucking at the crystal beads. Each one had been painstakingly hand-sewn by the royal dressmaker, but they were now doomed to meet the floor as the Princess brooded.

"I suppose this will have do for today," whined Rose, resigning to the fact she would be condemned to wearing this glistening *rag* until some new gowns were made for her.

☙ ☙ ☙

"Spoiled little snip!" Mildred grumbled in resentment as she guided Evelyn and Alice back to the kitchen to complete breakfast preparations. She charged away, waddling as fast as her short, stout legs could carry her round, plump body from the royal bedchamber, lest Rose summoned them back to verbally accost them again.

"You shouldn't say such things about the Princess, Miss Mildred," scolded Evelyn, shaking her head in disapproval.

"I know," admitted Mildred, with a disheartened sigh. "But I speak the truth."

"No, you are not," corrected Alice, still attempting to shake off the *royal* treatment dispensed by the Princess. The tall, thin woman stared down her long, narrow nose to gaze at Mildred. "If you were speaking the truth, you would be calling the Princess a spoiled rotten, ungrateful, insensitive brat who only knows how to bully and manipulate those around her, family included, to get her way!"

"Now, now, Miss Alice, I believe you're exaggerating!" declared Evelyn. "I know the Princess can be demanding at times, but she is young, after all."

"Don't you go making excuses for the Princess! With each passing year she becomes more impertinent, ruder than rude and – and –," stammered Mildred, trembling with anger as she searched for all the proper adjectives to describe the Princess. "And more!"

"You're her same age, Evelyn, but you have enough sense to treat others with decency," explained Alice. "You would think with her upbringing and privileged lifestyle, the Princess would be the very definition of diplomacy and civility. There are times when I cannot believe she is her mother's daughter!"

"That is rather harsh," responded Evelyn, cringing under Alice's sharp, unforgiving tone.

"You are relatively new to the palace staff, my dear girl," reminded Alice, patting Evelyn sympathetically on her shoulder. "However, if this is your mindset where she is concerned, you will be considered gullible, foolish or both. You do not know the Princess as we do. Regrettably for us, we know her all too well."

"True, you both have been in service much longer," conceded Evelyn, "but it may very well be that Princess Rose has had a hard life nonetheless."

Mildred and Alice stopped dead in their tracks. They stared wide-eyed with mouths agape as though the young girl's innocent words were a rude slap to the face. This moment of stunned silence was followed by a burst of laughter as the older women slapped their knees, guffawing heartily.

"My dear, sweet Evelyn, are you mad?" snorted Mildred; her tearing eyes rolling in dismay. "The only thing that pampered Princess has ever experienced that was hard had been cold toast too lightly buttered!"

"Or a tasty dessert that sat in the icebox for too long, becoming hard with the cold to bother her royal sweet tooth," scoffed Alice.

"You make Princess Rose sound so very spoiled."

"She *is* spoiled!" exclaimed Alice and Mildred, in total agreement.

"And in your short time here, you have experienced only a small taste of her obnoxious behaviour," warned Alice.

"But suppose her life has been hard in other ways," reasoned Evelyn, still attempting to find some good in the Princess.

"Oh yes, being waited on hand and foot; having servants at her constant beck and call," teased Mildred.

"Having her every whim catered to," added Alice, her thin lips pursing together in annoyance as her pinched nostrils flared ever so slightly. "I only wish my life was even half as *hard* as that!"

"The Princess has all these things and more, but perhaps she is lacking in other areas of her life," responded the kind-hearted Evelyn.

"The only thing she is lacking in is some good old-fashioned discipline!" grunted Mildred. "If the Princess was my daughter – "

"Heaven forbid!" interjected Alice, grimacing at the very thought.

"As I was saying," continued Mildred, her pudgy finger pressing against her plump lips as she considered Rose, "the young Princess would be learning some manners from me if she were my daughter."

"Well, if you ask me, I would say she is lacking in a good dose of common sense," decided Alice.

"There you go then! How can you be so hard on Princess Rose?" asked Evelyn, blinking innocently as she pondered this mystery.

"She makes it all too easy, my dear," responded Mildred, as she and Alice burst into a fit of giggles as they rounded the corridor into the dining hall.

"Good morning, ladies," greeted Queen Beatrice.

They jumped with a start, immediately recognizing the Queen's voice.

"Good morning, Your Majesty!" All three offered their salutations as they respectfully bowed before her.

"You must be having a wonderful start to your day," commented Beatrice. "You ladies are in such a jovial mood this morning."

"We are?" responded Mildred, her eyes arching up in surprise at this remark.

"Yes, I heard laughter coming from down the corridor. Perhaps my ears deceived me, but I was certain it was you three."

"You heard correctly, Your Majesty," assured Alice, her sharp features becoming more accentuated as her face flushed with embarrassment.

"Lovely!" exclaimed Beatrice, as she nodded in approval. "It is wonderful to hear such joy so early in the day."

"Wonderful, indeed," agreed Mildred.

"However, I was certain you had been tending to my daughter," said Beatrice, smiling politely as she studied the worried faces before her.

"That, we were," admitted Alice.

All members of the domestic staff had a soft spot for Queen Beatrice and her husband, King William. They truly respected and honoured the royal couple, but the Princess, because of her demanding and forceful ways, only garnered respect because of her title. Out of love and loyalty to the monarchs, the staff felt compelled to downplay the Princess' abrasive nature.

"Odd…" sighed the Queen. "I just know how difficult my daughter can be at times. She is not in the best of moods first thing in the morning."

"Oh, not Princess Rose!" exclaimed Mildred, her pudgy, nails-chewed-to-the-quick fingers waving off the Queen's concern as Beatrice headed to the breakfast table to wait for the King and Rose to join her. "Your daughter was not being difficult at all. She's a royal charmer, she is!"

"A royal *deadbeat* is more like it." Alice muttered beneath her breath as Evelyn's brows discreetly knitted into a frown of disapproval.

"You were saying?" questioned Beatrice, staring over at Alice.

"It was nothing, Your Majesty," replied Alice. "I was just saying your daughter is *loyal* and *upbeat*."

"You are too kind, Alice."

"Oh no, Your Majesty, not at all!" exclaimed Alice.

"Oh yes, and I do know what I speak of," admitted Beatrice.

"Pardon me, Your Majesty, but may we be excused?" asked Mildred. "We were just on our way to complete breakfast preparations."

"Of course, Mildred." The Queen nodded in approval. "And please make sure you serve up a healthy portion of stewed prunes with my daughter's breakfast."

"I mean no disrespect, but are you sure of this, Your Majesty?" questioned Mildred. "The Princess always raises such a fuss when you make her eat prunes."

"I am quite sure," responded the Queen. "One day she will thank me for promoting healthy eating habits in her quest to stay regular."

"Nothing wrong with that!" agreed Mildred, but she was more pleased the Princess would be forced to grovel, whine and fuss before finally being made to eat the dreaded prunes anyway. She curtsied once more before herding Alice and Evelyn to the kitchen.

And such was the daily routine in Pepperton Palace. As the demands of the day mounted, Princess Rose made sure to add to them.

"Bloody hell!" cursed Mildred. She clutched her heart, dropping the bucket and mop as an anxious face suddenly appeared from behind the collection of brooms and other cleaning tools. "Tagius Oliver Yairet, what in heaven's name are you doing in this closet?"

For a fleeting instant, the young man cringed. His father used to address him by his full name. Of course, that was only when he was in big trouble, but it was long ago since he last heard his father's voice echoing through the corridors of this great palace.

"Shhh!" Tag, as he was usually called, pressed a finger to his lips! Remaining crouched on the floor amongst the clutter, he answered in a hushed voice, "I'm hiding."

"No... You don't say! I thought you were writing the next great literary masterpiece," rebuked the matronly woman. "Of course, you're hiding!"

"Keep your voice down, Millie," ordered Tag, glancing nervously around the woman's rotund form. "I don't want her to find me."

"*Her?*" repeated Mildred, her curious eyes darting about.

"You know whom I speak of," said Tag, his words matter-of-fact. "The royal Princess Pain in the Patootie!"

"Well, I shall make you a deal, young sir," offered Mildred, collecting her mop and bucket from the floor. "I won't tell if you don't."

"You've got a good heart, Millie," praised Tag, slouching against the wall of the closet as he relaxed. "In fact, you've got such a kind heart, I'm sure you won't mind giving me one of those biscuits to eat while I bide my time in here."

She gazed at Tag's eyes as they stared hungrily at the leftovers on the kitchen table.

"Feeling a bit peckish, are we?"

"Yes, ma'am," admitted Tag.

"I suppose it won't hurt. It'll only be added to the pigs' slop anyway," decided Mildred. Snatching up two buttery biscuits, she thrust her hand through the stand of the broom and mop handles to pass the food on to him.

"Thanks, Millie." Tag nodded in appreciation.

"You are most welcome, young sir. And I won't breathe word as to your whereabouts either."

"I'd appreciate that," said Tag, his teeth sinking into the flaky crust of the round, crumbly biscuit.

"The door... Open or closed?"

"Closed, please," replied Tag, using his finger to steer a stray crumb back into his mouth.

"As you wish."

Alone in the clutter with nothing more than the seam of light pouring in from between the door and the floor to illuminate this tiny room, Tag enjoyed his solitude. He happily munched on the biscuits as he listened for the hard, sharp telltale sounds of heels striking against the flagstone floor to forewarn him of impending doom.

He took the opportunity to recall yesterday's studies: lessons in the language arts, mathematics and history he had learned on the sly. Restricted by what he could see and hear through the open window of the palace library where Princess Rose begrudgingly endured the intellectual droning of the scholars appointed to educate her, the young man soaked up this knowledge. He craved and revelled in what details the Princess considered irrelevant and mundane for a young lady of her royal standing.

In a roundabout way, Tag felt it was fair compensation for having his plans of following in his father's footsteps rudely thwarted by the Princess. Still, he could not deny he yearned to learn all he could of the knighthood, taking up a broken broom handle in place of his father's sword to assault the neighbouring farmers' scarecrows to practice his skills with this *weapon*.

Happily surrounded by his many thoughts as he sat on the hard floor of this cramped, dim-lit closet, he brushed the crumbs from his shirt.

"Here you go, Squeakers," whispered Tag. He placed these morsels in front of a hole in the corner of the room for the resident kitchen mouse to feast on.

Now, had this been any other mouse, Tag would not have bothered with this small gesture of kindness, however this rodent was unique. A small, white star on its brown forehead made it stand out from all the others Tag had seen darting about on the palace grounds. This clever mouse had managed to elude every trap ever set, not to mention the hungry cat that vigilantly patrolled the kitchen, pantry and root cellar. For this reason, Tag felt inclined to reward the tiny creature for its ingenuity and will to survive in spite of the odds.

Tag suddenly froze.

The hairs on the back of his neck stood up. Crouching motionless, his ears strained to hear through the closed door.

"Damn it all!" Tag cursed beneath his breath as the distinct *click, click, click* of designer heels striking against the stone flooring echoed and reverberated through the ground to rattle his nerves. "Why can she not leave me be?"

"Where is he?" Rose demanded to know, her arms crossing her chest as the toe of her shoe tapped impatiently on the freshly cleaned floor.

"Pardon me, my lady?" responded Mildred, barely glancing up as she continued her chores.

Grabbing the mop in Mildred's hands to make her stop cleaning, Rose snapped at her, "Where is he?"

"Whom do you speak of, my lady?" asked Mildred, attempting to maintain her composure even as she winced under the Princess' sharp tone.

"You know exactly whom I speak of! Now where is the court jester?"

"Which one?" probed Mildred.

"*My* jester! Tag, of course. Now, where is he hiding?"

"Young Master Yairet can be anywhere in the palace, my lady," replied Mildred. Deliberately slapping the sopping wet mop against the floor, she knew the Princess would back away than to get her precious shoes wet with dirty water.

"That is rather vague," pouted Rose. "The palace is a big place."

"Indeed, it is," agreed Mildred, glancing about the spacious royal residence. "I suggest you keep looking, my lady."

"And you have not seen Tag?" probed Rose, staring doubtfully at the domestic help as Mildred collected the bucket.

"Not since earlier this morning," answered Mildred. She did not feel an ounce of guilt in disclosing this information, for in her mind, she spoke the truth. She just chose not to be specific on how recent it was.

"Come out, come out wherever you are," chirped Rose, ignoring Mildred as she left to toss the dirty water.

The Princess' inquisitive eyes searched about, scrutinizing all the possible hiding places in this usually bustling kitchen.

Her syrupy sweet voice made Tag cringe, shuddering involuntarily as he spied her through the keyhole.

"What are you staring at?" grumbled Rose. Snatching up a wooden mixing spoon from the table, she hurled it at the grey tomcat curled up by the fireplace.

The accosted feline meowed in protest, its amber eyes flashing in resentment as it fled her wrath. Tag breathed a sigh of relief as he observed the Princess sulk in defeat, stomping off as she departed from the kitchen.

All was quiet as he listened and watched.

Tag suddenly yelped in surprise. One of those unmistakable violet eyes abruptly appeared at the keyhole to stare back at him, catching him completely off guard.

"Ah-ha! I knew I would find you!" exclaimed Rose, her dainty hands clapping together in glee. She whipped the door open, peering into the shadows to spy upon Tag's disgruntled face. His eyes seemed to flash a deeper shade of blue as his hand swept back his chestnut hair he had hoped would help to conceal him in the darkness of his solitude.

"Come out of the closet," demanded Rose. Her index finger flexed, motioning for Tag to come hither.

"I'd rather not."

"This is an *order*, not a suggestion," insisted the Princess. "Now step out."

"Not ready to."

"You will do as I say," demanded Rose, her hands rolling into tight fists that threatened of a pummelling. "Now get out of the closet."

"Fine," grunted Tag, pushing aside the mop and broom handles.

"What were you doing in there? You were not hiding from me, were you?" questioned Rose, watching as the young man brushed the dust from his clothes.

"Indeed, I was."

"How dare you?" scolded Rose, appalled by his candid admission. "Who are you to think you can avoid me?"

"You were the one to demand I play hide-and-seek, not me, Princess Rose," explained Tag.

"That was two days ago."

"I know. You said I'd be made to play until *you* saw fit to end the game. You never said it was over, ergo, I remained in hiding. And I was quite enjoying myself."

"In there?" sniffed Rose, staring into the dusty, cramped closet.

"Loved the company," responded Tag. His voice was laced with sarcasm as he gave the Princess a smug grin.

"But you were alone." She was momentarily baffled by his words.

"I know."

Rose's eyes flashed with anger, and just as suddenly, they cooled as she giggled one of those irritatingly high-pitched, girlish giggles, "Oh, you were just teasing me."

Before Tag could respond, Rose unleashed a scream of fright to make the blood in his veins run cold. She hastily shoved the boy aside as she scrambled to stand on a stool.

"A mouse!" shrieked the Princess, pushing Tag toward the little creature trying to squeeze under the door to take refuge in the closet.

"So it is," agreed Tag, kneeling down to observe the tiny rodent squirming to wriggle between this narrow gap.

"Don't just stare at it! Do something!" demanded Rose. She quickly hiked up the hem of her gown to make sure the little creature had no way of reaching her. "Kill it!"

"It is only a mouse," rebuked Tag, "a harmless, little mouse."

The end of a broom suddenly swung down.

"Stop it!" shouted Tag, using one hand to intercept the blow as he used the other to scoop up the frightened creature. "It's only Squeakers."

"Make it stop squeaking!" demanded Rose. She backed away from the rodent as it eagerly sniffed the boy's hand. "Give it the broom! And use it with gusto!"

"Her name is Squeakers," explained Tag. He pushed away the broom the Princess was more than willing to use on the little animal. "She's my pet."

"Your *pet?*" gasped Rose, her face contorting in utter disgust as she watched the mouse climb the boy's arm up to his shoulder. "It is a filthy, little rodent!"

"She is small and a rodent, but she is not filthy," countered Tag, speaking with all certainty. "In fact, this particular mouse is cleaner than some people I know."

"That is probably true, but all it means is that you know some very filthy people. Now, be done with that disgusting vermin before it spreads some dreadful disease and kills us all!"

"Kill us?" groaned Tag, his eyes rolling in exasperation. "Mark my words, Princess, there may come a day this little mouse will save your life."

"And *you* mark *my* words, Tagius *Oddball* Yairet, like that will ever happen! What kind of fool do you take me for, anyway?" admonished the Princess. "That is a furry, little disease ball."

Squeakers calmly sat on the boy's shoulder, its tiny whiskers quivering with nervous energy as it sniffed Tag's earlobe.

"Just because she is insignificant to you, it does not mean Squeakers is nothing to me," grunted Tag, thoroughly annoyed by Rose's condescending attitude.

"It is only a mouse, for pity's sake!" rebuked Rose, cringing as she watched Squeakers' tiny paws feel about for secure footing on Tag's vest. "Kill the bloody thing!"

"Why? She's done nothing to you."

"Oh yes, it has," argued Rose, backing away with broom in hand. "I find that creature offensive! That loathsome animal deserves to die."

"I am sure there are those out there who find *you* offensive, but do you deserve to die?" countered Tag, lowering Squeakers to the floor so she could make good her escape.

"I cannot believe you just compared me to that revolting vermin!" exclaimed Rose. Her beautiful face abruptly scowled, taking on a hard edge as she absorbed the sting of Tag's insult. "And who finds me offensive? I want names!"

"Why? So you can have those people killed, too?" ridiculed Tag, shaking his head in dismay as he waited for Squeakers to disappear into the closet.

"Say… You were speaking in jest! After all, *everybody* loves me."

"Of course they do," said Tag, with a dreary sigh. "And while you bask in the glow of self-adoration, I really must be off."

"Not so fast," said Rose, pushing Tag out of the kitchen.

"Where are we going?"

"Follow me," ordered the Princess, steering the reluctant young man down the corridor.

"*Follow?* That'd imply you would be in front of me, leading the way," corrected Tag, stumbling along as she prodded him on. "Not herding me like an old goat."

"Never mind that, I have a grand plan," announced Rose, her eyes gleaming with mischief.

"A plan or a *scheme*, for there is a difference you know?"

"What difference does that make?" sniffed Rose. "The only thing that truly matters is that I benefit from it."

"Of course," sighed Tag. "But what does this have to do with me?"

"Plenty! I need you to help me."

"To do what?"

"I need you to get me a tooth."

"A *tooth?*" gasped Tag, frowning in confusion. "Even though you're a princess, I'm not about to give you one of my teeth!"

"Keep your voice down. And who said I wanted one of your rotters?" grunted Rose, grimacing in disgust. "I want a perfect, little baby tooth."

"Don't you have still have a whole bunch of them in that mouth of yours?"

"You fool! I am nearing my sixteenth birthday," muttered Rose, her hands on the curves of her hips to accentuate her blossoming feminine form. "I am almost a woman, so of course I have no baby teeth left in my mouth."

"Pity," said Tag, backing away from her. "Well, there goes your grand plan. Tootle-loo! See you later, Princess."

"Not so fast!" snapped Rose, seizing Tag by his ear. "I know where *you* can get one."

"*Me?*" He danced about on the tips of his toes as the Princess twisted a little more on his tender earlobe to make sure she had his undivided attention.

"Yes, you! Now, here is the plan. The scullery maid's boy, *what's-his-name* will be – "

"His name is Timothy," interjected Tag, annoyed the Princess never took the time to become personally acquainted with the palace staff.

"Yes, well… Timmy has a tooth that is coming loose. I want you to get it from him," demanded Rose.

"How do you suggest I do that?" questioned Tag.

"For some strange reason, the boy quite likes you. He will give that tooth if you ask it of him."

"And if he doesn't want to part with it, then what?"

"Then do what you must," replied the Princess, her shoulders shrugging with indifference.

"You will have me just snatch it from the boy's mouth?" gasped Tag, his eyes wide in disbelief.

"If he does not hand it over willingly, why not?" answered Rose, nodding enthusiastically.

"Because it is called *stealing*. Not to mention, assaulting the child to do so!"

"So what?"

"I will have you know, I do have some sense of honour and common decency!" declared Tag.

"You are not a knight. You are my court jester. Why would you have a need for honour when you do not even have dignity?"

"And *you* made sure of that," growled the young man, his hand slapping his forehead in frustration.

"My! You are bitter," noted Rose. "But it is a wasted emotion. A knight needs a sword and you do not have one, nor will you ever, since your father's weapon was lost."

"The point being, I refuse to steal the tooth, whether it was still lodged in his mouth, or not, just to appease you."

"Then make him give it to you," ordered Rose. "Tell him if he does not, you will tell the Queen you saw him nicking a bottle of wine from the cellar for his mother."

"But I didn't," argued Tag. "Something like that can get him *and* his mother expelled from the palace, or worse! And you know Timothy would never do something as underhanded as that."

"You might know that and I might know that, but my mother on the other hand... I do not believe the Queen knows the lowly, domestic staff as she should."

"Brilliant!" groaned Tag, throwing his hands up in exasperation.

"Yes, I am!" exclaimed Rose, nodding proudly.

"I was not speaking of you! And if I were, it was not meant as a compliment."

Rose's delicate brows furrowed in confusion as she asked: "So you refuse to carry out my order?"

"First, it was stealing. Now, it is extortion! Just what kind of princess are you?" questioned Tag, bewildered by her strange demand.

"I am the kind of princess who knows how to get what she wants, when she wants it. Now get me that tooth! Besides, I only want to *borrow* it, so it is not really stealing."

"Call it what you will, but I want no part in your deranged, little plot," declared Tag.

"But you must! And it is a *grand plan*, but I desperately need that tooth to make it so."

"Why? You want for naught. You're in no need of coins from the Tooth Fairy, or anyone else, for that matter."

"True," admitted Rose, her shoulders rolling in a shrug. "I just need to *speak* to the Tooth Fairy. The only way to make it happen is to lure her with a tooth."

"This is too bizarre. I'm afraid to ask what you intend to do with the Fairy once you meet her. In fact, I want nothing to do with whatever this plan is that you're hatching."

"You *will* help me!" declared Rose, her feet stamping in defiance.

"Why should I?" snapped Tag, thoroughly annoyed by her willfulness and outrageous demands.

"Because I say so. And as you so conveniently forgot, you are a *nobody* and I am a *princess,* so there! Besides, if you do not, it is one more day you will have to endure as my court jester. At the rate you are going, you may as well kiss the knighthood good-bye, for soon, you will be too old to be a squire to any knight!"

The same panic he felt in his heart when he was a boy of ten surfaced once more. That was the fateful day Princess Rose demanded he be removed from his post as his father's page because she wanted to be amused.

Tag's father, the captain of the King's army, at first agreed to Rose's demand that his son become her playmate and personal court jester to appease his King, but he believed the Princess would soon outgrow this stage to release Tag of this demeaning order. Unfortunately for father and son, he was killed in battle and Tag had been relegated to this undesirable posting for the past seven years, condemned to this lowly station for as long as the Princess saw fit.

"You would not dare!" groaned Tag.

"Oh yes, I will," threatened Rose. "And I have."

"Then what difference will it make to me? You've already ruined my life."

"If you refuse to do what I say, I shall punish you!"

"You already have!" snapped Tag, pushing by the Princess to escape her torment. "I should be training as a knight, instead, I am your fool appointed to amuse and entertain you! What more can you do to me?"

"Plenty!" sniffed Rose, speaking with all certainty.

"And to think, I used to like you," growled Tag, scowling in resentment.

"That was long ago, when we were children," reasoned Rose. "And as you are too thick to know it, I have changed since then."

"You most certainly have!" agreed Tag, not even glancing back to deliver this angry retort.

"Even if you do not like me now, what do I care? In the big scheme of things, you are an insignificant nobody. I have princes and other young men of noble lineage who would love to be in my esteemed company."

"Only because they do not know you as I do," grunted Tag. He stormed away down the long corridor to leave the Princess alone to sulk and plot her next course of action without him.

"Fine then!" hollered Rose, too dignified to chase after Tag. "I do not need you! If all else fails, I am confident that child can be bribed of his tooth."

As dusk surrendered to darkness, King William and Queen Beatrice braced themselves for their nightly routine, the arduous and onerous task of convincing their daughter to go to bed at a decent hour.

From the time Rose was a little girl, old enough to realize there was a designated bedtime to adhere to, she would do everything in her powers to forestall this event. If she had it her way, she'd be awake well into the night doing whatever she pleased. In many ways, it had become a ritual for the King and Queen to demand, cajole, beg and threaten Rose to go to bed on time.

Unfortunately for the Queen, she did most of the verbal jousting with her insolent daughter while her husband merely backed her up with the occasional, obligatory: *'listen to your mother, Rose'*.

It was not because William disagreed with his wife. In fact, he wholeheartedly agreed with the Queen. It was the backlash of dealing with his daughter that he truly dreaded. In many ways, it was easier to allow Rose to have her way than to deal with the terrible bouts of whining and pouting when she was in a foul mood, not to mention the furious temper tantrums they, and the domestic staff, had come to fear when Rose felt she had been wrongfully disciplined.

The Queen's efforts to instill some sense of order into Rose's privileged life was usually undermined by her husband's complacency. His reluctance to make his daughter comply with their wishes and to dole out punishment for her unruly behaviour was also driven by his lack of desire to be viewed as the bad guy in the family dynamics. He much preferred the role of the doting father.

Sharing an after-dinner cordial in the palace library, King William used this time to review the latest tax levees to fund local road repairs while Queen Beatrice passed the time with some needlepoint, working on an elaborate tapestry that would one day grace the main wall in the grand throne room.

"It is unusually quiet this eve," noted Beatrice, carefully measuring a golden strand to thread onto her needle.

"Thank God for that," responded William, not even glancing up from the sheets of parchment he was perusing.

"I am serious, William. I cannot help but sense Rose is up to something."

"You, my dear, are much too suspicious where our daughter is concerned."

It was obvious to Beatrice her husband chose to cling to his memories of Rose as the innocent, little daddy's girl than to acknowledge her descent into the willful, manipulative teenager she had now become.

"I love her dearly and it is not my intention to discredit Rose's character, but you know as well as I do her actions and attitude of late leaves much to be desired," reminded the Queen. "At this evening's dinner table, she barely fussed and complained about her meal as she usually does. And when she was done, she did not even wait to be excused, she simply dashed off."

"I admit Rose was not as vocal as she normally is, but perhaps, everything was to her liking?" responded William.

"Since when has *anything* been to her liking? I swear, Rose complains for the sake of complaining, just to hear her own voice. And why was she in such a rush to leave the dinner table?"

"So she was in a hurry?"

"That is just it," said Beatrice, pondering this mystery. "Why the hurry?"

"You worry all for naught, my dear. It could be absolutely nothing," dismissed the King, topping up his glass with the sweet, carmine liquid.

"We can only hope," prayed Beatrice.

"Why hope, when we can ask?" William placed his glass on the table as the sounds of rushed footsteps passing the library caught his attention. "Rose, my dear, please grace us with your presence."

"What is it, father?" asked Rose, peering into the room.

"You are in a hurry, my dear," commented her father. "Where are you off to?"

"To bed, of course," answered Rose, looking quite innocent.

"*To bed?*" responded her mother, her brows arching up in surprise. Where was the fuss? The fighting? Now she knew for sure her daughter was up to no good. "Are you not feeling well, Rose?"

"I feel fine, mother. I just think it prudent that I go to bed early tonight. Not that I need any beauty sleep, but I do want to look my very best for my upcoming birthday gala."

"Well then, off you go! Sweet dreams, my dear," bade her father, turning his cheek to receive a good night kiss.

Giving her mother and father a quick peck on the cheek, Rose headed directly to her bedchamber as she wished them both a good night.

"See, my dear, there was nothing to be concerned about," said

William, with a reassuring smile as he picked up the stack of parchment to resume reading. "I do believe Rose is beginning to mature with age."

"I pray you are correct, William. As sincere as her words seemed, I still have a niggling feeling deep down inside our daughter is up to no good."

"Is it merely a suspicious mind?"

"No… More like a mother's intuition," replied Beatrice, as she listened to the sounds of Rose scurrying off.

2
Be Careful What You Wish For

"That pillow better be perfumed with the attar of rose, not that dreadful lavender essence," grumbled Rose, watching as Mildred turned down her bed and plumped up her luxuriant, down pillow.

"Attar of rose it is, my lady," assured Mildred, holding up the crystal perfume decanter for the Princess to inspect.

"Lovely! Sweet smelling roses for a beautiful Rose. It is only fitting, after all. As far as I am concerned, lavender reeks. It is too heavy for my delicate senses. Its overpowering stench dulls my mind."

"The lavender is said to have relaxing, calming properties," commented Alice, as she hung Rose's dress in the wardrobe. "It is the perfect remedy to help a troubled or restless mind achieve a blissful night of sleep."

"By all means, help yourself! Take that wretched bottle. You can use it more than me," offered Rose. "After all, my mind has nothing to be troubled about."

"How very generous of you!" exclaimed Alice. It had been a long, trying day of appeasing the Princess, and at this point, she made no effort to disguise the sarcasm in her voice.

"Yes, it is," agreed Rose, oblivious to Alice's cynical tone. The Princess' lovely face suddenly contorted in disgust as she scolded Evelyn, "What is wrong with you? Can you not see this ribbon does not match my nightgown?"

"With respect, my lady, no one will see it. What difference does it make?" questioned Evelyn, shrinking away from the Princess' angry scowl.

"Mildred, when will you have this girl properly trained?" rebuked Rose, snatching the white ribbon from her head. "Of course it makes a difference! *I* know it does not match and that is all that truly matters!"

"My humble apologies, my lady," said Mildred. "You must give Evelyn some time. She is relatively new and there is just so much for her to learn."

"A feeble excuse!" admonished Rose, glaring at her servant.

"With all due respect, it is not an excuse, my lady. I merely speak the truth," countered Mildred.

"I beg of you, my lady, do not blame Miss Mildred. I am terribly sorry!" apologized Evelyn, hastily selecting a pale pink, satin ribbon to tie back the Princess' golden tresses. "This one matches perfectly."

"Hmph!" grunted Rose, sneering with resentment at the handmaiden. "I ask for so little, and yet, the simplest of requests go ignored."

"I will do better," promised Evelyn, carefully securing Rose's hair so there would be less tangles to contend with in the morning.

"I would prefer it if you did your *best*," snipped Rose, checking to see if her hair was tied high enough on her head so it did not get trapped under her shoulders as she slept.

"Of course, my lady," responded Evelyn. She turned to pick up the urn of fresh water to fill the crystal tumbler that always sat on the nightstand by the bed.

"No! No water," ordered Rose.

"But – but," stammered Evelyn, confused by this new demand. "You said you always require a glass of water in case you get thirsty in the middle of the night."

"Do not question me, Gwendolyn! I am a princess. It is my prerogative to change my mind as I see fit."

"Yes, my lady," responded Evelyn. She did not even bother to correct the Princess about her name, for at this point she felt her continued employment was now tenuous at best.

"Just leave the glass by my bedside," ordered Rose, pointing to the nightstand.

"Empty?" questioned Evelyn, her brows furrowing in curiosity.

"Do you have cloth ears or are you just a stupid girl?" snapped Rose. "Just leave the empty glass!"

"You heard the Princess," said Mildred, taking the crystal tumbler from Evelyn's trembling hand. "Glass on the nightstand."

Alice quickly steered Evelyn to the door as she made a suggestion, "And let us leave Princess Rose to sleep."

"Good night, Princess. Pleasant dreams," bade Mildred, motioning for Alice and Evelyn to retreat quickly and silently.

"They always are," responded Rose, as she crawled into the soft, warm bed.

As the door closed, the Princess nestled down. She pulled the counterpane up around her neck and waited a moment to make sure her attendants were well on their way to retiring for the night.

"Now to set the trap," whispered Rose. She rifled through the drawer, pushing aside embroidery supplies to pull out a tiny jar of adhesive and a silk kerchief. She carefully unwrapped the bait; a perfect, little incisor she managed to swindle from the scullery maid's son with the promise of doubling his profit should he lend her this tooth.

Using tree sap that had been boiled down to a thick, sticky consistency and utilized by the bindery shops to glue sheets of parchment to the spines of books, Rose set to work. She applied a tiny drop of this clear, amber liquid onto the center of the nightstand. With great care, she positioned the tooth just so on this congealing droplet.

"This should do quite nicely." Rose took a moment to admire her clever trap as she placed the empty tumbler next to the bait. "Now, I wait."

As the sky deepened to a deep cobalt blue and a dusting of tiny, glittering stars studded the night sky, Rose impatiently tossed and turned, waiting for the Tooth Fairy to make her grand entrance.

"Where is she?" Rose muttered beneath her breath as she glanced at the ever-shrinking candle. Its small flame flickered and danced, casting its light to illuminate the tooth positioned on the nightstand for the Fairy to see.

"I suppose I should look convincingly asleep," decided Rose, snuggling down into her bed. She pulled the counterpane high around her neck as she closed her eyes. The sleep was feigned, but not the great yawn Rose could stifle no longer.

For what felt like hours, the Princess waited, watching through narrowed eyes for her quarry to appear. And as the night grew longer and the candle's wick continued to shrink, Rose's half-closed eyes became heavier and heavier. They slowly drooped until they gradually shut and she drifted off into a dreamless sleep.

Just as the Princess' breathing became long and slow, wheezing out of her parted lips, a golden orb of light flickered, tentatively hovering at the open window before floating into the bedchamber. Cautiously circling the room, this glow of light maintained a respectable distance from the sleeping form, flying overhead to ascertain that she was indeed fast asleep.

The Fairy waited for the long sigh or heavy snore, indication of a human embraced in a deep slumber. As another jet of spent air was slowly expelled from Rose's gaping mouth, the diminutive being decided it was safe to make her move. Her shimmering wings hummed as she maneuvered closer, fluttering down to the object of her desire: the perfect, little tooth.

Alighting upon the nightstand, she inspected this seemingly pristine specimen. Under the glow of the candle's light, she saw the tooth was completely devoid of decay, lacking in the usual nicks or chips and it was unusually white coming from the mouth of a human child; a mortal relatively unconcerned about oral hygiene. This was a rare find!

On her nightly forays, the majority of teeth she collected were either utterly rotten or riddled with the onset of cavities. Those in the worst condition were used to line the dungeons of her grand palace. However, this perfect tooth, a rare specimen indeed, polished and gleaming white in the candlelight would be a suitable addition in the construction of the main watchtower of her dental edifice. With an incisor like this, her castle promised to shine like a dazzling pearl in the sunlight. She just had to have it!

With her eyes and heart set on this tooth, the Fairy made her claim. Her eager hands took hold, but just as she attempted to lift the tooth to make off with it, the incisor refused to budge. Wrapping her arms around it, she gave it a mighty heave, her wings fluttering madly to aid in this extrication. Instead of flying off with her prize, the Fairy lost her grip, tumbling head over heels. To her surprise, the tooth remained exactly where it was.

"This is odd," the Fairy muttered beneath her breath, as she suspiciously eyed the prize. Kneeling down, she was stunned to spy a clear, sticky substance. This tooth was stuck in this congealing drop, keeping it fixed to the surface of the nightstand.

"I can remedy this," whispered the Fairy. Holding forth her wand that sparkled with light, she called upon an incantation to dissolve this hardening adhesive.

As a loud boom exploded around her, the Fairy jumped with fright.

A voice rattled her body right down to the bones as it exclaimed: "Caught you!"

"What the?" gasped the Fairy. Launching into flight, she immediately slammed into an invisible barrier. Her stunned face, plastered against this clear wall made a strange, high pitched squealing sound where flesh met glass as she slid down against this clear barricade.

"There is no escaping me, little Fairy!" declared Rose. She pressed down on the overturned glass to secure her prisoner.

The Fairy's aura glowed with an intensity to match her outrage. The fine, iridescent scales of her wings floated around like a cloud of glittering dust as she buzzed about. She was like an angry bee, bouncing and banging against the wall of this invisible trap in a desperate bid to escape.

"Try, try, try to fly! It will only make you cry!" chanted the Princess, teasing her moth-sized prisoner.

Hearing this juvenile taunting, the Fairy ceased her frenetic flight.

Fear gave way to anger as it became obvious this human being had deliberately set out to capture her.

"Do you know who I am?" Her puny balled fists pounded against the crystal barrier.

"You are a Tooth Fairy, of course," responded Rose.

"*A Tooth Fairy?*" she gasped in exasperation. "I am Pancecilia Feldspar, the *Queen* of the Tooth Fairies!"

"Oh, goodie!" exclaimed Rose. "Then you can grant even better wishes!"

"Are you mad? What makes you think I would grant *you* a wish?"

"*Three* wishes," corrected Rose. "You owe me three of them if you want your freedom."

"You really are loopy! You have me mixed up with a genie, you horrid little twit!" admonished Pancecilia Feldspar, sputtering with rage.

"I am not the *little* one!" snorted Rose, staring mockingly at her prisoner. "You are!"

"That is what you think!" With a wave of her wand and a magical incantation, a surprising metamorphosis took place before this mortal's startled eyes. The entire room seemed to tremble with her fury as the glass rattled against the nightstand.

Rose dove under her quilt as the Fairy transmogrified into the size of an adult human with a stunning set of wings. She gracelessly tumbled off the nightstand as the crystal glass, too tight to fit, popped off her head to shatter on the floor. Scrambling to her feet, the Fairy snatched up the counterpane, yanking on it to expose the cowering mortal hiding beneath this quilt.

"Who'd have thought you were capable of that?" gasped Rose, stunned by the Fairy's unexpected transformation.

"Proves how little you know!" growled the Fairy. "How dare you?"

"How dare *you?*" snapped Rose, jumping up on her bed to stand nose to nose with the Fairy. "Do you even know who you have just insulted, Pancreas?"

"To start, do not insult me! It is Pancecilia, or Pance for short," corrected the Fairy. "And I know exactly who you are, young lady."

"If you did, you would not be speaking to me with such disrespect."

"You are Rose," grunted Pance, impatience tainting her voice as she glared at this human. "And I will give you the respect you are deserving of!"

"I am Rose-alyn Beatrice Elizabeth Wilhemina Pepperton, the Princess of Fleetwood. My parents are the King and Queen!"

"And that is supposed to matter to me?" questioned the Fairy, disgruntled by this mortal's arrogance. "Do you feel you are above being punished because you are a princess?"

"Maybe not, but you are a nobody to me," sniffed Rose, speaking with utmost confidence. "No one can punish me except my father or mother!"

"If that is the case, then we shall see just what punishment the King and Queen will dole out for your audacious act of impudence. If you are lucky, perhaps they will show you some mercy."

Instead of trembling in fear of the retribution in store for her, Rose began to giggle, dismissing the Fairy's words. "Now, *you* are being silly! These are my parents you speak of."

"Yes, and as your father is reputed to be a fair and just ruler, he will deal with you accordingly!"

"He will deal with me as any loving father would treat his precious daughter."

"That is exactly what I am hoping for!" stated Pance. "If he cares, King William will see fit to discipline you for your own good."

"Yes, yes, but first you will have to find him," taunted Rose, almost daring her to do just that. "He could be anywhere in this big, old castle. You will be searching for a very long time."

"That's what you think, missy!" grunted Pance. With a wave and a flick of her wand, she and the Princess vanished, vapourizing in a shower of sparkling, golden dust.

"Wh- what happened?" stammered Rose. Her hands hastily patted her body to make sure she was whole again as her startled eyes glanced about to see the stunned expression on her parent's faces as she and the Fairy suddenly materialized before them in the palace library.

"What is the meaning of this?" questioned King William. Startled by their abrupt appearance, he dropped the sheets of parchment he had been reviewing while the Queen nursed her finger, having pricked it on the embroidery needle.

"I am sorry to intrude on you at this ungodly hour, Your Highness," apologized the Tooth Fairy, bowing respectfully before the royal couple. "But I desire an audience with you."

"Pancecilia Feldspar, is that you?" asked Queen Beatrice, putting aside her needlework as she admired the glistening wings. It had been at William's coronation ball that she had last seen the Tooth Fairy in her full, regal size.

"Indeed, it is, Your Majesty," greeted Pance, nodding in respect to the Queen. "And I say again, I am sorry to intrude at this late hour, but there is an urgent matter requiring your immediate attention."

The King and Queen glanced over at their daughter as Rose attempted to sneak out of the library as the Fairy addressed her parents.

In a bright flash of light, Pance disappeared, only to reappear before Rose. She blocked the doorway of the library to prevent her escape.

"You are not going anywhere, young lady!" snapped Pance, thrusting the glowing tip of her wand into Rose's face to steer her back to her waiting parents. "I am not done with you!"

"Who said I was leaving?" grumbled Rose.

"Good gracious!" exclaimed the Queen. "What have you done now, Rose?"

"My dear, do not hasten to jump to any kind of conclusion just yet," urged her husband. "This may have absolutely nothing to do with our daughter."

"Unfortunately, Your Highness, I hate to be the bearer of bad tidings, but it has *everything* to do with your daughter," responded Pance.

"Pray tell, Pancecilia, what has Rose done now?" asked Beatrice. "And spare no details, for I want to know exactly what our daughter has been up to."

"To put it bluntly, Princess Rose took it upon herself to set a trap to capture me. And to make matters worse, she succeeded!"

"You did *what?*" The King and Queen gasped in unison, staring in utter disbelief at their errant daughter.

"She makes it sound so very bad, but it was not like that at all," insisted Rose, her eyes blinking innocently at her parents.

"How dare you downplay your actions!" denounced Pance. "Do not take her word as the truth."

"And you expect my mother and father to believe in you? A Fairy with a name like *Pants?*" snorted Rose, rolling her eyes in ridicule.

"It is pronounced Pance, like dance! Not like *underpants,*" explained the agitated Fairy.

"Rose, enough with your rudeness!" admonished her mother. "How dare you speak to Pancecilia Feldspar with such disrespect? And how dare you do such a despicable thing to her?"

For a moment, Rose's eyes glazed over, brimming with tears. Her lower lip protruded in a sad pout as she blinked helplessly at her father in a bid to solicit his sympathy.

"Now, now my dear," said William, patting his wife's hand in a bid to calm her down. "I am positive there is a logical explanation for what had happened."

Before Rose could respond, Pance spoke up, "I will have you know your daughter deliberately laid a trap; a perfect baby tooth to be exact, to lure me into her bedchamber, where upon she trapped me in a drinking glass when I attempted to claim the *bait* she left on her nightstand!"

"Good gracious, Rose! How can you do such a terrible thing?" rebuked her mother, her face burning with embarrassment upon learning of her daughter's latest scheme.

"It must be a mistake, my dear friend," decided the King. "Rose had shed the last of her baby teeth quite some time ago."

"But I speak the truth, King William," insisted Pance.

"The only way Rose would be able to use a baby tooth to lure you is to physically remove it from another child," stated the Queen. She suddenly blanched, the colour draining from her face as she stared in horror at her daughter. "Tell me it is not so! Do not tell me you plucked a tooth from the mouth of an unsuspecting child!"

"He was not *unsuspecting*. He parted with it willingly," explained Rose, in her own defense.

"Ah-ha! So you do admit to placing a tooth out to trap me!" declared Pance, staring accusingly at the Princess.

"Well, what do you have to say for yourself, young lady?" interrogated her mother, her arms crossing her chest in annoyance as she eyed her daughter.

"Not much, really," said Rose; her tone indifferent.

"There must be some misunderstanding," decided the King, hoping this was the case so he would not be condemned to face his daughter's wrath and the ensuing feelings of guilt should he be forced to punish her.

"It is obvious Rose has done the Fairy wrong! Why must you constantly come to her defense?" groaned his exasperated wife.

"Because she is my daughter," reasoned the King. "Which begs the question, why do you not, when you are her mother?"

"You know as well as I do, *our* daughter has been less than forthright on more than one occasion," reminded Beatrice.

"Oh, mother," sighed Rose, disappointment lacing her voice. "I was young and foolish then, I have matured greatly since. You really must learn to trust me."

"And anyone with even a hint of maturity would know trust is earned, not given freely," reminded her mother. "Sadly, your actions of late do not warrant trust, my dear."

Realizing her efforts would not garner her mother's backing, Rose gazed over at her father, peering at him with those sad, doleful eyes to garner his sympathy.

The King squirmed uncomfortably in his chair. Trapped by the Fairy's stare of condemnation on one side; his wife's look of resentment for not supporting her on the other; while his daughter stood before him, pulling her saddest face ever, he could take no more. William rose from his chair and began to pace. He hoped those in his company would take this abrupt action as his need to seriously consider all parties concerned, rather than to be viewed as no longer being able to bear up to their scrutiny. He adopted a pensive expression on his face as he tried his best to appear deep in thought.

"So, Your Highness, in all your wisdom, how do you intend to handle this matter?" questioned the Fairy.

"Well, we must be sensible. We must not be hasty in passing judgment nor in delivering punishment."

"Now see here, William, I pray this is not your way of avoiding the issue at hand," admonished his wife. "As unsavoury as this whole matter of punishing Rose is, she must be dealt with! You are doing her no favour in not disciplining her. She must learn to be accountable for her words and actions. Nothing will be learned if you shrug this matter off, pretending it never happened."

"Quite right, my dear," agreed her husband. "Rose must be punished!"

"*What?*" gasped Rose, her eyes widening in utter surprise as her mother breathed a sigh of relief.

Pance gave Rose a smug smile, pleased that her father was willing to take appropriate measures to condemn her wretched actions.

In typical fashion, the Princess knew there was only one of two ways to handle this situation: issue a royal tantrum unlike no other or open the floodgates to unleash a torrent of tears. Her flushed face, which had instinctively screwed up in anger and frustration suddenly softened, dissolving in a sad trail of tears. She began to sob uncontrollably as she sputtered: "I- I- I am *sorrrry!* I promise I will never do that again!"

"Rose, enough with this silliness!" scolded her mother, her nerves worn thin with this whining. "You have shed crocodile tears once too often and there is no sincerity in this apology. You have repeatedly promised to change, however, it is apparent by your actions you cannot be held to your promises."

"But I *will* change," whined Rose, stamping her feet in frustration.

"Yes, you most definitely will, but only after you receive just punishment, my dear daughter," cautioned her mother.

Rose glanced over to her father, seeking pity as great tears tumbled down her burning cheeks. Her lower lip quivered as she whimpered: "Father… It's not fair."

Unable to endure her mournful cry, King William turned away from his daughter's pleading eyes. He pulled Pance aside as he whispered to her, "My dear friend, I urge you not to take deliberate action in punishing Rose."

"Am I mistaken, or are you allowing me to dole out punishment on your behalf?" questioned the Fairy.

"Well, I feel it is only fitting, as you are the one who was wronged," justified the King, willingly transferring this distasteful task on to Pance. "But as I said, I urge you not to take deliberate action, if you get my meaning?"

"Do you mean to say I am *not* to cast an enchantment on your daughter to teach her a lesson?"

"Yes! I do believe a strong threat of punishment, perhaps a moral lesson of what will happen if she does not change will be the best way to handle this dilemma," suggested William, hoping this would appease both the Fairy and his wife.

For a moment, Pance's blood boiled at the mere thought the obnoxious, young Princess would get away with her appalling actions and then, the Fairy had a change of heart.

"Perhaps you are correct, Your Highness," decided Pance, giving William a judicious nod. "A lesson in humility, a strong warning of what can happen if the Princess does not change her errant ways, will be just the medicine to cure her need to act on these ill-conceived ideas."

"There you go then, a satisfactory solution all the way around!" exclaimed the King.

He was thoroughly pleased he would not have to be the one to dole out punishment to his daughter. Neither would his wife chastise him for not taking appropriate measures to discipline Rose and at the same time, neither was the Fairy going to place a hex or spell on his daughter as a form of retribution for capturing her.

"So be it!" consented Pance, nodding in approval. "Allow me speak to your daughter on my own. In fact, we will discuss the repercussions of her actions while I tuck her back into bed."

"A brilliant idea!" praised King William. "Go to it, my friend. Deal with my daughter as you see fit."

"But- but- but" stuttered Rose.

"You heard your father, Rose! Accept your punishment with grace, and be done with it," urged the Queen. "I pray you will learn your lesson this time."

"Come along, Princess Rose, I shall escort you back to your bedchamber," offered Pance.

"It is so late and I am too tired," whined Rose, deliberately dragging her feet as she feigned a yawn. "I do not believe I have the energy to walk all the way back to my room."

"Worry not," responded the Fairy. With a wave of her wand and a magical enchantment, in a glittering shower of golden light, she and the Princess vanished from the palace library. Just as quickly, they materialized in Rose's bedchamber.

"Will you stop it with that!" scolded Rose, unaccustomed to this mode of transportation. She hastily wiped the phony tears from her eyes that failed to absolve her of the impending punishment.

"You claimed you were too tired to walk these great halls. I merely expedited the return to your bedchamber."

"I was not really tired," snapped Rose.

"I know."

"Really?" questioned Rose, as she clambered into her bed.

Pance righted the overturned nightstand. Using an incantation, the tiny shards from the shattered crystal tumbler sparkled as they floated off the floor. A flick of her wand sent these glistening fragments out the open window, skyward to become one with the stars bejeweling the night sky.

"Do you take me for some kind of fool?" responded the Fairy. "I was just waiting for an excuse to get you here – alone! And the sooner, the better!"

"Sorry to disappoint, but I am not intimidated by you. You made a promise to my father you would not cast a spell on me. So there!"

"You silly, silly girl! It is a pity you do not even listen to your father as you should. He agreed to me issuing you a strong warning, to threaten you with the consequences of your insolent behaviour if you do not change."

"You are the silly one! And you will be disappointed to know I am not frightened of useless threats issued by a lowly Fairy."

"You nasty, impudent girl!" snapped Pance, her wings quivering with mounting rage. "How dare you?"

"*Dare me?* I am no ordinary girl! You are speaking to a princess!" reminded Rose, her balled fists pummelling her pillow. "I can do and say whatever I wish, whenever I want, to whomever I please."

"Do not hide behind your title. Though it is true you are royalty, you are cursed with a sense of entitlement."

"I *am* entitled," snipped Rose, her tone smug. "And how can getting what I want, when I want it, be a curse? It is something everyone dreams of!"

"That is not the curse," responded the Fairy. "Though you get whatever you desire, in your heart, you appreciate nothing and you take *everything* for granted. *That* is the curse. You are in need of nothing, yet you want everything!"

"Oh, boo-hoo! You are just jealous!"

"Of you? Absolutely not!" declared Pance, her words defiant.

"Believe what you want, but I know everybody wishes they were me," stated Rose, speaking with all certainty. "There is not one person outside these castle walls, you included, who is not jealous of me."

"Damn it all! I have had it with you, Rose!" cursed Pance, the wand trembling in her grip as her anger mounted.

"How dare you address me so informally? It is Princess Rose-alyn Beatrice Elizabeth Wilhemina Pepperton to you, Tooth Fairy!"

"In my eyes, you are just Rose. I see you for exactly what you are; a prickly, thorny rose in dire need of a good pruning to cut her down to size!"

"And you are nothing but a tatty, old pair of under*pants* nobody wants!" ridiculed the Princess.

"Do not test me, young lady! I have a wand and I know how to use it."

"Go ahead!" taunted Rose, daring Pance to retaliate. "Unless your promise to my father means nothing, you will be in big trouble if you cast a spell on me. Mind you, if your powers are as wanting as I suspect, the best you would be able to do is to turn me into a warty, old toad. And even at that, I would still look prettier than you!"

"Looks are not everything, Princess."

"Yes," agreed Rose, eyeing Pance with obvious contempt, "especially when you have none."

"You are as reckless with your words as you are with your actions," denounced the Fairy.

"And you know nothing about keeping your word," countered Rose.

"You know not what you speak of. I have not defied the promise I made to your father."

"That is not what I am speaking of. I was referring to the promise of granting me three wishes," reminded Rose.

"I never made such a promise to you."

"Ah, but I did catch you, so you owe me three wishes for setting you free," stated the Princess.

"You did no such thing! And it is a bloody good thing you mortals do not lose your tongue each time you lie, otherwise, yours would have fallen off long ago!"

"So you set yourself free. That is a minor detail," snorted Rose. "The point is, I captured you. Now you are free. You owe me three wishes."

"And where in heaven's name did you hear this cockamamie story that a Fairy would grant wishes in exchange for freedom?"

"It is common knowledge. Everybody knows that," replied Rose, her words matter-of-fact.

"You are a fool! It is common knowledge a Fairy will grant a wish for a good deed done," corrected Pance.

"I set you free! That was a good deed."

"Get it through your thick head! I set myself free," rebuked the Fairy.

"Well, whatever the case, you will make an exception for me," ordered Rose, as demanding as ever.

"Why should I? Is it not good enough I will not dispense punishment in the form of a spell? Because I can be extremely wicked about it if I wanted to be."

"You will do so because I am a princess. Now, make it so!"

"And if I grant you a wish, what is in it for me?"

"If you do, I will permit you to do what my father suggested: warn me of the ramifications of my so-called ill-conceived actions," negotiated Rose.

"*You* will permit *me?*" scoffed the Fairy, her brows arching up in dismay. "As you have a selective memory, it was your father who authorized me to do this, not you! And a king always supersedes a princess."

"Ah, but when he and my mother are not in our presence, what I say, goes," explained Rose.

"Nice try, but not good enough. You will listen to my words of caution whether you want to or not."

"La, la, la, la, la, la! Can't hear you!" chanted Rose, her hands clamped firmly over her ears.

"Good gracious! You are behaving like a child! Exactly how *young* are you?" questioned the Fairy, frowning in disgust at the Princess' infantile display.

"I am a young lady – almost sixteen," responded Rose, her hands still covering her ears.

"Ah-ha, so you can hear me!" exclaimed the Fairy, pointing her wand accusingly at the Princess.

"No, I can't."

"See! You did it again! You can hear me. Either you listen, and listen carefully, or you will face my wrath."

"Wah, wah, wah!" mocked Rose, pretending to wipe a tear from her eye. "Talk all you want. I shall decide if you are worthy of an audience."

"You are impossible! How dare you test my patience?"

"And how dare you waste my precious time!" snapped Rose.

"This is going nowhere fast," groaned the Fairy, appalled by this pretentious mortal's attitude.

"Yes, so you better go *somewhere* now," suggested Rose, showing her the door.

"The nerve!" snapped Pance.

"The gall, the audacity, the insolence, blah, blah, blah," sniffed Rose. "I have heard it all before."

"And it does not bother you?"

"Why should it? I may be all these things and more, but above all else, I am a genuine princess."

"Not if I turn you into a toad or some other lowly creature. I believe it would be a vast improvement."

"Eek!" shrieked Rose, diving behind her bed for cover as the Fairy pointed the glowing wand at her. "You dare not do it! You promised my father: No spells!"

Pance drew a deep breath. Gathering her composure once more, she considered this promise she made to King William.

"You are quite right," admitted the Fairy, lowering her wand. "I respect your father too much to disregard our agreement."

"Farewell then," bade Rose, peering over the edge of her bed as she waved the Fairy off.

"Who said I was leaving? I am not yet done with you."

"I am most definitely done with you. And if you stay, I will not listen to you anyway," stated Rose.

"What must I do to make you listen to my warning?"

"If you grant me three wishes, I will hear you out," bargained Rose.

"I said it before and I will say it again: One wish for one good deed done. You have done nothing but infuriate me from the start and I cannot foresee any good deeds coming from you anytime soon."

"How about just *one* wish?"

"My, you are persistent, I will give you that."

"I would prefer it if you gave me a wish," responded Rose.

"And if I did grant you this, what in the world would a princess like you ever wish for?" asked Pance.

For the longest moment, Rose was silent as she pondered this question.

"Now, give it serious consideration, and remember, be care–"

"I know, I know," interjected the Princess, nodding thoughtfully. "Be careful what I wish for."

"Precisely!"

"If that is the case, then I know exactly what I would request," announced the Princess, basking in her moment of brilliance.

"Let me guess, you would wish for three more wishes," determined Pance.

"How did you know?"

"I was not born yesterday. You are not the first, and you will certainly not be the last, to try and stretch out one wish. However, it is usually the poor and down-trodden making this request, not the rich and the privileged."

"Of course those lowly peasants would make such demands," stated Rose. "They are greedy by nature."

"That is an unfair claim. How can you say such a terrible thing about the poor?"

"They are poor because they are lazy," denounced the Princess. "They refuse to work hard to elevate their status, after all, they are not called commoners for no reason, you know?"

"These are your father's people – his subjects, you speak of in such a derogatory manner!" gasped Pance, exasperated by her disparaging words.

"So? I hate the common people," admitted Rose, shrugging with indifference. "They are so... so... common."

"*Hate* makes you ugly," warned Pance, shaking her head in disgrace as she was made witness to the Princess' true nature.

"When you are as rich and beautiful as I am, there is no such thing as being ugly. So, do I get my wish?"

"No! I am not about to break the Fairies' code just to appease you."

"Then you can waste your breath, for I am not about to listen to whatever it was you were going to say," grunted Rose, stamping her feet like a belligerent child on the verge of a tantrum.

Reaching this stalemate, the Fairy made an offer: "Suppose you listen to me and if you do, I will tell you how you can get all the wishes you can ever dream of?"

"Truly?" asked Rose, her eyes narrowing in suspicion as she stared at Pance. "Whatever I dream of?"

"Literally and figuratively," promised the Fairy, her hand over her heart as she made this vow. "Think on it! A never-ending supply of wishes, if that is what you desire!"

"It is much better than three measly wishes!" declared Rose, her hands clapping together in glee.

"So, will you listen to what I have to say to you?"

"I will lend you my ear, both in fact, if you swear on my father's good name you will tell me how to get whatever I dream of when you are done," offered the Princess, hoping to strike up a bargain.

"First of all, as your father had suggested, a lesson in humility," decided Pance, her finger tapping her chin as she gave this grave thought.

"Remember, no spells! Not one enchantment."

"I will not do a thing to you, but *you* most certainly will if you do not change your ways," cautioned the Fairy.

"So I was a bit zealous in my efforts to capture you. Suppose I promise never to do that again?"

"Bloody right you will not be doing that again!" declared Pance. "But it is not just about that. It is how you treat others in general I mean to address."

"And what would you know of my treatment of others?"

"I know plenty, young lady! Being that I can be quite small when I want to be, I can move about unnoticed by most. And I will tell you now, what I have heard spoken of you has not been flattering."

"So what? I treat others exactly as they deserve or expect to be treated."

"No one, not even the palace staff, deserve or expect to be treated with such disregard as you have treated them. And do not deny it, for I have heard the whispering in the halls of the palace. I know how you deal with others, those in stations lower than yours, those you despise because you feel they are less of a person than you are, because you are royalty and they are not."

"So what? It is not as though I killed anyone. And if someone does get hurt, at least it will be some lowly commoner," justified Rose. "What harm is that?"

"Words can kill, as surely as action," cautioned the Fairy. "There are those who cater to your every whim, and yet, you treat these people with such disregard. Why is that?"

"Because they expect it from a princess and sometimes, one must remind them of their place in the world otherwise, they will come to believe they are just as good as us."

"You sound as though you despise the common people," noted Pance.

"Usually, I am indifferent to them. However, what I truly do hate are the commoners who do not know their place in society," corrected Rose.

"That is a horrible thing to say! It is no wonder you are despised by so many."

"That is a lie! *Everybody* loves me," insisted Rose, shielding herself behind a sturdy wall of denial. "After all, what is there not to love?"

"Plenty!" snapped Pance. "And just because your subjects bow down to you, catering to your every whim, it *does not* mean they love you. In fact, they do not even respect you."

"Of course they do! That is why these people do whatever I tell them."

"Make no mistake, they do not do these things willingly," argued the Fairy. "They only cow to you because it is expected of them. From what I understand, you make their lives miserable if they do not comply. If anything, those made to cater to you, actually loath you!"

"Oh, no, no! They do it because they love me and want to make me happy."

"There is no getting through to you, is there?" gasped the Fairy, astounded by this mortal's ignorance. "And how would you feel if you were one of those common people you so despise?"

"I am the Princess of Fleetwood. As if that will ever happen!" scoffed Rose, as she shook her head at the Fairy.

"If you do not change your ways, you shall unleash a curse unto yourself. You shall become what you hate the most. Your indifference will be your undoing," cautioned Pance.

"And that is it? That is my warning?" Rose's eyes narrowed in suspicion as she stared at the Fairy.

"Yes, but do not take it lightly, Princess Rose, for at the midnight hour, from henceforth you shall be held accountable for your words and actions. Your indifference to others will cause you to suffer. The only way to make it stop is for you to find your heart."

"So… you are not putting a spell on me?"

"Whatever happens will be of your own doing, not mine. Your choices will determine the outcome."

"I have been known to make some very wise choices, so I can live with that," decided Rose.

"Mark my words, Princess," warned Pance, the tip of her wand throbbing with light, "if you do not change your ways, all who know you will see you for what you truly are. You will remain as such until the day you come to understand and appreciate what it means when nobody loves you."

"As if! I am the fairest in all the lands. All will bow to my magnificent glory, for I am as lovely and lovable as they come!"

"I am speaking, but obviously you are not hearing me," muttered Pance, groaning in disbelief. "Often, the hardest lessons to learn in life are the ones thrust upon us. Perhaps it is not such a bad thing for you to experience *life*."

"If you mean for me to endure some hardship to better appreciate my lifestyle, I know all about hardship," declared Rose.

"Do you now?"

"Oh yes," said the Princess. "I am made to suffer each day! There are times when I feel as though I am drowning in a sea of incompetence. The lowly staff appointed as my attendants consistently fail to meet my expectations."

"As I said, keep this up and you will be made to learn the hard way. Swallowing a bitter pill shall either fix your ills or make you choke. You have a heart of stone, Princess Rose. Where is your compassion?"

"Make no mistake, it is there, but it is reserved for those deserving of it."

"It shall come to pass those who love you will turn on you if you do not find your heart," warned Pance, sensing her lack of compassion.

"Yes, yes!" Rose urged the Fairy to spill this great secret. "Now, what about the promise of telling me how to get all my dreams fulfilled? You are still going to keep your promise to me, are you not?"

"I always keep my promise. As you accept this wish without performing a good deed, to make this deal binding, you must give me the one thing you value above all others in exchange."

Without a moment's thought, Rose dashed over to her dresser. Rummaging through the contents of a large jewellery box, she found a simple, heart-shaped locket she once wore as a little girl. It was a birthday gift she received as a child, but she could no longer remember who gave it to her. Obviously, this inexpensive bauble had no sentimental value or personal relevance to her anymore. It now lay buried beneath a regular treasure trove of expensive pieces of diamond and ruby encrusted jewellery.

"This should do quite nicely," Rose muttered beneath her breath. "And I will not even miss it."

"I do not have all night, Princess. Do you have something you wish to exchange?"

"Here you go," offered Rose, presenting the silver chain and locket to the Tooth Fairy as she blatantly lied. "It is very dear to me, and for this reason, I believe it will be a fair trade."

Pance inspected the locket suspended on this thread of fine, silver links. "Are you sure of this?"

"Of course I am," assured Rose, giddy with excitement. "Now how do I make all my wishes come true?"

"To obtain all you can ever dream of or ever wish for, you must make a special deal with the Dream Merchant," revealed Pance, speaking in a whisper so no others would hear this secret.

"The Dream Merchant? Who is this person, if indeed he is a person?" asked Rose, gazing suspiciously at the Tooth Fairy.

"This *person* happens to be a very powerful Wizard. He specializes in magic that allows dreams to come true, hence, the moniker the *Dream Merchant*. And as with any merchant, there is a price to be paid for his services."

"And what might that be?" questioned Rose, intrigued by the possibilities.

"That, I cannot say," replied Pance.

"Because you will not say? Or because you do not know?"

"The price is totally at his discretion. Just be warned, Princess, it might be greater than what you bargained for."

"That is of little concern, for money is no object to me," said Rose, shrugging off the Fairy's warning.

"Who said the price was monetary?" Pance responded with a shrewd smile.

"What are you *not* telling me?"

"I have told you all you need to know. As for the price, as I said, it is at the Wizard's discretion to ask, and it is at your discretion to accept or decline his offer."

"Fair enough then," decided Rose. "Now, where do I find this Dream Merchant? Is the Wizard in some faraway land or is he somewhere in Fleetwood? And can he be summoned or must I go to him?"

"If you are in need of his services, *he* will come to *you*," disclosed Pance.

"But where shall we meet?" asked Rose, bewildered by this response.

"Where else, but in your dreams," revealed the Fairy, giving the Princess a knowing smile as she placed the locket in her bag along with the collection of teeth. "For now, I will take this silver heart and hide it away in a very special place."

"And if I should want it back?"

"Trust me, if that should ever happen, and I highly doubt it will, it will not be worth the effort for you to retrieve it," replied Pance, as she shrank down to her usual size that allowed her to steal into bedchambers unnoticed in the still of the night. "Besides, you do not have the heart to undertake any kind of quest, no matter how simple."

"You can think what you want. Now, are you telling me that all I must do is dream of the Wizard, this so-called Dream Merchant, and he will come to me?" questioned Rose, unleashing a great yawn as she crawled back into her cozy bed.

"Yes, but be warned, Princess, even the sweetest of dreams can have a dark side," cautioned Pance, as she hovered before Rose.

With that said, the Fairy's translucent wings shimmered, humming as they carried her out the window and into the tranquil night. She drifted away until her golden light became one with the stars twinkling in the cobalt sky.

A Strange Encounter

Rose woke with a start. Bolting upright from her bed, her eyes quickly grew accustomed to the darkened room as she glanced about, searching for evidence of the Tooth Fairy.

"That was strange... Either I dreamed the whole thing or that Fairy lied to me," grumbled Rose. Her eyes narrowed as she scrutinized the nightstand for the tooth she had set out.

"Pancecilia Feldspar does not lie!"

An agitated voice growled at her, rumbling from beneath the bed.

"What was that?" gasped Rose, now wide-awake. Dangling over the edge of her bed, the Princess cautiously lifted the dust ruffle to peer beneath it. For a moment, her eyes adjusted to the complete and utter darkness consuming this small area of the bedchamber. She saw nothing. Only silence and a suffocating blackness greeted her eyes.

"See something interesting down there?"

Rose shrieked in surprise, somersaulting off the bed to land flat on her back onto the floor. She stared up to see a strange man lying across her bed where she, just seconds before, lay. Even in the darkness, his blue-gray eyes sparkled with mischief as they stared down at her startled face. These eyes were framed by a wild tangle of grizzled hair and a long silvery moustache cascading down to become one with his beard.

"That is an odd way to greet me," he snorted in disapproval.

"Who are you?" yelped Rose. In a frightened panic, she did not even wait for an answer. She quickly dove beneath her bed to get away from this intruder.

"Who am *I?* What a silly question!"

Rose unleashed a bloodcurdling shriek yet again as this man suddenly appeared next to her beneath the bed.

In absolute fright, the Princess scrambled away, dashing to the door to escape. Yanking it open, she screamed as this odd-looking man appeared before her, standing in the corridor to impede her way.

"Will you stop it with that bloody screaming!" He admonished her just as she rudely slammed the door in his disgruntled face.

Turning to dive under her quilt, this man abruptly reappeared in her room. He cupped his hand over her mouth just as she was about to unleash another shriek.

"For pity's sake, shut your royal gob and stop with that incessant screaming!" he demanded, pressing a finger to his lips for silence. "It is damned annoying."

It was a strange encounter the Princess was ill prepared for. Rose backed away, snatching up the urn of water sitting on her dresser, she threatened him, "Be gone or I will hurt you!"

"Many try, all failed," dismissed the stranger, nonchalantly flicking the dust from his dark robe that was adorned with a plethora of eye-catching, embroidered appliqués of glowing moons and stars.

"Not me!" declared Rose, daring him to take a step closer.

Just as she hoisted the urn to hurl it at him, the man abruptly vanished, only to reappear behind her. Seizing the pitcher from her hands, he scolded her, "No need to get your knickers royally twisted, young lady! Now calm down!"

"If you do not leave, I shall scream at the top of my lungs!" warned Rose, as her hands blindly groped about the top of the dresser for another potential weapon to throw at him. "The knights guarding the keep will come running!"

"What is wrong with you?" grumbled the stranger, as he shook his head in dismay. "You *have* been screaming. Do you see anyone coming to your aid? Anyone at all: knight, soldier or servant, coming to answer your call?"

"What have you done to them?" asked Rose, palming a hefty crystal decanter of her favourite, rose-scented perfume. "I demand to know!"

"I made it so they will not hear you. After all, you are not the first human to scream bloody murder upon seeing me."

"How did you do that?" Rose dared to ask as she clutched the decanter in her trembling hands, raising it in a threatening gesture. "Did you kill them?"

"What do you take me for? A murderous thug on a killing spree?"

"Are you?" questioned Rose. The decanter was poised in her hand, ready to launch at him as she cautiously backed away.

"My, you are rather big on high drama! Of course I am not a mass murderer. And I am only here because *you* were the one to summon *me*."

"I did not ask for *you!*" retorted the Princess, grimacing in disgust as she eyed him with certain contempt. "I asked for the *Dream Merchant*, not some strange, wizened old man with a scruffy beard down to his knees, dressed in a gaudy robe that glows in the dark."

"Good gracious, you are rather thick in the head for a Princess! And I will have you know, this is *not* gaudy. This robe is quite tasteful, perhaps a little extravagant, but I think it is quite fetching on me. It is very appropriate, especially if one is the aforementioned Dream Merchant."

"You are *him*?" gasped Rose, reluctantly lowering the perfume bottle she had planned to lob at him.

With a polite bow, the old man formally introduced himself, "Silas Agincor, Master Wizard - third level, a.k.a. the Dream Merchant, at your service, my lady!"

With a snap of his fingers, the candle on the nightstand was instantly ignited with a bright amber flame. Its steady light peeled back the gloom so she could better see him in all his glory.

"You are not at all how I imagined," grumbled Rose, heaving a disenchanted sigh as she took a tentative step closer to inspect this Wizard by candlelight.

"Well, I am sorry to disappoint you, but this is your own doing," responded Silas, his old hands smoothing out his unkempt beard. Feeling slighted by her words, he turned his short, bulbous nose up at the Princess. "You were rather vague when you summoned me in your dream – vacillating back and forth with how you pictured me."

"I was?"

"Most definitely! And the hour grows late; time was wasting away. I took it upon myself to arrive as I normally appear to those with limited imaginations."

"Are you telling me that you appear as I had dreamed you?"

"Pretty much."

"That is impossible! I would never dream up such hideous clothing on anyone. It is a crime of fashion!" disputed Rose, shaking her head in disgust.

"Oh, this is my doing! I quite like my usual attire," explained Silas. He was unrepentant as he lovingly adjusted his eye-catching apparel. "I chose to overrule your desire of dressing me in that opulent, crushed velvet robe that screamed of snobbery. I also did away with the conventional, pointy hat you mortals seem to associate with us Wizardly types."

"You do not wear a hat?" questioned Rose.

"Not now," explained Silas, pointing to his balding head. "Look at what an eon of bad hat-hair has done to me. Besides, it is my personal taste in clothing that allows me stand out from other Wizards, if you get my meaning?"

"Well, had I known that I could conjure you up however I please, I would have dreamed up something much better than this!" exclaimed Rose, pursing her lips in disapproval. "And it is not so much that ghastly robe I find distasteful, the entire package is somewhat wanting."

"If you find me so abhorrent, it is not too late," informed Silas. A trace of a mischievous smile appeared beneath the lush growth of silvery whiskers.

"Now you are the thick one. How can I dream when I am wide awake?"

"My dear girl, there are those in the world who can dream with their eyes wide open," stated the Wizard, raising the tip of his glowing index finger to her forehead. "Obviously, you are not one of them. Try this."

As his fingertip touched lightly against her forehead, a strange tingling sensation expanded from this point of contact. Like a pebble tossed onto the mirror-like surface of a tranquil pond, it rippled, expanding outward to migrate through her body. It was the same prickly feeling when one's foot falls asleep, but this time, it felt as though her head was abuzz with this numbing sensation.

"Now, close your eyes and relax completely. Deep in your mind's eye, conjure up an image of exactly how you would imagine me to look."

"And I can truly imagine you *any way* I want?" queried Rose, as one of her eyes popped open as she searched the Wizard's face for the truth.

"Yes! I can appear more eye-pleasing if that is your wish, or however you want me to be; taller, shorter, fatter, younger and so on. Just be sure you have a clear image in your mind."

"You can make it so? However I imagine?"

"It sounds rather dubious, but yes. I will warn you though, do not get silly with this magic," cautioned Silas. "Calling me up is serious business, after all."

"I must try this!" exclaimed Rose, squeezing her eyes shut.

"Take a deep breath, clear your mind and create a picture in your head of exactly how you would like to see me," instructed the Wizard. "The more vivid the image, the more real it shall become."

Rose did exactly as Silas requested, clearing her mind as she exhaled a slow, deep breath. Pushing away the occasional random thought that wandered into her mind, she conjured up a new and improved image for the Wizard. As her eyes snapped open, she leapt back, squealing in surprise and horror.

The Wizard stood before her, the head of a goat with a long, scruffy beard protruded from a human body still draped in the gaudy robe she so disliked.

"*Baa-ad* girl!" he bleated. "I warned you not to get silly."

"*Ewww!* I hate goats!" exclaimed Rose, staring in repulsion.

"Then why did you not think of something more pleasant?" scolded the goat-headed Wizard.

"I did not think it would actually work."

"Well, try again," urged Silas, fighting the urge to chow down on the linen sheets. "Before I take to eating everything in sight."

Squeezing her eyes shut, another image popped into her head, but before it could take full form, Rose opened her eyes. She gasped, stumbling back as she stared at Silas in this new form.

"This is truly disturbing!" gasped Rose, leaping onto the bed to get away from the Wizard. Instead of the goat head on a human body, this time, he had a human head on the body of a basset hound.

"What is the meaning of this!" growled Silas, frantically spinning about like a dog chasing its tail as he tried to inspect his flea-bitten, canine body. The claws tipping his stumpy legs clattered loudly against the floor as he spun in a patchwork blur of black, tan and white fur as he tried not to trip over his beard.

"You said to think of something more pleasant," argued Rose. "I like dogs, but not like this! You are like a man and an animal – a *manimal!*"

"Just calm down!" snapped Silas, his new tail wagging enthusiastically. "Try it again, but please, this time restore my dignity and make the change an actual improvement, not some aberration of nature. Think of how you would truly like me to appear. Think carefully, think clearly and stop with this nonsense – no more conjuring up thoughts of animals."

Rose closed her eyes, drew in a deep, cleansing breath and as she exhaled, her mind was cleared. As she conjured up a fresh image, her lips curled into a mischievous smile.

Before Silas could stop her, he was transformed once again. To his pleasant surprise, he was no longer a quadruped with a wagging tail. Instead, he was standing on his own two feet and still donning his eye-catching ensemble.

"This is better," praised the Wizard, preferring his original form.

Rose said nothing in response, she merely stood before him, giggling quite loudly.

"What?" snapped Silas, his eyes narrowing in suspicion as he glanced at her.

His hands instinctively smoothed out his beard to make himself look more presentable, but half way down its length, his hands came to an abrupt halt. They were met by what he first thought was a line of knots tangled in his beard.

Peering down, a neat row of dainty, pink, satin bows met his eyes; each perfectly spaced and tied to decorate his freshly groomed beard.

"What have you done now?" gasped Silas, spinning about to look at his reflection in the mirror positioned over the dresser. His jaw dropped in shock, stunned by what he saw. The Princess had gone overboard in her efforts to conjure up a neater looking, well-groomed Wizard.

"This is most unbecoming! I look like a fancy show horse being readied for dressage!" admonished Silas, yanking at the bows adorning what hair he had left. They encircled his head like an odd-looking, pink crown.

Rose ceased her fit of giggles only when the Wizard threatened to leave, "I have had enough of this foolishness! If you refuse to treat me with the respect and dignity I am deserving of, then neither are you deserving of my gift!"

"Wait!" pleaded the Princess, biting her lower lip to stop laughing. "I could not help myself. I promise, it will not happen again! Give me another chance!"

Silas scowled in disapproval. The long, wiry hairs of his grizzled brows knitted together in an angry frown, but this harshness was somehow lost to her by the decorative bows adorning his beard and thinning head of hair.

"You are utterly lacking in self-control and discipline," scolded the Wizard. "I hardly think you are worthy of another chance."

"I swear on my father's good name, I will do better," vowed Rose; hand over heart as she made this solemn promise.

"No more shenanigans?" questioned the flustered Wizard.

"I promise!"

"Very well, then. This is your last opportunity, but if I do not see a concerted effort on your part, I will take my leave immediately."

"I promise to conjure up a more dignified image for you. Something even you will be pleased with."

"I will be the judge of that. Now, start again," ordered Silas. "Close your eyes, inhale deeply and as you exhale, clear your mind of all thoughts. Concentrate only on how you truly want to see me."

This time, Rose did exactly as she was instructed. She focused on this new image to create a concise picture in her mind's eyes.

"That is more like it," decided the Princess. She opened her eyes to check out her latest creation.

Gone were the garish robe, the long, silvery beard, the wrinkled, liver-spotted skin and the prominent, bulbous nose. Instead, Silas now appeared before her as a handsome, young man dressed in princely finery. He had stunning sapphire eyes, wonderfully chiselled features, and a flowing mane of golden hair even she would envy. However, he now stood no taller than her largest doll.

"I must say! I look quite dapper, but now I am no bigger than a garden gnome," Silas squeaked in a small voice that perfectly matched his diminutive stature as his hands caressed the youthful, wrinkle-free skin on his face.

"It is much better, but not anywhere near the height I had hoped for," decided Rose, shutting her eyes once more.

When she opened them again, the Wizard now stood six-feet tall and he was irresistibly handsome.

Rose clapped her hands with glee as she skipped over to the Wizard. "Oh, this is so much better! I *like* this!"

And then he spoke: "Well, I am duly flattered!"

The same stern, gruff voice came out of that perfect mouth to effectively shatter this grand illusion.

The Princess released a dreary sigh of disappointment as she gazed at this seemingly improved version of the Dream Merchant. "I take it, you are still you?"

"Of course I am! Otherwise, I would not be able to make your dreams come true. Instead, I would be just another dashing gadabout that you'd undoubtedly expect to charm you off your feet."

As visually pleasing as this transformation was, Rose could not get over that grating, know-it-all voice, now synonymous with the Wizard. She shuddered, disgusted by the thought of cozying up to this mysterious being disguised as a charming prince.

"Can I turn you back into a dog?"

"Not if you want your dreams to come true," cautioned Silas, issuing a stern warning to the Princess. "You turn me into a mutt and depending on how strong your imagination is, I shall probably spend the entire time begging for food, chasing my tail or heaven-forbid, licking my *you-know-what* as dogs often do."

"Will you stop it with that talk!" snapped Rose, as she tried to erase this disturbing image from her mind. "You are giving me a bad case of the willies!"

"We must get down to business, for there are others in need of my services, after all," suggested the now-handsome Wizard with the old man's voice.

"Just give me a moment," ordered Rose.

She closed her eyes, drew in a deep breath and as she exhaled, she gave her body a quick shake, right down to her manicured fingertips. Her eyes popped open once more as she announced, "We may now proceed. My mind is clear."

"Oh, goodie!" responded Silas, in feigned enthusiasm as he sat down on the fine wool area rug by her bed. "Then proceed, we shall."

"Hold on," said Rose. She fetched the goose down pillow from the bed, placing it on the rug. Feeling more at ease with this eye-pleasing version of the Dream Merchant to deal with, she made herself comfortable, her royal bottom now suitably cushioned. "Now I am ready."

"Are you positive?"

"Absolutely," confirmed the Princess, her eyes shining bright with eager anticipation of what was to come. "Now, how does all this work? Can I truly get any and all of my dreams fulfilled?"

"To put it simply, if you dream it, you can make it so," confirmed Silas, sweeping the golden locks from his dazzling sapphire eyes as he took a moment to enjoy his new, youthful form. "Even the strange and the fantastical can happen if that is your wish. For example, if you dream of making this rug fly, whisking you off to wherever you please, it can be done."

"Now that is downright silly," scoffed Rose, with a giggle. "Who in their right mind would ever wish to ride on a flying carpet?"

"Fine! The point being, it was just an example of what can be achieved no matter how extravagant or wild your dreams are."

"Point taken, now get to the important stuff," ordered the Princess. Her hand gesturing for him to hurry up as the clock in the watchtower sounded to announce the first stroke of midnight. "How do I make my dreams come true?"

"Typically, when you summon me in your dreams to grant your wish, I appear just as I did on this eve."

"Hold on here! This leads me to believe I am only getting *one*. I thought I was entitled to *all* the wishes I could ever dream of," protested Rose, her eyes narrowing in suspicion.

"That you are, but I am a very busy Wizard, I cannot be at your constant beck and call for each and every little wish."

"I have been duped!" gasped Rose. "I am a princess, therefore, I am entitled to more than just one stinking wish!"

"It is only a *stinking wish* if that is how you dream it up. And besides, the wise need only a single wish, one dream to come true to be truly happy, but I sense you shall be more demanding than most."

"Are you saying I am not wise because I have many I wish to be fulfilled?" queried Rose. "Or is this your way of cheating me of what is rightfully mine?"

"You can have as many as you please, Princess, but a time will come when an embarrassment of riches shall become just plain, simple embarrassment."

"Are you wealthy?" questioned the Princess.

"By no means in the monetary sense, but I do have an abundance of loyal and loving friends and I want for naught. Overall, I get by quite nicely."

"Now that is rather pathetic! *Getting by* implies just that. You *are* poor," snorted Rose, rolling her eyes as she responded in an incredulous tone. "And that explains much about your sentiments!"

"What about them?" questioned Silas.

"It is like the way homely people have *great personalities* to compensate for their ugliness," explained the Princess, her words matter-of-fact. "In your case, you use these so-called *loyal friends* to make up for your impoverished state. It is meant to make you feel better despite living in destitute squalor."

"What are you speaking of, girl?"

"Listen up! If you really knew what *you* were speaking of, you would know great wealth can buy you all the friends you'd ever want, not to mention those in the higher echelons of society, plus so much more," explained Rose. "You would know there is absolutely nothing embarrassing about being rich."

"Well, it is apparent to me that you only know of excess. The meaning of moderation is quite foreign to you, so for your own good, I must enforce specific restrictions in dispensing these wishes," decided Silas.

"Like what? Are you going back on your promise that I can have all the wishes I can dream up?"

"I am a man of my word," swore Silas. "You can have whatever you dream up, however, they will be doled out accordingly. In your case, no more than three wishes per day."

"*Three per day?* Do you mean three during the hours of daylight?" asked Rose, wishing for clarification. "And then three more in the evening?"

"I mean three in a twenty-four hour period. And I am wise to your ways, young lady! No manipulation of taking one of these wishes and wishing for three more in its place. Such violation of the enforced rules shall effectively nullify our deal and you shall be allotted only one wish per day."

"Still, three is a bit stingy, don't you think?" responded Rose, her lower lip protruding in a pout.

"Not if there is a great deal of thought and consideration in the making of these wishes," corrected Silas. "One can be as good as one dozen if you know what you are doing."

"Well, I think you should give it more thought and consider giving me more than three wishes."

"Are you sure you are a princess? For I swear, your humorous comments are more fitting of a court jester."

"Ha, ha!" scoffed Rose, in mock laughter. "There is a court jester, but sadly, he is not that funny."

"And why is that?"

"How would I know? Tag is none of my concern."

"Perhaps he should be," responded Silas.

Rose unleashed a dreary sigh as she sulked, "I thought we were going to discuss the business of making *my* dreams come true?"

"Fair enough," conceded Silas, his hands fishing about the pockets of his new, fancy trousers. "Let us get down to business. First, you shall be in need of this."

He presented to the Princess a perfectly round, highly polished, marble-sized stone of the clearest quartz crystal.

"What is this?" asked Rose, staring at the flawless orb nestled in the palm of his hand.

"This is a dreamstone," revealed Silas, holding it before her eyes.

"And exactly what does this quaint, little rock do?" questioned Rose, eyeing the crystal with a degree of suspicion. In her mind, it looked quite ordinary. There was nothing about it that appeared magical.

"As I said before, because I cannot be at your constant beck and call for each and every little wish percolating in that fecund imagination of yours, I have vested this special crystal with magical powers. It will allow this stone to make your dreams become reality."

"Oh! I am liking this!" squealed Rose, giddy with excitement.

"There is a warning that comes with this magic crystal," cautioned Silas.

"What is it?"

"You must always keep it safe on your person, for if it should fall into the wrong hands, the consequences can be dire," warned the Dream Merchant, his voice became foreboding and grave.

"How dire?" Rose stared at the lovely, but innocuous-looking stone that had the power to potentially do so much for her.

"Dire as in *'we're all gonna die'* dire!" exclaimed the Wizard. He pretended to tear out his hair in a fretful bout of anxiety as though the world was about to come to a cataclysmic end.

"That bad?" questioned Rose, her hand recoiling at this unexpected news.

"Maybe not," responded Silas, with a shrug of his shoulders. "That shall depend on whose hands it falls into."

"Well then, my first wish, and you will be pleased to know it is a wise one, is that you make it so I do not lose this dreamstone," decided Rose.

"Not bad," praised Silas, giving her a prudent nod as he worked his magic. "Will this do?"

Opening his hand once more, this time the crystal orb was suspended on a delicate, filigree bead cap. It dangled from a matching chain that glistened like the highest quality silver. "You can wear it as a necklace, plus, it will always be close to you and within your sight."

"This will simply not do," dismissed Rose. Shaking her head in disapproval, it was as if it was a tawdry piece of jewellery unworthy of her consideration; a cheap bauble that had fallen out of fashion and she'd never be caught dead wearing.

"And just why not?" asked Silas.

"It is not *gold*. Everyone knows I wear only the highest quality gold."

"But this is platinum, more rare than the yellow gold you are accustomed to."

"I know, but the average person will mistake it for lowly silver. I cannot allow the people to think I am dressing below my means," explained Rose, turning her nose up at the silvery necklace.

"Very well," groaned the Dream Merchant, his hand rolling into a tight fist as he reworked his magic. "Gold, it is."

As he unclenched his fist, he presented to Rose the magic crystal dangling from a fine strand of gold. It shone in the candlelight for her to admire in all its understated glory.

"I suppose this will have to do," decided Rose, slipping the gold necklace over her head. "Considering I only wear the finest diamonds and other precious gems, and not cheap pieces of quartz crystal, I suppose I can get used to it, considering its potential value."

"Its true value will be entirely dependent upon the bearer," stated Silas.

"And how long do I have it?"

"It is yours for however long you feel it is necessary. Once you no longer have a need for the dreamstone, you must return it to me. You cannot simply give it to another, nor can you pawn, trade or sell it. It *must* come back to me or else – "

"I know, I have heard it before," interjected Rose, with a dreary sigh. "I will be cursed."

"No, but that is a bloody good idea if it keeps you on the straight and narrow," responded Silas, giving her a thoughtful nod. "I was going to say that if you foolishly give it to another, not knowing what his intentions are, you can bring about the doom of innocent people. Great harm can come to others; their fate altered because of your negligence."

"Doom... great harm... altered fate," repeated Rose, nodding as though she was acknowledging the Wizard's every word when, in all honesty, she really didn't care as long it was not her fate that was going to be doomed or altered in a negative way. "I understand. Now, the hour grows late. We do not have all night. How does this magic crystal work?"

"First of all, you should know the dreams you conjure up in your head while you are fast asleep often reveal your deepest desires. However, the best ones are created when you dream while you are awake," explained Silas.

"So I can just *wish* for what I want," determined the Princess, staring intently at the dreamstone.

"Oh, no, it is not as simple as that! Dreaming while asleep is easy, but as I said, to dream while you are wide-awake is a whole other matter. It is a skill that must be mastered and requires great focus."

"How do I do this once you leave?"

"A master storyteller can have entire tales unfold in their mind, each character as real as you or I, every action and reaction played out in exquisite detail as they commit these stories to parchment. So, too, can you dream in this manner."

"It sounds difficult," decided Rose.

"True, but it is a skill that can be mastered. It is like daydreaming, but this time, you must put thought and intention into your imaginings. They must be crystal clear in your mind's eye, and not only must you see it, you must believe it to be real. It must be tangible on all levels for it to become reality."

"And if I am not able to devote this kind of concentration to this wakeful dreaming, then what?" Never one to dedicate herself to any of her studies, in her heart, Rose sensed she would lack the discipline to master this skill, too.

"If you do not concentrate, your thoughts will be scattered, and so will the magic required to make it real," cautioned Silas. "You shall end up wasting wishes correcting the ones that fall short of your expectations."

"I do suppose that dreaming while asleep can produce rather random results, for there are times when my dreams can be quite odd, but considering the amount of effort to dream otherwise, maybe that is not such a bad thing."

"If you are lazy and unconcerned about the quality of the end results, then it really does not matter," agreed Silas. "However, if you have focus and direction, a single, well-thought-out dream can be far more satisfying than a multitude of insignificant, random ones."

"But it seems so much easier to dream while asleep," whined Rose. She balked at the idea of being made to work, even if it was not manual labour she was confronted with. "Are these dreams not as easy to fulfill as the wakeful ones?"

"Yes, they are, but, it is only because they are conjured up by your true self," responded Silas, debating whether this girl even had a conscience and functioning moral compass to steer her through the obstacles of life.

"Well, my *true self* cautions me against exerting more effort than I must when there is a faster, easier way of achieving results," decided Rose.

"As I said, these nocturnal wanderings in your mind's eye can reveal some of your deepest desires, but so too, can they expose some of your darkest secrets," cautioned the Dream Merchant.

"Not that I have any *dark secrets* to be worried about, but how do I prevent the undesirable dreams from coming true?" questioned Rose.

"That is easy, Princess. Only the dreams conjured up while you sleep, the ones you are the most deserving of, tend to come to fruition," revealed Silas, flashing Rose a dashing smile with the perfect set of pearly white teeth she had imagined him with. "If there are no dark secrets as you claim; no reason for concern."

"Brilliant!" squealed the Princess. Pleased with this knowledge, her hands clapped together in delight, for in her mind, she was most deserving of only her grandest wishes, not those pesky dreams that sometimes played out in her mind after a particularly trying day of ordering the staff about. "But suppose I simply change my mind and decide I do not like the dream that had come true?"

"To undo a wish will require you to use another to correct it, if indeed you have another left during the twenty-four hour cycle. That is why I urge you to use utmost discretion to employ this magic."

"I suppose that will do. As long as it can be undone if I am not pleased with the results, that is all that matters."

"Now, ask me what the catch is," urged Silas, giving the Princess a shrewd wink.

"Is there a catch?"

"Always! Nothing is for free, my dear girl. After all, I am the Dream *Merchant,* not the Dream *Giver-Awayer,*" grunted Silas, his eyes rolling in frustration. "I do not know about you, but in my world, the word *merchant* implies commerce and trade."

"So, there is a price to be paid if I want the magic imbued in this crystal," determined Rose.

"Everything has a price," cautioned the purveyor of dreams.

"What is this price? Whatever it is, I will pay it."

"You are still young, possessing nothing you yourself had earned to truly appreciate its worth. I desire something money cannot buy, but is priceless to you, nonetheless."

"And what would that be?"

"The love of your parents," answered Silas.

It was always his goal to set the price so high, it became a very real deterrent to those who were indiscriminate or careless about what they wish for. As was usually the case, the average person with any scruples would rescind the offer, thinking better of striking up a deal with this Wizard.

"Say again?" Rose gasped in surprise.

"I know the price is steep, but it must be equal to, if not greater, than the value of the dreamstone and all the powers it is imbued with. Let me just say, it is a way of putting your priorities in order. Of course, if you feel it is not a fair trade, then we will conclude negotiations and I shall be on my way."

For a lingering moment, Rose pondered his offer in silence.

Silas Agincor was sure he had effectively squelched her desire now that the price seemed exorbitant.

"Well, I suppose I shall take my leave now," announced the Wizard. He reached to reclaim the crystal hanging about Rose's neck, only to have the Princess abruptly step away to avoid his grasp.

"Hold on!" snapped the Princess. "I am still considering your offer."

"What is there to consider?" grunted Silas. "Your parent's love for the magic crystal... the price is far too great!"

"You said that, not me," retorted Rose, mulling over this trade.

He was momentarily stunned to discover this mortal was willing to give up what other lonely and neglected children would die for.

"In fact, I would say you are the one who is about to be short-changed in this deal," decided Rose.

"Good gracious! That is a terrible thing to say about your mother and father," chastised Silas.

"Think what you want. I know my parents do not truly love me.

That is why they are so mean to me."

"Do they beat, starve or verbally abuse you? Do they treat you like an orphaned child subjected to a gruelling life as a slave in a work house?"

"They might as well," grumbled the Princess, completely disenchanted with her royal life. "If they truly loved me, they would stop nagging at me to mind my manners and to *behave as a Princess should*. They would allow me to do as I please, when I please. I would not be made to endure long hours of study to, as they put it, *broaden my horizons and to challenge me intellectually* 'nor would they subject me to incompetent staff that fail to treat me with the respect I am deserving of."

"And I suppose there is more," said the Wizard, rolling his eyes in dismay as the Princess drew a deep breath.

"Oh, I have only just begun," spouted Rose, as she continued on her little tirade to justify her stance. "I am bound by stifling rules and strict orders just to please my mother and father. They try to control what I say and how I say it! They tell me when I should go to bed, even when I am not tired. They even choose when and what I eat, ignoring my wishes of changing my diet to suit me."

"You wish to become a vegetarian?" questioned Silas, as he struggled to better understand this mortal's dilemma.

"Are you mad? I wish to become a dessertarian!"

"A *what*?" asked Silas. "I have never heard of such a thing."

"For the uneducated, it means I would like to subsist on a diet consisting of only desserts. I'd take my sticky toffee puddings and treacle-smothered cakes over a *healthy* serving of meat and vegetables, any day."

"My goodness, a daughter of privilege so hard done by -- made to suffer nonetheless!" declared Silas, his tone mocking as he pretended to blot away a non-existent tear of sympathy. "Did it ever occur to you the King and Queen do what they must because they *love* you?"

"If this is *love*, I can do without it!" sniffed Rose, her words tainted with bitterness. "It would be so much better if they just ignored me – pretended I did not exist. I would be free to do whatever I please, come and go as I desire, and get away with bloody murder if that was what I wanted."

"Is this your wish? For the ones who love you to treat you like you no longer exist?" questioned Silas. "Think carefully, Princess, for the ramifications of such of wish can have grave consequences."

"It would be a bloody good start," decided Rose. "But I suppose I am being a bit rash. It does sound rather extreme when you really think about it."

"Indeed, it is," agreed the Wizard, relieved to see the Princess was finally beginning to understand the importance of wishing, and wishing well.

"Maybe if my mother and father, and those in their service who constantly hover around me, just *ignored* the things I say and do, it would be a better wish. I would be able to do whatever I please."

Silas' hand slapped his forehead in frustration, groaning in disbelief upon hearing this revision.

"Well? Can this wish be granted?" asked Rose.

"I suppose as I am restricting you to three wishes per day, a lesser trade of being ignored will suffice than to forfeit their love entirely. The question is, are you willing to pay the price?"

"Absolutely! However, love is not tangible like money or jewels," countered the Princess. "It is not as if it can be stuffed into a purse and traded away in exchange for something that is real."

"Though you cannot see the wind, it is still very real. On a hot summer day, you can feel its cooling breeze on your face or be witness to its devastating powers if it chose to unleash its wrath in a terrible storm."

"I will give you that, but it does not explain how you intend to exchange this so-called *love* or in my case, going by ignored so I may do as I please, for this wondrous dreamstone," argued Rose, her fingers fondling the crystal she now coveted.

"I am a Wizard! I have my ways," responded Silas, giving the Princess a sly smile. "But are you sure of this? Is the price truly worth it?"

"Believe me, if they loved me, they would allow me to do what I please. The only way that will ever happen is if they ignore me. I would be free to do whatever I want – to make my own decisions and act on my own free will."

"Just know that their concern and love comes from the heart. Without it, there is no compassion," warned the Wizard. "This is what separates man from beast. Are you still willing to barter it away so easily?"

"To get whatever I desire? It is more than a fair trade," decided Rose, her head nodding judiciously.

"As you sound so confident, here is advice you must heed as you willingly engage in this transaction," offered Silas.

"What is that?"

"Just because your dreams come true, it does not guarantee happiness. Sometimes, it is a wish squandered. In fact, the best you can do is to wish good things for others, for when you do, good things will come back to you many fold. But for that to happen, it must be a selfless wish, a random act of kindness if you will, made freely from the heart *without* the intention you shall gain something in return."

"To make a wish for another *is* to squander a wish," corrected Rose.

"You say that now, but there will come a day when you will truly understand what I speak of," cautioned Silas. "You might even discover that wishes made for you by others can bring you tremendous contentment – true happiness. It can even mean your salvation."

For a moment, Rose silently mulled over his words of warning, and then she began to giggle, "I think not! I am the only one who can dream up the best wishes for me. The only things other people wish for me is that I behave like an obedient, well-mannered princess, treat the lowly commoners with greater respect, take to my studies with greater zeal and so on and so forth. And that is just my mother's wishes!"

"Queen Beatrice is respected for her wisdom and compassion," responded Silas. "You would be wise to heed her words."

"Whose side are you on?" grumbled the Princess, stomping her feet in frustration as she glared at the Dream Merchant. "This is supposed to be about me and my wish!"

"Yes, yes! So you have no reservations in receiving the dreamstone at the said price?" queried Silas, making certain she was clear on this deal.

"None, whatsoever," confirmed Rose, her hand wrapping around the crystal pendant to make sure he did not renege on his offer.

"Then our negotiations have come to a conclusion. The stone is yours for however long you wish to keep it," announced Silas, bowing in acknowledgement of this deal.

"That is it?" asked Rose, her eyes nervously darting about, searching for a spectacular show of the Dream Merchant's powers. "No thunder and lightning? No great earthquake to herald this event?"

"Not all magic requires a grand display to unleash its powers. I prefer a more subtle approach," explained Silas, with a shrug of his now broad, manly shoulders. He playfully tossed his luxuriant mane of golden hair he'll be made to relinquish once this deal was complete and he vanished from this bedchamber to appear in another mortal's dream.

"So, it is done?" questioned Rose. She felt oddly the same for one who had been granted such a wondrous gift.

"Indeed, it is," confirmed Silas.

"And you were serious when you said I am only allotted three wishes per day?" questioned Rose.

"For your own good, yes! And as it is just after the midnight hour, the twenty-four hour cycle has already commenced. You have until the stroke of midnight to use this allotted quota, if it pleases you."

"And suppose I use only two and still have one left? Can I bank it? Carry it forward to the next cycle?" asked Rose, hopefully.

"Must you push it?" groaned Silas, shaking his head in frustration as he waved three fingers before her face to make it absolutely clear. "Three per day means just that! It will not be my fault if you chose not to use your quota on whatever given day."

"But suppose I lose count and I accidentally wish for more than three," asked the Princess, still searching for a loophole that would allow her to exceed this daily quota.

"Then you, my dear Princess, are an idiot in need of a wish to better your basic mathematical skills. For now, consider yourself duly warned."

"So be it," said Rose, nodding in agreement. "Consider me warned."

"Then, I shall wish you well and I pray you learn to temper your wants and your needs, and more importantly, you come to know the difference or this whole experience can all go to hell in a hand-basket for you, if you are not careful."

"Well that sounds rather dark and foreboding," responded Rose, uncertain if this Wizard was speaking in jest.

"It was meant to be."

"Oh… I suppose if it should, even though it won't, I really should know how to return this dreamstone to you."

"That is easy to do," responded Silas, giving her a knowing smile. "If you ever wish to summon me for this purpose, you must, and I cannot emphasize it enough, you must say: *Oh, great Wizard, the Merchant of Dreams, please answer this wish to put an end to my schemes.*"

"That is it? I must recite this dreadful rhyme?" mocked Rose.

"So revoke my artistic license! I will be the first to admit I have no career as a great poet, but at least it is easy to remember. That was the whole point of it," explained Silas, his cheeks blushing with embarrassment as this mortal ridiculed him. "Just be sure you say it *exactly* as I did. Now, shall I repeat it for your benefit?"

"That will not be necessary," assured Rose, shooing the princely-looking Wizard away from her bedchamber. "Take your leave. Do so now!"

"Just be careful what you wish for, Princess," cautioned Silas, as he faded away like a wisp of smoke.

"I have already heard that warning before! Now, go!" grumbled Rose, her hands reaching out to fan away this swirling vapour as it vanished into the night. "I have some serious dreaming to do."

Curse This Cursed Curse

"Stupid, old bed! Much too hard for my liking," Rose muttered as she stretched, her entire body aching. Rolling over from her back onto her side, she pulled the quilt up around her neck. Instead of the soft, down counterpane swathing her in its billowy warmth, fringed tassels tickled her under the chin.

Rose's bleary eyes eased open, only to be stabbed by the glaring morning light shining through the window. Squeezing her tired eyes shut, the Princess yanked the pillow from beneath her head to use it as a shield against the impending sun. Rather than a soft mattress, her head fell with a *'thud'*, thumping against a hard surface.

"What happened?" gasped Rose.

Her eyes snapped open upon this rude awakening, glancing about in a confused daze. Her world seemed to have tipped sideways. Everything seemed so tall, or she had gotten very small as she stared over at the foot of the dresser and the bright seam of light passing under the closed door. Pushing away the tassels brushing her face as she rolled onto her back, Rose suddenly realized her world had not turned on its side, nor had she shrunk. Instead, she had fallen asleep on the rug by her bed, tossing it over her body like it was a quilt.

She breathed a sigh of relief as she stared up at the familiar ceiling of her bedchamber.

"Now, how did I get here? Did I fall out of bed last night?" she wondered aloud as she stretched her tortured muscles. Like an old, arthritic woman trying to right herself, the Princess grabbed the edge of the bed, pulling herself onto her feet.

Glancing about, all appeared as it did before she went to bed last night, except for the tumbler she had used to capture the Tooth Fairy. It had vanished, not even a single crystal shard remained on the floor.

"Damn it all!" cursed Rose. "The Fairy tricked me! Nothing has changed. I shall have to report her to father! But first, I must get dressed."

For the longest moment, Rose stood in the middle of her room, waiting for her attendants to come to her aid, but Mildred, Alice and Evelyn did not arrive. They were always annoyingly punctual, but on this morning, it was well after their appointed time.

"Those lazy sods!" grumbled Rose, clanging the service bell. "Where are they?"

The Princess went ignored. Not one servant came running to answer her call. Rose opened the door of her bedchamber, peering down the long corridor. She listened for the sounds of rushed footsteps eagerly racing to her room. Instead, there was only profound silence.

"Unbelievable!" muttered Rose. She shook her head in disgrace, uncertain if this was part of her punishment. "Mother and father have gone too far this time. How dare they relieve me of my attendants? Well, I will show them. I am perfectly capable of dressing myself!"

Rose stormed over to her wardrobe closet, throwing the double doors open to select her own dress to wear this morning. Rather than a closet burgeoning with sumptuous gowns and lovely shoes to match, the wardrobe was stripped bare.

The Princess stood there dumbfounded, her mouth agape as she took in this unexpected sight.

"Hmph! I suppose I did tell Mildred to have the dressmaker replace all my old gowns. That is what happened," decided Rose, nodding her head in approval. "Finally, at least one of them had the smarts to do as she is told."

Then it suddenly dawned on the Princess. The Dream Merchant! The great purveyor of grand wishes. But nothing seemed very different at all. Rose still felt the same as she did yesterday and all the days before. Glancing at the large mirror over her dresser, she noticed she even looked the same. She was still her beautiful self, in spite of her tangled mop of golden tresses and now-wrinkled nightgown.

Was it all a bizarre dream? Or did she have a run-in with the ill-tempered Tooth Fairy? She had to be sure. Rose dashed over to the other side of the bed, searching for the tooth she had set out last night to trap the Fairy. Oddly enough, there was no tooth. There was not even a trace of the adhesive she had used to secure the bait.

"It seemed so real," groaned Rose.

The disappointment in her voice was obvious as she glanced at down at her reflection in the porcelain washbasin. Tears brimmed her eyes as she washed them away with a splash of the tepid water. Blotting her face dry, Rose released a dreary sigh, clutching the towel to her chest as though it was a doll meant to comfort her. It was at this very moment she felt something hard beneath her nightgown. It pressed uncomfortably against her tender skin.

"Stupid button!" cursed the Princess. Reaching down into the lacy neckline of her nightgown to remove the offending adornment, Rose gasped in surprise as her fingers fished out a crystal pendant dangling from a gold chain.

This moment of stunned silence was fleeting as the Princess erupted into an unbecoming display of elation.

"The dreamstone! It is real! *Woo-hoo!*" Rose whooped in euphoria, dancing about with the precious stone in her hand. "It happened! It really happened!"

She plucked it up by the bead cap, kissing the smooth, round crystal as though it was a long, lost heirloom rediscovered. This moment of impropriety came to an end as Rose composed herself.

"I am going to take care of you, my precious, little charm!" vowed Rose, holding forth the crystal to better admire it.

Exhaling a puff of air from her mouth, the dreamstone's lip-smudged surface was immediately clouded by condensation. She hastily wiped away all traces of lip and fingerprints so the crystal was in pristine condition once more.

"First thing first," decided Rose. "As I cannot traipse around in this nightgown all day while a new wardrobe is being made for me, I shall have to dream up an entirely new gown, one to suit this auspicious occasion."

Recalling the Dream Merchant's instructions, Rose closed her eyes. She drew in a long, slow breath, filling her lungs to capacity. As she slowly exhaled, pushing away all other thoughts from her mind, a vision took form. It was a beautiful white, taffeta gown with lavender accents to highlight her eyes. The satin bows, sparkling sequins and glistening crystal beads encrusting the gown were so plentiful, it not only weighed the dress down, it bordered on obscene decadence.

Rose scrutinized this image, shaking her head in disapproval, "Too much glitz and glitter to the point of being tasteless."

One by one, the satin bows vanished as she decided to do away with the sequins too, but she retained the crystal beads, after all, they did match her new pendant.

"Much better," decided Rose, approving of this new gown she created in her mind. "But why settle for crystals when I can have diamonds?"

Envisioning this upgrade, the gown shimmered. It glistened with the kind of radiance that only comes from the best quality, flawless brilliant-cut diamonds.

"Absolutely exquisite!" exclaimed Rose. She now imagined how this dress would look on her, imagining how it flattered her body, fitting perfectly to the curves of her waist and over her hips. "But something is still missing."

In her mind's eye, lovely satin shoes bejewelled with diamond beads appeared on her feet. And these shoes not only matched her new gown, they fit her dainty, little feet perfectly!

"A beautiful gown and shoes must be properly complemented by the right pieces of jewellery," decided Rose. After giving it much thought, she decided on an exquisite, gold band with a large, solitary diamond to adorn her right index finger, that way, when she pointed at people or things, not one person would be able to ignore this five-carat, Princess-cut stunner on her digit of power.

"Oh, and I must have a tiara to match."

As though tended to by an invisible hairstylist, the pink satin ribbon tying Rose's bed-head mop of hair vanished. These golden tresses tumbled down around her shoulders to magically twist, twirl and tease into a hairdo befitting a princess of her regal loveliness. And to top off her crowning glory of impeccably coiffed hair, a magnificent tiara held all the delicate strands perfectly in place.

Before making this dream into reality, Rose inspected this image, giving it a critical once-over to make certain it was *exactly* what she wished for.

"Perfect!" Rose whispered to herself.

As she opened her eyes, she gasped in astonishment as this gown, complemented by the pieces of jewellery she had conjured up in her mind, now adorned her body. She stood before her reflection in the mirror to admire her creation. It was everything she had imagined, but even more beautiful now that she was actually wearing it.

"This is so much better than what the royal dressmaker is capable of!" declared Rose. "If I plan it just right, I will never have to contend with her useless fussing, careless primping and boring designs! And, I can wish for a new outfit each and every morning! What a perfect start to a perfect day."

Rose pranced out of her bedchamber, ready to greet the world. Her light steps delivered her down the stairs where she skipped to the dining hall to join her mother and father for a morning meal.

"I must be early," said Rose, glancing about the empty room. It was obvious the servants were only now preparing for breakfast. The table was set, but the entire course was yet to be delivered.

"I do hope they are not tardy this morning. All this dreaming has made me hungry," sighed Rose. Stepping over to the dining table, she lifted the cover of one of the dishes, only to grimace in disgust.

"What is wrong with Mildred? Good help is so hard to find these days," groaned Rose, staring with utter disdain at the serving dish filled with stewed prunes. "She knows I hate these things!"

"Good gracious! How did you get in here?" asked Mildred, almost dropping her serving tray onto the floor. Alice and Evelyn were just as shocked to see this uninvited guest in the dining hall.

"How did *I* get in here?" snorted Rose, scowling in disapproval.

"Unless you have been invited, beggars are not permitted in the palace!" declared Mildred.

"How dare you insult me?" rebuked Rose. "And what is wrong with you? Since when does a beggar dress so exquisitely?"

"If you call that tatty, old frock *exquisite*, then you're not right up here," scolded Alice, her finger tapping her forehead. "Now, I suggest you leave on your own accord, or I will call the guards to have you escorted from the palace."

"But I live here!"

"Unless the King and Queen have hired additional staff that we are unaware of, then no, you do not!" corrected Mildred, her pudgy hands resting defiantly on her abundant hips. "Ladies, are you aware of any new hires?"

"No, Miss Mildred, not that I have heard," answered Evelyn, shaking her head in response.

"We are always the first to know," added Alice, staring down her nose at the stranger. "There had been no new staff members called into service of late, at least none who would stay after being verbally accosted by the Princess."

"Are you mad? I live here! I am Princess Rose! This is my home!"

"You are an imposter! And a poor one at that!" admonished Mildred. "Now, leave before we have you physically removed!"

"The insolence! I will not put up with such rude behaviour from lowly servants!" raged the Princess. "How dare you speak to me like I am nothing more than a common… commoner!"

"That is because you are!" snapped Mildred.

"Mind you, she does have the Princess' abrasive nature down pat," admitted Alice. "Her shrewish personality is quite convincing."

"I *am* the Princess!" shouted Rose, stamping her feet in frustration.

"My, my! She even has the temper tantrum down perfectly," noted Mildred, shaking her head in disgust.

"Not quite," corrected Alice. "Princess Rose would not only stamp her feet like a spoiled child, she would be holding her breath until she turned blue in the face."

"I would not!" disputed Rose.

"Please leave," urged Evelyn. "We do not want any trouble. Just leave before the King and Queen arrive for breakfast. If you do, we will not report you."

"I have had it with the three of you! I shall report you to my mother and father," snapped Rose. Plopping down onto her chair, she refused to budge from the table.

"Look here! I do not know who your parents are, but you must leave, and do so immediately," demanded Mildred. "You will not be granted an audience with the King and Queen. They have no time for vagrants like you."

"But they *will* see me," insisted Rose, her hands wrapping tightly around the armrests of the chair to secure her place.

"Please ma'am, go before there's trouble," pleaded Evelyn.

"Come now, Gwendolyn, you must know it is me!" Rose stared pleadingly into this young woman's eyes.

"I have never met you before and my name is not Gwendolyn."

"The Princess would know her staff and it is obvious to me that you do not," stated Mildred, her words matter-of-fact. "Now, take your leave before I take my broom to your backside!"

"You must believe me! I am Princess Rose."

"I believe you are on an unscheduled leave from the local mental asylum," countered Alice.

"Nobody speaks to me with such disrespect, especially you three! Have you all taken leave of your senses?" gasped Rose, shaking her head in disbelief.

"No, but I do believe *you* have," responded Mildred. "I suggest you leave before the authorities come looking for you to lock you away for good!"

"I swear! I *am* the Princess!"

"You look nothing like the Princess," argued Alice.

"Oh, I know what it is!" decided Rose. "It is this new dress and the tiara! The new hairdo! That is why you do not recognize me. I will have you know I created this outfit myself."

"Do you take us for fools? The Princess does not even know how to thread a needle, let alone sew on a button," disputed Mildred.

"And I do not believe she even knows how to brush her own hair," added Alice. "Now leave at once!"

"That was uncalled for! Just look beyond this dress and these jewels! You will see it is *me*: Princess Rose."

"See for yourself, ma'am," said Evelyn, tilting a silver, serving tray for this stranger to gaze into. "I believe you are very confused. Perhaps, you only wish you were the Princess."

Rose's eyes opened wide in surprise. She almost jumped out of her fancy, new shoes upon discovering what the three women were seeing. Not even she recognized the reflection staring back at her.

True to the Tooth Fairy's words, Rose had indeed become what she hated the most! Not only did she appear in the slovenly rags of a peasant, apparel befitting the most downtrodden of society, she was as withered and shrivelled as the prunes she hated so much. Her hands touched her face to discover her skin, especially around her eyes and mouth, had become deeply creased. Even her hands were wrinkled and flecked with dark liver spots like that of an old woman.

"There must be something wrong with this tray!" decided Rose.

"I hardly think so," responded Evelyn, staring at their reflections in the tray. "I look as I always do, just as you do."

"Please, listen to me," begged Rose, her heart racing in sheer panic. "This is a terrible mistake! I truly am Princess Rose-alyn. Please do not judge me by my appearance! A terrible trick had been played on me! I've been cursed!"

"A likely story!" disputed Alice, dismissing this claim.

"In fact, we know for sure you are not Princess Rose," growled Mildred, taking up the broom. "She would never say *please* to – what does she call us? Oh, yes, *lowly commoners!* Now take your leave before you are thrown into the dungeon for trespassing!"

"I suppose you are right," conceded Rose. With a disheartened sigh, she stood up from the chair she had sat in since she was a toddler. "I will leave… right after I see my parents!"

The Princess dashed from the dining hall, but instead of heading to the main entrance of the palace, she was setting a course to the throne room.

"Stop her!" hollered Mildred, broom in hand as she led the charge with Alice and Evelyn following close behind. "Intruder in the keep!"

Sprinting down the corridor, their cries for the guards to intervene echoed behind Rose.

As the captain of the King's army and several of the soldiers stationed in the castle keep suddenly appeared at the end of the hall to intercept her, Rose abruptly turned, racing down another corridor.

"Halt!" shouted the captain, urging his men to give chase. "Halt or you will be forced to stop!"

Ignoring this order, Rose sprinted away from them, confident she could outrun her ironclad foes.

Joining the pursuit, the soldiers' heavy armour rattled and clanged as they gave chase. Even weighed down by their suits of steel and armed with swords and long pikes, they were quickly gaining on her.

In a mad scramble, Rose leaped up. Tearing down a huge wall tapestry, she hoped to slow her pursuers down. It billowed like the collapsing sail of a tall ship, falling to the floor. Instead of being deterred by this obstacle, the men merely trampled over the wall decor in a bid to stop this intruder.

"Good God! For an old biddy, she's fast!" noted one of the soldiers.

"Don't waste your breath talking," ordered the captain. "Stop her before she gets to the throne room!"

As the heavy footfalls racing up behind her grew louder, Rose refused to surrender. She charged off toward the main hall where a historical display decorated this great chamber. It consisted of weapons and full stands of antique armour representing Fleetwood through the ages.

With a burst of speed fuelled by desperation, Rose dashed past this display, stopping only to send the first stand of armour crashing over into the next. In a cavalcade of smashing armour and crashing weapons toppling to the floor, the soldiers were slowed only nominally. The captain vaulted over the chaos, ordering his men on, "Stop that hag! She mustn't get to the King and Queen!"

Just as Rose burst into the throne room, her chest heaving, her eyes looking wild, the royal couple jumped with a start upon seeing her. Before the Princess could utter a single word, the knight rushed up, subduing the intruder.

"What is going on here?" King William demanded to know.

"No need for concern, my liege," assured the captain. The knight bowed apologetically as one of the soldiers helped to restrain their feisty captive. "Just escorting this woman out."

"Mother! Father!" She called out as she frantically struggled against the captain's powerful grip as another soldier moved in to subdue her. "It's me, your daughter, Rose!"

The King and Queen exchanged quizzical glances, and then stared at this old peasant they had never before laid eyes on.

"Remove this poor imitation of the Princess from the palace immediately," ordered King William, waving this stranger off. "It is obvious this woman is greatly disturbed."

"Yes, my liege, right away!" The captain bowed as he motioned the soldiers to escort the peasant out.

"Do you suppose Rose invited that woman into the palace?" asked the King, turning to his wife.

"Why would she? After all, she hates the common people," answered the Queen, her shoulders shrugging with indifference. "If she did, then Rose will have to deal with this matter in her own way and in her own time, as she always does."

"Where is our daughter, by the way?" questioned William.

"Your guess is as good as mine, dear," replied Beatrice, watching as one of the soldiers pried the woman's hands from the corner of the hallway as this trespasser refused to leave willingly. "I imagine she will show up when she gets back from doing whatever it is she does."

Kicking and screaming, Rose put up an incredible fight. She even contemplated biting her assailants. The only thing that stopped her was remembering how infrequently these commoners bathed and washed their hands.

"How dare you?" shrieked Rose, spitting mad as she struggled against their hold. "Unhand me! I am a princess – *the* Princess!"

"And I am the King of Fleetwood," the captain snorted in ridicule, watching as his men shoved her out the gateway. With a wave of his hand, the captain ordered for the portcullis to be dropped.

As this heavy iron grate slammed down with a resounding clatter, Rose came to the terrible realization this barrier would effectively prevent her entry into her rightful home.

"Come back here!" demanded Rose, her hands banging against the portcullis as she watched the captain and his soldiers march away. "Let me in!"

"If you know what's good for you, you'll bugger off and do so now!" snarled the captain. "If you insist on making a commotion, I am confident my liege will have no qualms about making room for you in the dungeon, if that's what you insist on."

"But I am Princess Rose-alyn Beatrice Elizabeth Wilhemina Pepperton!"

"You are nuttier than a fruitcake, that's what you are!" hollered the captain, as he turned his back on her to address the soldiers. "Keep your eyes on her. She's a real nutter, that one. Make sure she does not enter the palace. If she attempts it, you have my permission to raise the drawbridge, with her on it."

"Yes, sir!" The soldiers responded in unison as they saluted to their parting captain.

"I am the Princess! Do you hear me!" shouted Rose.

As her words went ignored, panic and frustration rose to an all-new level. The frightening prospect she'd be forced to spend the night in the company of strangers, and worse yet, in the presence of the vagrants, vagabonds and the other sordid cast of characters making up the dregs of society, seeped into the back of her mind.

Resigning to the fact these men were unsympathetic to her plight, Rose crumpled into a dejected heap. Plopping down on the bridge over the moat, hot tears streamed down her face. Peering up at the soldiers guarding the way, she realized her best puppy eyes would do nothing. They'd probably see an ugly, old wrinkled hound as they were unmoved by this prodigious show of tears. It caused her to sob all the louder, weeping inconsolably into her hands.

"What in the world are you crying about?"

"Wh- what?" sniffled Rose. She glanced up to see her personal court jester standing over her.

"Did you break a fingernail sorting through your jewels this morning?" asked Tag, squinting as the morning sun reflected off the diamond ring to momentarily blind him with its dazzling glare. He stared down at her, leaning against his walking stick that doubled as his training sword whenever he took to accosting the local scarecrows.

Rose stopped sobbing long enough to stare up at Tag as she asked, "You know me?"

"That's an odd question."

"I ask again! Do you know me?"

"There are times when I would rather not admit to it, but of course I do," answered Tag.

"Then, who am I?"

"Are you daft? If you have to ask, then you've been sitting in this sun longer than you should," responded Tag, his eyes shone like sapphire as they glanced up at the yellow orb burning through the wisps of cloud.

"Who am I?"

"Depending upon your mood, you are either Princess Rose or Rose-alyn Beatrice Elizabeth Wilhemina Pepperton the Princess of Fleetwood, if you want the whole world to know *exactly* who you are. Why do you ask?"

"Do I look odd to you?" asked Rose, blotting away the salty tears on the hem of her fancy gown.

"No more so than usual."

"I am serious!" snapped Rose, in no mood for any of his smart remarks.

"So was I."

"Seriously, do I look like myself?"

"Aside from your weepy eyes and your cheeks turning red from all that blubbering, you look like you always do," responded Tag, his shoulders shrugging with indifference. "And as your looks are so bloody important to you, I suggest you go back into the palace; make yourself presentable. In all honesty, this is a rather sorry state you're in."

"Perhaps you can sneak me back in?"

"What in the world are you talking about? Why do you need me for that? You have more right to be in there than I do."

"True, but not according to *them*," grunted Rose, her eyes like daggers as they shot a hostile glance at those guarding the palace grounds.

"You are making no sense, whatsoever!"

"Maybe to you, but the whole world has gone crazy," responded the Princess, heaving a disheartened sigh.

"The world is the same. Perhaps you're the crazy one," suggested Tag, his words matter-of-fact. Sitting down next to the Princess, he let his legs dangle over the side of the drawbridge.

"Do not tease!" scolded Rose, using the back of her hands to wipe away the tears trickling down her cheeks. "Because of that stupid Tooth Fairy, I am now banished from the palace."

"You do realize with every word you speak, our conversation just keeps getting more bizarre?"

"Remember yesterday when I tried to enlist your aid in meeting the Tooth Fairy?"

"Oh yes… your so-called *grand plan*, the one I denounced as a devious *scheme*," recalled her jester.

"Well, things did not go quite as planned."

"Bloody hell! Are you telling me that you succeeded in talking to the Fairy?" asked Tag, stunned by this surprising bit of news.

"In truth, I succeeded in *capturing* her, but that wretched little Fairy did not take well to being taken prisoner."

"Can you blame her? I'd be beyond angry if you tried something stupid like that on me!"

"Well, to make matters worse, it just so happened I captured the *Queen* of the Tooth Fairies and she had a few powers I was not expecting. And to complicate the whole situation, the Fairy confronted my parents. She demanded I be punished for trapping her."

Instead of offering sympathy, Tag began to laugh. Rarely was the Princess ever called on her ill-conceived plans to dupe or manipulate others.

"This is not funny!" snapped Rose, smacking Tag on his arm. "Because of Pancecilia Feldspar, I am cursed."

"Yeah, yeah… I know. You are cursed with beauty," mocked Tag, shaking his head in disbelief.

"True, but it is more than that! She told me if I did not change my ways, I would be cursed and now, I have been utterly vanquished from the palace."

"This sounds serious."

"It *is* serious! Worse yet, this morning *everybody* in the palace failed to recognize me," continued Rose, as she fought back another wave of tears. "When they looked at me, all they saw was a shrivelled up, prune of a peasant. That is why they cast me out!"

"Too strange!" declared Tag, staring into the moat to gaze at her reflection. "I still see the same, spoiled princess I've always known. So how is it that everyone sees a stranger and I still see you?"

Rose thought on this question for a moment, and then it dawned on her: "Where were you last night?"

"What does that have to do with anything?"

"Just answer my question! Were you in the palace last night?"

"As I do not consider myself to be in your service when you're asleep, I chose to take care of a personal matter that is none of your business, by the way," disclosed Tag.

"So you were gone all night?"

"Just returning now," admitted Tag. "Thought I'd sneak back in before you summoned me to entertain you."

"That must be it! This curse seemed to have only affected those who remained in the palace last night."

"But as an old peasant woman?" questioned Tag, scratching his head in bewilderment. "That is too bizarre!"

"Well, the Fairy did say I would become what I hate the most," admitted Rose.

"Let me guess… prunes and peasants," decided Tag.

"Yes! That is why the palace staff, even my own parents, did not recognize me!"

"The Fairy, this Pancecilia Feldspar, warned you this would happen if you *did not* change your ways?" queried Tag, trying to understand the circumstances.

"Well… yes."

"So you brought this curse unto yourself?" determined the young man. "This is your own doing?"

"Not on purpose."

"And I take it, the more you talked and antagonized her, the more severe the Fairy decided the punishment should be?"

"She was pretty vindictive when I think about it," answered the Princess.

"You captured her, for pity's sake! It bloody well serves you right," declared Tag. "You've finally received your comeuppance! You got exactly what you deserve. Mind you, your *hate list* is pretty extensive. If what you say is true, you best be careful of what you say aloud."

Rose's eyes grew wide in surprise as her hands slapped over her mouth in case she blurted out another word to exacerbate an already bad situation.

"This is good," decided Tag, nodding in approval. "It is better you do not prattle on about all the people and things you so despise. Bad enough being a peasant, even worse to be one of those *poor* peasants made to get by on the generosity of others."

"Curse this cursed curse!" swore Rose. "I shall get even with that blasted Tooth Fairy for doing this to me."

"You did this to yourself," corrected Tag.

"That wretched Fairy tricked me!" growled Rose, still refusing to accept responsibility for her actions.

"No trick here! Just your own stupidity working at its best."

"How dare you speak to me in this insolent manner? I am still the Princess, after all."

"If your own parents refuse to acknowledge you, then why should I? Had I only remained in the keep last night. I would be seeing a ragged, slovenly peasant sitting next to me, too."

"I suppose that is true."

"Damn it all, what cruel irony is this?" groaned Tag, his fingers snapping in disappointment. "Why did I not stay last eve?"

"For a court jester, you are not funny at all," dismissed Rose, rolling her eyes in frustration.

"That is because I never wanted to be a jester, especially for you! And as none, except for me, recognize you for whom you really are, as far as everyone is concerned, you are *not* Princess Rose. You are, as you so eloquently put it, a nobody!"

"That is a mean thing to say!"

"I speak the truth! And as you have been ousted from the palace as a lowly commoner, I am no longer in your service," reasoned Tag.

"Meaning?"

"Woo-hoo!" exclaimed the young man, his fists pumping the air. "I'm free – free, I tell you! I am no longer your fool! Good-bye, common peasant girl!"

"Where are you going? You cannot leave me here to fend for myself."

"Wanna bet? See? My feet are moving, I am stepping away," announced Tag, taking a deliberate step back as he bowed in parting salutation.

"Farewell! So long! See you later, and if I am lucky, maybe not!"

"But you must help me!"

"Quoting *your* famous last words: *'What's in it for me?'*"

"It is reward enough to be in my service," answered the Princess. "What more can you ask for?"

"I don't know what else this curse did to you, but you've truly lost your mind! I will never become a knight, no thanks to you, but at least I'm now free of you. I need not put up with any of your ill treatment and demeaning words. Farewell!" said Tag. Spinning about on his heels to beat a hasty retreat, he waved good-bye over his shoulder.

Rose did not utter another word. Drawing her knees up to her chest, her arms wrapped around her legs. She rested her forehead on bended knees to hide the tears streaming down her face as she began to sob.

It was not her usual, contrived *boo-hoo I-feel-sorry-for-me* crying Tag was so used to. There was true fear and desperation seated in this weeping and it was enough to force him to stop dead in his tracks.

"For pity's sake, will you stop it with those tears!" groaned Tag, shaking his head in disgust as he dug into his pocket, searching for a kerchief. "It is so pathetic."

"I – I can't h- he- help it!" stammered Rose, choking out the words between gasping sobs. "I – I know not what to do."

"To start, put a stop to the waterworks!" ordered Tag, handing her a worn, tattered kerchief. "Your tears are going to flood this moat."

Without even bothering to examine this ragged cloth to see if it was clean, Rose quickly blotted her tears, blowing her nose into the now damp kerchief. Drawing in a deep breath to compose herself, she thrust the well-used cloth into Tag's face as she announced, "There! No more tears. Now will you help me?"

Tag recoiled from this soggy offering, motioning the Princess to keep it.

"Give me one good reason why I should. And it better not be your usual *'because I am a princess and you are a nobody'* rubbish. That is a lame reason, now even more so than ever."

"You should help me because your father, a great and noble knight, would expect you to come to the aid of a damsel-in-distress."

"I am not a knight, therefore, I have no code of honour to abide by where you are concerned."

"Then where is your sense of compassion for a fellow human being?" asked Rose, staring with pleading eyes at Tag.

"It fell to the wayside when you destroyed my dreams of following in my father's footsteps. As for showing you some compassion? Perhaps if you treated others with respect, I'd be more inclined to help, but of late, your treatment of others, particularly those of a lower station in life, does not inspire me."

"I tell you what. If you promise to help me, I will more than make it up to you," offered Rose.

"As far as I am concerned, there is nothing you can say or do that will set things right," countered Tag.

"What if I see to it you get your father's sword back?"

"You're a wretched one! It's just like you to stoop to whatever level you deem necessary to get what you want," denounced Tag, his eyes flashing in anger. "How dare you make a promise you cannot keep?"

"On my father's good name, I swear if you help me, I shall see to it your father's sword is returned to you," vowed Rose, her hand over her heart in solemn promise.

"How dare you swear on the King's good name when you are lying? You told me long ago that sword was lost in battle when my father died."

"That was not quite true," revealed Rose. Unable to meet his eyes, the Princess stared down at her hands. "I stored your father's sword in my dowry chest. I meant to return it to you when the time was right."

"So you lied to me! You had been lying to me all these years!" growled Tag, unable to believe his ears. "And when would you have deemed the time as being right? When I was too old to become a knight?"

"I do believe the time is right at this very moment," decided Rose, hoping to pacify her jester. "And if I lied, it was a harmless lie."

"Harmless to whom? You never cared for what became of my father's prized possession! It meant nothing to you, but it was *everything* to me. It was all I had left of him."

"Well, now that I understand how truly precious that old sword is to you, you can have it," promised Rose, "*if* you help me."

Tag just glared at the Princess, snorting a loud, angry breath as he shook his head in despair and resentment. "Until now, you never intended to give that sword to me. You are a horrid little… little… princess!"

"You make it sound like being a princess is such a bad thing!"

"In your case, it is."

"You are just angry."

"You're bloody right I am! I want my father's sword *now!*" demanded Tag, infuriated by her irreverent attitude.

"I would give it to you now, if it were not for this curse," explained Rose. "Until it is broken and those in the palace allow me back in, I cannot retrieve it for you."

"So... if I help you to break this curse, you will promise to return my father's sword to me?" questioned Tag, seriously considering Rose's offer.

"I swear," vowed Rose, her hand over her heart.

"In addition, not only will you return my father's sword to me, you shall release me as your jester."

"I suppose it can be done," said Rose. "But only if you are successful."

"Of course, it can be done! As for success, I can do whatever I put my mind to as long as you return my father's sword to me when this curse is undone."

"I promise!"

"You swear?" asked Tag, searching her eyes for the truth.

"On my father's good name," vowed Rose.

"Well, your name is no good to me, however, your father's will do," decided Tag, determined to reclaim the family heirloom. "So, what is involved in undoing this curse?"

"How would I know?" groaned Rose. "I was not paying particular attention when the Fairy rambled on."

"Figures!" grunted Tag. "Do you think a knock on your noddle will help you remember?"

"Do not come near me!" scolded Rose, ducking his hand that was eager to take a flick at her perfectly coiffed head.

"Then I recommend you think and think hard. Now focus! What did the Tooth Fairy say?"

"I am trying, but I am having difficulty sorting out what she said and what the Dream Merchant warned me of," responded Rose, picking through her selective memory.

"The Dream Merchant? Who is that?"

"I am not about to bore you with the details of this Wizard. It is a whole other matter."

"If I am expected to help you, you better tell me everything that happened last night," ordered Tag. "If this so-called Dream Merchant has anything to do with the curse you are under, it is best to tell me all you remember."

"Fine! This Wizard, the Dream Merchant as he is called, appeared after the Tooth Fairy revealed how to summon him."

"And what is he? Evil or something?"

"As best as I can tell, he was rather eccentric, but benign. He specializes in magic that allows dreams to come true. Whatever you can dream up, whatever you can wish for, he can make it come true. He appeared last night in my dreams to grant me all that I can ever wish for."

"Well, if this is what you wished for, to be treated like a commoner and banished from your palace, then I believe the Tooth Fairy absconded with more than just your tooth," decided Tag. His knuckles rapped against his forehead as though his skull was now devoid of a brain.

"I did not wish for this to happen!" groaned Rose. "I had wished for this new gown and these fine jewels."

"Wow!" marvelled Tag, staring at her beautiful gown, tiara and its matching accessories. "That is quite the wish. And this Dream Merchant made it so?"

"Yes," moped the Princess.

"Well then, just make another wish to undo the curse," suggested Tag.

"That cannot be done," informed Rose.

"I don't understand. You just said the Dream Merchant could make your wishes come true."

"That part is true, however, Silas Agincor – "

"Who is Silas Agincor?" interrupted Tag.

"The Dream Merchant's name is Silas Agincor. Anyway, what I was saying is, he felt it was prudent to restrict me to three wishes per day. I thought he was being stingy. He claims he was being prudent."

"If that is the case, just wish yourself back into the palace or wish for this curse to be undone," said Tag.

"I already tried."

"So the Wizard lied to you. Either he only granted you one wish or the gown, shoes and jewels constituted three wishes," determined Tag.

"Well, actually this outfit was one wish. I had already used the other two wishes."

"On what, pray tell?"

"The first wish was for my parents to ignore what I say and do, that way, I am free to do as I please."

"Well, that explains why the King and Queen have not come looking for you. And what was your second wish?"

From behind the bodice of her lovely gown, Rose produced the dreamstone for Tag to see.

"You wished for a crystal pendant?" asked Tag, surprised she would want something as ordinary and cheap as this bauble.

"This is a dreamstone," explained the Princess. "The Dream Merchant had imbued it with powers to make all the wishes I can dream of come true. He warned me that it must never fall into the hands of another or there could be dire consequences, so I wished he would make it so I would never lose this magic crystal. That is why it now hangs from this golden necklace."

"First wish: stupid idea. Second wish: it makes sense somewhat, I suppose," decided Tag. "So when are you granted another three wishes?"

"I must wait until midnight."

"Then it's simple! You'll just have to be patient and wait until tonight to wish for this curse to be undone."

"If it were only that simple," groaned Rose, with a dreary sigh.

"Are you saying it's not?"

"I am under a curse! I would never *wish* to be an old peasant woman. And as you are too thick to know it, a curse is quite different from a wish."

"So, am I wrong to believe this curse can be undone?" queried Tag.

"This curse, becoming what I hate the most, can be undone, but not with a wish. The Tooth Fairy said that until I find my heart and I am loved by none... or nobody, I would remain cursed."

"Which is it? None or nobody?" interjected Tag.

"What difference does it make? Nobody in the palace loves me now. That is why I am here."

"And what of this heart?" queried Tag.

"It must have something to do with the locket I gave her, for she warned I would not have the heart to seek it out to reclaim it."

"Well, this should be easy. We are halfway there as we speak."

"What do you mean?" queried the Princess, glancing up hopefully.

"Nobody loves you, that's pretty obvious," grunted Tag.

"That is not quite true!" protested Rose. "I am loved by all in Fleetwood, except for those in the palace whose minds had been addled by the Fairy's curse."

"Now you are being delusional," reasoned Tag. "And as for your heart, I didn't think you had one to begin with, so there lies the challenge."

"I am not amused!" scolded Rose, frowning in anger.

"Who said I was being funny?"

"Never mind that. The silver locket she took is in the shape of a *heart*," explained Rose. "Perhaps that is what she meant when she said I would have to find my heart – that I must find the will and the heart to endure a quest to reclaim it."

"Well, I suppose you have none other to consider, so that must be it," decided Tag.

"Pance said she was going to put it in a special place, but I imagine it must be difficult to access as she warned me it would not be worth my effort to try."

"Did she say where?"

"No, at least I do not recall her mentioning that."

"I suppose that will be our first mission, to find out where your heart is," decided Tag, as he thought on this missing locket.

"So you will help me?"

"I am helping myself," disclosed Tag, unashamed to make this admission. "I just want my father's sword back."

"I swear, it is yours once we break this curse," promised Rose. "If you help me and we succeed, I will give it to you."

"Then we best be on our way."

"To where?"

"To see the Tooth Fairy, of course," responded Tag, hoisting the Princess onto her feet.

Well, That Was Stupid...

"So, do you know where to find the Tooth Fairy's castle?" questioned Rose, as she daintily lifted the hem of her gown so it would not get dirty.

"Nope."

Tag's answer was brisk. He did not even slow down to address the Princess as he should, but at this point, he really didn't care.

"For someone who does not know where to go, you sure act like you do," grunted Rose, struggling to keep up with her jester's deliberate strides.

"I never said I didn't know where I'm going. You just assumed so."

"But you said *no*," reminded Rose.

"All I admitted to was not knowing the location of the Fairy's castle."

"Very well then. Where are you taking me?"

"Away from here," he responded, glancing over his shoulder at the great battlement surrounding Pepperton Palace.

"I would much rather stay here, close to home."

"And I would prefer to let you stay than to have you follow me about all day, but you heard the soldiers guarding the palace grounds. If you loiter about the gateway any longer, they'd have reason to lock you into the dungeon."

"*Ewww!*" groaned Rose, shuddering in disgust. "I have never been down there before, but I have not heard one good thing about that place."

"Were you expecting maid service and three square meals a day? It's a prison, for pity's sake," grumbled Tag, annoyed by her ignorance. "So of course you'd hear nothing good about it."

"Fine! But you have not answered my question. Where are you taking me?"

"If you must know, we're going to wander around the County of Wren until the day is done."

"Are you serious? We are going to wander until nightfall?" gasped Rose. She dreaded the prospects, for never in her entire life had she been made to walk *anywhere*.

"Until the midnight hour or however long it takes for you to make those wishes again," explained Tag.

"Just remember, you cannot ask me to wish for your father's sword. You promised to help me break this curse first. This is my guarantee you will help me."

"I know," groaned Tag, unleashing a dismal sigh. "I just said that so I could watch you squirm."

"Ha, ha!" snorted the Princess, in mock laughter. "Still not funny."

"All the more reason to release me as your court jester. There are others more suitable for the job than me, you know?"

"Seriously! Are we going to walk all day? For nightfall is a long way's off," reminded Rose, staring up at the morning sun. It crept ever so slowly across the sky, and even more so now that she desperately wanted it to be midnight.

"We're heading to the nearest village. Although you're unaccustomed to suffering, today you'll be made to walk on your own two feet. I'm not some beast of burden, so don't even think of asking me to carry you."

"Who said I was? I am quite capable, you know? So we are heading to Cadboll in Wren. Why there?"

"To kill some time, as we have so much time to kill," responded Tag, picking up his pace.

"Do you know someone in Cadboll?"

"I know a few of the villagers."

"I mean to say, anyone who can help us find the Fairy's castle," said Rose, trotting along behind him.

"No, but I know of a special place where we can bide our time, as I'm sure your royal, little feet can't take to walking for any real distance."

"Well, as comfy as these new shoes are, I must admit, a carriage to ride in would suit me better."

Tag glanced over his shoulder, frowning in annoyance at the Princess.

"But at this point, it is neither here nor there," finished Rose. "So, where is this place you have in mind? Is it close?"

"We are going to the best pub this side of Fleetwood, but it is clear on the other side of Cadboll," answered Tag. The thought of a frothy pint of dark ale motivated him to march on.

Rose came to a dead stop.

"Hold on! Are you saying you are taking me, a princess, to a public drinking house? A place where commoners gather to imbibe in libation?"

"No, I'm taking you to a place where ordinary folks like *me* like to congregate to share in a friendly drink. And worry not, Princess. This pub is the finest drinking establishment in all of Wren."

"Somehow, coming from you, it does not sound impressive."

"Trust me, it'll be fine," promised Tag.

"Do lords and ladies of nobility frequent this place?" questioned Rose.

"Why do you ask?"

"If they do, it must be a fine establishment worthy of my presence."

"No such hoity-toity, upper-crust types at this pub, only peasants and lowly commoners like me. And for this reason, it's great!"

"It better not be patronized by rogues and scoundrels or you will hear about it," warned Rose.

"Oh, I'm sure I will," sighed Tag.

"Slow down!" ordered Rose.

She tiptoed around clumps of horse manure scattered across the roadway like a regular obstacle course meant to hamper her. Stepping gingerly, it was as though she'd somehow be contaminated if this excrement should touch her shoes.

"No, *you* hurry up," responded Tag, marching along at a steady pace. "Remember, I'm on a mission."

"You are on your way to a pub," corrected the Princess.

"Same thing."

"Slow down, I command you!" Rose stamped her feet in defiance as she huffed and puffed to catch her breath.

Tag came to an abrupt halt, spinning about on his heels to confront her. "If the palace staff and your own parents do not acknowledge you as being a princess, why should I? There's no need for me to follow any of your commands!"

"You will do as I say, for you know who I am, therefore, you must treat me accordingly."

"According to protocol, I should, but until this curse is broken, I'll treat you no different than I would a regular girl. In this case, a pesky, demanding one. So there!"

"But – but-" stammered Rose. "I have seen you treat that peasant girl with more respect and kindness than you do me."

"Which one?" asked Tag.

"You know the one! She delivers the basket of eggs to the palace every other morning. I have seen you smiling and laughing with her, helping to carry that basket into the kitchen for her. And I have also seen you carrying buckets of water for my handmaiden Gwendolyn, when that is her job."

"Her name is *Evelyn*," corrected Tag. "And those buckets are heavy. I was only trying to be helpful. Besides, unlike you, they have manners and they are respectful to me!"

"The point is, you treat these peasants and servants with greater kindness than you do me, and I am royalty!"

"Oh… so you're jealous," noted Tag, with a smirk of a grin as he stared at Rose's scowling face.

"*Jealous?* I am angry! I deserve more respect than both of those lowly wenches combined, and yet, you treat me like I am deserving of less."

"Well, here is some news for you, *Princess*. Your parents hold a royal title far greater than yours, but they have the wisdom to know the respect of their subjects is earned, not given freely by the people."

"So you say, but I prefer ruling through fear and intimidation," countered Rose. "It has worked for me. I always get what I want."

"Perhaps, in your crazy world, but in the *real* world, outside the walls of the castle, *please* and *thank you* can go a long ways. It's a simple concept to grasp, but I do not believe it's within your character to be gracious."

"The insolence!" snapped Rose, her perfect brows furrowing in anger. "You have raised my ire for the last time! I will no longer put up with the impudence of a simple court jester!"

"Good for you," responded Tag, shrugging with indifference. "Farewell! Good luck finding the Tooth Fairy."

Rose watched in stunned disbelief as Tag turned. Without a second thought, he promptly marched away. By his tone and actions, it was apparent he had every intention of leaving her behind.

"Wait!" hollered Rose. She picked up the hem of her gown to run after him. "I command you to wait!"

Her order went unheeded. Tag continued on his merry way, not even glancing back.

"Wait… p-pl- please!"

For a moment, Tag could not believe his ears. Did the Princess really choke out the '*p*' word? He stopped. Turning about, he watched as Rose dodged the clumps of drying road apples littering the way as she rushed after him.

"Did I hear you correctly? Did you say *please?*"

"So I did," admitted Rose. Her cheeks were flushed and to her benefit, Tag would not know if it was from sprinting or from embarrassment. "It is no big deal."

"Then you should say it more often. Now what do you want?"

"Th- tha- thank you," sputtered Rose, choking on her attempt to show gratitude to her jester.

"*For?*"

"For waiting for me," replied the Princess. Panting, she struggled to catch her breath after exerting that short burst of energy she was so unaccustomed to doing.

"You're welcome," responded Tag. "See, that wasn't so hard, was it? Now, what do you want from me?"

"I demand... I mean to say, I *need* you to help with this quest. I cannot do it on my own. Please, will you help me?"

Knowing the Princess was forced to swallow her pride, and it was probably so big it could choke a horse, Tag decided to honour his vow to assist her. In his own mind, he had no intention of breaking his promise to begin with, but the threat he was willing to walk away from this commitment was a useful bargaining tool in keeping Rose on her best behaviour.

"Before you try pulling those *puppy eyes* on me, don't bother," grunted Tag. "I will help, but from now on, you will treat me with the respect I'm deserving of. It works both ways, you know?"

"This is all very new to me, being spoken to like a commoner and worse yet, being treated like one," Rose gasped between deep breaths. "It goes against convention."

"New is good. So, do we have a deal, Princess?"

"Deal!" agreed Rose, nodding in approval.

"Then shake on it," ordered Tag, extending his hand to make the deal binding. "I want your word."

Instead of eagerly taking his sweaty hand into hers, Rose stared at the calloused, dirt-smudged paw presented to her, inwardly debating on if it was sanitary enough to touch.

"Do you want me to spit on it? Is that what you're waiting for?" asked Tag, swishing about a copious gob of saliva in his mouth to help solidify the deal.

"No!" gasped Rose. Before he could contaminate the palm of his hand with spit, she snatched it up into hers, giving it a firm shake. "We have a deal!"

"Good! Now let's be on our way," said Tag.

To her disgust, he spat out the excess saliva. She jumped back as Tag launched it in the general direction of her precious, new shoes.

Rose hastily wiped her hand on her gown as she inhaled deeply to catch her breath.

"Just give me a moment to compose myself," requested the Princess. She adjusted the tiara that now sat slightly tilted on her head after being made to run after him.

"You have one minute, not a second more."

"Good gracious! What is this?" Rose gasped in alarm. Her fingertips touched the beads of moisture gathering on her forehead. "My head is leaking!"

"It's called sweat."

"I am a Princess! I *glow*, but I certainly do not sweat."

"It comes from hard work or expending a great deal of energy, both of which are quite foreign to one as pampered as you," explained Tag, biting his tongue to keep from laughing. "Now walk. We still have a distance to go."

And so, the unlikely couple journeyed on, Tag leading the way as Princess Rose trudged along behind him.

"I wonder what time it is?" asked Rose, inhaling deeply as the tantalizing aroma of freshly baked bread and sizzling sausages filled the air as they entered the village of Cadboll.

Glancing at the sun, Tag determined it was at the highest point in the sky. "I'd say it's about twelve o'clock or a little there after."

"How can you tell?" questioned Rose, intrigued by his assumption. "By the position of the sun?"

"That, and the fact I can hear your stomach rumbling from where I stand. You always eat promptly at noon. Your stomach is sounding the alarm."

"Oh, so that is the noise," said Rose, her hands pressing against her belly as another audible rumble sounded from deep within. Having never gone hungry in her young life, the Princess had never before heard her stomach growl with pangs of hunger. "I never thought my stomach could talk."

"Yes, and it's demanding to be fed."

"If this is what it feels to be hungry, I do not like it, not at all. Can we have a meal at this establishment?" asked Rose.

"Food is served, but I hardly think pub fare; simple, rib-sticking stews or greasy fried sausages served up with a heap of boiled potatoes are to your royal tastes."

"You are right! However, at this moment I am willing to allow my delicate taste buds to suffer in order to squelch these hunger pains," decided Rose.

"If you are not going to be fussy, then you're welcome to order a meal," responded Tag.

"Then I will do just that," decided Rose.

"So, how do you intend to pay for it?"

"What do you mean?"

"You know? Money," he answered. "It is not as though you can order food and not pay for it."

"Perhaps you can lend me some? I will repay you once this quest is done," suggested Rose.

"Do I look wealthy to you?" Tag snorted in laughter as he jingled the loose change in his pocket. "You are the rich one. I can barely scrape together enough to pay for two pints of ale!"

"That is it? That is all you have?" gasped Rose.

"What can I say? My monthly wage as your personal fool leaves much to be desired and leaves even less to enjoy some of life's simple pleasures. But as you are always quick to point out, the free room and board offsets any discrepancy in my pay scale as established by the union of court jesters."

"There is a union representing court jesters?"

"There should be, considering the amount of respect we garner matches our wages," lamented Tag.

"You are not supposed to be respected. Laughed at, yes, but respected?" scoffed Rose, with a dismissive chortle.

"There you go! Hence, I am cash poor." Tag jingled the coins in his pocket to add to the effect.

"If that is the case, I shall request an increase to your monthly stipend," said Rose, feeling generous.

"That will not be necessary," declined Tag, speaking with all certainty.

"You are refusing my kind and generous offer?"

"Only because I'll be free of my appointed vocation once I break this bloody curse."

"I suppose it is good to be optimistic," decided Rose, but only because his success would be to her ultimate benefit. "But that does not help my – I mean *our* present situation. We need to eat."

"Not necessarily! The ale at this pub is so rich and hearty, it will be like drinking a liquid meal," promised Tag, as his mouth watered.

"You have no idea how disgusting that sounds," groaned Rose, grimacing in revulsion.

"I guarantee a pint will fill you right up. It will effectively quench your thirst and at the same time, kill your hunger."

"As well as my taste buds, no doubt." The Princess shuddered at the thought. "Only the finest wines cross this discerning palate; not ales and stouts consumed by the masses."

"You're just being fussy."

"At this moment, I need something more substantial – solid food to quell my hunger," countered Rose.

"Well, you have between here and the pub to come up with a solution. Otherwise, the most I can do is buy you a pint."

"I know!" exclaimed Rose. "The barkeep will see I am Princess Rose. He will feed me for free, and possibly you, too, if I tell him that you are my servant."

"I know who you are. You know who you are, but as you regularly refuse to *mingle with the commoners* as you so eloquently put it, only a rare few outside the palace know what you look like. I hardly think they will take your word for it that you are the Princess of Fleetwood."

"But how many peasants dress as elegantly as I do? How many wear diamond encrusted tiaras as well as I can?"

"Well, here's a solution that's guaranteed to work. Use that tiara of yours to pay for a meal," suggested Tag. "If you do, you'll have more than enough left to buy a horse and carriage, not to mention a small army of coachmen to serve you. That way, you can travel in the style you're accustomed to."

"If that idea were not so laughable, I would consider it," giggled Rose, waving off his recommendation. "Do you honestly think I would part with my tiara? It is what makes me, *me!*"

"Then that's a rather sad commentary on your life; to be defined by what you wear."

"You are a boy. You do not understand," argued Rose, firmly affixing her bejewelled tiara onto the crown of her head.

"Nor do I wish to, for if there's logic in your words, then that means I finally understand your mindset. And *that* would be a sad commentary on *my life* and my way of thinking."

"Say what you want, but I will not be parting with any piece of jewellery!" declared Rose. "I designed them to match the diamonds adorning this gown."

"You mean to say these are *not* crystal beads on your dress?" gasped Tag, staring at the ensemble that glittered in the sunlight.

"Do you honestly think, given the choice, I would wish for ordinary crystal over precious, beautiful gems?"

"Point well taken," said Tag, with a nod of understanding. "But you do realize you're literally a walking diamond mine? Even one of those beads will pay for a decent meal and then some."

"True, but to remove even one diamond will ruin the overall appearance of this gown. I cannot have that!"

"Think of what you're saying," reasoned Tag. "I'm speaking of a single, little diamond. No one will notice one missing bead."

"I have thought about it and the answer is a resounding *no! I* would notice and that is all that truly matters. I refuse to damage this lovely gown I created."

"Your choice: one slightly flawed dress for a wonderful meal in the best inn in all of Cadboll or you can go without food until who knows when."

"The choice is easy. The gown shall remain unspoiled."

When it came right down to it, Tag was not surprised by her decision. With a shrug of his shoulders, he grunted, "Therefore, you shall go hungry. It's that simple."

"Not necessarily," responded Rose, giving him a knowing smile. "I know how to get a meal without parting with any of my jewels or damaging my gown."

"I know that look. I'm almost afraid to ask what you have in mind."

"Then, do not ask. Just follow me," instructed the Princess, following the delectable aroma of freshly baked goods. Just off the main road where vendors and merchants gathered to sell their wares in the marketplace, Rose traced the irresistible scent of warm cheese biscuits, crusty loaves of bread and freshly baked apple pies.

"Ah, the local bakery!" announced Rose, peering around the building to eye the stall and its table covered with today's selection for sale to the public. "I knew I smelled something delicious."

"Good gracious, Princess! Don't tell me you intend to steal something to eat?" groaned Tag.

"As far as I am concerned, it is only considered stealing if the person you are stealing from knows something was stolen. Believe me, he has so many goods for sale, he will not notice if one item goes missing."

"That sounds logical."

"It does?" asked Rose, stunned to hear he agreed with her definition of theft.

"Of course it doesn't! And if you do this, I want no part of it," stated Tag. "At least I have morals and scruples!"

"Well, so do I. However, at this moment, all other senses are overruled by my sense of hunger," reasoned the Princess. "Besides, even if the baker is not aware I am about to *borrow* from him, I intend to pay him back when I can. So there! It will not be like stealing at all."

"I don't approve, but if you're so intent on doing this, you bloody well better help yourself to the smallest thing on that table," warned Tag, hoping to minimize the loss to the baker.

"That man is so rotund from eating all the leftovers he cannot sell, I will be doing him a favour," decided Rose, attempting to justify her actions. She watched as the baker replenished a basket with freshly baked buns. His flour dusted apron barely wrapped around his corpulent form as he waddled around the table to conduct business.

"That's not the point," admonished Tag, thoroughly annoyed by her indifference and strange reasoning.

"Just keep your voice down. Wait here," ordered Rose. "If anything, there is a chance I will be able to charm him into giving me something to eat."

"So, you mean to beg like a poor peasant?"

"I will not demean myself," stated the Princess. "I am sure if I explain my situation, he will show me some compassion and offer me something to eat."

"Begging..." stated Tag, with a disgruntled sigh as he watched Rose weave through the growing crowd gathering in the marketplace.

For the longest moment, Rose stood before the table of plenty. Her mouth watered as the tantalizing aromas swirling all about were heightened by her growing hunger. Seduced by these scents, she cautiously inched her way closer to the baked goods. Her trance was broken as the baker addressed her.

"So, what can I get for you today, young miss?"

"It all smells so very good," said Rose, her eyes scrutinizing each and every loaf of bread, crusty roll and fruit-filled pie.

"All freshly baked this morning, so I promise you, they're better than good," swore the baker, proud of his many hours of labour. "The apples pies are especially scrumptious. The fruits are from the early crop, just picked last evening from the local orchard."

"Oh, they do look delectable," agreed Rose, hungrily eyeing a pie burgeoning with so much fruit, the sticky, sweet apple juices seeping out of the ventilating slits in the pie crust caramelized and flowed over the side of the baking pan. She smelled the hint of cinnamon and nutmeg mingling with the apple's tart juices to make her mouth water all the more. Her need to satisfy her sweet tooth compelled her to take action. "They smell so delicious!"

"Would you be wanting one?" asked the baker; pleased she could detect quality without even sampling a bite. "They're usually the first to be sold out and I won't be making any more until next week."

"Most definitely," stated Rose, licking her lips in anticipation. "However, there is one minor problem."

"What might that be?"

"Well, I am a long way from the palace and my father, King William controls my purse strings, so at this very moment I have no coins to pay for this pie. If you would be so kind to give me one now, I will be sure to pay you three times its worth later."

"You certainly dress like a princess and you may very well be Princess Rose-alyn, but I have no way of knowing for sure, having never been invited to the palace to see her with mine own eyes."

"But I *am* Princess Rose," she insisted.

"Sorry, miss. You know what they say? Fool me once, shame on you! Fool me twice, then shame on me! I've had others, paupers disguised in noblemen's finery trying to pass themselves off as royalty to get something for nothing. They all promise to pay when they return from their castle, but in all this time, I've yet to recoup my losses. I'm not about to fall for that trick again."

"But I speak the truth! I really am the Princess of Fleetwood."

"Yes, and if I told you that I'm the Duke of Farnwick, would you believe me?"

Staring at his tattered shirt, the worn trousers and the flour and batter stained apron stretched tightly over his ample form, Rose's answer was prompt: "No, but I – "

"So why should I believe you're the Princess when I don't even know for sure what she looks like? Sorry, young lady, but if you don't have the money to pay for this pie, then you best make room for the other customers," requested the baker, dismissing her with a wave of his pudgy hand.

"Please, sir, I am so famished. I feel faint with hunger! I have not eaten a bite since yesterday. I'll take anything, even a day-old biscuit."

"No money, no food! It's as simple as that, so make room for those wishing to buy," ordered the man.

Rose's plea fell on deaf ears as the baker turned to help a paying customer as other patrons were drawn to his table by the smell of warm breads and cooling pies.

"I can see that went over well," Tag muttered beneath his breath as he watched the baker turn his back on Rose.

Inwardly, he was pleased to see the Princess was reduced to grovelling. It was not because he wanted to see her embarrassed, but for once, he wanted to see Rose humbled. And as far as Tag was concerned, there was no better way, for this was something she detested about the peasants who, in desperation, resorted to begging for a handout when they were unable to work to keep food on the table.

Just when he thought Rose had erased all thoughts of stealing, Tag was appalled to see what happened next. She continued to hover over the table while the baker was preoccupied with other customers clamouring to be served next. And not only did she go against his warning to pilfer the smallest of bun or biscuit, he watched as Rose discreetly picked up a whole apple pie. Turning away from the table, she attempted to push through the crowd before the baker could take notice.

"Hey! I wanted that one!" cried out a waiting customer, pointing accusingly at the Princess. "You can't just take it!"

The baker turned in time to see the Princess rushing away, pie in hand.

"Come back!" he shouted, struggling to push through the crowd gathering around his table. "Stop that thief!"

With the bad timing of the truly cursed, Rose spied upon the captain of her father's army. He appeared with a small contingent of knights and soldiers as they marched straight toward the marketplace. Unbeknownst to the Princess, they were sent forth to search her out, as she had not been seen since late last night. The King and Queen believed their daughter's disappearance coincided with the arrival of the early morning intruder.

"Thief!" hollered the baker. Huffing and puffing as he fought to work his way through the crowd, he waved the knights on. "Stop that pie thief!"

"Hey! It's that old peasant woman we tossed out of the palace this morning!" announced one of the soldiers, pointing an accusing finger at Rose.

"Maybe she knows what happened to the Princess," said another.

"Stop her!" shouted the baker, as he lagged far behind the fleet-footed Rose as she darted off.

"You heard him! Stop that woman!" ordered the captain, urging his men on. "If anything, she must be questioned."

With the deafening clamour of weapons and armours rattling behind her, Rose froze for a split-second. The very men appointed to protect her were chasing her down once more.

"Oh, no! Not again!" cried Rose.

She sprinted away, pie in hand. Just as she was about to dash by the building she had left Tag hiding behind, he grabbed her arm, yanking her around the corner.

"A *pie?* What is wrong with you? I told you to take the smallest item on the table, not dessert for ten!" groaned Tag, his hand slapping his forehead in frustration.

"But I grabbed the *smallest pie*," insisted Rose, hoping it would somehow lessen the gravity of the crime. "I thought you'd want some."

"Well, that was stupid! I told you I wanted nothing to do with anything criminal! Stealing this pie *is* a crime!"

"I didn't mean to get caught."

"Neither do any of the other thieves being hauled off to prison," chastised Tag, pushing away the pie Rose offered to him.

"I don't want to go to prison!" gasped Rose, only now realizing how much trouble she was in.

"Brilliant! Absolutely brilliant! You should of thought of that first!" Tag snapped as he shook his head in dismay. He glanced around the corner to see the captain and his men, pushing and jostling to get through the crowd. "They are coming and they are quite intent on capturing you!"

"What should I do?" asked Rose, her eyes anxiously darting about, searching for an escape route.

"Shut your pie-hole so I can think!" ordered Tag.

"With a bite of pie?" asked Rose, hoping to steal at least one mouthful if she was going to be punished anyway.

"Don't you dare!" snapped Tag.

"Fine, but what am I to do?" asked Rose. She glanced around the corner to see the captain and his men fast approaching, but now there was a growing mob following behind them.

"I don't know! Give back the pie! You can't be accused of stealing if you give it back."

"You're right!" agreed Rose. Leaping out from cover, she turned to face the angry mob coming toward her. "Wait! I want to return this pie that somehow followed me."

"Don't let her get away," hollered the captain. He leapt over a spilled basket of tomatoes he accidentally knocked over from a farmer's stall.

"They mean business!" shouted Tag. He watched as the King's men scrambled to clear the crowd standing in their way as they raced toward the Princess, but this time, their swords were drawn. "Don't just stand there! Give them the pie! Just give it to them!"

Seeing the scowl on the captain's face and the equally angry baker waddling behind as he coaxed the men on to capture her, Rose panicked.

She threw the pie, eager to be rid of it. And had this dessert been a weapon capable of dispensing death, it was with deadly accuracy it hit its mark.

As the soldiers in front of him ducked, the sticky, sweet pie struck the captain square in his startled face. Catching him by surprise, it bowled him over flat on his back.

Rose's mouth dropped open in shock, her eyes wide-open in disbelief.

"Now you did it! I said to *give* it back! Not *throw* it in the captain's face!" admonished Tag, grabbing Rose by her hand to force her to run. "Now you can add assault to your growing list of crimes."

"I did not mean for that to happen!"

"Get them!" hollered the captain, scrambling back onto his feet. Using his hands to wipe the remnants of pie from his face, he waved his men on to give chase. "Capture that damned woman!"

"Bloody hell!" cursed Tag, running as Rose struggled to keep up. "Now you're a wanted criminal and I'm guilty by association, no thanks to you!"

"Should we surrender?" asked Rose.

"By all means, you go right ahead, after all, *you* are the guilty one," reminded Tag, turning off the road to dash across a field in a bid to lose the angry mob. "It'll give me a chance to escape."

"That was not funny! Where are we going?"

"We have to shake them off, lose them somehow," explained Tag, darting behind a huge haystack.

"We should hide," suggested Rose, but more so because she was out of breath and tired from running.

"Where?" asked Tag, his eyes darted about, searching for a hiding place.

"Anywhere! They're coming for us!" cried Rose, as she peered around the haystack. "We must hide."

A pair of hands suddenly slapped over their mouths. Rose and Tag were yanked deep into the great mountain of drying alfalfa. They disappeared from sight just as the knights and soldiers, followed by the unruly mob of villagers eager to watch the outcome of this pursuit, charged into the field.

6

Cankles Mayron, V.I.

"Shhh!"

A muffled voice buried deep inside this huge mound of alfalfa whispered as his hands came away from their mouths, *"Quiet!"*

Rose and Tag complied, not speaking another word. They remained still, not even breathing, as the angry voices and hurried footfalls stopped momentarily, only to rush on by to fade away in the direction of a neighbouring field.

"It's safe now," announced the voice coming from somewhere within this haystack. "I'm sure of it."

Tag pushed the blades and stalks aside, peering out to see if they were indeed safe from capture.

"Check, will you?" ordered the Princess.

"That's what I'm doing," responded Tag.

"So, what do you see?" whispered Rose. She blindly groped about, tapping Tag's arm to get his attention.

"Hush!" ordered Tag. His ears strained to listen for signs of their adversaries coming back their way.

Impatient for news, Rose did not speak. Instead, she persistently tapped on his arm. When her efforts did not garner his attention, she shook him as she growled beneath her breath, "I will not be ignored!"

"What are you talking about?" grumbled Tag, still peering out from his grassy hiding place.

"I had been poking and shaking you, but you choose to ignore me," rebuked Rose. "The nerve of you!"

"Now I know for sure you've lost your mind. If you were touching me, I didn't feel a bloody thing."

For a moment, Rose was silent as she absorbed her jester's bizarre words.

"What is wrong with you?" Rose's hand, feeling about in the darkness of this drying mountain of alfalfa, squeezed his arm once more. "You cannot feel this?"

"No… Why? What are you doing?"

"Squeezing your arm."

"Surely you jest," countered Tag. "I can't feel it."

"I can!" chirped an unfamiliar voice. "An' that isn't my arm you're squeezin', miss."

Rose's eyes had remained shut to protect them from being jabbed by the stalks of grass, but now they flew wide-open. She shrieked in disgust upon discovering she had been manhandling the stranger who had pulled them into this hiding place.

"*Yuck! Ewww!*" she yelped in disgust.

As though she had squashed a big, slimy slug with her bare hand, Rose wiped it on her gown as she dove head first from the haystack.

Tag crawled out, laughing heartily as he watched the Princess frantically jump about. She dragged her hands over her diamond and alfalfa covered gown as if it would somehow miraculously vanquish whatever it was she thought she may have contracted from touching this stranger.

"Come out at once!" ordered Rose. "I demand to see who it is that I had the ill fortune of making contact with!"

As angry as the Princess sounded, she was hoping this stranger would turn out to be a handsome, young man with the charms and intelligence to match; a regular knight in shining armour, as Tag proved to be rather useless to her.

"Hold on!" The voice called out. "You got rid of the worst of the cramp in my calf with all your proddin', but it's still botherin' me."

Instead of a dashing, Prince Charming-type leaping forth to reveal his identity to Rose, in the most undignified manner imaginable, the droopy, back-end of a well-worn pair of trousers was the first thing to greet her eyes. The stranger crawled out backwards from the hiding place. Like a lowly animal, he emerged before her on his hands and knees. When he stood upright, shaking the drying alfalfa from his raiment, he towered above the petite Princess, but in reality, it was his lean build that made him appear taller than he really was.

As her eyes took in his drab attire in a single, scrutinizing glance, it was immediately apparent this man was no prince, and if he was, he had no doubt earned the title of the Prince of all Paupers.

Shaking the last of the grass from his mop of hair, the stalks fell like shedding fur falling from a mange-infested mutt. Rose stared at his feet to notice something odd about this man. A beaten up leather shoe clad his right foot, while his left was dressed in nothing more than a thread-bare wool sock bearing a hole from which his big toe protruded like a baby potato escaping from a burlap sack. After closer examination, she discovered his missing shoe was tucked securely under his left arm.

"You wretched soul! What is your name, you poor man?" asked Rose, taking a wary step back from this bedraggled stranger.

"Cankles Mayron at your service, young miss!" He bowed politely before her. "An' why feel pity for me? I'm quite fine, you know?"

"She doesn't feel sorry for you. She means *poor* as in *not wealthy,*" explained Tag, removing a handful of drying grasses from his shirt. "Anyone who is not of royal blood falls into her definition of a *poor* person."

"Oh, I see… It sounds rather odd to me, but who am I to say?" responded Cankles, as he scratched his head in thought. "Meanin' no disrespect to you, but it'd be like me assumin' you're a princess jus' 'cause you dress like one."

"I dress like a princess because I *am* a Princess!" grunted Rose, as she attempted to turn the skirt of her gown to hide the grass and mud stains now smudging one side after she dove from the haystack.

"Are you jus' sayin' that?" questioned the man, eyeing her sparkling apparel and tiara that now sat a-skewed on her drooping hairdo.

"Are you daft?" asked Rose, her brows furrowing in agitation as she adjusted her tiara. "How many peasants dress in such finery?"

"Not many, I suppose. Mind you, I've peeked in on the annual masquerade ball hosted by the Mayor of Cadboll an' I swear I saw some of the local girls dressed up all fancy, pretendin' ta be princesses."

"Come to think of it, I've seen that, too," stated Tag, nodding in agreement.

"What is wrong with the two of you?" grunted Rose. "There is a difference between *pretending to be* and actually *being* a genuine princess. And I will have you know, sir, I am a genuine princess!"

"Sure, if you believe it, then so do I," said Cankles, giving Tag a wink as he played along with her.

Rose's eyes narrowed in resentment as her nostrils flared like an angry bull. "I am Princess Rose."

"Yeah… an' I'm the village fool," responded Cankles, giving her an affable grin.

"Seriously! I am Princess Rose-alyn of Fleetwood," she insisted, stamping her feet as if it would somehow lend some credibility to her claim.

"Accordin' to some, I'm serious, too," he responded with a

modest shrug.

"*Arrrgh!*" grunted Rose, her face reddening with anger. "You are impossible!"

"Not really, but *that* sure is!" declared Cankles, his thumb jabbing over his shoulder as he pointed to the haystack.

"What are you talking about?" asked Rose, peering around him at the huge mound of alfalfa.

"Try findin' a needle in that! Now that's pretty near impossible," explained Cankles, shaking an angry fist at the mountain of drying grass.

"What were you doing in there?" queried Rose.

"Like I said, I was searchin' for a needle. A boy told me it was impossible. I believe it can be done, but it'd jus' be real difficult."

"You were looking for a needle in that stack of hay?" gasped Rose.

"Good gracious! Do you need me to say it again? An' people say I have cloth ears!" snorted Cankles, chuckling as he glanced over at her companion. "Your girl is worse than I am!"

"Oh, no! She's not *my girl!*" gasped Tag, shuddering in disgust. "I'm no fool and I have better taste than that!"

"You are *my fool* and I will have you know I have enough scruples *not* to associate with a commoner like you," snapped Rose, her finger jabbing Tag in his chest.

"Now, now! No need for such hostile words between lovers," admonished Cankles. "Life's too short to be angry at each other. You should kiss an' make up."

As though they read each other's thoughts, simultaneously, Tag and Rose groaned in repulsion.

"I'd rather kiss a pig!" declared Tag.

"I heard you do that all the time!" snapped Rose. "And rumour has it, you actually enjoy it!"

"What nastiness is this?" exclaimed Cankles, shaking his head in disapproval. "What is wrong with the two of you? Don't let pride stand in the way of young love!"

"Love her?" gasped Tag, mortified by the thought. "That self-centered excuse for a princess? Never!"

"Well, I have taste! I would never stoop to his level, if there was one as low as that," muttered Rose, turning her nose up at her jester.

"I'm nothing but a – a – joke to you!" sputtered Tag, infuriated by her insult.

"A joke, yes, but alas, you are not funny," corrected Rose, as she gave him a smug smile.

"I've heard that when a girl pesters a man like that, she's actually quite fond of him," stated Cankles, giving Tag a knowing smile and a friendly jab of his elbow.

"Well, you heard wrong! And besides," snorted Rose, as she glared at Tag, "he is no man! He is a *boy!*"

"That's it! I'm done with your insults!" snapped Tag. Turning his back on the Princess, he stormed away in anger.

"Tag Yairet!" Rose hollered, pushing past Cankles as she gave chase.

"Oh, I love this game!" exclaimed Cankles. He dashed by the Princess, one shoe still tucked under his arm as he tackled the young man. *"Tag!* Now you're it!"

Knocked to the ground, Tag groaned in pain.

"What are you doing?" asked Rose.

"Have you lost your mind?" snapped Tag, pushing Cankles off his body.

"Some tell me so, but I can't rightly say," he responded, leaping back onto his feet as he pranced about in victory. "Now run! I'll be it again if you want. I'll even give you both a head start."

"You are an idiot! An absolute idiot!" admonished Rose.

"So I've been told," responded Cankles.

"I said Tag Yairet, not *tag, you're it!*"

"Terribly sorry! So that's your *name?*" determined Cankles. His face glowed red with embarrassment as he pulled the young man back onto his feet.

"Actually, it's Tagius, but she insists on calling me Tag."

"And this is not some childish game we are playing," stated Rose. "We are on an important mission."

"Oooh! I love missions! Never been on one myself, but I do love 'em!"

"When I say *we*, I mean to say: Tag and I. Nowhere, and at no time, did I say Crinkles."

"My name is *Cankles*," he corrected her. "Cankles Mayron."

"The point being, you were not invited on this quest," snapped the Princess, as she yanked Tag back onto his feet.

"Quiet, I hear voices," warned Tag, motioning Rose and Cankles to be silent. "I think our *friends* are coming back!"

"Oh, wonderful!" groaned Rose, heaving a disgruntled sigh.

"Quickly! We need to hide," ordered Tag. Glancing about, his eyes searched for a safe sanctuary.

"I refuse to go back in there!" declared the Princess, her words adamant as she stared at the haystack.

"We don't have a choice at this moment," grumbled Tag, scowling in frustration at Rose. "Do you prefer to be captured?"

"I know!" exclaimed Cankles. "Follow me. I know where you can hide an' you'll both be quite safe!"

"Ladies first," invited Cankles, giving the door a nudge with his shoulder to force it open. "Step right in."

"What is this place?" asked Rose. Her face grimaced in revulsion as Cankles held the rickety door open for her to pass through.

"Be it so humble, this is my home," answered Cankles, as he motioned for Tag to enter. "Welcome, my friends! You can stay for however long you wish."

"It is rather disg-"

"Decidedly *quaint!* That's what it is," interjected Tag, as he gave Rose a poke with his elbow. "And it's much better than hiding in that prickly haystack, right Princess?"

"Oh, yes! Much better," agreed Rose, pulling another stalk of drying grass from her hair.

"Don't you go mindin' the mess," said Cankles. He apologized as he hastily brushed the crumbs from yesterday's dinner and this morning's breakfast off the table. "Don't usually have guests in my home, so I didn't bother tidyin' up all the time."

"Worry not," said Tag, stepping over a large, sleeping dog. The beast barely twitched, not even lifting its head in acknowledgement of these guests. A long, low snort wheezed from its gaping mouth as its flappy, pink tongue lolled, leaving a growing puddle of drool on the floor.

"Watch where you step," cautioned Cankles, attempting to steer Rose around the hound's long, bony tail that was slowly thumping against the wooden floor as it dreamed its doggie dreams. "Don't want to be stepping on Puke."

"*Ewww!* Where?" asked Rose, groaning in disgust as her foot recoiled from the floor. "Were you sick?"

"Puke's my dog's name," explained Cankles, stooping to pat the old mongrel on its scabby head. In response, the animal barely opened its eyes as it wheezed loudly, only to settle back down to sleep.

"That's an unusual name for a dog, or *anything* for that matter," commented Tag, staring at the mangy-looking mutt as its gangly hind legs twitched as though it was on the hunt for rabbits in its dream.

"Not really. The name suits him perfectly," responded Cankles.

"He's not the brightest dog in these parts. He eats jus' about anything that'll fit in his mouth an' it's not always the most edible stuff either. The worst thing is when he eats Honk's hairballs. That really gets him pukin' up a storm, hence the name, Puke."

"What in heaven's name is a *Honk?*" queried Rose, staring with profound disgust at the sleeping dog.

"Honk is my cat," explained Cankles, glancing about for the stray, ginger tabby he had adopted several winters ago. "She's not here right now, probably out huntin' for field mice."

"Goodness! You're rather original when it comes to naming your pets," noted Tag.

"Well, the name Puke was already taken so I had to come up with something else that was suitable for my cat."

"I am afraid to ask," responded Rose, hoping this man would take the hint she really did not want to know the details of the feline's name.

"Don't be! It's jus' that ev'ry time Honk coughs up a big wad of hair from her gut, she sounds like a goose chokin' on its own tongue."

"That is disgusting!" groaned Rose.

"Don't I know it! *Ho- hon- hooonk!*" demonstrated Cankles. A horrendous noise bellowed forth as though he was gagging on a barbed fishhook caught in the back of his throat. "Honk coughs up a hairball about the size of the biggest dust bunny you can imagine! But before I can get rid of it, the dog gobbles it up like it's nobody's business. He eats the damned thing an' the next thing you know, he's pukin' his guts out."

"I take it, this happens frequently," decided Tag.

"Too often," admitted Cankles. "But what can I say? Friends are hard to come by these days an' without question, these animals love me no matter what. It's only right I take good care of 'em an' love 'em back. Besides, there aren't many who'd put up with their bad habits."

"For good reason," grumbled Rose; examining the floor for any unwanted surprises she did not want to tread on.

As though her negative feelings were powerful enough to wake the old hound, forcing it up onto its lanky legs. With a vigorous shake, its loose skin flapped and rolled over a bony frame to send loose fur flying, while threads of drool hanging from its slobbering jowls splattered Rose's gown.

"Get away from me, you disgusting beast!" cursed the Princess, as she pulled Tag in front to shield her.

"Come on, Puke, get out! Get some fresh air," ordered Cankles, pushing the dog out the door. "See if you can catch a nice, big rabbit for dinner."

"Thank goodness!" exclaimed Rose, watching as the hound lumbered out, a bony, wagging tail smacking against the door as it exited. "For a moment, I thought that dog was going to attack me."

"Oh, Puke's friendly! If anything, he'd lick you to death if he had a chance."

"Now that would be truly disgusting!" groaned Rose, shuddering at the thought.

"Enough about my animals! Come, sit down. I'll serve up some refreshments. I'm sure you're both parched."

"Something refreshing to drink would be lovely," said Rose, as her eyes glanced about the small hovel.

"Make yourself cozy," invited Cankles.

The sun, filtered by a thick layer of grime coating the windows, managed to seep through to shed some light on their modest, but cluttered surroundings. A narrow cot with a thick mattress overstuffed with straw and covered by a tattered patchwork quilt and a single dresser-drawer were pushed up against the far wall. Rows of dusty shelves that bowed, threatening to collapse from the weight of his eclectic collection of personal treasures lined the wall just above this simple bed. In the center of this room was a rickety wooden table surrounded by the crudest looking chairs the Princess had ever seen.

"Where do we sit?" asked Rose. Her eyes roamed about, searching for a comfy sofa.

"On the chairs, where else?" responded Tag, plopping down on a wobbly stump carved out to resemble a simple chair.

"Well?" said Rose. She waited for Tag to do the gentlemanly thing by pulling the chair out from the table for her to sit on.

"Well, what? If you do not want to sit on the chair, the floor looks clean enough."

"So much for being a gallant knight," snipped Rose.

"I'm not a knight. And you are always so quick to point that out when it suits you."

"Allow me," offered Cankles. He placed his left shoe on the mantle over the fireplace before pulling the chair out for Rose to sit upon.

As she folded her gown neatly beneath her to take her place at the table, Tag glared at her as he grunted, "Go on, say it. Or have you already forgotten your manners?"

"Th- tha- thank you," sputtered the Princess, spitting out the words that were never a part of her day-to-day vocabulary.

"Oh my, you have a bit of a stutter," noted Cankles.

"She only has a speech impediment when it comes to saying certain words," explained Tag. "It'll be cured once she gets used to saying them."

"I've never heard of such a malady, but you're more than welcome, Princess," said Cankles. "Now, make yourself at home. I won't be long."

Resting her elbows on the edge of the table, Rose squeaked in surprise. She abruptly discovered this piece of furniture was just as wobbly as the hard chair she was sitting on.

"This will simply not do," groaned the Princess, her hand rocking the old table back and forth. "How can anyone live like this?"

"Some people have no choice. And if this does not appeal to you, will the haystack suit you better? You're more than welcome to wait it out in that heap of alfalfa until the midnight hour," offered Tag.

"I did not say that," countered Rose. "It is just that this rundown shack is hardly the place for a person like me."

"At this time, neither is your palace. If you're smart, you'll hold your tongue and take care not to insult our gracious host."

"Fine!" conceded Rose, watching Cankles shake out a little spider nesting in one of the ceramic mugs he was about to fill. "I was just thinking aloud."

"Try not to. I'd rather not hear what you're thinking about," urged Tag.

"So, Candles – " said Rose, addressing the man.

"Cankles," he corrected her again as he poured from a badly chipped pitcher to top up the three mugs.

"Yes well, I could not help but notice you wear only one foot apparel," said the Princess, glancing up at the left shoe on the fireplace mantle. "Is there something wrong with the other shoe that prevents you from wearing it? Or is there some kind of impediment, perhaps a painful bunion that afflicts you peasant-types preventing you from wearing it?"

"Oh, no! It's nothing like that!" chortled Cankles, his hands wrapping around the three drinking vessels to deliver to the table. "I use it as my man-bag."

"Say again!" responded Rose, frowning with curiosity.

"I was told if I keep my money in my shoe, I'd never lose it an' potential thieves wouldn't think of lookin' there to rob me," explained Cankles. "I wasn't 'bout to chance losin' another ha'penny an' I sure as heck wasn't about to tote a girlie purse. It jus' made perfect sense to me."

"I do believe you're actually supposed to *wear* your shoe with the coin *in it*. That way, it will not fall out and thieves will be truly dissuaded from stealing it," recommended Tag.

"Hmph!" grunted Cankles, giving his guest a thoughtful nod of his head. "I suppose it does make more sense than keepin' it tucked under my arm."

"And I'm confident your foot would appreciate it, too," said Tag, accepting the mug Cankles placed before him. "Thank you very much."

"Th- thank you," said Rose, but only after Tag shot a baleful glance her way to remind the Princess to use her manners. "You wouldn't happen to have any food, would you?"

"Oh, dear! How rude of me!" exclaimed Cankles, his hand slapping his forehead for being so forgetful. "Of course I do! I've got something special cookin' up even as we speak."

He dashed over to the fireplace, eager to please his guests. Here, smoldering embers continued to exude just enough heat to keep his supper warm without burning it. Cankles balanced a cracked platter on one hand as the other carefully plucked up the hot skewers of meat from an iron cooking rack.

"Good gracious! That man is a bit of a dolt," muttered Rose, glancing over Tag's shoulder to spy on Cankles.

"Hush! Keep your voice down. He's a little slow and he seems to take things quite literally, but so what? He's no dolt!" snapped Tag, his voice in a hush. "I think it unfair the local people have labeled him the local V. I."

"*V. I.?*" repeated Rose, her delicate brows frowning in curiosity. "What does that stand for?"

"You know? *Village idiot,*" whispered Tag.

"Oh… I see," responded Rose, her head nodded in understanding. "Cankles Mayron, V. I."

"Shhh!" ordered Tag, as he glanced at their host.

Cankles' ears pricked up upon hearing his name.

"Were you speakin' about me?" he asked, as his hand recoiled from a hot spot flaring from the embers.

"Just trying to teach the Princess the proper pronunciation of your name," lied Tag, speaking up before Rose could say something else to insult him.

"Nothin' hard about my name," stated Cankles. "But what's this *V. I.* thing you're talkin' about?"

"It means vil- "

Before Rose could finish, Tag interrupted her: "Virtually indispensable! You are virtually indispensable to this quest, and us. If you had not pulled us into the haystack, we'd probably be locked up by now."

"Well, jus' for that, I'll have to join you two on this mission. See it to its right an' proper end," decided Cankles. "But we'll eat first. Jus' as soon as I can serve this up."

"Great! Just great!" groaned Rose, rolling her eyes in frustration as she muttered beneath her breath. "Now look what you have done. This idiot will only slow us down."

"No more than you already do," disputed Tag, taking a swig of ale. "At least he is kind enough to feed you when others would not."

"Oooh, food!" exclaimed the Princess, licking her lips in anticipation of a tasty meal. "Do you require some help?"

"That'd be nice," responded Cankles, nursing his burned thumb.

"Tag, go help the man," ordered Rose, waving her hand to dismiss him from her presence.

Her jester rolled his eyes as he stood up from his chair. Tag knelt by Cankles, holding the platter steady for him.

Placing the food on the table between his guests, Cankles invited them to indulge, "Help yourself! Tuck in while they're nice an' hot."

"I am absolutely famished!" declared Rose, selecting the largest portion. She daintily picked up each end of the skewer; cautiously blowing on the tantalizing morsel to make sure it did not burn her delicate mouth. Sinking her teeth into the tender, savoury, fire-roasted meat, the taste and the smell worked in tandem to make her mouth water.

"This is absolutely delicious!" declared Rose, trying to consume this fare as elegantly as possible in these primitive conditions. Having not eaten since last evening, she was fighting a tremendous urge to stuff as much into her mouth as she could.

"I'm glad you like it. It's all in the seasonin', ya know? Fresh rosemary an' tarragon does wonders when mixed with minced garlic. They help to reduce the gaminess of the meat," explained their host. "Eat more. There's plenty."

"This is truly delectable," praised Rose, licking the greasy but flavourful juices from her fingers before indulging in another bite. "I think I will have more."

"Go right ahead," urged Cankles, pushing the platter closer to the Princess.

"This is the best squab I have ever had the good fortune of dining on," noted Rose, taking another eager bite. "These ones are of a good size! And here, I thought it was a bit early in the spring for baby pigeons."

"Oh, I don't like the notion of eatin' any type of baby birds, but since some folks refer to pigeons as flyin' rats, I suppose it's pretty, darn close to tastin' like squab," decided Cankles.

"What are you talking about?" asked Rose, as she stuffed another bite into her mouth.

"Your meal, of course," responded Cankles. He tore off a mouthful of meat to devour.

"Are you saying this is *not* a pigeon? I am actually eating a *rat?*" she gasped.

"I'd never think of feedin' an ordinary rat to a princess. I'd only serve up the freshest, plumpest, locally caught water rats found in these parts. An' this spring, they're plentiful, so there's a lot more where I got these."

Rose's eyes grew wide with disbelief as her mouth fell agape. The meat she was in the midst of chewing rolled off her tongue to plop onto her lap, this time, adding a greasy stain to her gown.

Mortified, she stared at the roasted carcasses skewered onto these sticks.

With thin ears burned to a crisp and pointed snouts that can easily be mistaken for a bird's beak, once denuded of fur and skin, and then roasted beyond recognition, the Princess was appalled as she dared to better scrutinize her meal.

"The water rats, or muskrats as they're called in some parts, are quite bountiful this spring," responded Cankles. "They're plump from a good feed of hyacinth and bulrush tubers that are plentiful this time of year."

"This does not look like a rat!" insisted Rose, in firm denial. "Where is the long, scaly tail? Even I know all rats have tails."

"Oh, that! I cut 'em off. They jus' get in the way when you're cookin' 'em up," explained her host. "They tend to burn an' fall off, an' there's really no meat on that part, anyway."

Tag deliberately sank his teeth into the skewered morsel, watching with amusement as the colour drained from the Princess' face as the rat-on-a-stick dropped from her hands.

"*Ugh!* I ate a rodent!" Rose shrieked in disgust as she jumped up from the table. Her hands slapped at her tongue, frantically trying to remove all traces of the tainted meat from her royal palate.

"What's up with her?" asked Cankles, watching in fascination as the Princess raced about his tiny abode, wiping her tongue against the doorjamb like she was a horse taking to a saltlick.

"Methinks this roast is too rich for her fussy taste," decided Tag, attempting to be diplomatic so as not to insult their host as he took another bite of his dinner.

"Arrrgh!" groaned Rose. Her tongue dangled from her mouth as though she was waiting for it to swell to grand proportions, like the meat would somehow cause a severe allergic reaction.

"Will you stop with the dramatics!" ordered Tag. "It's a strange thing it was so delicious until you found out what it was."

"Here, Princess. Wash it down with this," suggested Cankles, offering her one of the ceramic mugs.

Rose snatched the cracked vessel from his grasp, taking in a mouthful of the beverage to wash away all evidence of roasted rat. The swishing came to an abrupt halt as the unfamiliar flavour of yeasty, tepid ale accosted her delicate taste buds to send her senses reeling. Her eyes flew wide open in disgust as the foul tasting brew assaulted her tongue and threatened to kick her tonsils if she swallowed it.

Tag immediately grabbed Cankles by the edge of his ragged vest, pulling him out of the line of fire just as a mouthful of ale and a copious quantity of saliva erupted from Rose's mouth, spewing forth in a fine spray like a dragon unleashing liquid fire.

"What in heaven's name is this swill?" gasped the Princess, using the back of her hand to wipe away the dribble of dark brown liquid running down her chin.

"It's only the best thing to ever come from the Gelded Pony," stated Cankles.

"Good gracious! This foul concoction came from a castrated horse?" gasped Rose, in utter revulsion. Her eyes searched for water, even puddle water, to wash out her mouth.

"The *Gelded Pony* is the best public drinking house in the County of Wren. It's the one I was telling you about that's situated on the outskirts of this village," explained Tag, laughing heartily upon witnessing the Princess' reaction to sampling this beverage.

"It's all I could strain from the dregs at the bottom of the casks, but it's quite drinkable if you're not too fussy," added Cankles.

"How disgusting!" groaned Rose.

"And you just had your first taste of ale. The choice drink of the common folks, far and wide."

"This is what *you* people might drink, however, I am not in the habit of putting just anything into my body. It is like a sacred temple, while yours is a regular carnival!"

"At least I have fun eating and drinking whatever I want," responded Tag, taking another deliberate swig of ale.

"I prefer wine – vintage wine, if you have it," sulked Rose, still cringing from the bitter aftertaste that continued to assault her sensitive tongue.

"Sorry, Princess. Don't have no wine, vintage or otherwise," apologized Cankles. "Can get you some fresh milk if you like, but it'll take me awhile as I'd have to corral the neighbour's cow first."

"That will not be necessary," insisted Tag. "Until she can break this curse, she is like one of us, a commoner. She should just get used to it."

"Good gracious!" exclaimed Cankles. He stopped eating to focus his attention on this bit of news. "What curse are you speakin' of, Master Yairet?"

"It is a long, sad tale of woe," lamented Rose, plopping back down in her chair as she unleashed a dreary sigh.

"Yes," interjected Tag. "So I will keep it short by saying that due to the Princess foolishly capturing the Tooth Fairy, and then accepting a magic crystal from the Dream Merchant, she is now cursed. Thanks to her brilliant mind and infinite wisdom, the palace staff and her own parents believe she is a vagrant, nothing more than a lowly peasant woman they ousted from the palace."

"That's terrible! Is that why you were being chased by those knights an' soldiers this morn?" queried Cankles, as he listened with great interest.

"Well that... and the fact that I was wrongfully accused of stealing." She pushed away the rat she had been eating, having lost her appetite.

"Do not trivialize your actions," admonished Tag. "Speak the truth, for once in your privileged life. You did steal! You brazenly stole a whole, not a slice, but I repeat, a whole apple pie from the local baker."

"Tsk! Tsk! For shame!" exclaimed Cankles, shaking his head in disgrace. "I admit I'm not the smartest person in the world, but I'm tellin' you, even I know it's wrong to steal."

"It is morally reprehensible, that's what it is," added Tag, giving the Princess the evil eye as he stared at her diamond-studded gown. "Especially when there was a way to pay for the pie she nicked!"

"Fine! I get it! I already feel funny about the whole incident," groaned Rose, shuddering involuntarily to shake off this sensation gnawing at the back of her mind and prodding at her stony heart.

"That funny feeling is called *guilt*," explained Tag.

"Well, I do not like it," said Rose, "not in the least."

"Good, because if you did not feel guilty and was not bothered by it, I'd say there is more wrong with you than I originally thought possible," grunted Tag.

"Well, I already told you I was going to pay the baker back three times its worth," countered Rose, trying to minimize the gravity of the crime.

"That's not quite so bad, then," rationalized Cankles, feeling some sympathy for the Princess.

"Still stealing," reminded Tag.

"Well, I tried to give the pie back, but it accidentally ended up in the captain's face," Rose continued with her explanation.

"*Accidentally?*" snorted Tag, his tone incredulous. "That pie hit the man spot-on! With an aim like that, I'd say it was pretty deliberate."

"I say again! It was an accident. The point being, that is when things went from bad to worse. Not only was I chased out of the palace, I am now wanted for theft."

"So, what did you steal, Master Yairet?" asked Cankles.

"Me? Nothing! I know better than that. Thanks to the Princess though, I am now considered guilty by association. Hence, we are both on the run."

"An' this quest the Princess was speakin' of, what's that about? Is it to break this curse?"

"Cankles, my good man, we are on a quest to find the Queen of the Tooth Fairies," revealed Tag. "However, that would entail finding someone who can tell us where she resides."

"Well, you're in luck!" exclaimed Cankles, smiling broadly. "I know exactly who can tell you."

"Who?" Tag and Rose asked in unison, eager to learn more.

"*Me!* That's who!" declared Cankles. His thumb proudly jabbed his chest to make sure there was no mistaking whom he was speaking of.

"You know where Pancecilia Feldspar lives?" questioned Rose, staring suspiciously at the man.

"She prefers to be called Pance by her friends," insisted Cankles.

"So you say, but do you truly know where she lives?" asked Rose.

"I know where her palace is. She told me, but more importantly, I've been there a few times."

"You know that devious little being, personally?" gasped Rose.

"Sure do, but if you took the time to know her, there's really nothing devious about the Fairy. I had tea with her couple of months ago an' I can honestly say she's really quite nice."

"This is too bizarre! How is it that you had tea with this Fairy?" queried the Princess.

"She came by for a tooth."

"Hold on! You are an adult. The Tooth Fairy only comes by to pick up teeth from children," argued Rose, frowning in confusion.

"That's what most believe, but the Tooth Fairy only comes to those who believe she'll come by. All children believe she will, but for some reason when they grow up, many stop believin'. If you stop believin', then why should she come? In my case, I believe an' I always will."

"The man does have a point," said Tag, with a nod of agreement.

"But where did you come across a tooth?" questioned Rose. "Did you swindle it from a child?"

"That's your department, Princess," Tag snorted in disgust.

"I lost a molar. It got pushed out when my wisdom tooth grew in," explained Cankles, his mouth agape as he pointed to the new tooth shining white against the other dingy, cavity-riddled teeth. "Funny thing is though, I don't feel any smarter for havin' this new one, being called a wisdom tooth an' all."

"Never mind that! You have actually seen the Fairy?" probed Rose.

"With my own two eyes, I did. An' she left me only a ha'penny cause my tooth was only fit to line the dungeon of her palace. Even as we speak, that coin's safely tucked away in my shoe," stated Cankles, pointing to his footwear resting on the mantle over the fireplace.

"So she told you where her palace is?" asked Tag.

"Told me? As I said before, I've been there!" declared Cankles, proud to share this bit of information with his guests.

"You must be good friends," decided Rose.

"When you consider how many teeth I've lost, I'm pretty well acquainted with Pance. An' I never set out to capture her either. Jus' a friendly old invite an' she accepted. We had tea at this very table!"

"So, where is the Tooth Fairy's palace?" asked Rose.

"Where else, but in the Fairy's Vale," responded Cankles, speaking as though it was common knowledge.

"Fine, but just where is this place?" asked Tag.

"Head two leagues north as straight as the crow flies. As you reach the Dimbolt Forest, follow the edge of the forest for another two leagues or so. This time, you'd have to be headin' east 'til you come across a huge, fallen pine tree. It toppled over durin' a great storm, but it's still very much alive."

"And the Fairy's Vale is there?" asked Rose. "By this fallen tree?"

"Oh, no! From there, follow the direction of the largest branch that's twistin' northward into the forest. It points the way —"

"To the Fairy's Vale?" probed Tag.

"Not quite, it points you to the trail that leads to the Vale. Once you find this trail, you must stay the course. Make sure you don't stray off this path or you'll get yourself good an' lost," warned Cankles.

"And the Fairy's Vale is somewhere along here?" queried Rose.

"Yes... about three leagues, if you stay on the correct trail, that is. An' jus' make sure you don't step in the Fairy Ring or you'll be askin' for big trouble," cautioned Cankles. "The Fairies don't take lightly to any human tramplin' over their ring, 'specially if you squish any of the toadstools surroundin' it."

"What are you talking about? What is this Fairy Ring?" questioned Rose.

Cankles began prancing about, tiptoeing in a circle to demonstrate.

"What the heck is that?" asked Rose. She stared at this tall, lanky man as he awkwardly pirouetted around the table. "Is he having a fit?"

"Good gracious, Princess! Have you learned nothing during your studies on local Fairy lore? He's trying to tell you a Fairy Ring is where those tiny beings congregate to dance under the moonlight," explained Tag, motioning Cankles to sit down.

"Yes, an' you must take care not to trample this magic circle or bad things will happen to you," warned Cankles.

"Like what?" asked Rose, still skeptical as ever.

"I've heard you can be come very ill, stricken by some kind of fever," answered Tag.

"What a bunch of malarkey!" scoffed Rose. "I do not believe it."

"Oh, I've heard worse than that! I've been told that if a man pees in their circle, even if it's by accident, to really desecrate their magic place in the worst way possible, he'll be plagued by a terrible rash down there," added Cankles.

"Down where?" asked Rose, bewildered by these words.

"You know, down *there*," replied Cankles, his eyes discreetly glancing down at his nether-region.

"The legs?" queried Rose.

"He means to say the part of the anatomy *between* a man's legs," explained Tag, pointing to his groin so there was no misunderstanding. "His manhood to be exact."

"Oh, so you have nothing to worry about," sniffed Rose, with a smirk directed at her jester.

"You are so humorous!" chortled Tag, in feigned laughter. "You are the one who should be the court jester, not me!"

"Whoa! Hold on here! Did I hear you right? You're a court jester?" marvelled Cankles, staring with wide-eyed, newfound admiration.

"Not by choice," replied Tag, with a dismal shake of his head.

"A noble vocation, to entertain an' make others laugh! I envy you, Master Yairet!" exclaimed Cankles.

"Envy me? Why?"

"It's a talent, an absolute talent! True skill is needed to be a jester in a royal court. How did you land such a prestigious posting?" queried Cankles, his eyes a-glint with excitement.

"It is a long story and the Princess will tell you –"

"That it is a long and *boring* story you will not want to hear about," interjected Rose. "And we digress yet again. We were talking about the Fairy's Vale and the Tooth Fairy's palace. Remember?"

"Oh, yes!" exclaimed Cankles. "Her palace is easy to find if you don't get lost along the way. It's too bad I'm not part of this quest. I'd be showing you how to get there. It'd be so much faster, but alas, my services aren't required."

Rose grabbed Tag by his arm, pulling him into the corner of the room for a private conversation.

"What do you think? Should we invite him along?" asked Rose, speaking in a whisper.

"Did you not say he would only slow us down?" responded Tag, his words in a hush so Cankles would not hear, and therefore, would not be offended if the decision were to be a resounding no.

"In my way of thinking, if we use him to get us to the Vale to find the Tooth Fairy's palace, it will be much faster than following his vague directions," suggested Rose. "Once we do, we can ditch him and be on our merry way."

"Just abandon the man? That's rather harsh, even for you, considering you are the one asking for his help."

"Fine, I shall graciously thank him first, and then I shall shake him off."

"That's still bloody rude of you. Either accept his help and be genuinely gracious about it or don't bother."

"Fine then! He can come along with us, but if he fails us along the way, I will ditch him so quickly, his loose noggin will be spinning," vowed the Princess.

"*Woo-hoo!* I won't fail you, Princess!" promised Cankles, gleefully slapping them on their backs.

Tag and Rose jumped in surprise, unaware he had been hovering directly behind them all along.

"I take it, you heard what we said?" questioned Rose.

"Every word, being that I was standin' right behind you," explained Cankles, excited by the prospects of joining them on this quest. "An' I swear, I won't be lettin' you down, Princess Rose. We can leave right away, if it pleases you!"

"I commend you on your eagerness to get this mission underway, but we must wait until dark," responded Tag.

"Oh, yes… the knights an' soldiers searchin' for you," recalled Cankles.

"I would rather avoid them altogether, if possible," stated Rose. "I am not suited for life in a dungeon."

"Understandably so," agreed Cankles. "I take it, you need to see the Tooth Fairy to break this curse."

"It is not quite that simple, but it is a start," replied Rose. "And it just occurred to me, if we wait until midnight, I can use my dreamstone to get us to the Fairy's Vale."

"Why waste a wish on something like that?" asked Tag.

"It will not be a waste," disputed Rose. "If I wish for us to be transported to this place, it will be far less time consuming."

"Oh, so in other words, we would save time because you would be spared the long, gruelling trek in those fancy shoes of yours," determined Tag.

"Well, that too, but it will be much faster to wish us there," insisted Rose.

"An' what's this dreamstone you're speakin' about?" questioned Cankles, listening with keen interest.

"This," replied Rose, pulling out the gold chain from behind the bodice of her dress to reveal the magic crystal.

"No offence, but it looks like an ordinary bead of quartz to me," commented Cankles.

"True, it is a crystal, but it is far from ordinary," explained Rose, holding it forth for them to see, but not touch. "It was given to me by Silas Agincor, the Wizard better known as the Dream Merchant."

"So, it's full of magic?" asked Cankles.

"Very much so," stated the Princess. "This dreamstone allows me to make three, and only three, wishes in a twenty-four hour cycle. So, even if I used one wish to get us there to the Fairy's Vale, I shall still have two more left."

"So exactly how does it work?" queried Tag.

"The Dream Merchant was very specific in his instructions. It is of the utmost importance that I form a clear, concise image in my mind's eye of exactly what I desire," explained Rose.

"An' that's it?" queried Cankles. "It sounds simple 'nough."

"There is nothing simple about it. He said if I am unable to focus on this technique, to conjure up dreams while wide-awake, it would be when I sleep that dreams can potentially become reality."

"Oh… so you've got to be careful of them nightmares," decided Cankles.

"You would think, but the Dream Merchant did make it clear that only the dreams I am most deserving of will be the ones to come true."

"Oh my! This is truly astoundin'!" marvelled Cankles.

"It is," agreed Rose. "And I should take full advantage of the magic imbued in this crystal as I see fit."

"Well, your earlier attempts at dreaming up these wishes fell short of expectations, but I sense there was not a lot of foresight involved when you made the one to go ignored by your parents and the palace staff," surmised Tag.

"To the contrary," disputed Rose. "It was a good wish, had it not been for the Tooth Fairy's curse that made me look like a shrivelled old prune of a peasant in their eyes."

"If that's the case, why can't you jus' use one of them wishes to turn you back to the way you were in their eyes?" questioned Cankles.

"The Tooth Fairy's curse cannot be broken with a wish granted by the Wizard," explained Rose. "As I understand it, the power of one magical being cannot be undone by another when set upon a mortal. That is why we are on our way to see Pancecilia Feldspar."

"Interesting," responded Cankles, scratching his head in thought. "Then perhaps we should use one of those wishes to get to the Fairy's Vale so you can see Pance right away."

"Not so fast! Think on this, Princess," urged Tag. "You already said you must conjure up a precise image. Is that not so?"

"I did. What of it?"

"Do you know what Pancecilia Feldspar's castle looks like, right down to its last turret and window? Even with Cankles' directions, can you truly conjure up an accurate image of this Fairy's Vale? For if not, we can end up who-knows-where standing in front of the castle belonging to one of her distant relatives. It will be a wish wasted and in all likelihood, another will be wasted in the process of getting us back here to start over again."

"Oh my! You're a smart one, Master Yairet," praised Cankles. "Waste not, want not, I always say! We're better to walk the distance."

"But if we wait until midnight, I can try. If it does not work, then we can walk," suggested Rose.

"And what happens if we land in a strange place that our friend here does not recognize and we become utterly lost looking for the Fairy's Vale?" questioned Tag.

"Then I will simply wish for us to return to this very spot, and then we shall walk from here," replied Rose.

"As I said, two wishes wasted and just as much time lost," stated Tag. "We are better off walking to our destination. Besides, if we depart this evening, instead of waiting until the midnight hour to employ one of your wishes, we will get there in roughly the same time, if not sooner."

"Master Yairet is quite right, Princess," agreed Cankles. "If we leave after dusk, we can be there well before midnight."

"Hold on here," demanded Rose. "You two should be doing as I say, being that I am a princess."

"True, but you are fast developing a reputation for being a regular slacker," warned Tag. "If you insist on using that dreamstone, then Cankles and I will walk. You'll have to deal with the ramifications of a wish gone bad all by yourself if things are not dreamed up in that mind of yours exactly as they should be."

"No disrespect to you, Princess Rose, but Master Yairet did make for a good case," reasoned Cankles. "I think it prudent that we walk instead of usin' magic."

"What good is my title if no one does as I command?"

"What good are your commands if your title gets you thrown into your parent's dungeon?" Tag answered with a question of his own. "You should think about that!"

Rose unleashed a dreary sigh of resignation as she muttered, "Fine... we walk."

"First, we wait until dark," reminded Tag.

"And what do you suggest we do in the meantime?" questioned Rose.

"Since it's not safe for the two of you to be wanderin' around out there right now, I'd say jus' make yourselves comfortable in my home until then," suggested Cankles.

"I am easily bored," stated Rose. "There must be something to do than to sit here twiddling my thumbs?"

"I can call Puke an' Honk in," offered Cankles. "They can keep you good an' amused for a while, 'specially when my cat takes to chasin' Puke around."

"Do not bother," declined Rose, shuddering in disgust. "Leave your animals to roam outside where they belong."

"Well, don't look to me, Princess. I'm your personal fool no more, so don't even think I'll keep you entertained!" Tag's arms crossed his chest in defiance.

"We can finish eating," offered Cankles, pointing to the platter of roast rat still waiting to be consumed.

"Good plan," praised Tag, selecting another rat-on-a-stick morsel. "No point in wasting perfectly good food."

"I have lost my appetite," groaned Rose, turning her nose up at the exotic fare. Instead of sitting at the table with Cankles and Tag as they resumed eating, the Princess wandered over to the shelves lining the wall over their host's bed.

The smallest item was a well-used porcelain thimble and the largest was a basket filled with old, used candles burned down to a nub of a wick. They had solidified into misshapen blobs of wax.

"What is all this?" asked Rose, eyeing the clutter of worthless odds and ends; some stacked, others scattered on the shelves in seemingly chaotic fashion.

"Those are my knick-knacks," explained Cankles, and then pointing to the lower shelf. "An' those are my paddy-wacks."

"Your *paddy-whats*?" questioned Rose, frowning in curiosity.

"They're like knick-knacks, but bigger an' worth a heckuva lot more," explained Cankles.

"Oh, I suppose that makes sense, in a strange sort of way," responded the Princess. She peered at one long object sheathed in a leather-wrapped case protruding from the bottom of this collection. It was buried beneath several broken coal oil lamps, a collection of ceramic bowls and platters and a stack of tattered, worn leather-bound books Cankles had never read, but had eagerly studied the etchings enclosed within the pages to make up stories in his mind.

"And just what is this?" queried Rose. She pointed to, but dare not touch the dust and cobweb covered object that intrigued her.

"Oh, *that* old thing," responded Cankles. He carefully pried it free from beneath his other treasures to show the Princess. "It's jus' an old sword."

"I figured that out, but where did it come from? It is my understanding swords are handed down from father to son."

"So they say, but I don't rightly know 'bout this one. I always jus' had it. Been with me for longer than I can remember," answered Cankles, scratching his head in thought as he pondered the origin of this weapon.

"I've always wanted a sword," said Tag, admiring the leather-wrapped hilt decorated with brass detailing that matched the brass chape protecting the tip of the scabbard. "My father had one he had wished to hand down to me, but I was told by an *unreliable source* it had been lost in battle when he was killed."

"And now it is safely stored away at Pepperton Palace, waiting for you to reclaim it once this quest is done." Rose was quick to say before Tag could add to her burden of guilt.

"May I have a look?" asked Tag, marvelling at the workmanship that had gone into the creation of the scabbard alone.

"Of course! Jus' don't go an' cut yourself," cautioned Cankles, passing the sword on to Tag. "It's pretty old, but the blade's still deadly sharp. Almost cut my fingers off once when I tried to used it to chop kindling for my fireplace."

"Good gracious! This is a sword, not an axe! It should be treated with utmost respect," admonished Tag, his fingers caressing the hilt. The tang of the blade was enclosed between two pieces of oak, held in place by rings of brass and wrapped in a fine, thin strip of leather to enhance the grip of the hilt. All these elements, as well as the brass detailing helped to give it a bit more weight to provide the weapon its perfect balance.

"Go on! Take it," urged Cankles. "Jus' be careful. It's quite the formidable sword, if I do say so myself."

Tag eagerly took the weapon into his hands. Cautiously unsheathing the blade, the highly polished double-edged sword filled his eyes with wonder. The diminishing rays of the sun's light filtered in through the grimy windows to dance off the forged steel, reflecting off the fuller.

"Would the sword not be stronger if it did not have this dent down the center of the blade?" questioned Rose, pointing to the long, narrow groove worked into the sword. It ran almost the entire length of the blade.

"My father told me the strength of the sword is determined by the elements added to the iron ore in the forging process," explained Tag. "This *dent* is called a fuller and it allows the blade to be easily extracted from the body it is embedded in."

"How?" asked Rose.

"Care for a demonstration?" teased Tag, hoisting the sword in his hand.

"Not really," responded the Princess, taking a wary step back.

As Tag carefully housed the blade back into its scabbard, he noticed the initials *M K* worked into the cross-guard used to protect the hand from an assault. These two, highly stylized letters were slightly overlaid and entwined.

"There are initials here. Who is MK?" queried Tag.

"Hell if I know," responded Cankles. His eyes scrutinized the detailing Tag took notice of, but had always passed by his eyes. "I always thought it was jus' a fancy design."

"For the uneducated, perhaps," sniffed Rose, staring at the distinct lettering. "But those are definitely the initials M and K."

"I suppose it could've belonged to someone in the family an' then gifted to me, but I can't rightly say, being that I don't know if I have any family to speak of," stated the perplexed man, shrugging his shoulders in bewilderment. "Not much else I can tell you about it."

"Odd," commented Tag.

"Yes, he is," agreed Rose, glancing over at their host.

"No, not *him!* This," explained Tag, scowling at the Princess as he held the sword before her. "If I did not know better, I'd say this is a fine sword worthy of a great knight, but if that was the case, what is it doing here? A knight does not simply abandon his weapon. It is as much a part of him as his hands or his soul."

"I bet he stole it," decided Rose, staring with eyes narrowed in suspicion.

"Me?" gasped Cankles, his hand seizing his heart as through these words were like a dagger thrust into his chest. "Steal? Never!"

"Come off it, Princess," scolded Tag. "He may be a simple man, but he's not a thief."

"Thanks… I think," responded Cankles, scratching his head in thought.

"How else would a person like *him* get his hands on something as valuable as this," argued Rose.

"By accident? By bartering? Anything but stealing," rebuked Tag. "I don't believe it is in his nature to steal."

"You're quite right, young sir. Might borrow an' forget to return something every now an' then, but I don't take to stealin' from no one," vowed Cankles, his hand resting over his heart in solemn promise.

"So you say," grumbled Rose.

"I believe him," decided Tag. "Maybe it belonged to one of his kinfolk from a long time ago."

"I do not know about kings in other countries, but I will tell you this," grunted Rose, turning her perfect nose up at Cankles, "my father would never be foolish enough to find protection within a circle of *idiots.* Only the bravest, most noble of men who are *not* intellectually challenged would serve as one of his knights. This fellow hardly fits the description and I doubt his kin was any different."

"May not be smart, but at least I'm honest," said Cankles, attempting to salvage his dignity that Rose had no problems trampling on.

"Never mind her words. The point is, this is a grand sword you should treasure," praised Tag, handing the weapon back to Cankles. "I know I'd be proud to call it my own, if I were so fortunate."

"If you like it so much, why don't you keep it?" offered Cankles, pushing the sword back to Tag. "As you can see, it was buried beneath all my belongings jus' collectin' dust. I don't have much use for it myself, 'specially since I'm not too keen on fightin' an' all that dangerous stuff. It's yours if you want it."

"Mine?" gasped Tag, uncertain if he heard correctly. "Are you positive?"

"Sure! After all, if you're leadin' us on this grand quest, it's only fittin' the hero have a proper sword should the need arise," decided Cankles. "That's the way it works in all the tales I've ever heard."

"Well, thank you, my friend," said Tag, honoured to have this weapon gifted to him. "I swear I shall take good care of it."

"I know you will," responded Cankles. He glanced out the window to see the shadows cast by the sun lengthen, stretching across the landscape. "Dusk will be upon us in a few hours and night will follow quickly. We best get ready now."

7

The Fairy's Vale

Under the twilight sky, Cankles led the way, cutting through neighbouring pastures and planted fields as he escorted his new comrades northward. As a velvety darkness settled on the lands and a dusting of stars twinkled against the deepening cobalt sky, Cankles and Tag marched on. Their steps were deliberate as the Princess trailed behind them, trudging along as she intermittently whined about her ordeal.

"Keep up, will you?" ordered Tag. He glanced over his shoulder to spy on Rose as she lagged behind, grumbling longer and louder the further she was made to travel. "We still have a ways to go."

"It is bad enough I am being made to walk," complained Rose, stumbling as the ground dipped slightly before her. "Why can we not take to the roads? It would make it so much easier."

"Easier, yes, but you should just keep on walking," responded Tag, "I'm sure there are those still looking for us. We best keep off the well-used roads for now, at least until we're closer to the cover of forest."

"It is not so much the arduous trek as it is the wretched smell," whined Rose, her hand coming up over her mouth and nose to filter out the stench wafting around them.

"Sorry, Princess. As tasty as those water rats are, they're a bit rich for my stomach if I eat too many of 'em," apologized Cankles, hoping she wouldn't notice his face redden with embarrassment in this growing darkness. "Perhaps you shouldn't be walkin' downwind of me."

"I think she means the reek of cattle," determined Tag.

"As in *cows*?" asked Rose, her eyes nervously darting about for signs of bovine beasties lurking nearby.

"We *are* in a pasture," reminded Tag, marching on through the knee-high grasses.

"So? That does not explain how you know there are cows in this field," said Rose, annoyed by her jester's know-it-all tone.

Just as Tag turned about to address her, Rose shrieked in surprise, falling flat on her back to disappear in the tall grasses.

"Princess!" called out Cankles. He dropped his pack as he dashed to her aid. Offering his hand, he hoisted her back onto her feet.

"How do you fare?" asked Cankles, as he brushed the dirt and grass from her gown.

"I've been better," groaned Rose, pushing her drooping tiara back onto her dishevelled head of hair.

"What do you know? Master Yairet is right," noted Cankles, staring at the footprint the Princess left in a steaming pile of cow manure.

"Now that is truly disgusting!" declared Rose. She dragged her foot through the grass to scrape off the fresh dung clinging to the sole of her shoe.

"Could have been worse," stated Tag, speaking with all certainty.

"How can it be worse than this?" snapped Rose.

"You could have fallen face-first into that heaping, big pile," responded Tag, biting his lower lip to keep from laughing aloud.

"Very funny!" She scowled in anger.

"Master Yairet does have a good point, Princess," noted Cankles, standing steady as Rose used his shoulder for balance as she wiped her shoe clean. "When you think about it, that would've been way more disgustin'."

"Well, here is a point that might register in that simple mind of yours," grunted Rose. "If we were walking on the road, this would not have happened in the first place!"

"Just calm down," urged Tag. "It is only manure."

"You only say that because you are used to treading in this stuff. I am a Princess, therefore, I am not even accustomed to being made to walk!"

"Unfortunately, you will be made to suffer a little longer," advised Tag. "Just be careful where you tread."

"I cannot even see where I am stepping in this darkness," grumbled Rose, her eyes squinting to exaggerate her case.

"Jus' follow close behind me," suggested Cankles, offering to lead the way.

"I tell you what, Princess. If you can hold your tongue and stop complaining until we reach that fence over there, then I will consider travelling by way of road," offered Tag. "Unfortunately for you, I cannot foresee that happening as you're such a fervent whiner, so proficient at complaining about every little thing there is."

"I am not! I can hold my tongue if I want to."

"Prove it!" snapped Tag, daring her to accept this challenge.

"I will!" Rose pursed her lips together, using her hand to motion that she was locking them shut and throwing away the key.

"This will be interesting," commented Tag, turning to address Cankles. "If I were a betting man, I'd say she will not even make it half way before she begins complaining again."

Rose did not utter a single word in her defense, giving her jester another angry scowl as she motioned for Tag to continue on.

"I'd say she looks pretty determined to prove you wrong, Master Yairet," stated Cankles, giving the Princess a nod of approval.

"We shall see," said Tag, giving Rose a smirk of a grin. "Now, move on."

Under the cold, silvery light cast by the stars and a sliver of a crescent moon, they marched on across this wide pasture. Although she uttered not a single word, Rose stewed in her resentment. With an anger fuelled by Tag's taunting words, she stubbornly pressed on, lifting the hem of her gown to limit the grass stains.

As Tag set the pace, Cankles walked slightly slower to allow Rose to follow in his footsteps. She struggled to keep up on this uneven terrain as she dodged the piles of cow manure scattered about as Cankles had the good sense to warn her about them.

Rose glanced up to see the outline of the split-rail fence silhouetted against the night as they drew closer. She smiled, pleased she was about to prove Tag wrong. Rushing along, just as she scampered by a small grove of trees in the corner of the pasture, a subtle movement – a shadow within the shadows, caught her eyes.

For a fleeting instant, the Princess froze. Her eyes probed the darkness to better scrutinize this object. To her horror, she watched as this large shadow became even bigger as it stood up on its four, stout legs. A flick of a tail and the sway of its head armed with massive horns filled her heart with immediate dread as the creature's hulking form filled her terrified eyes.

Instead of calling out in warning, Rose rushed on ahead of her companions.

"That a-girl! You can do it, Princess!" praised Cankles, cheering her on as he watched her push by Tag. "Jus' gotta put your mind to it."

"What's up with her?" grumbled Tag. He frowned in curiosity, for he knew Rose was never one to run unless her life depended on it.

Before Cankles could respond, a loud, angry snort rattled the night air. He and Tag turned, glancing behind just as a big brute of a beast lowered its head to present an impressive set of horns. The agitated creature pawed the ground, threatening to charge at the intruders.

"*Cow!*" hollered Tag.

"Actually, it's a bull," corrected Cankles, noting the high, muscular shoulders lending power to its intimidating form and the large horns designed for goring prospective rivals.

"Who cares? *Run!*" ordered Tag, charging behind Rose as she raced to the fence. "Don't just stand there! Run!"

Seeing Tag race off, dashing past the Princess to escape, it dawned on Cankles that he, too, should run for his life as the thunder of hooves drew closer, heading straight for him.

"*Aaaaah!*" bellowed Cankles. Throwing his hands up in the air, he bolted as the bull charged full tilt. Its head, lowered; the points of its horns aimed at his backside, ready to skewer him.

With arms flapping and legs flying, Cankles scrambled, running with all his might. His long, lanky legs carried him with speed, allowing him to sprint past Tag and Rose. With the grace of a yearling buck, he easily sailed over the fence, only to land like a hobbled donkey. Crashing down on the other side, he stumbled, tripped and then somersaulted, coming to a skidding stop in the tall grasses.

Tag raced close behind. Grabbing the top rail, he vaulted over the fence, landing easily on the other side. As he glanced over his shoulder, he spotted Rose. She was panting hard as she ran. The whites of her eyes were aglow in the dark as the bull quickly gained on her.

"Come on, Princess!" urged Tag, frantically waving her on. "Don't look back! Just run!"

Knowing instinctively that her long gown was going to hamper her efforts to climb, Rose dove between the rails. As the frothing mad bull barrelled down on her, Cankles and Tag grabbed the Princess by her hands, yanking Rose through to the other side, just in time.

Charging at top speed, the bull's hooves sank into the earth to slow it down, but the forward momentum as too great. Even as the angry bovine attempted to veer away, the tips of its horns rammed into the fence as its moving target was pulled through to safety. The bull snorted with indignation, bellowing in rage as it momentarily struggled to dislodge its horns from the fence.

Rose tumbled to the ground as Tag and Cankles fell backwards. For the longest moment, they lay there motionless. All they could hear were the sounds of their own hearts hammering wildly and their ragged breath, gasping to fill their aching lungs.

Confident these intruders would dare not trespass through its territory again, the bull stomped its hooves in warning. Snorting loudly, it turned tail to trot off into the night.

"Good God!" cursed Rose, breaking the silence. "We could have been killed!"

Instead of sharing her concern, Tag and Cankles lay breathless, snorting and coughing with laughter after the exhilarating run.

"I am serious! We could have died!"

"But we didn't!" countered Tag.

"These near-death experiences always make me feel so alive! It's like a jolt to the senses!" exclaimed Cankles, his arms wrapping around his belly as he guffawed heartily.

"By God! That was fun!" declared Tag.

"Are you mad?" snapped Rose. Her balled, quivering fist punched his arm. "That was not fun, nor was it funny!"

"You didn't see the look on your face," scoffed Tag. "*That* was funny!"

"Don't mean to be rude, Princess, but I gotta admit you were quite the sight to behold. Your eyes looked like they were gonna pop clear out of your head," added Cankles.

"Well, you *are* being rude! You both are," admonished Rose, examining the tear in her dress where it had snagged onto the fence. "And now look at this. My gown is ruined! There is a rip in it."

"Better the dress than your body," declared Tag.

"Quite right!" agreed Cankles, wiping the thread of saliva from his chin as he sputtered in laughter.

"Har-dee, har, har, har!" mocked Rose. "Laugh if you want, but this gown was special to me."

"Well, now that rip goes perfectly with the dog slobber, grass, mud and food stains you've acquired so far," teased Tag.

"Shut it!" snapped the Princess. "You are making me mad!"

"Cankles and I are the ones who should be mad at you. Why didn't you say a rampaging bull was ready to gore us?"

"And what? Lose the bet that I could hold my tongue when I want to? I think not! If anything, I have proven you wrong! Wrong! Wrong! Wrong!"

"Say, she did jus' that!" declared Cankles, nodding his head in approval. "She didn't even let out a peep when you'd think she'd be screamin' for dear life."

"So there!" grunted Rose, glaring at her jester.

"I am big enough to admit when I'm wrong," responded Tag, giving the Princess a thoughtful nod. "In many ways, I'm dumbfounded."

"That's a good thing, right?" asked Cankles, looking to Tag for confirmation. "Cause usually, it's bad to be found dumb."

"In this case, it's good," stated Tag. "In fact, as much as I am mad, I must admit, I'm duly impressed."

"You are?" gasped Rose, stunned to hear his admission.

"Yes," admitted Tag. "You actually proved me wrong and I can't say I'm sorry for that."

Rose beamed with pride upon hearing these words of praise, for seldom of late had her jester had anything positive to say about her.

"I wonder what other miracles will be in store for us on this quest," pondered Tag, as he picked up Cankles' pack from the ground, handing it to him.

"Methinks the Princess can put her mind to whatever she wants, when she wants to," determined Cankles. "I'll bet she wouldn't even say a word, not one, if something like a fire-breathin' dragon took to chasin' us down."

"That would not be a good thing, then," countered Tag. "In all likelihood, we would all be killed if she chose to be quiet for once in her life."

"Actually, it'd be twice then," noted Cankles.

"Never mind that!" snapped Rose. "That crazed beast could have been the death of us. Why did you not use your sword to kill that animal?"

"You're the crazy one to think I would take this fine weapon to that bull," admonished Tag, his hand patting the scabbard.

"In other words, you do not know how to handle a real sword," ridiculed the Princess.

"Not at all. I refuse to kill that animal for behaving as it should. Just as the knights of your palace are trained to expel unwelcome intruders, so too, is that animal reacting to those trespassing through its territory."

"But I am a Princess! I can understand it charging after you two, but me? How dare you, you mad cow? You loathsome beast!" Rose cursed as she shook an angry fist at the massive creature, lumbering away to chew its cud.

"Bull," corrected Cankles, positioning his fingers over his head to display his version of the wide, larger horns possessed by the male bovine species.

"It will be whatever I choose to called it," sniffed Rose.

"Does that belong to you?" questioned Tag, pointing into the fenced pasture. "Because if you've lost it, you better go back and retrieve it."

"Lost what?" asked Rose. Her brows furrowed in curiosity as she stared into the dark field.

"Your mind!" replied Tag, snorting with laughter. "Do you honestly think a simple animal can tell a princess from a pauper?"

"Quite right, Master Yairet!" chuckled Cankles. "I certainly couldn't tell you were a princess when I first set my eyes on you."

"That is because you *are* a simple animal," grumbled Rose, scowling at Cankles. "You would think that in my princess finery, any creature, man or beast, would know my standing in life."

"Ripped, stained, drooled upon by a hound! That is some finery, Princess," teased Tag. "When it comes right down to it, that bull really doesn't care."

"Well, it should!" snapped Rose.

"Why? Were you expecting it to curtsy to you before it charged?" asked Tag, rolling his eyes in frustration.

"Curtsy, yes. Charge, no!"

"Now that'd be a sight to behold," mused Cankles. "I've never seen a cow or bull curtsy to anyone."

"We can debate the nature of that beast and why it wouldn't yield to your will or we can venture on to the Fairy's Vale," offered Tag, growing tired of Rose's grumbling.

"We venture on. And as I had proven you wrong, we shall take to the road," reminded the Princess.

"I was going to recommend that anyway," responded Tag, laughing inwardly at Rose's wasted exercise in self-control. "After all, it is dark enough now."

Hot, sweaty and stinking of cow manure, Rose sulked as she trudged along the roadway, struggling to keep up with her comrades. It was bad enough being made to walk, but to do so in these conditions? It was nothing short of deplorable and now she longed for a nice, hot bath and luxuriant soap scented with the attar of rose.

As Cankles stopped to gain his bearings, Rose drew in a deep, weary breath. It was at this very moment she detected something that was oh-so familiar to her.

"Do you smell that?" asked Rose. She sniffed the air, trying to home in on this scent.

"Smell what?" asked Tag.

"Can't blame me this time," said Cankles.

"It is too pleasant to be you," responded Rose, dismissing him with a wave of her hand. "I smell lavender. I am sure of it."

"It grows wild in these parts," stated Tag. He pointed to the low-growing clumps of vegetation with spikes of mauve coloured flowers growing by the roadside. "What's the big deal?"

"The big deal is, it is the sweetest, most beautiful perfume I have ever had the good fortune of smelling!"

"You *hate* lavender," argued Tag, scratching his head in frustration.

"Not anymore!" declared Rose.

Like a dog rolling in fresh cow dung, the Princess pitched her body onto the mounds of lavender. She writhed about, crushing and bruising the leaves, stems and flowers to transfer its essence to her gown and body. "Aaah! Never has there been a scent sweeter than lavender!"

"You should try this, Master Yairet," recommended Cankles, as he rolled about on his own lavender clump. "The Princess is right! It's quite the refreshin' smell, indeed!"

"Do you know how insane you both look rolling about like that? People coming by will think you're having a fit! Enough of this silliness. Let's move on."

Cankles promptly hopped up onto his feet, pulling Rose onto hers.

"Time's a-wastin' away," agreed Cankles. "Follow me. We enter the forest from here. Keep close now. It gets pretty dark in there."

"This is disgusting!" groaned Rose, brushing away the sticky, dew-laden web that clung to her hair and tiara.

"It's only a spider web," said Cankles. "And it's not like that puny spider would do anything to you. If anything, being that you're so much bigger, the poor thing would be frightened of you."

"I did not say I was *frightened*," argued Rose, ducking under a branch he held up for her. "I said this web, along with all the other bugs, slugs and all manner of beasties we have come across thus far, are disgusting."

"Oh my, you do not get out much, do you, Princess?" asked Cankles, surprised she'd be so disturbed by the presence of these creatures that were a part of his day-to-day life.

"I much prefer the splendid surroundings of my palace. This is repulsive, being out-of-doors," complained Rose.

"It is called nature," responded Tag, his eyes rolling in exasperation. "And it's about time you got back in touch with it."

"I will not touch *it!* Neither will I allow it to touch *me!*" snapped Rose, grimacing in repulsion as she was forced to dodge another web in her path.

The Princess froze as a small shadow on the forest floor darted toward her. A ball of frenetic energy, its nervous movements were quick and jerky, stopping and starting as it advanced.

Rose recoiled in disgust as a curious little chipmunk with dark, liquid eyes and a twitching nose scampered toward her, coming into full view in the light of the cold, silvery moon. Eager for a handout, the rodent peered up at her, begging for a nut or a seed. Instead of offering food, just as the chipmunk scrambled onto her shoe, Rose's foot flew out to send the creature flying. It sailed through the air, squeaking all the way as it flew past Tag, just missing his head.

"What was that?" gasped Tag, his eyes staring into the darkness as twigs and branches swayed in the wake of the airborne rodent.

"Methinks that chipmunk is now a flying squirrel," answered Cankles, looking aghast at the Princess.

"That animal attacked me!" insisted Rose, attempting to justify her actions. "It had crazy, little eyes that forewarned of its intent to scamper up my gown. I could not have that, you know?"

"You kicked an innocent, little chipmunk?" groaned Tag. "For shame!"

"It was not like that! I did not actually *kick it*," explained Rose. Her face was flushed with embarrassment. "It was more like I *flung it* from my foot when it pounced on me."

"Kick, flung, it matters not," grunted Tag, shaking his head in disapproval. "I only hope that poor creature didn't get hurt because of you."

"I am sure it is fine, but what about *me?* That little beast gave me quite the scare!"

"I'd say that chipmunk was the one that looked more terrified," decided Cankles. "Its whiskers were all a-quiver as it flew by Master Yairet's head."

"If we had only traded a diamond or two from that gown for some horses," lamented Tag. "We would be done with this trek faster, plus, the creatures of this forest would be safe from you."

"We can still do that," decided Rose. "The next farm we come across, I will exchange some of these beads for fine horses."

Tag came to a dead stop upon hearing these words. "We've come this far and only now, when we are well into this forest and far from any farms, do you decide on this?"

"How was I to know we would be made to travel for this long?" grumbled Rose, her shoulders rolling in a shrug.

"Even before we started, Cankles told you how many leagues we'd be made to walk to reach the Fairy's Vale."

"I know, but I had no idea it was *this* far, being that I had never been made to walk before. Destinations seem so much closer when riding in a carriage," explained Rose. "I suppose my perception of distance is not up to snuff when compared to the common folk who are used to walking everywhere."

"I would have to agree with that," conceded Tag.

"Don't fret, Princess. It's not too late to trade for horses on our way home," said Cankles.

"True," said Tag, "but I am curious, Princess. Why now? Why are you willing to part with some of those diamonds when you were so adamant about not ruining your dress to pay for that pie you are now accused of stealing?"

"For one, we are in the middle of nowhere, so there is little chance I will encounter anyone I need to impress. Plus, in an hour or two, I can wish for a new and better gown. I shall wish for one that is much prettier than this tired, tatty thing," explained Rose.

"I'm confident there are better, more worthy things to wish for than another jewel-encrusted dress," grumbled Tag.

"True, but surely you do not expect me to be seen in this outfit again, especially if we should head back to Cadboll? That will set the people's tongues wagging if they see their Princess wearing the same dress two days in a row."

"Oh, we can't have that, can we?" responded Tag, his tone cynical.

"Definitely not! The only thing this dress is good for now is to use these diamonds to purchase the horses we will need for the remainder of this quest."

"A wise plan, but we really should move on," stated Cankles. Waving his comrades on to follow him. "That fallen pine tree I told you about is just up yonder."

As they approached this directional landmark, Tag took a moment to admire the tenacity of this old, gnarled pine. Blown over during a powerful windstorm, its trunk grew parallel to the ground before stubbornly twisting upward to follow the sun once more.

"So where to go from here?" asked Tag.

For a moment, Cankles stared at the toppled tree, deciding which of the low-hanging branches was the biggest of those that still survived.

"This way," determined Cankles. "This one's pointin' the way to the trail."

Trekking on through the darkness with nothing more than the celestial light to guide them, the trio made their way northward through the forest.

"Look, fireflies!" marvelled Rose, pointing through the stand of trees as golden orbs of light floated about, gracefully weaving and dancing between the high branches.

"No, that can't be," disputed Tag. "They are too bright; much too big to be fireflies."

"Quite right, Master Yairet," responded Cankles. "We're near to the Fairy's Vale."

"Those are Fairies?" gasped Rose, watching in fascination as the splendid show of golden light abruptly vanished as her excited voice rang through the forest.

"Shhh!" said Cankles, pressing a finger to his lips. "Keep your voice down. The Fairies aren't used to strangers coming to these parts. They're kinda timid."

Rose merely nodded in understanding as she followed behind Tag and Cankles.

"Over there, in that meadow," disclosed Cankles, pointing to a small clearing up ahead. "That's the Fairy's Vale."

"Well, it is about time!" exclaimed the Princess.

Pushing between her comrades, Rose rushed ahead, calling for the Tooth Fairy, "Pancecilia Feldspar, I want a word with you!"

"Hold on!" hollered Cankles. "Wait, Princess!"

"Where are you!" shouted Rose, spinning about in this meadow as her eyes searched the darkness for the Tooth Fairy. "I demand an audience with you this very minute!"

"Watch where you st- "

Before Cankles could issue his warning, Rose stumbled, falling to her knees.

"Oh, no!" groaned Cankles, staring in disbelief as he ran toward the Princess.

"What?" asked Rose, brushing the dirt from her hands as she sat up. "What did I do?"

Tag dashed after Cankles. As he entered the meadow, he saw a number of toadstools, each with a red cap flecked with white spots. Several were broken, the shattered caps up-ended to reveal the gill-like filaments beneath. These damaged fungi were now destined for reclamation by the earth.

"This is not good," gulped Tag.

"Indeed!" confirmed Cankles, his eyes darting about nervously. "Not good at all!"

"What are you talking about?" asked Rose, flicking off the grass and dirt clinging to her gown.

"Do you not see it?" asked Tag, pointing to the ground at her feet. "You are standing smack-dab in the middle of a Fairy Ring!"

Rose glanced down, slowly turning about as her eyes focused on the ground. They followed the perfect circle of toadstools growing around a faint path worn into the earth by the feet of many dancing Fairies.

"What is the big deal? So a few toadstools got trampled? They will grow back," responded Rose, with a shrug of indifference.

"They'll grow back for sure, but remember what we told you about what can happen if you desecrate their magic circle?" reminded Cankles, pointing to his nether-region.

"Oh, that? I am not a man, so I have nothing to worry about," snorted Rose, dismissing his concern.

Just as she was about to step out of the damaged ring, a golden aura swelled from beneath the caps of the remaining toadstools as orbs of light glowed from the dark shadows of the surrounding forest.

"Oooh... This doesn't bode well for you," groaned Cankles. He listened with nervous anticipation as the thrum of Fairy wings grew louder.

"Worry not," urged Rose. "I can make them understand it was an accident. If anything, they can probably be bribed to appease them."

"Angry Fairies aren't easy to appease," warned Cankles, as he stared at the glowing spheres swirling through the forest. They converged in a great show of light floating ever closer to the Princess.

Realizing how incensed these tiny beings were, Rose spoke up. Before she could make an offer, her voice was drowned out, lost in the angry drone of hundreds of rattling wings descending on the meadow to surround her. Cankles and Tag dove to the ground, ducking beneath this bold show of force as the Fairies flew from the forest and emerged from beneath the ring of toadstools to attack this intruder.

To Rose's surprise and horror, she was swarmed by a multitude of thoroughly agitated Fairies. They dove at her with astonishing speed, coming in from all sides. Rose shrieked in fright as tiny hands yanked at her hair and tugged at her gown in a frenzied, aerial assault.

In a matter of seconds, it was over. As quickly as they lay siege, the Fairies dispersed into the forest, their shimmering, golden light vanishing into the night.

"Thank goodness they are gone!" exclaimed the breathless Princess as her eyes nervously glanced about for signs of another assault.

"I can see why," noted Tag, scrutinizing Rose's dishevelled apparel. Along with her jewel-encrusted tiara, the matching necklace, bracelet and diamond ring that adorned her body were now conspicuously absent. Gone, too, was every diamond bead that decorated her gown.

"Oh no!" groaned Rose, realizing she had been stripped of every glittering pieces of jewellery that once adorned her person. "Gone! All gone! I might as well be naked."

"Please, no!" yelped Tag, grimacing at the thought.

"I forgot to mention one small detail: Fairies like shiny," stated Cankles, scrambling onto his feet. "It appears you were able to appease 'em after all, Princess."

"The dreamstone!" gasped Rose, her eyes filled with dread.

"Did they take it, too?" asked Tag.

Her hands flew up to her chest, frantically feeling about. Beneath the bodice of her gown, nestled between her breasts, she felt the hard, smooth crystal pendant press against her skin. Safely tucked away from the sight of the Fairies, it was safe. She sighed with relief.

"Thank goodness!" exclaimed Rose, clutching the magic crystal to her chest. "It is still here."

"For one unlucky Princess, you were lucky this time," decided Cankles.

"It was not luck," responded Tag. "Do you honestly think *anything* would want to venture down *there* to steal away with it?"

"Very funny!" scoffed Rose, as her hand adjusted the gold necklace still hanging about her neck.

"I was not being funny," insisted Tag. "I was speaking the truth. Now, before the Princess adds insult to injury, causing that angry mob to descend upon us once more, let's find the Tooth Fairy's castle."

"Quickly then!" exclaimed Cankles. "Follow me."

He deliberately skirted around the Fairy Ring to lead the way to the edge of the meadow where a majestic oak tree grew. It was the largest in all of Dimbolt Forest. With a wide buttress to support the weight of the massive trunk and the many great, sprawling branches stretching up into the sky, this magnificent oak filled their eyes with wonder.

"In all my life, I've never seen such a huge oak tree!" marvelled Tag, staring up to see the highest branches become one with the night sky.

"It is a big tree. So what? We are here to find the Tooth Fairy," grunted Rose, glancing about. Her eyes searched the base of this tree for the famous, white castle. "Now where is it?"

"It's in there, Princess," revealed Cankles. He pointed into a large hollow in the trunk of the oak tree.

"What? The Queen of the Tooth Fairies lives in a tree?" gasped Rose, her tone incredulous. "I thought her castle was supposed to be a magnificent structure to be envied by all."

"It is," insisted Cankles. "Take a look."

Rose stood up on her toes, straining to peer into the dark hollow. Her eyes opened wide in surprise.

A gleaming white castle, constructed entirely of perfectly polished teeth Pancecilia Feldspar had collected on her nightly forays, glistened in the starlight. It practically glowed before her very eyes. The many turrets gave rise to an unusual architectural design like no other she had ever seen. The tiny banners emblazoned with the image of a perfect bicuspid donned the spires of the watchtowers, but on this breezeless eve, they drooped pathetically.

"That is it? That puny dollhouse?"

Tag stared inside to see this miniature palace filling the tree hollow. "It'd say it is pretty impressive. Small, but impressive nonetheless."

"So now that we have found it, call the Tooth Fairy out. I demand to have a word with her," ordered Rose.

"You can't do that," responded Cankles. "If you want to meet with Pance, you gotta follow Fairy protocol."

"What do you mean?" asked Rose.

"If you want to meet her, you gotta go in there an' politely request, *not demand*, an audience with her."

"It makes sense to me," stated Tag. "After all, we are in the Fairy's Vale. It's best to abide by their customs if we do not wish to offend them. And as you have already offended Pance and now her people, I strongly recommend you take Cankles' advice."

"Do you realize you are now sounding as foolish as he does," sniffed Rose, addressing her jester as her eyes darted over to the village idiot in their company. "Look how big we are! Just how do you propose we go into that tiny domicile?"

"There's nothing to it, really. You jus' gotta know what to do," confided Cankles. "Watch this, Princess!"

With one ear pressed firmly to the tree's trunk, Cankles' knuckles rapped lightly against the hollow. A series of knocks in a rhythm akin to an old folk tune drummed out a special code known to only those granted permission to access this palace.

To Tag and Rose's surprise, a globe of golden light appeared at the mouth of the tree hollow as a tiny voice called out, "Who dare ask permission to enter the royal residence of Queen Pancecilia Feldspar?"

"Hello, Sparks!" greeted Cankles, bowing politely before the Fairy guarding the way. "It's only me, Cankles."

"Well, good evening, Master Mayron. What a pleasant surprise to see you again," responded the Fairy.

"I've come by with my friends. They're seekin' an audience with your Queen."

For a moment, the tiny being scrutinized the two mortals in Cankles' company. Tag smiled politely at the Fairy as he used his elbow to nudge Rose, urging her to do the same.

With a forced smile, Rose spoke up, "I urgently need to speak to Pancecilia Feldspar."

"Well, I suppose if you are friends of Cankles Mayron, then you must be friends of the Queen," decided Sparks, hovering before them. "You may enter."

"And just how do we do that?" grumbled Rose. "I hardly think my hand, as dainty as it is, will even fit into the keep."

"Jus' be patient, Princess," urged Cankles. "Allow my friend to work his magic."

Sparks circled overhead and as he did so, his wings rattled, vibrating to release a shower of glittering, golden dust that floated down upon the mortals. He dispensed this magic with a special incantation to activate these sparkling particles.

"Close your eyes. You don't want to get any of this Fairy dust in them," warned Cankles. "It can sting a bit."

"And then what?" questioned Rose, her eyes squeezing shut.

"Breathe in," instructed Cankles, inhaling loudly. "You gotta fill your lungs with this magic dust for it to work properly."

"What will it do?" asked Tag, breathing in deeply.

"It'll make us small. You'll see how it works," responded Cankles.

"Well, I feel no different," grumbled Rose, inhaling another deep breath.

Just as she opened her eyes, she watched in astonishment. Everything around her seemed to abruptly grow to massive proportions as she shrunk down. She, Tag and Cankles disappeared into the grass growing around the base of the oak tree.

"Wow! This is absolutely incredible!" exclaimed Tag, in awe as he glanced up at the blades and stalks of grasses towering above them like a great forest.

"Look out!" hollered Cankles, pulling the Princess out of the way.

A large, black beetle trundled along, its snapping mandibles held low to the ground as it scavenged for food buried in the leaf litter. The ebony, armoured beast was deliberate in its actions, unwavering in its course as it lumbered on by, ignoring the tiny humans.

"What a horrid creature!" gasped Rose, shaken by the sight of this gargantuan, six-legged monster ambling past them.

"No worries, Princess, it's only a carrion beetle. It prefers to eat things that are already dead," said Cankles.

"That's a relief," said Tag, as he watched the beetle disappear into the dense jungle of grass on its determined quest for a meal. "But I suggest we get up to the palace before something does come along that's hunting for a live meal."

"Brilliant idea, Master Yairet," approved Cankles, nodding in agreement.

"Surely, you do not expect me to climb all the way up there," gasped Rose, staring up to the tree hollow that now seemed impossibly far from her reach.

"I've made the climb before," revealed Cankles. "It isn't easy, but it can be done."

"Oh, no!" groaned Rose, releasing a dismal sigh. "After travelling this far I am really not up to this gruelling task."

"I'm not 'xpectin' you to climb, Princess. There's an easier way to get up there."

"Then make it so," urged Rose.

With a sharp whistle, Cankles summoned their ride.

In response, there was a rustling of leaves and the skittering clatter of sharp claws scrambling down the tree trunk. Rose shrieked in surprise as a dormouse plopped to the ground before them.

"Your ride awaits, Princess," announced Cankles. He scratched the furry ball of nervous energy behind its large, quivering ears.

"I am not going to ride on a disgusting rat!" gasped Rose, shrinking away from the rodent.

"It is not a rat at all," argued Tag. He cautiously approached the creature with nervously trembling whiskers and large, liquid eyes that shone even in this darkness. "It is obviously a common dormouse, and a cute one at that!"

"There is nothing *common about it!* It is as big as a horse. And there is nothing cute about it either," disputed Rose, grimacing in repulsion.

"Oh, come now, Princess! From our new perspective it looks to be as large as a draft horse, but look at those adorable eyes," countered Tag, his hand gliding through the soft, dense fur to pet the creature.

"Hop on," urged Cankles, as he climbed onto the rodent's rounded back. "I know it's not the grand carriage you're used to, Princess, but it'll do the trick. There's plenty of room up here, so come on."

Without hesitation, Tag grabbed a fistful of fur, pulling himself up behind Cankles as Rose stood there, her mouth agape as she stared dumbfounded at her male comrades.

"You best hurry, Princess," said Cankles, waving her on to join them. "This magic won't last forever, you know? If you wait for too long, you'll be too big to ride. You'll end up squashing the poor thing."

"Come on, Princess! You're wasting precious time," coaxed Tag, extending his hand to pull Rose up. "Let's get this over with."

"Very well," conceded Rose, taking Tag's hand into hers. Given the options, she had no intention of embarking on the monumental climb up the tree's rough, deeply fissured bark to reach the tree hollow.

Tag and Cankles hoisted Rose onto the animal's back. Even through its coat of plush fur, they could feel its muscles twitching rapidly with nervous energy.

"Now hold on tight! She tends to move quickly," warned Cankles, bracing himself for the ride. His legs tightening around this unconventional mount as he leaned forward, clinging to the rodent's fur. With a gentle prod of his heels, he spurred the creature on.

"*Eeeee!*" Rose shrieked in surprise as the dormouse leapt into action, easily bounding up the tree trunk.

Tag's legs were clamped around the dormouse's body while his hands clutched a fistful of fur to secure his hold. He suddenly groaned in pain as the Princess' arms wrapped around his chest, her fingernails sinking into his clothes, skin and flesh as she held on for dear life. Like a powerful snake constricting around his body, Rose effectively stifled his ability to breathe as his eardrums were assaulted by her piercing screams of terror.

With rapid, energetic spurts, the dormouse darted up the oak tree to disappear into the hollow where Sparks awaited their arrival at the stairs leading into the castle keep.

"I will never do that again!" gasped a terrified Rose. "That was absolutely traumatic! That beast could have been the death of us."

"Come now, Princess, it wasn't that bad. Aside from going deaf and not being able to breathe thanks to you, that was rather fun!" declared Tag. Hopping off the dormouse's back, he rubbed his aching ribcage to vanquish the pain inflicted by the terrified Princess. "In fact, it was quite the thrilling ride, more so than any horse I've ever ridden."

"I'll say!" agreed Cankles, climbing down from their shared mount.

"Are you daft? Why is it that every time we undertake a harrowing, death-defying task, you deem it to be fun?" scolded Rose, sputtering in anger. The colour had all but drained from her face long before they had reached their destination.

"Because it *was* harrowing *and* we did defy death," reasoned Tag, slapping Cankles on his back in thanks for this exhilarating, once-in-a-lifetime experience.

"You are both quite insane!" denounced Rose, as she struggled to dismount.

There was nothing graceful about her style as she slipped off the dormouse, sliding down its rounded back to land on its fluffy tail. With a flick of this appendage, the dormouse unceremoniously dislodged the Princess before darting back up the oak tree to disappear in the high branches.

"You'd have to be mad to think that was fun!" snapped Rose, as she struggled to stand.

Tag and Cankles pulled the Princess back onto her feet.

"Just calm down," urged Tag. "You're fine. That's the most important thing. Plus, we made it to the Tooth Fairy's palace in one piece and in short time."

"I suppose," grumbled the Princess. "But as I said before, I will never do that again."

"If all goes as planned, there'll be no need to," responded Tag, waving her on to follow behind Cankles.

8

A Leap of Faith

"Now *this* is impressive!" admitted Rose, glancing up at the white palace walls towering before her. From this altered perspective, Pancecilia Feldspar's abode had taken on a regal quality of magnificent proportions.

"Welcome! I suppose a formal introduction is in order," The Fairy bowed in salutation as the trio approached. "My name is Sparks Firestar."

"And just where do you stand in the grand pecking order of royal hierarchy?" questioned Rose, staring at the Fairy who now stood taller than her.

"Oh, no! I am far from royal, young miss. I am merely a trusted aide and humble servant to the Queen."

"So you work here?" queried Rose.

"Yes, I work under Pance."

Cankles burst out laughing, "It's still funny every time you say that, Sparks!"

"Yes, yes, I know," responded the Fairy, his cheeks flushing with embarrassment.

"What are you talking about?" asked Tag, giving his friend a quizzical look.

"He works *under Pance*," responded Cankles, sharing the joke as he pointed to the Fairy. "Get it? *Underpants!*"

Tag and Rose just stared with raised eyebrows.

"It's a play on words," explained Cankles, attempting to stifle his laughter. "Get it?"

"Got it, but don't want it," groaned Tag, shaking his head in dismay.

"Perhaps you should go stand over there," suggested Rose, pointing to the far side of the courtyard as her eyes rolled in frustration. "Finish having a chuckle on your own. We are in the midst of conducting some important business."

"Do not be concerned with him. I am quite used to Master Mayron's sense of humor. And lest he breaks out laughing again, it is better to say I am the Queen's personal assistant," corrected Sparks, motioning them to follow. "My job is to give the Queen's busy life a semblance of order."

"I figured out that much," responded Rose.

"And just who might you be?" queried Sparks. He stared at this mortal's dishevelled head of hair and the plain, shabby gown she wore. Seeing the stains and tears that so conspicuous, he automatically assumed she was a peasant.

"You do not know?"

"Should I?"

"Absolutely! My name is Princess Rose-alyn Beatrice Elizabeth Wilhemina Pepperton from the Kingdom of Fleetwood. And this boy, Tag Yairet, is my servant."

"The name is Tagius and I am *not* your servant," he protested, his nerves bristling in annoyance with this introduction.

"Would you prefer if I introduced you as my court jester?" snipped Rose. Her tone was sharp as she attempted to put Tag in his place.

Tag held his tongue as the Princess continued, "And obviously, you are already acquainted with Crinkles Moron."

"Cankles Mayron," corrected the Fairy, giving this returning visitor a polite nod of his head. "Welcome, one and all, to the grand palace of Pancecilia Feldspar, Queen of the Tooth Fairies."

"This is quite incredible," marvelled Tag, staring at the dentine stonework forming the majestic archway into the castle keep. Each tooth was of uniform size and shape; unmarred by chips, scratches or cavities.

"When you consider perfect teeth are a rare commodity these days and the Queen pays a premium for flawless specimens, it better be incredible," responded Sparks, leading the unexpected guests into the palace and through the main hall. With a nod of his head a Fairy maiden darted away to retrieve some refreshments.

Sparks escorted them into the royal library. As they walked into this darkened room, with a snap of Sparks' fingers, fireflies perched on an overhead chandelier and the wall sconces immediately glowed, illuminating the library with their golden light.

"Please have a seat," offered Sparks. "Make yourselves comfortable."

In this great room, a collection of books stacked from floor to ceiling lined the walls of this chamber.

"So many books!" gasped Tag. "This is truly astounding!"

"The Queen is a firm believer that reading is the cornerstone of knowledge," explained Sparks.

"Well, with books like *One Hundred and One Ways to Remove a Tooth, The ABC's of Dental Care,* and *Flossing for Dimwits,* I do believe your Queen's knowledge is somewhat limited," assessed Rose, as her eyes scrutinized some of the titles of this collection.

"I believe it is *your* understanding of my Queen that is somewhat limited," countered Sparks, his translucent wings rattling with annoyance at her audacious comment. "Let me assure you, Pancecilia is knowledgeable in many things pertaining to our world and that of the human realm. This is not her main library. This one happens to feature books pertaining to her vocation."

"I suppose that is a good thing," said Rose, making herself comfortable on a sofa over stuffed with bulrush fluff.

"Of course it is," stated Tag, glaring at the Princess. "After all, ignorance is not necessarily bliss. In some cases, it can get you killed."

Rose gave the Fairy a feeble smile as she added, "It was not my intention to insult the Queen. It was merely an observation."

"And a poor one at that," grunted Tag.

"No need for concern," responded Sparks. "Just be grateful my Queen was not present to hear this *observation.* Now, what brings you to this palace?"

"I am here to request an audience with your Queen," replied Rose. "Due to a terrible misunderstanding, a curse had been set upon me."

The Fairy's brows arched up as he scrutinized this mortal and her tattered apparel. "She cursed you with poor taste in fashion?"

Rose's face flushed with embarrassment. The palms of her now-grimy hands ran down the skirt of her crumpled, stained gown in an attempt to smooth out the wrinkles, but her efforts to look more presentable failed miserably.

"This gown was quite fine at the start of the day, but due to the curse, I am made to suffer. This is the result of my suffering."

"Let me assure you, Princess Rose-alyn, there are far worse things to endure in life than to be made to wear a less-than-flattering gown," responded Sparks.

"It is much more than that. And I am here now to put things right."

"I understand my Queen well enough to know she would never subject a living soul to the misery of one of her curses unless there was good reason to do so."

"There was good reason all right," interjected Tag, as Rose shot a hostile glance in his direction.

Before he could share in the details that led up to this curse being unleashed upon her, Rose spoke up, "I assure you, good sir, it was a terrible misunderstanding, nothing more. It is one I am confident can be rectified once I meet with your Queen."

"I hope for your sake you are correct," responded the Fairy. "Unfortunately, Pance is not available at this very moment. She is out on one of her nightly forays, harvesting teeth as she has done for hundreds of years."

"Can you not call her home?" asked Rose. Her voice tightened with concern, her back straightening as she listened to his words. "It is very urgent that I speak to her immediately."

"Alas, my Queen will return, but only prior to the break of dawn, possibly sooner if it is an unproductive night."

"That will not do!" exclaimed Rose, standing as though it would somehow prompt the Fairy to act on her behalf.

"I am sure this is a major inconvenience for you, however, she will return in due course. If it is urgent that you meet with her, then I recommend you be patient and wait for her return."

"It's been a long night an' you've travelled far, Princess. There's no harm in waitin' for a few more hours," urged Cankles. "You should take this time to rest while you can."

"I agree. You seem to have no difficulty in making others wait for you, urging them to be patient," reminded Tag. "I believe it is time for *you* to learn some patience."

"This shall make your wait less tedious," said Sparks. The beautiful Fairy maiden they had seen upon their arrival in the keep flew into the library. She delivered a tray of drinks to serve to the mortals.

With a flutter of gossamer wings, she set the tray down on a table before departing.

"Let me offer you some refreshments and a little something to eat while you wait," said Sparks. "I am sure you are thirsty and famished after your long trek."

"That would be lovely! But please, tell me it is not ale," whined Rose. The memory of the foul beverage Cankles had served still left a bitter taste in her mouth.

"I believe I have something better than ale or stout," promised Sparks, as another lovely Fairy maiden soon followed. Her tray was laden with delicate, pressed cookies made of flower pollen and sweetened with honey. They filled an overturned cap of an acorn husk. She set the platter of cookies down next to the wooden holder that prevented the drinking vessels from tipping over.

"This is... quaint," decided Rose, selecting her words carefully to not offend the Fairy.

She stared at four lilac flowers arranged on the drink holder. Each tubular floret formed the perfect-sized beverage container for one as small as a Fairy. Peering into the drinking vessels, each flower was filled with a clear liquid.

"Undoubtedly, you are accustomed to fine crystal," stated Sparks, serving a drink to her first.

"Quite true," confirmed Rose.

"But she's quite open to new experiences," interjected Tag, nodding in appreciation to the Fairy as he accepted the offering.

"From a practical point of view, the flower of the lilac bush is not only the perfect size for serving refreshments, but the drop of nectar produced by the lilac, and its perfume too, actually enhances the flavour of this special beverage," said Sparks.

"What is this?" asked Rose, sniffing the distinct floral bouquet emanating from this refreshment.

"It is called honeydew. It is sweet like honey, but as silky as early morning dew as it goes down one's throat," explained the Fairy, motioning his guests to indulge.

Rose was rather reluctant to partake, even as she watched Cankles and Tag eagerly join their host in a drink.

"You really ought to try this, Princess," encouraged Tag. "It's delicious!"

Raising the flower to her lips, Rose took a cautious sip. As the sweet liquid rolled over her tongue, her eyes opened wide in surprise. "For once in your life, you are correct, Tag! This is positively delectable!"

Having been made to quench her thirst from streams and creeks along the way, Rose gulped down the honeydew. She emptied the liquid from this floral vessel while her male comrades stared in amazement, watching as she used the back of her hand to wipe away the dribble running down her chin.

"Delicious! You must tell me how it is made," urged Rose, slipping the lilac floret back into its stand. "I am confident my mother would love it as much as I do."

"I am sure she would," responded Sparks, with a nod of his head. "However, unless you are a Fairy, honeydew can be difficult to harvest."

"Whatever do you mean?" questioned Rose. "Like harvesting grapes?"

"For lack of a better word, it is *milked* from aphids."

"You mean those sap-sucking insects I find on my rose bushes?" queried the Princess, her brows furrowing in curiosity.

"Yes."

"Who would have thought tiny aphids have udders like a cow?" marvelled Rose. The fingers and thumbs of her hands squeezed as though she was milking a tiny, invisible cow.

"They don't," responded Sparks, topping up her drinking vessel.

"I fail to understand," said Rose, eagerly taking up the lilac floret to indulge in another sip.

"We found out long ago by watching ants tending to aphid herds, if you gently stroke the backside of the aphid, it would secrete a sweet solution," explained Sparks.

"No udder is involved?" asked Rose, seeking confirmation as she stared suspiciously at the clear liquid.

"Not one teat," revealed the Fairy. "Honeydew is secreted from the aphid's *posterior.*"

"You are serious?" Rose's complexion took on a sickly pallor as the colour drained from her face.

"Quite," confirmed Sparks, as he topped up Cankles and Tag's drinking vessel.

"Don't look so appalled," scolded Tag, as he enjoyed another sip. "You said yourself it was delectable. So much so, you guzzled it down with no reservations."

"That was before I found out it comes from an insect, and worse yet, from which part of the aphid this liquid is secreted from," argued Rose.

"Do you eat honey?" asked Sparks.

"Of course I do," answered Rose. "It is the sweetener of choice for most of the desserts I favour."

"Do you know where honey comes from, Princess?" questioned the Fairy.

"I can assure you, Master Firestar, I am no fool. Of course I know," replied the Princess. "Honey is made by bees."

"That is so. Apparently, you have no qualms about consuming bee vomit, and yet, you are repulsed by the notion of drinking a sweet liquid milked from the back-end of aphids?"

"*Bee vomit?*" repeated Rose, her tone incredulous as her eyes narrowed in doubt.

"To be precise, yes! Bees harvest nectar from flowers. They return to their hives where they regurgitate it into cells of wax," explained Sparks. "Hence, it is quite literally bee vomit."

"Makes perfect sense to me," said Cankles, taking a deep draught from his floral drinking vessel. "Everything tastes better with bee vomit on it!"

"Drink the beverage and be gracious about it," urged Tag, scowling in annoyance at the spoiled Princess.

"No need for concern, Master Yairet," said the Fairy.

"Please, just call me Tagius."

"Then Tagius, it is," responded Sparks, giving the mortal a polite nod. "And the Princess need not feel it necessary to partake just to be courteous. It is a matter of personal taste and cultural differences. Where mortals take to consuming the flesh of animals, we Fairies prefer to subsist on fruits, vegetables, nuts and seeds."

"And this tasty liquid that oozes out from the bottom of a sap-sucking insect," added Cankles, raising his vessel in praise of the honeydew before taking another drink.

"That, too!" declared Sparks, toasting the merits of this fine beverage.

"Well, I am not here to drink honeydoo-doos," responded Rose, in a disgruntled huff. "I am here to see Pance."

"As I said before, she will return once she is done for the night, so you must be patient, Princess."

Rose released a dreary sigh, "I wonder what time it is?"

Sparks glanced out the high window of the library to spy the sliver of moon as it continued its steady journey across the sky. "We are approaching the midnight hour."

"Already?" asked Rose.

"Yes, but as I said, Pance will not return until dawn. If it is an especially unproductive night, she will be back early," reminded the Fairy.

"Dawn is a while away," determined Rose, standing up from the sofa. "Do you mind if I stretched my legs a bit? Perhaps visit your Queen's main library to admire her extensive collection of books?"

"It is down the main hall, first door to your left," said Sparks, replacing his drinking vessel back onto its stand. "I will escort you."

"It is kind of you to offer, but I believe I know my right from my left. I am confident I can find it."

"Very well then," said Sparks, with a polite nod of his head. "If you feel the need to rest, please let me know. I will show you to the guest bedchamber."

"I am quite fine for now. Perhaps later."

Rose stood up, and with as much grace as she could muster in her torn and dirty gown, she proudly marched from this room into the hall. As she walked away, she could hear Cankles laughing, snorting loudly as Tag shared in a joke with him and the Fairy. Confident they were preoccupied, Rose headed straight to the main library. Pushing open the double doors, she peered inside. Aside from the books, this room was dark and empty.

"Lights on!" demanded Rose, closing the door behind her.

The library remained dark.

The Princess clapped her hands together as she demanded once again, "Lights on!"

Much to her chagrin, again, this order went ignored. The library remained immersed in darkness.

"Now what did that Fairy do?" Rose grumbled beneath her breath as she recalled Sparks' entrance into the library. "I know!"

With a snap of her fingers the fireflies glowed brightly, filling the library with their golden light.

"Much better!"

Glancing about, Rose made sure she was alone.

"It must be just past midnight now," determined Rose. Pulling on the gold chain hanging about her neck, she lifted the dreamstone out. Pressing her ear to the library door, she listened. Down the hall, she could hear Tag conversing with the Fairy.

"I must hurry," whispered Rose, clutching the magic crystal tightly in her hand.

Closing her eyes, the Princess breathed in deeply. She slowly exhaled as she cleared her mind. As the distant voices faded and her expelled breath carried with it all the woes of this dreadful day, she set to work conjuring up a concise image.

Recalling her last memory of Pancecilia Feldspar, Rose recreated the Fairy's image in her mind's eye. From her scowl of reproach and the translucent wings that would quiver in anger to the intricate design carved into her wand, Rose focused on the Tooth Fairy. However, instead of envisioning Pance in her royal bedchamber, Rose recreated the details of this very library she now stood in.

"I wish for Pancecilia Feldspar to be here *now!*" demanded Rose, squeezing the dreamstone in the palm of her hand as though it would somehow help.

A golden aura swelled, suddenly erupting into a dazzling show of light that penetrated through Rose's closed eyelids.

"What the pearly hell is going on here?" snapped Pance, as she appeared before Rose. The Tooth Fairy dropped the coin she was just about to place under a child's pillow in exchange for the tooth. "Sparks! What is – "

She gasped in surprise, turning to find Princess Rose standing in her library.

"Your Majesty! We saw a flash of light coming from here!" exclaimed Sparks, as he burst into the chamber. "What are you doing back so soon?"

The Tooth Fairy's face reddened with anger as she glared at the female mortal. "It would appear I had been summoned, and obviously, not by you."

"I had travelled a long way to speak with you," stated Rose. "This meeting could not wait any longer."

"Did you do this, Princess?" gasped Tag. "Did you wish for the Tooth Fairy to return, just because you know nothing of patience?"

"I know plenty about patience! Enough to know mine has been worn thin," retorted Rose. "I had waited long enough for this meeting."

"Tut, tut!" responded Cankles, shaking his head in disapproval. "You shouldn't have done that, Princess."

"Don't you *tut* me! Only donkeys tut," grumbled Rose.

"That made no sense," ridiculed Tag.

"Neither does he, so we're even!" sniffed Rose, as she glared at Cankles. "Anyway, I only did what I had to do."

"Cankles Mayron? Is that you?" asked Pance, staring at this mortal man in Rose's company.

"Good evenin', m'lady," greeted Cankles, offering a respectful bow to the Tooth Fairy.

"What brings you here? And with her, at that! Surely ill fortune had frowned upon you to embroil you in matters concerning this Princess."

"Oh, no embroilin' here, m'lady," assured Cankles.

"How about entrapment? Coercion? Or perhaps, extortion on her part played a hand in your involvement?" probed Pance, bewildered by Cankles' presence.

"Don't rightly know what those fancy words mean, but it wasn't ill fortune at work here. Fate brought us together. I rescued the Princess when she and her friend needed rescuin'!"

"Well, sometimes, fate can be a cruel prankster," sympathized Pance, with a disheartened sigh as she glanced over at Cankles and the Princess.

"My sincerest apologies, Your Majesty," offered Tag, bowing with utmost respect to the Tooth Fairy. "I tried to warn Princess Rose against summoning you before your time. I had asked her to be patient, to wait for you. Unfortunately, my words went ignored, yet again."

"And who you might you be, young man?" questioned Pance.

"My name is Tagius Yairet, and yes, ill fortune frowned upon me long ago when I first met the Princess."

"Oh, hush!" snapped Rose. "Why is everyone getting so upset? So I disrupted the Tooth Fairy's schedule a wee bit? This is more important than those stupid, little chompers she insists on collecting."

A stunned silence fell upon this room as all eyes turned on the Princess as her abrasive words insulted the Fairy.

"Holy halitosis!" gasped Pance. Her wings trembled in agitation as her wand swelled with light. "Did I hear you correctly, Princess Rose?"

Pulling her jester in front as a human shield in case Pance vented her wrath, Rose peered over Tag's shoulder to address the Fairy. "I mean to say, there is no point in getting upset now. Those teeth can wait. You are here now, so you should tend to my needs first."

Tag jumped away, pushing Rose in front of him. "Here you go! She asked for it! Do your worst! Maybe turn her into a toad for a day or two. That will teach her a lesson in abusing her wishes."

"Actually, a frog would be better," interjected Cankles. "Frogs are way cuter and less warty."

"Enough talk about turning me into an amphibian!" snapped Rose. "Besides, Pance already knows where her magic is concerned, I am untouchable! My father made sure of that!"

Pance drew a deep breath, slowly exhaling to release this tide of anger swelling in her heart.

"You are quite right, Princess," acknowledged Pance. "Unlike you, I respect your father enough *not* to go against his wishes."

"I do so respect my father!"

"If you truly did, you would not be in the trouble you are in now," responded Pance, her words unsympathetic as she stared at the Princess.

"I respect *and* love him, so there!"

"You only love your parents when it suits you," rebuked Pance. "It is not given freely and it is withheld if you do not get what you want."

"*Wow!* You really do know the Princess," marvelled Tag, nodding in agreement with the Fairy.

"Through her actions and her indifference, Princess Rose has had a profound effect on all she encounters, yourself included, young master," stated Pance. "And it is obvious to me, Princess Rose, you have yet to find your heart."

"That's what brings us here in the first place," revealed Cankles. "Master Yairet an' I are tryin' to help the Princess."

"I am afraid she may be beyond help, nor will she find it here, my friend," responded Pance.

"Well, if I cannot find it, I will use the dreamstone to wish for it," decided Rose, seeking a fast and easy way to achieve her goal.

"Too bad for you, but just as I cannot undo a Wizard's magic with a simple incantation, neither can you use the Dream Merchant's powers to undo my magic," stated Pance, confirming Rose's greatest fear.

"This is not fair! You and that old curmudgeon are in cahoots," snapped Rose. "I have been overwhelmed and undermined!"

"Need I remind you that you activated this curse?" questioned Pance. "I had warned you that unless you made a concerted effort to change, you would become what you hate the most."

"Hence the prunie peasant," teased Tag, biting his lower lips to prevent from laughing.

"You hate prunes?" asked Cankles, scratching his head in bewilderment.

It was obvious to all in his presence that it had not yet registered in Cankles' simple mind that she also detested peasants.

"They are disgusting to look at and just as disgusting to eat," explained Rose.

"But prunes are our friends," insisted Cankles. "They're yummy an' they help keep you regular."

"Forget the prunes!" snapped Rose. "Where can I find my heart? You said once I find it, the curse will be lifted."

"Your heart?" repeated Pance.

"Yes, you know the one! The silver, heart-shaped locket you so eagerly took from me to seal this miserable deal," reminded Rose.

"Oh, *that* heart! The one you so willingly traded away. If you are so intent on reclaiming that trinket, you should know, it is far to the east."

"How far?" asked Tag.

"In the Land of Big," responded Pance.

"Where?" asked Rose.

"It's near to the Land of Small," answered Cankles. "I know where it is."

"You do?" queried Rose.

"Yep! Been there before," confirmed Cankles, with a nod of his head. "It's far, far, *farrr* away. It'll be quite the journey an' a perilous one at that."

"It will?" responded Rose.

"I had warned you before, to reclaim the locket would be no easy task," reminded the Tooth Fairy.

"Fine! Just tell me where it is in the Land of Big," demanded Rose.

"As I said, it will not be a task for the faint of heart. If you are so determined to reclaim it, then all you must do is follow your heart."

"Why must you always speak in riddles?" grumbled the Princess. "You are not making this easy for me, are you?"

"And deliberately so. If is it so important to you, you will find a way to reclaim your locket."

"So you will make me struggle?" groaned Rose. "You will do nothing to help me."

"I will help you by offering you the gift of struggle," said Pance, giving Rose a prudent nod of her head.

"What kind of stupid gift is that?" snapped Rose. "I have no need of this!"

"I have never met a more needy mortal. Struggle in the form of hardship will build character and I have never met one more in need of character building than you!"

"*Needy?* I want for naught! In fact, I have everything I could ever possibly want," retorted Rose.

"You say that now, and yet, you are the bearer of the dreamstone," reminded the Tooth Fairy.

"There are some things that cannot be bought," responded Rose. "But you would not understand."

"It is apparent to me that you are ungrateful for this gift I am offering to you," commented Pance.

"I am royalty! I should not be made to struggle! If anything, I have already been tricked into accepting this deal," argued Rose.

Sparks listened in silence to this hostile exchange, shaking his head in dismay as the outspoken Princess voiced her candid opinion.

"If your intention is to have the Tooth Fairy compound your curse, just keep this up," groaned Tag, his hand slapping his forehead in utter frustration.

"Be assured, young Master Yairet, this curse is as only as difficult as Princess Rose perceives it to be," responded Pance, giving Tag a knowing smile.

"Well, I can honestly say, for reasons of my own, I'm rather unsympathetic to her plight," admitted Tag. "I believe you are right about this *gift of struggle*. If the Princess intends to take on this quest, it may as well help to build her moral fibre if nothing else, for she is definitely wanting in character."

"Nothing wrong with a little hard work an' sweat," agreed Cankles, nodding in approval.

"I am a Princess! I am not meant to sweat! What is wrong with you two?" gasped Rose, her eyes like daggers as she glared in frustration at Tag and Cankles. "You are supposed to be helping me, not making this all the more difficult!"

Just as she was about to declare before all, *I hate you both!* Rose stayed her tongue. The threat of becoming what she hates, being transformed into an idiot-of-a-court-jester weighed heavy on her mind.

"It is apparent to me that you do not even understand the true value of friendship, Princess," noted Pance, shaking her head in disappointment. "If you did, you would consider yourself extremely lucky to have the likes of these two fellows by your side as you embark on this quest."

"Make no mistake, they are *not* my friends," explained Rose. Pointing first at Cankles, and then at Tag as she denounced them. "He is too bizarre for my liking, while Tag is just plain insolent and stubborn. Besides, as far as class goes, we are worlds apart, especially *him*. Cankles is merely helping us because he has nothing better to do with his time."

"Princess Rose, let it be said that only a true friend would put himself in such a position to help another," reminded Pance.

"Well, if he fancies me a friend, then who can blame him?"

Pance released a sigh of resignation, "My words fall on deaf ears! Do not waste any more of my time, or yours, for what you seek is not here. And until you find it, do not call upon me again!"

"At least tell me where you hid my locket," demanded Rose.

"If you are so intent on reclaiming it, then your determination alone will help you find it. For now, I have had enough of you! I have work to do before the night is done."

"I beg of you, remove this curse from me," pleaded Rose.

"Begging does not constitute a change of heart. It merely voices your desire to change your situation so you are not made to suffer the consequences of your actions."

In a dazzling flash of golden light, Pancecilia Feldspar vanished.

"Well... that went as planned," said Tag, in a mocking tone as he glared at Rose.

"Maybe if you had only said *please*," offered Cankles. "Maybe she would've changed her mind."

Rose's only response was to release a disheartened sigh.

"If anything, at least we kinda know where the silver locket is," stated Cankles, trying to sound optimistic for the Princess.

"I suppose," said Rose.

"In light of the Princess' actions, I fear another careless act will be forthcoming. With this in mind, I suggest you leave before Pance returns," recommended Sparks. "You do not want to raise her ire more than you already have."

"What does that mean: *to raise her ire?*" questioned Cankles.

"To make her angry," replied Tag.

"I know that," said Cankles. "I mean, why do they not say *poke* or *prod* her ire, instead? It sounds more deliberate than to *raise* it."

"Good point," responded Tag. "But for now, I think we should take Sparks' advice and leave immediately. There is no point in overstaying our welcome."

"Quite right, Master Yairet," agreed the Fairy. "Pance can be very reasonable, however, if she returns to find the Princess still here, I am afraid she will be as mad as a witch on the rag, if you get my meaning?"

"I can't say I'd blame her," responded Tag. He nodded in understanding as he motioned for Rose to move.

"With the approach of dawn, when the first ray of sunlight touches the lands, the spell will be broken. You shall be restored to your original size," warned the Fairy. "You best leave now."

"Oh, quite right, my friend," agreed Cankles. "Don't want to grow big, gettin' your noggin stuck in this hollow."

"Why? Has that happened to you before?" questioned Rose, staring at Cankles.

His face reddened with embarrassment as he responded, "Won't admit it! Won't deny it! Jus' believe me when I say you don't want to get your head stuck in this tree."

"We shall leave now," decided Tag, as he turned to the Fairy. "Thank you for your kind hospitality, Sparks Firestar. It was a pleasure meeting you."

"You are most welcome, Master Yairet. I pray you and your comrades have a safe journey as you embark on this quest. If luck will have it, perhaps, our paths shall cross again one day."

"If we don't go an' get killed along the way, we should be safe," responded Cankles, clasping Sparks' wrist in fond farewell. "If so, maybe I'll be seein' you again, my friend!"

"That would be wonderful," said the Fairy, as he leaned into Cankles' ear to whisper. "Just do not come back with the Princess, is that understood?"

Cankles really didn't, but he shook his head in agreement anyway. The trio watched as the Fairy disappeared through the arch of the castle keep.

Staring up to the predawn sky, the stars were already beginning to lose their brilliance with the impending sun.

"We best be on our way," suggested Tag, standing at the mouth of the hollow to stare down to the ground below.

"If you think I am going to ride down on that disgusting rodent, think again," grunted Rose, shuddering at the thought of the harrowing ride on the dormouse.

"By all means, Princess, you are welcome to climb down instead," offered Tag, waving her on.

Rose glanced down. From this dizzying height, the ground seemed so much farther away.

"Are you mad?" snapped the Princess.

"Well, you certainly cannot stay in this hollow until the magic wears off to restore you to your normal height," reminded Tag.

"Oh, you won't be wantin' that!" exclaimed Cankles, massaging his temples as though erasing a phantom pain.

"There must be an easier way to get back down to earth." Rose thought aloud as her palm pressed against the dreamstone.

"You foolishly wasted one wish already," cautioned Tag, giving her a stern look of reproach. "I will be bloody mad if you use another one just to get down this tree."

"Fine!" snapped Rose. She dropped the dreamstone down the front of her dress. "Then what would you recommend I do?"

Tag and Rose turned with a start as Cankles whooped before dashing between them. With an exuberant *woo-hoo*, he launched himself into the air. A large oak leaf was clutched firmly in his hands as he threw his body from the mouth of the tree hollow.

"He is crazy! Crazy I tell you!" gasped Rose, watching in dismay as this village idiot lived up to his title.

Instead of crashing to the ground, a gentle breeze caught the leaf just so, allowing Cankles to float to earth.

"What a novel idea, Cankles!" praised Tag, as he searched about for a leaf of his own. "Brilliant! Absolutely brilliant!"

"If you are going to copy him, then you are just as crazy as he is!" denounced Rose, appalled Tag would even consider taking this leap.

"Jump or climb down. It's your choice," grunted Tag, plucking up a perfect leaf for this task. Taking an end in each hand, he was poised to jump. "See you down there!"

"You do this and it will be suicide! Dare you place your life in a flimsy oak leaf and an act of spontaneity because the idiot of Cadboll makes it look fun?"

"Stop calling him that!" snapped Tag, edging closer to the mouth of the hollow to see Cankles skillfully tilting the leaf like a kite to guide it down. "And I consider this a leap of faith. I firmly believe I can land safely."

"So you say," scolded Rose. "Just do not expect me to waste a wish to mend your broken body when this leap of faith ends badly."

Without so much as a *'farewell'* or a *'so long'*, Tag jumped. Like a sail on a tall ship, the leaf seemed to billow, catching the breeze. His downward free-fall came to an abrupt halt as he gently drifted to the ground.

"See! Nothing to it!" called Tag, landing lightly near the base of this oak tree.

"You can do it, Princess!" hollered Cankles. "But you better do it before Sparks' magic wears off an' you get stuck in there."

Rose stared down at her comrades, and then, she glanced up to the waning night sky. The light of the impending sun was rapidly leaching away the darkness.

"Either climb or jump!" shouted Tag. "Whatever you do, just do so quickly!"

Fearing the consequences of her indecision, Rose grabbed the closest leaf, yanking it free from the branch.

"If this doesn't work, you better promise to catch me!" ordered the Princess, as she inched closer to the edge.

"Don't worry about that!" hollered Tag. "We'll break your fall if we have to. Just do it!"

Closing her eyes and holding her breath, Rose steeled her nerves. She jumped, screaming hysterically as she fell. The sudden rush of air rising around her became a gentle breeze as her leaf served as a parachute, allowing the Princess to float down.

Screwing up her courage, Rose pried one eye open. To her relief, the earth was not rushing to meet her.

"This is not so bad," decided Rose, releasing a sigh of relief.

"Told you so," said Tag. "Just hold the leaf steady."

"What did you say?" called Rose. She glanced down, at the same time, tilting the leaf forward.

The results were immediate. Rose descended rapidly.

"Keep that bloody leaf straight!" shouted Tag, holding his own leaf up to demonstrate.

Rose struggled to hold the foliage aloft just so, allowing the air to fill the leaf and slow her fall.

Just as quickly, she began to float down once more.

"That was close!" gasped Rose, staring up at her parachute. With growing confidence, she attempted to control her landing. Where Cankles and Tag chose to float straight down, Rose tilted the leaf's edge to and fro, causing her to pirouette in graceful circles.

"Stop showing off! Get down here," ordered Tag.

"You are just jealous!" shouted Rose. Feeling exhilarated by this ride, she twirled through the air.

"Not if you crash!" hollered Tag. "Now hurry up."

Being lighter than her comrades, Rose had greater maneuverability. She was relishing this sense of freedom when a gust of wind swirled around her, causing the skirt of her gown to balloon out.

Had she been her full size, this gust would have amounted to nothing more than a gentle breeze, but being so small, it took on the power of a gale force wind. Rose screamed in fright as a tiny hole in the leaf became a gaping tear, growing larger with the growing pressure of air trapped against its surface. Her graceful circles now became erratic, uncontrolled spinning as the wind pushed her away from those waiting below.

Watching her disappear over the tall grasses, Tag hollered at her, "Let go, Princess! Just let go!"

He and Cankles gave chase, pushing through the towering forest of grass as they followed Rose's terrified screams.

"Bloody hell!" cursed Tag. "Why did she not listen to me?"

"Maybe she didn't hear you," responded Cankles, following hot on his heels.

"Oh, she heard me, alright!" snapped Tag, listening to her frightened cries becoming more distant as she drifted away. "Follow me! Quickly!"

Rose's eyes squeezed shut as her aerial travels sent her crashing through the stalks of grass.

"Not good! Not good!" sputtered Rose, wincing in pain as the blades of grass thrashed her as she lost elevation.

She watched, her eyes wide-open in terror as the hole in the leaf snagged onto a piece of grass, tearing it in half. Her eyes snapped shut again as she plunged straight down, screaming all the way. Her heart was pounding, ready to burst from her chest as she braced for a deadly fall! Expecting a bone-breaking, body-jarring collision with the ground, she gasped in surprise as her fall was broken by a soft landing that went *splat* like she had fallen on squishy, gelatinous dough.

Her screams of terror became shrieks of disgust as the stalked eyes of the largest, ugliest slug she had ever seen twisted about to stare unblinkingly at her as she straddled its back.

Just as surprised and frightened by her presence, the slug responded accordingly when threatened by a predator. Racing away only as a belly-crawler could, it oozed a copious quantity of slimy mucous from its yellowish-brown, mottled skin. Strings of sticky mucous clung to Rose's hands and gummed up her gown as she struggled to be free of this elongated, undulating mass of moist, slime-covered muscle. The more she squirmed about, the more mucous the slug extruded as it slid away, heading to a rotten log at top speed to escape this monster clinging to its back.

"This way!" shouted Tag, fighting through the grasses as Rose's screams reach an all-new pitch.

"At least we know she's still alive," said Cankles, rushing along behind him.

"Alive, but she's in some kind of danger."

Tag came to a skidding stop. A barrier of harvester ants marched in single file on an unerring course to their colony, refusing to budge from his path. Above their heads, each ant carried a neatly cut piece of leaf or colourful flower petal in their pincer-like jaws, holding it on high like a great flag.

"Move! Shoo!" hollered Tag, frantically waving at these dog-sized insects to get out of his way.

Following a pheromone trail set out by the scout ant, this army was unswerving, marching along this chemical-scented trail that prevented them from going astray. They were undeterred by Tag's wild gesturing and shouts, ignoring both mortals as they continued on their relentless, determined quest for foliage.

As Tag tried to push his way through this wall of ants, these powerful insects merely used one of their six legs to shove him away.

"My! They're awfully strong!" noted Cankles, pulling Tag back onto his feet.

"Just look at the size of the leaves they're carrying! It's bigger than they are!" stated Tag, amazed by the strength of these ants.

Attempting to push through this line, Tag made a run. Again, he was met with resistance as an ant easily shoved him aside as it marched on.

"We'll never catch up to the Princess now!" cried Tag, picking himself up from the ground.

"This way!" hollered Cankles, as he climbed a stalk of grass.

"But she's not up there!" called Tag.

"I know!"

The higher Cankles climbed, the more the grass bent.

Tag realized what his friend was attempting to do. He proceeded to follow, climbing a stalk of grass. As they neared the slender, seeded crown, their weight caused the grass to bend, lowering them to the ground on the other side of this imposing wall of ants.

The stalks of grass sprang back up as Cankles and Tag hopped off.

"Follow me!" shouted Tag, pushing through the forest of grass in the direction of Rose's screams.

"Look! Up there!" Cankles pointed to the remnants of the leaf Rose had used to parachute down. "There's her leaf, but where's the Princess?"

Tag glances about, searching for signs of Rose. All he found was a long mucous trail left by a giant slug or snail.

"There's nothing here but this slime," noted Cankles.

"You don't suppose she landed on a slug, do you?" wondered Tag.

"Could've… It'd explain all that screamin' when you consider jus' how squeamish she is," decided Cankles, struggling to yank his foot free from the sticky residue.

"Let's follow this trail," ordered Tag. "Just don't step in it."

"Right-o!" said Cankles, as he nodded in understanding. "If she's glued to a slug, she couldn't have gone far. After all, how fast can a slug crawl?"

"Considering how small we are, probably pretty darned fast," determined Tag, racing after the gastropod in question. "I'd never thought I'd live to say this, but *RUN! After that slug!*"

"Whoa sluggie! Stop!" squealed Rose, as her frantic struggle caused the slug to glide along all the faster. It was heading to the safety of a hole in the rotten log that was only as big as the slug's body. If it were able to squeeze into this opening, it would be rid of this unwanted pest on its back for good.

Realizing help would not be forth coming, at least not in time to prevent her body from being crushed against the log, Rose did the only thing she could do.

"She's up ahead!" shouted Cankles. "I can hear her!"

"Faster!" ordered Tag, unsheathing his sword as he charged ahead.

"Who'd a thunk a slug could move so fast!" gasped Cankles, struggling to keep up with his younger comrade.

"She's not that far ahead! I'm sure of it."

Cankles' weary, faltering steps forced him to stop and catch his breath. "Run ahead, Master Yairet, I'll catch up."

Just as Tag turned to coax his friend on, he gasped in horror.

Seized by his left ankle, Cankles screamed in fright. Hoisted upside-down into the air, he dangled helplessly from the powerful front legs of a monstrous praying mantis. He was about to become its next meal.

"Run! Save yourself!" hollered Cankles, kicking with his one free foot at the mantis' pincer-like mandibles each time it tried to take a bite of him.

Instead of escaping, Tag rushed at the monster. His sword clanged loudly as it barely made a dent on the insect's skeletal armour as he struck at its legs.

"Run!" shouted Cankles. "That sword won't work!"

Rather than give up his friend to this insatiable monster, Tag used the barbs on the mantis' legs to hoist himself up onto its back. Holding on with one hand, he struggled to pull himself up the insect's carapace until he straddled its thorax.

With an angry cry, the sword swung about in Tag's hand. The blade easily sliced through the vulnerable connective tissue joining the head to the thorax. As the mantis' head tumbled to the ground, its front legs released its hold on Cankles. He yelped in surprise as he landed next to the monster's head, its compound eyes staring through him as its jaws snapped in defiance even now.

To Tag's surprise, this beast did not simply die as he thought it would. Even decapitated, this body continued to act independently. It blindly scrambled about, fighting to dump Tag from its back.

As the mantis spun about, Tag slid down its slender back, landing on the ground next to Cankles. He pulled his friend onto his feet, urging Cankles to run than risk being trampled by the huge insect.

"This way!" shouted Tag, following the drying sheen of slime left by the slug.

As they rounded a bend in the trail, to their utter surprise, there stood Rose. She was still quaking from her ordeal.

"What happened to you?" asked Tag, watching as salt poured out from her gown and shook free from her tangled tresses.

"That slug happened to me, that's what!" Rose snapped as her thumb angrily jabbed over her shoulder to point at the shrivelled remains of a giant gastropod buried beneath a mountain of salt.

"Oh my!" gasped Cankles, grimacing in disgust at the sight of the slug that had died a briny death.

Tag shook his head in disapproval.

"So I used a wish! You did not come to my rescue, so you gave me no choice," grunted Rose, washing her hands in drops of dew to be rid of the slime before drying them on a blade of grass. "It was terrible ordeal! It was like being stuck to a giant, nose-blown kerchief!"

"*I* gave you no choice?" grumbled Tag, as he sheathed his sword. "Don't blame me because you wasted another wish!"

"If you had caught up and used your stupid sword to slay that beast, I would not have been forced to use a wish to rescue myself!"

"If you had only listened to me when I was yelling at you to let go of the leaf!' snapped Tag.

"Now, now! No need to get angry, my friends," urged Cankles, motioning for calm to prevail. "The important thing is, we're all alive!"

The trio froze as a dark shadow glided over them. An owl was on the hunt.

"At this moment, our time is better spent finding shelter than arguing," decided Tag, speaking in a whisper as he led them to the cover of a large toadstool. "There are dangers still lurking near to us until this magic wears off."

"And just what makes you believe we will be safe hiding under the caps of these toadstools?" questioned Rose. "If a bear or wild boar comes along, we shall be eaten up along with these mushrooms."

"I hardly think so," replied Tag, staring up at the bright red caps and distinct white spots that served as a warning to all. "These toadstools are highly poisonous."

Less Than Kind

"Are you still mad at me, Tag?" asked Rose, her lower lip protruding in a pathetic pout.

"I should be, but in retrospect, it was rather clever of you to wish for salt, enough of it to kill the slug."

"Are you serious?" Her words were doubtful as she glanced over at her jester.

"Well, as sharp as my sword is, I hardly think it would have killed the beast. Slow it down a bit, but probably not much more than that."

"I'm thinkin' if you had, you probably wouldn't be able to free your sword from that slimy body," determined Cankles, shuddering in repulsion as his mind replayed the image of the salt encrusted, mucous slathered carnage Rose had left for them to find.

"That is probably true! And as I said before, I had no choice," reiterated Rose. "That slug was heading straight for a rotten log. I was sure to become a smear on its back if it had squeezed into the hole it was heading for."

"The important thing is, you're alive and there's still one more wish we can call upon before day's end, if we need it," resolved Tag.

"So all is well?" questioned Rose.

"All is well, considering. We should move now while we have the light of day to travel by."

"Which way do we go?" queried the Princess.

"We journey that way," announced Tag, squinting as he gazed to the golden orb peeking over the distant horizon, "to the east."

"So, we follow the sun?" asked Rose, raising her hand to shield her eyes from its dazzling glare.

"If we do, doesn't that mean we'll be heading west then?" questioned Cankles, thinking on how the sun migrated across the sky to eventually set behind the grand pinnacles of the Cascade Mountains bordering Fleetwood on the western horizon.

"We head in the general direction of the sun where it rises and we move accordingly," explained Tag. He wiped his sword clean on a handful of dew-moistened leaves before sheathing it back in its protective scabbard.

"What was that mess on the blade?" queried Rose, staring at the coagulating yellowish-green ooze smeared on the leaves Tag tossed aside.

"Praying mantis blood," replied Tag, "if you can call it that."

"You used that sword to squash a bug?" grunted the Princess, her voice taking on a sarcastic tone. "That is a rather extreme! Did the little mantis scare you?"

"I was bloody scared, but not Master Yairet!" declared Cankles. "That beast almost killed me! If it wasn't for him coming to my rescue, I'd be as good as dead! That's the reason why we couldn't get to you as fast as we wanted to."

"What are you talking about?" asked Rose, stepping away from Cankles' animated gestures.

"You thought that slug was big. This praying mantis was *huge!*" exclaimed Cankles. "An' worse yet, it was one hungry beast. It seized me by my ankle an' hoisted me on high! Tried to eat me, but Master Yairet wouldn't have it. Lopped the beast's head clean off, he did!"

"You did?" asked Rose, staring in surprise at Tag.

He smiled with satisfaction as he heard the distinct click of the scabbard's locket accepting the blade to perfectly couple the sword in its protective housing.

"I suppose I did," responded Tag, his shoulders rolling in a modest shrug. It suddenly dawned on him that he had committed his first truly heroic deed with a real sword: a deed worthy of a great knight. He stood a little taller and prouder before his company.

"Oh, don't be so modest, Master Yairet. It was a monster! You may've well had slain a great dragon."

"It was *that* big?" probed Rose.

"When you consider how small we were shrunk down to, yes!" insisted Cankles, stretching his arms far out to his sides to demonstrate the immense size of the insect's head. "Its noggin alone was yeh big! An' those snappin' jaws were powerful strong, waitin' to make an easy meal of me. If it wasn't for our friend here, that mantis would've cut me in half!"

"And this is no exaggeration? Tag actually killed this beast with his own hands?"

"He was braver than brave, Princess! There was no hesitation the way he charged straight for the monster. He boldly climbed onto the mantis' back," recounted Cankles, as he drew his index finger across his throat. "An' then he cut its head off!"

"I am truly amazed!" marvelled Rose, nodding in approval to her jester.

"That I killed the mantis?"

"That," answered the Princess, "and I am surprised you even had it in you to do the deed."

"I suppose my father's blood flows strong through my veins," decided Tag, smiling inwardly as he thought on how proud his father would have been had he seen him in action.

"Well, whether it was a selfless act of courage or a foolish act fuelled by thoughtless panic, I am duly impressed," praised Rose. "I suppose all the scarecrows that had met their demise by your broomstick had enabled you to improve your skills with that sword."

"No doubt," responded Tag.

"You might come in handy after all," decided Rose.

For a moment, Tag silently mulled over her comment.

"Somewhere in those words, I do believe there was a compliment," determined the young man. "Thank you. Now, we should really be on our way."

"Well, I do not know about you, but I have not slept in over twenty-four hours now," groaned Rose, through a great yawn. "I am utterly exhausted. Can we not rest for a little while?"

"I take it, if I said no, you will put your foot down and demand we rest anyway?" assumed Tag.

"I've gotta admit, Master Yairet, I'm pretty tired myself," confided Cankles, his hand coming up to his mouth to stifle a weary yawn. "Now that we're all back to our normal size, if we sleep, it's not like a monster insect is gonna try to eat us."

"I suppose we can rest for a couple of hours," decided Tag. "But we should be on our way well before mid-morning."

"How about we rest until noon?" bargained Rose, hoping to sneak in a few extra hours of beauty sleep.

"The amount of sleep is non-negotiable," replied Tag. "Take advantage of it now or we move on."

"Fine!" snapped Rose. She plopped down onto the moss-covered ground in defeat.

"Don't worry, Princess, it'll be adequate time," promised Cankles. "You'll feel nice an' refreshed when you wake."

"So you say," grumbled Rose, heaving a disgruntled sigh. "Just keep in mind, you peasant types can function with little sleep. You are used to waking early and going to bed only after you've toiled all day long. However, people like me are a different breed. We are taxed emotionally and mentally dealing with your kind, so it stands to reason we would require far more sleep."

"Well, now that you are one of *us,* it is high time you get used to functioning as a commoner," responded Tag. Unsympathetic to her plight, he leaned his back against a tree and closed his eyes. "Take this time to get some sleep, rather than waste it whining."

"I would, but you keep talking!" snorted Rose.

Drawing her knees up to her chest, her arms wrapped around her legs. With a weary sigh and a great yawn, she rested her forehead on her bended knees. Rose was too tired to complain about her stained, torn gown stripped of all its finery and now covered in dried slug mucous or about the cold and hard ground. She just wanted to sleep.

Well before Tag and Cankles could settle into a fitful slumber, Rose was immersed in a deep sleep where she languished in a strange dream.

It started off well enough as she savoured the tangy, sweet chunks of apple bursting forth from the flaky piecrust as she indulged in her first, tempting bite of the baker's pie she had longed for since her ill-fated attempt at pastry pilfering. With this single bite, the tender fruit filled every corner of her watering mouth. The intoxicating aroma of ripe apples mingling with spicy, freshly ground nutmeg and cinnamon filled her nostrils, making her drunk with this tantalizing combination.

Before she finished swallowing her first bite, she wedged another huge piece into her mouth. It was so much, she could barely breathe as she stuffed her face. This was the best pie she had ever eaten and she was determined to devour every last bite of this ill-gotten pastry. Even as her belly swelled with the delicious pie, she could not sate her voracious appetite as her stomach growled like never before, demanding to be fed. Like a ravenous animal, she hungrily crammed more and more of this pie into her mouth.

She froze at mid-bite as the baker, his rotund body squatting low to the ground, appeared before her. He peeked under his table to spy upon this thief.

Rose, scrambling with pie in hand to escape the angry baker, pushed through the crowd as Tag followed behind her, shouting, *"I told you so!"*

As though reliving a nightmarish moment in her recent past, just as she fled, rounding the corner of a building to escape the baker, Rose was confronted by the captain of her father's army. This time, there were four times as many knights and soldiers in his company and each one was just as determined as before to capture her. They gave chase, shouting at the villagers to help them detain her as Rose raced away with pie in hand.

With her heart pounding in her chest and hammering in her ears, she ran with all her might. She swore she could hear Tag's heavy, distorted voice as he yelled, *"Give him the pie, Rose! Give him the pie!"*

It was as though she knew what was going to happen next. Even as she waged an internal war, her arms acted independently of her will. She gasped in horror as the remnants of the pie flew from her hand, striking the captain square in his face. Somehow, the apple pie had transformed into a huge monster of a pastry the size of a wheel of cheese weighing one stone, if not more. It slammed into the captain's startled face, bowling him over and all those caught in the wake of this explosive collision between man and pastry.

"Now look what you did!" Tag's angry words echoed in her ears as she dashed across a field of freshly mowed alfalfa. Rose's legs ached with every step as she sprinted on with Tag following close behind. Just as they darted behind a haystack to evade the angry mob, her three attendants abruptly appeared to confront Rose. Mildred, Alice and the young one whose name she could never remember stood before her, looking thoroughly agitated.

"Evelyn, her name is Evelyn!" snapped Tag, rolling his eyes in frustration.

"What are you three doing here?" asked Rose. "Shouldn't you be scrubbing floors or something?"

"You tell us," responded Mildred, in a disgruntled huff. "Obviously, we are here for a reason."

"If you are going to ask for an increase to your monthly stipend, now is not a good time."

"The only thing we would ever ask of you is to be treated with little respect, though in your eyes, we are unworthy commoners," grunted Alice, shaking her head in disapproval.

"You do not even have the courtesy to address me by my name," added Evelyn, boldly speaking up for once in her young life.

"That's all we want," chanted dozens of other voices, "just a little respect!"

"You want what?" gasped Rose.

"You heard us!" snapped Mildred, waving a stern finger in the Princess' face as Alice and Evelyn joined her to make their demand clear, spelling out the word, *"R-E-S-P-E-C-T!"*

Rose tried to run as every member of the domestic staff, from the royal dressmaker to the palace groundskeeper, joined her attendants. They surrounded the Princess, but before they could hurl another angry word or do something truly bizarre like break out in song, a knight in silver armour mounted on a magnificent white steed burst forth from the haystack. He reached down, his powerful arm scooping the Princess up onto his stallion. With a thundering of hooves, they charged off, leaving the angry mob behind in a cloud of dust.

"Fear not, beautiful Princess, for you are safe with me," vowed the knight, steering his stallion through rolling pastures.

"Thank you for coming to my rescue, good sir!" said Rose, wrapping her arms around this brave knight.

"All in a day's work for a knight," he quipped as he hopped off his mount. He extended his hands to help Rose down. "Allow me."

Gently lowering her to the ground, he motioned her to follow, "Come with me. You will be safe inside."

The small, ram-shackled hut was strangely familiar to Rose. The knight used his shoulder to push the rickety door open, inviting the Princess in. Just as she stepped into the room, an ugly hound jumped up to greet her. The mutt drooled, slobbering on her bejeweled gown as dirty paws ravaged her dress. In the corner of the cluttered room, Rose spied a ginger-coloured cat. Hunched over as it made a horrific retching sound, the feline was too busy coughing up a hairball to even look at her or take notice of the hyper dog leaping about.

"Get away from me, you disgusting beast!" hollered Rose, as she shoved the dog away.

The mutt snorted in disappointment. Shaking its body, the loose skin rolled and flapped over its lanky frame as though trying to shake off this rejection. With loose fur a-flying and jowls a-flapping, it splattered her gown with more drool before bounding out the door.

"Forgive me, Princess Rose-alyn. I shall teach that hound some manners if it pleases you," offered the knight.

"Please do! But first, a name," said Rose, her eyes peering through the narrow slit of the helmet's visor.

"Surprise, Princess!" said the knight, as he raised the visor to reveal his face. "Cankles Mayron at your service!"

Rose's eyes were wide-open in disbelief. The daring knight who had come to her rescue was none other than the Village Idiot of Cadboll.

"This cannot be!" gasped Rose, backing away from her rescuer. "I cannot believe it's you!"

"Oh, but it is. It's pretty grand what a full stand of armour can do for a man!" exclaimed Cankles. His knuckles rapped on the cuirass, thumping the shell of steel protecting his torso, front and back.

"This is not right! You are a fool! An idiot – not a knight!"

"I've been called worse, but still, it was less than kind comin' from you, Princess. Of course I'm a knight!"

"Only in *your* dreams, not in mine!" retorted Rose. She backed away to the door to escape this bizarre situation that was only becoming stranger by the minute.

"If you go out there, jus' watch out for the Fairy Ring," warned Cankles, removing the gauntlet that protected each hand.

Rose raced out the door only to stumble into a dark forest. She cried out as she tripped, falling to her knees.

As her eyes snapped open, she immediately recognized the shattered toadstools scattered before her. No sooner than she stood up, a swirling mass of golden light swarmed her like angry bees forced from their hive.

"Shoo! Go away!" hollered Rose, her hands clamping over her ears as the drone of hundreds of wings filled her ears. She could feel a multitude of tiny hands yanking at her hair and tugging on her gown. "Be gone!"

She lashed out, her eyes snapping open. In a confused daze, Rose woke to find herself staring at Cankles and Tag.

"Oh, no!" groaned Tag. "This is not good!"

"Wh- what?" stammered Rose, relieved to see Tag and to notice that Cankles was not kneeling before her, donning a knight's armour.

"Either you're travellin' with a wardrobe an' bakery we didn't know about, or you used your last wish of the day," answered Cankles, lifting a huge apple pie from her lap. It was the largest pie they had ever seen. Its golden crust baked to flaky perfection bulged with an abundance of ripe fruit. Sticky, sweet apple juice, its sugar caramelized to a golden brown as it vented from the slits in the crust, made this pastry all the more tantalizing.

"What is this?" gasped Rose, struggling to sit up.

"It's a pie, of course!" snorted Tag.

"No! I mean this!" Rose jumped up, her hands holding up the apron and simple frock she now wore.

"Now, even I know it's a dress an' apron," replied Cankles. He salivated over this delectable dessert he cradled in his arms like a bulging, disc-shaped baby.

"I know that! I mean why am I wearing this rag? This is something befitting a peasant girl, not me! Only the finest silk, velvet and crinoline touches this body!"

"So you did not wish for this?" questioned Tag.

"Are you mad? Of course not! Not in a million years would I wish to look like a peasant, let alone become one. As for that pie! After all the trouble it caused me yesterday, I swore to never eat another pie for as long I live."

"I suppose that makes sense," determined Tag.

"It makes perfect sense!" snapped Rose. "Mind you, I know as I fell asleep, I was upset my gown was utterly ruined after landing on the slug, but make no mistake, if I had wished for a new dress, it would not have been this peasant garb."

"Did you not say if you dreamed while you slept, the dreams you are most deserving of are the ones that will come true?" asked Tag.

"So I did…" responded Rose. "What of it?"

"Do you not see? You got *exactly* what you were deserving of!" declared Tag, an amused grin spreading across his face.

"You are as bad as the Tooth Fairy! Now you are the one speaking in riddles," denounced Rose.

"Oh, no riddle here, Princess!" teased Tag, with a lighthearted chuckle. "If I am correct in my assumption, the pie appeared because you are overwhelmed with guilt for stealing one and the *peasant* dress is undoubtedly because the Dream Merchant, in all his wisdom, felt you deserved to live as one of us commoners, starting with the right apparel."

"Laugh now, funny boy, but you assume too much!" cursed Rose. "Come midnight, I shall wish for a new gown and be done with this rag. It will be more opulent than the first."

"Well, I think you look quite fetchin' in that outfit, Princess," praised Cankles, attempting to lift her spirits.

"Of course I do! But that is not the point!"

"Before you waste another wish, keep in mind, if you dress as decadently as you normally do, you might as well march through the countryside wearing a placard announcing to the whole world: *Rob me, please*!" said Tag.

"What do you mean?"

"You'll invite the attention of every thief and scoundrel looking to turn over a quick coin!" explained Tag.

"You are trying to trick me," decided Rose, shuddering in disgust as she felt the wool fabric touching roughly against her delicate skin.

"Oh, Master Yairet wasn't speakin' in jest, Princess," averred Cankles. "The further we head from the borders of Fleetwood, the worse it'll get. You'll be meetin' up with all sorts of unscrupulous folks who'd think nothing of robbin' you blind of all that's valuable."

"In fact, it would not surprise me if they make off with your entire dress, than to waste time plucking off all the diamond beads one-by-one," stated Tag. "They're definitely the type to just leave you there in the middle of the road in your knickers!"

Rose's face flushed with embarrassment. She envisioned herself standing there in her undergarment as Tag pointed, laughing at her ill fortune.

"Perhaps it is better to keep a low profile as we move through the lands," decided Rose, as she shook this disturbing image from her head.

"The lower, the better," assured Tag, glancing up to see the sun had advanced from the eastern sky. "We are awake now. We should get going. And as our plans to wish for horses have been pre-empted, we shall be made to walk for now."

"How about a little breakfast first," suggested Cankles, holding up the humongous pie. "After all, we shouldn't let this fine pastry go to waste."

"Quite right, my friend," agreed Tag. He licked his lips as he pulled out his hunting knife to slice the pie into manageable wedges.

"Ladies first," offered Cankles, passing to her a piece of pie served up on a large leaf.

Rose pushed away the pastry. "I have had my fill of pie to last me a lifetime. You go right ahead. Indulge without me."

"I would never have thought such an ugly, simple pair of suede shoes could be so comfortable," commented Rose. She hiked along with purpose as she followed behind Cankles while Tag took up the rear.

"Anything is better than those fancy shoes with stacked heels you usually wear," stated Tag, standing up on his toes. "It's unnatural to be walking about like this. And how you even traipse around in them without falling and breaking your neck is a bloody miracle."

"It is no miracle," explained the Princess, moving with ease. "It is a matter of breeding. People like me, being of noble blood, are designed to don such fine apparel. It is in how we carry ourselves – with poise and grace."

"Oh, and I thought it was with fallen arches and hammertoes," teased Tag.

"Har, har!" grunted Rose, in mock laughter. "You really are not funny."

"Never said I was. Right now, I'm just grateful we have not had to endure listening to you whine about being made to walk. So, thank goodness for *ugly, simple shoes.*"

"Well, being fashionable does require some sacrifice," admitted Rose, breathing easier as she was no longer confined in the suffocating grip of a corset.

"I'd take comfort over style any day," chirped up Cankles.

"That is quite obvious," sniffed the Princess, frowning at his attire that consisted of a simple cotton shirt and wool trousers, topped up by a course, wool cloak. She was only glad this fool now wore both his shoes on his feet than to carry one tucked under his arm.

"Thanks for noticing, Princess!"

Rose issued another frustrated sigh as she ducked under the tree bough Cankles held up for her.

"Not that I am complaining, but how much further do we walk?" she asked.

"We shall go on until nightfall," answered Tag. "We'll take advantage of the daylight while we can."

"Are we going to stop and eat?"

"Not any time soon," replied Tag. "We are still full up on pie."

"But what about me? My stomach is starting to make noises again," whined Rose.

"You should have had some pie when you had the chance," responded Tag. His words were far from sympathetic.

"It would have left a sour taste in my mouth," decided Rose. "I would rather chew on a stick than to ever eat a pie again."

"Lucky you!" exclaimed Tag, glancing about the forest. "Take your pick! There's plenty of sticks to be had."

"If you're feelin' a bit peckish, I've got some food in this pack of mine," offered Cankles, stopping to accommodate the Princess.

"It better not be rat-on-a-stick," grumbled Rose.

"Oh, no! Wouldn't think of it! They're better eatin' hot," responded Cankles, as he rummaged through his bag. "Here we go."

With grubby hands, he tore off a ragged piece from a round loaf. He offered the bread to her with a modest chunk of aged cheese.

"This should do you nicely 'til supper time," said Cankles. "Tuck in!"

Rose stared at this meager offering of food, sniffing it first to determine how safe it was to eat.

"This is it?" asked Rose.

"Silly me! I forgot!" exclaimed Cankles, his hand fishing about in his pack. "Can't forget about this."

Just as the Princess extended her hand, waiting for something she considered truly edible, he pressed a water flask into her hand.

Her look of hope dissolved into an anguished expression of

utter disappointment.

"Have a drink. It'll help to wash it down," said Cankles, not understanding her reluctance to eat.

"Don't worry about her. She's just being fussy," grumbled Tag. "And if she was truly hungry, she'd eat it, no problem."

"The problem is, this is not *real food*," argued Rose.

"Perhaps in your world, but for everyone else scraping by to make ends meet, especially after paying their taxes to keep you in the lifestyle you're accustomed to, sometimes, this is all there is left to eat."

"How about some gruel then?" offered Cankles, holding up a cloth bag.

"What is gruel?" asked Rose.

"It's rolled oats. The oatmeal is boiled into a mush. Don't need to eat much of it 'cause it's really quite fillin' – guaranteed to stick to your ribs."

"It sounds disgusting!" groaned the Princess.

"If you complain about eating that bread and cheese, I'll be happy to force some gruel down your throat so you'll better appreciate what *real people* eat," growled Tag.

"No need for that! It is just that there is much for me to get used to in these primitive conditions, the food included. I just need more time to adapt and become accustomed to the bland."

As her empty stomach rumbled, turning on itself for nourishment, Rose felt the first true pangs of genuine hunger. It was not the typical *you've missed afternoon tea and snacks before dinnertime* munchies. It was the terrible, hollow feeling that gnaws at the very pit of one's stomach type pain, threatening to worsen all the more if an offering was not made to quell this need.

Driven by sheer hunger, Rose forced herself to do what she would have believed to be unthinkable, even one day ago! She ate this stale piece of bread and rancid smelling cheese. Nibbling tentatively at first, after she overcame the initial shock of consuming bread without a liberal slathering of creamy butter and sweet berry preserves, Rose devoured her food.

"Whoa! Slow down, Princess!" exclaimed Cankles. "There's no rush. If you eat like that, you won't taste a single bite."

"That is the idea!" sputtered Rose, choking down the bread and hard cheese with a swig of water.

"See! It wasn't that bad!" said Tag, with an amused smile. "And your stomach will thank you for it."

"It was bad enough! Perhaps my appetite has been sated for now, but I cannot subsist on a diet like this forever," warned Rose, surprised that the rumblings and the hunger pangs were vanquished instantly. "A princess needs to eat, and to eat properly."

"Actually, we all do," reminded Cankles.

"I tell you what," said Tag, "before we stop for the night, I'll make sure we catch some game for dinner. This is the perfect habitat for grouse and quail, so I'm confident we can catch a few when they roost for the night."

"You swear?"

"I promise on my father's good name," vowed Tag, his hand over his heart.

"I shall hold you to your words, Tag Yairet," stated Rose.

"You do that," responded her jester. "Now, let's move on."

"How do you know we are still heading in the right direction?" asked Rose, glancing about the unfamiliar forest.

"When the sun is not visible, it can be rather confusing to travel through these tall stands of fir and spruce. So when in doubt, check for moss growing on the north side of the trees," answered Tag.

"Really now?" sniffed Rose. "If that is so, you have had us travelling in circles all this time! There is moss growing all around this tree."

"Oh, she's quite right, Master Yairet," noted Cankles, staring at the base of a large fir tree. On all sides a thick carpet of sphagnum moss clung to its deeply fissured bark.

"For these trees growing in perpetual shadow, yes. But in the more open areas where the sunlight reaches the forest floor, like over there," explained Tag, pointing just ahead, "you'll notice the moss grows most densely on the north side, away from the drying rays of the sun."

"You're a smart one!" praised Cankles, dashing up ahead to inspect the trees that basked in the sun's light for a good part of the day. "It certainly does grow more on this one side. So this must be north an' that can only mean we're headin' east after all!"

"As the sun is already so low in the sky, can we not rest for now?" asked Rose. "After all, you did promise you would hunt for game birds to sup on."

"I did," agreed Tag, glancing toward the western sky where the sun settled ever lower, its waning light casting long shadows stretching along the forest floor. "I tell you what, Princess. Cankles and I will do the hunting. You can get a fire ready for roasting our grouse."

"You sound very optimistic about catching a bird," determined Rose.

"I have seen signs a-plenty this forest is teeming with them. Plus, grouse are not the most intelligent birds to begin with. They are easy prey for both man and beast."

"Well, why do I not just wait for you to return with a bird first before I even bother with building a fire?" suggested Rose.

"You are just being lazy," denounced Tag. "Or are you afraid to get your hands dirty?"

"Neither!" snapped Rose. "I just prefer not to waste my time."

"It will not be wasted," argued Tag.

"It will be, if there is no grouse to cook."

"There will be grouse! And if you refuse to build a fire, then you can clean the birds for roasting instead, while I get a fire going. So choose!"

"Fire! I would rather build a fire," said Rose, repulsed by the whole idea of plucking and gutting their meal.

"Well, then! Get to it," ordered Tag. "If you want to eat, you better learn to start pulling your weight."

"It is just that..." her voice trailed off as her gaze fell to the ground.

"What is it, Princess?" probed Cankles.

"I have never built a fire before," admitted Rose. "I do not even know where to begin or what to do."

"There's nothing to it!" exclaimed Cankles.

"Don't you go taking over her chores, my friend," warned Tag. "If we should somehow become separated, she must learn to at least make fire if she wishes to survive out here on her own."

"Quite right, Master Yairet! I'll get the fire pit started an' the Princess can take care of the rest. I'll jus' teach her what to do."

Cankles used his hands to clear off the highly flammable leaf litter and dried pine needles, scraping away until he reached bare earth. He and Tag gathered some rocks, placing them in a circle around this clearing.

"What are the rocks for?" questioned Rose, watching as they neatly arranged their collection.

"These rocks help to keep the fire contained," explained Tag.

"Plus, if the night gets really cold, you can drop 'em down your shirt an' pants to keep you warm," added Cankles.

"Now there's a lovely thought," groaned Rose.

"Listen up, Princess," ordered Tag. "Gather some dried moss, needles, leaves... whatever you can find that's easy to burn."

"But he just cleared that stuff away!" gasped Rose, staring at Cankles.

"Of course he did," grunted Tag. "If he hadn't, not only would we have a roaring bonfire to contend with, we would also be faced with a bloody big inferno if this fire spreads through the forest."

"Oh," responded Rose. "Then what do I do next?"

"Put the tinder in the center of this circle, and then, once you get a spark to catch, carefully place small, dried twigs and sticks over top. Once the embers turn into steady burning flames, put a log or two on top," explained Tag. "Wait to make sure they actually catch on fire before you place more on top, or you will end up smothering the flames instead."

"And just how do I ignite the tinder?" questioned Rose.

"With one of these," said Cankles, digging up a small, hard object from his pack.

"A rock?"

"It's flint," explained Tag, pulling out his hunting knife. "Use the blade to strike against it to create sparks."

With a quick demonstration, the blade scraped sharply against the rough, flat surface of the flint to create a flash of sparkling light.

"Just be careful once the sparks take to the tinder," warned Tag. "When it starts to smoke, blow gently. If you do it just right, the ember will catch, setting the tinder on fire. If you blow too hard, you'll extinguish it."

"This is sounding more and more complicated," groaned Rose, taking the flint and knife from Tag's hands.

"It's really simple," assured Cankles. "Even I can build a fire."

Sensing this man had issued a challenge, Rose was not about to be outdone by a village idiot. "Well then, so can I!"

"I'm confident you'll give it a valiant attempt," responded Tag. "However, if I were a betting man, I'd say I'll be returning with dinner long before you even have the tinder lit."

"It is a good thing you do not bet then," sniffed Rose, her words confident. "For I shall have a fire well under way long before you return empty-handed!"

"I'll believe it when I see it," grunted Tag.

"I am a princess! I can do whatever I set my mind to," insisted Rose, her finger poking Tag in his chest to lend emphasis to her claim. "Mark my words, it will be done!"

"Are they to be underlined?" questioned Cankles, searching for a quill and inkwell in his pack.

"Pardon me?" responded Rose, frowning in confusion.

"Your words," answered Cankles. "How do you want 'em marked?"

Rose gave no answer. Her eyes narrowed in contempt as her face scowled in agitation. Turning her back to him, she addressed Tag.

"As I was saying, I can do whatever I set my mind to."

"You mean to say, you can get *other people* to do whatever you set your mind to," corrected Tag.

"Not so!" protested Rose. "I shall have a fire underway well before you catch even one grouse!"

"You're on!" declared Tag, eager to undertake this challenge. "See you back here in a few minutes."

"I will be waiting," stated Rose, hurriedly scooping up dried leaves into her apron, "and so will the fire!"

As Cankles and Tag rushed off to begin their hunt, the Princess wasted no time, dumping a loose, heaping mound of leaves and pine needles into the center of the fire pit. Determined to prove Tag wrong, Rose snatched up as many pieces of sticks and twigs she could fit in her arms, dumping this load next to the circle of rocks.

Crouching low to the ground, Rose was poised for action. With knife in one hand, flint in the other, she struck the two objects together. To her surprise, golden sparks appeared on contact, but as quickly as they appeared, they vanished from sight, not even touching down on the tinder.

Again, knife met flint with violent intent as another explosive show of sparks flashed, and just as quickly disappeared.

"This is so stupid!" Rose grumbled beneath her breath. She lashed out at the flint, angrily striking it with the knife. This repeat performance yielded little in the way of results. The small hill of tinder was intact and as cold as when she first began this exercise.

"Maybe if I held the flint closer," mumbled Rose, as she rethought her strategy.

With the same zeal, blade met flint, but this time, the sparks made contact with the dried needles and leaves. Instead of bursting into flames, the few sparks that landed, merely smoked, dying out quickly.

"That was a little better. There's still hope for me yet. I can win this little contest."

Rose leaned in closer, pressing the flint against the tinder. Drawing a deep breath to focus on the task at hand, Rose slowly exhaled as she muttered, "I can do this."

Gripping the knife and flint firmly, the two objects clashed. To Rose's surprise, tiny golden sparks leapt from flint to tinder, smoldering with intention.

Dropping her tools in excitement, she crouched low to the ground, blowing a gentle, steady breath on the tinder.

Instead of fire, there was only smoke.

Rose made another attempt to breathe life into the smoldering ember. It glowed brighter, vapourizing needles and leaves, but still no flames.

"Gentle is not working," decided Rose. "Maybe it needs more air."

Determined to master this skill, Rose got down on her hands and knees. She leaned in closer over the smoldering mass. Filling her lungs, she blew harder, causing some of the needles to fly off. A growing pillar of gray smoke swirled, increasing with her efforts. Just as Rose inhaled, leaning in to unleash another breath, she squealed in surprise as the tinder erupted into flames right before her face.

She fell back with a start, watching as the rapacious fire eagerly devoured the dried needles and leaves. An acrid odour suddenly filled her nostrils, giving rise to panic.

Her hair was on fire!

The golden strands curled, turning black before disintegrating to a fine ash as she used her hands to smother the flames. To her relief, the damage was minimal.

Even at the expense of sacrificing her beautiful hair, Rose was absolutely thrilled she had finally accomplished what deep down inside she was beginning to fear was impossible. Carefully, she placed the sticks and twigs she had gathered over top of the burning tinder. Once she was confident the fire would take, she rushed off to find more and larger pieces of wood.

Making several trips, Rose piled a heap of wood close to the fire pit. Tossing a log on the ever-growing flames, she took a moment to revel in her success. Her heart filled with pride, for more than she proved to Tag she could undertake this task with success, she had proven it to herself she can accomplish whatever she set her mind to – even if it was only a menial task.

"Look! Up there!" Tag whispered excitedly, as he pointed to a branch about twenty feet above. "There are two birds, one perched next to the other."

"Wonderful!" exclaimed Cankles, peering up at the dimming sky through the tangle of branches. There, he spied upon the pair of grouse roosting peacefully on the spruce tree's bough. "Nice an' plump. They should make for a lovely meal."

"Now, all we have to do is catch them," said Tag, searching the ground for something to throw.

"You mean to down 'em with a rock?"

"An arrow would be easier, but we must make do with what we have at hand. In this case, rocks."

"Aren't grouse like pheasants? If you miss, won't they jus' fly off?" queried Cankles. He stared up hungrily as the birds sat motionless high above, huddled close together for shared warmth.

"They're nowhere near as smart as a pheasant. I've heard these birds are too stupid to know they're in danger until it's too late," disclosed Tag, palming a rock in his hand as he determined the best angle of trajectory to take down his prey.

"Do you think it's fair to go at 'em when they're fast asleep?" questioned Cankles. He felt a pang of guilt, staring at the birds that remained frozen on their lofty perch in spite of the activity below them.

"They're not asleep," insisted Tag. "They are keeping still in hopes they'll go unnoticed by us."

"Well, I'd say they're pretty clever then."

"Not really! We did take notice, but they haven't figured that out yet," countered Tag, as he took aim. "Now, just be ready to rush in and grab them when they fall."

Cankles stood poised like a cat, waiting to pounce on its dinner in case the birds were just stunned, rather than outright killed.

"Ready?" asked Tag. He pulled his arm back to put some speed and power behind the throw.

"You bet!"

Tag let the rock fly, but to his embarrassment, it came nowhere near to hitting the intended targets.

"I was just warming up," insisted Tag, picking up another stone. "This is the one that'll bring them down."

Of course, it was only the second of many to be airborne on this eve. Every rock within their reach that was not too heavy to propel skyward became part of this barrage. Alas, they were thrown either too high, too low, or too far to the left or right to even come close to dislodging one of the birds from its perch.

"See! Too stupid to move!" declared Tag, frustrated by his failed attempts. His only consolation was the birds had yet to take flight.

"Either that or they're real smart an' figured out we're bloody bad shots," determined Cankles, rubbing his shoulder that was starting to ache.

"They're not smart, nor are we bad shots," argued Tag. "We were just unlucky, but I sense our luck will soon change."

"How about standin' right beneath an' tossin' a rock straight up?" asked Cankles. "That might work."

"At this moment, I'm willing to try anything. I'm not about to let the Princess prove me wrong or she'll never let me live it down."

Maneuvering directly beneath the birds, Tag and Cankles assessed their new position.

"See," whispered Cankles, as he palmed his stone. "Fewer branches in our way. We can get a clear shot at 'em now."

"Ready?" asked Tag, feeling the smooth, cold surface of the rock in his sweaty palm as his heart swelled with renewed confidence.

"Yep!"

"On the count of three," ordered Tag. *"One!"*

They set their sights.

"Two!"

Poised, they were ready to hurl their projectiles.

"Three!"

He and Cankles unleashed their wrath, propelling their rocks with utmost purpose. Jettisoned, the rocks sped toward the birds with deadly intent, but disappointingly dismal results. In another pathetic attempt, they were much closer, but still, they missed.

One grouse merely ruffled its feathers as the other flapped its wings in the wake of the flying projectiles lobbed their way. Their heads cocked from side to side, gazing down with seemingly vacant eyes.

Simultaneously, Tag moaned in pain as Cankles groaned in disgust. The rock Tag had launched at his intended meal came straight back down to earth. It struck him atop his head as he tried to duck, but too late, while a fresh dollop of bird-droppings christened his comrade. It landed with a loud, wet *splat*, falling smack-dap on the middle of Cankles' forehead.

"Well, that was interestin'!" commented Cankles, as he wiped the white and green smear from his forehead.

"How can this be interesting?" queried Tag, rubbing the crown of his head as his face reddened with embarrassment and annoyance.

"Who'd a believe a rock an' bird poop would come down at the same speed?" marvelled Cankles.

"Never mind that!" grumbled Tag, glaring angrily at the birds that had remained unscathed thus far. "I am not ready to give up."

"Maybe they're jus' not meant to be eaten on this night," reasoned Cankles.

"Not that the Princess had succeeded in building a fire, which I'm sure she has not, but I'm not about to be bested by a girl. Especially, *that* girl!"

"So, you're not gonna give up?"

"In this contest, my hunting prowess will be in question if I walk away now. I refuse to accept defeat to those blasted birds!" declared Tag. "I am determined to get those damned grouse, even if it kills me!"

"Well, they seem to be winnin' the contest so far," determined Cankles. "After all, they haven't been hit once! You have, an' they didn't even throw the rock at you."

"Well, I am about to get my revenge, and it will taste oh-so sweet when those birds are roasting on a spit over an open fire," growled Tag.

"Well, maybe you're right an' they aren't that smart at all," decided Cankles. "They haven't moved, even with all those rocks flyin' by. Maybe if one of us climbed up this tree an' just bopped 'em on their noggins with a stick, that'd be easier?"

"Hey… I think you're on to something, my friend," responded Tag, nodding in approval.

"I am?"

"Sure! All we need to do is climb this tree and get them!"

"Well, I don't mean to come across soundin' like a coward, but I don't take to heights too well. I can give you a boost up there though, if it'd help," offered Cankles. He laced his fingers together to give Tag a leg up to reach the lowest branches that were out of reach otherwise.

Pulling himself up against the spruce tree, Tag struggled to grab the branches.

"Stand a little closer!" ordered Tag. "Now stand tall! Just a little higher."

Cankles grunted and groaned as he fought to lift his friend up.

"Almost there!" hollered Tag, his fingertips straining to grab hold.

"What are you two doing?"

Cankles gasped in surprise, falling to the ground as Tag yelped in fright, hanging from the limb he just managed to seize.

"I thought you were hunting for grouse, not playing in the trees," admonished Rose, shaking her head in shame.

"Shhh!" whispered Cankles, scrambling back onto his feet as he pointed to the high branches. "The food is up there. We jus' haven't got them down yet."

"A little help here!" hollered Tag, dangling helplessly from the branch.

Cankles rushed over, wrapping his arms around Tag's legs to lift him higher.

"Thanks! That's more like it," praised Tag, making his way up into this towering spruce.

"What are you trying to do? Scare them away?" asked Rose, watching as Tag inched his way along.

"I am going to catch us some grouse for dinner."

"There is an easier way, you know?" stated the Princess.

"And how's that?" questioned Tag, his tone skeptical as he glanced down at her scowling face.

Without another word, Rose selected one of the rocks Tag and Cankles had deployed in their failed arsenal. After taking a moment to check the angle of the two birds perched on the bough; she took aim and simply hurled the stone. The projectile flew in a perfect line, hitting the closer grouse first. The impact sent its little head smashing into its roosting partner. In a small blizzard of brown and grey feathers, the two birds fell to the ground, landing at Cankles' feet.

Both he and Tag were absolutely dumbfounded, staring with their mouths agape at the Princess, and then the downed birds.

"Better shut your pie-hole before feathers go in," laughed Rose, motioning for Tag to close his mouth.

"I'm fit to be tied!" gasped Tag, shaking his head in disbelief.

"Shall I find some rope?" offered Cankles, hoping to be useful.

"I mean to say, I am completely flabbergasted! With an aim like that, I can't help but think your pie was thrown into the captain's face quite deliberately."

"As precise as it was, that throw was not deliberate," insisted Rose, failing to disclose she's had years of practice, lobbing her shoes at her attendants.

"All I can say is, that was brilliant!" praised Cankles, holding up the grouse, one in each hand for Tag to see. "Absolutely brilliant!"

"Lucky is more like it," responded Tag, testing his footing as he made his way back down.

"Luck had nothing to do with it. Nor did I need any luck in building the fire," said Rose, suitably pleased with herself.

"No!" gasped Tag, glancing down at her. "You did it? You actually built a fire on your own?"

"Well, it was not as if there was anyone around to help, had I asked," responded Rose.

"I do believe she speaks the truth, Master Yairet," determined Cankles. "It appears she used her hair as tinder. How very clever of you, Princess!"

"There is a fire burning as we speak?" questioned Tag, still skeptical.

"It is ready and waiting to cook the birds _I_ just downed."

"Oh, I've gotta see this for myself!" exclaimed Cankles, delighted by this news.

"By all means," invited Rose, showing the way. "Just follow me!"

As Cankles and the Princess disappeared, Tag called out from his high perch, "Hey! What about me? A little help here!"

"I am not about to pluck those birds! Nor will I gut them," protested Rose. Her words were adamant as she recoiled in disgust from the dead grouse Tag thrust into her face.

"Why not? You're so good at *eviscerating* a person's dignity, I just thought it would be easy for you."

"You are just a sore loser!" snapped Rose.

"No worries, Princess," said Cankles, taking the fowl from Tag's hand. "I'll be pleased to dress 'em for you, especially as you were the one to kill 'em *an'* build this fire."

"By all means! You are welcome to undertake this task!" insisted Rose, using her hands to shoo him away.

Cankles eagerly set to work. Using his knife, he removed the head, feet and wingtips of each grouse. With carefully placed incisions to the skin around the ankles and the base of the wings, and then along the length of the breastbone, he turned the skin, feathers and all, inside-out. It allowed him to literally *pop* the body out of its skin so there was no need for plucking.

Rose found this strangely fascinating. Once the skin was flipped back out again, the feathers remained attached to look like a small, feathered jacket waiting to be worn by a naked bird, should one happen along.

As Cankles proceeded to gut the birds, Rose looked away. She was too squeamish to watch as he used his fingers to remove the organs from the body cavity, saving the small heart, liver and kidneys so they can be roasted, too.

In less time it took for Tag and Cankles to locate the grouse and attempt to kill them in a useless hail of stones, the tasty little game birds were roasted to perfection and ready to eat.

Huddled around the warmth of the campfire, the trio shared in this hard-earned meal. It was a simple fare, and yet, Rose savoured every bite. There were no fancy spices or rich, creamy sauces smothering the meat to disguise any imperfections. The grouse were seasoned with a bit of sea salt Cankles carried with him and fresh sprigs of herbs he was able to gather from the forest floor. In all its understated glory, the meal was absolutely delicious.

"That was most satisfying!" declared Rose, daintily blotting the corners of her mouth on the apron.

"That was the best, my friend," praised Tag, issuing a sigh of contentment as he gave Cankles a nod of approval. "Even tastier than the water rat you had served us!"

"Kind of you to say so, young master!" Cankles responded graciously as he flopped onto his back to stare up at the stars. He rested his head on his pack as he surveyed the deepening sky. "Even I gotta admit I out did myself on this night. It was a grand meal even though we didn't have much to start with. Mind you, even if the Princess didn't down those grouse, there's always something we can find to eat in this forest."

"I would have to say you are a glass-half-full kind of fellow," decided Tag, nodding in approval to his new friend.

"Half full of what?" questioned Cankles. "Ale, I hope? 'Cause I'm more of an ale man, than wine or spirits."

"What Tag means to say is you are more the optimistic sort, refusing to view the world with constant doom and gloom," explained Rose.

"Yes," said Tag. "While the Princess here is a glass-half-empty sort."

"Meaning the opposite?" probed Cankles.

"At times, she's so pessimistic, not only does she view the world as such, she *is* the very incarnation of doom and gloom," teased Tag.

"I am not!" disputed Rose, as her lower lip protruding in a pout.

"Then what are you?" asked Tag, his eyes scrutinizing the Princess. "An optimist or a pessimist?"

"Neither," responded Rose. "I am a *realist*. I walk the fine line between the two, so consider me the voice of reason."

"Then this voice of reason must have been talking crazy talk to you," mocked Tag. "Look at the mess you find yourself in now!"

"That was almost funny, but not quite," sniffed Rose.

"I thought it was," stated Tag.

"What do you know? But enough of this silly talk. What do we do now?"

"We sleep, Princess," replied Tag, flopping onto his back to stare at the multitude of stars dotting the cobalt sky.

"Now?" gasped Rose, ever the night owl. "It is much too early."

"Not when you consider we'll be leaving at first light," reminded Tag, carefully removing the sword and its scabbard from his belt.

"Why so early? Why can we not just sleep in for a little bit?" groaned Rose.

"Because the early bird gets the worm," responded Tag.

"Oh, I'm not keen on worms, not unless I plan to use them for bait when I go fishin'," stated Cankles.

"That's not what I'm talking about," explained Tag.

"But you jus' said something about birds an' worms, an' early worms," insisted Cankles, scratching his head in bewilderment.

"I mean to say, you can get more accomplished *and* reap the rewards if you are willing to get an earlier start than others."

"Well, I'm still not keen on the worms, but the other stuff you said makes sense to me," decided Cankles.

"Good," said Tag.

"Jus' don't know why people speak in such riddles."

"It is just an old saying," said Rose, laughing lightly. "The problem is, you are a simpleton and you tend to take things quite literally."

Cankles stared at the Princess, uncertain if she was laughing at him in ridicule or in good fun.

"Think nothing of her, my friend. You know what they say?" said Tag, giving Cankles a shrewd nod and a wink of his eye. "He who laughs last..."

"Is the slowest to understand?" concluded his new friend.

"Not quite," explained Tag, seeing the baffled look on Cankles' face. "But never mind."

"Well, I jus' believe a person should be direct. Say what they mean an' mean what they say," explained Cankles. "It'd put an end to a whole lot of misunderstandings, if you get my meanin'?"

"What is apparent to me is that you seem blissfully ignorant of most things," responded the Princess.

"Do not listen to her," dismissed Tag, scowling at Rose in disapproval. "You may not understand all that we speak of, but as least you are not morally repugnant like someone I know!"

"No need to get testy!" rebuked Rose. "I was merely making an observation."

"I'm not sure I like what you're observin', Princess," responded Cankles.

"If anything, I am truly amazed by your ignorance," said Rose.

"You're *amazed*?" questioned Cankles, scratching his head in thought as his eyes scrutinized the Princess for the truth. "Well thank you! Most people tell me I'm quite un-amazing."

"She was being *sarcastic*," corrected Tag, his elbow poking Rose in her ribs to dissuade her from issuing another insult.

"I'm not sure I follow," admitted Cankles.

"As I said, *amazing!*" teased Rose.

"Shut it, Princess!" scolded Tag. "As my father used to say: '*If you can't say something nice, then don't bother speaking at all!*'"

Rose sulked, pouting in silence.

"No harm done, Master Yairet," insisted Cankles, offering the Princess a congenial smile. "She was jus' teasin' me. I'm sure of it."

"Why do you insist on coming to her defense?" questioned Tag, flustered by this man's willingness to give Rose the benefit of doubt. "Are you not bothered by her disparaging remarks? What she said was less than kind. In fact, most would say her words can cut the average person to the quick."

"Well, I suppose I'm not average," decided Cankles.

"Most definitely, and in more ways than one," agreed Rose, as Tag shot another baleful glance in her direction.

"Truth be told, the whole world can be rather unkind. Folks have said worse things about me," revealed Cankles, his shoulders rolling in a shrug. "But if I felt bad every time someone said something demeanin' about me, I might as well jus' crawl under a rock an' never see the light of day again."

"The world can be cruel," agreed Tag. "It must be hard at times."

"Well, I can't help what other people say or do to me, I can only control how I respond an' how I choose to treat others."

For a lingering moment, Tag mulled over Cankles' words. For such a simple man, he was capable of saying such profound things, and yet, Tag was quite certain Cankles was rather oblivious as to just how insightful he could truly be.

"You are absolutely correct, my friend," agreed Tag, still glaring at the Princess. "It is best to ignore what others will say, especially if it is less than constructive."

Throughout this brief, but revealing exchange, Rose had been unusually silent. The tip of her finger was wedged in her mouth as she sat quietly, staring at the fire.

"What's wrong with you?" asked Tag, watching Rose as she nursed her index finger.

"*This* is what's wrong," whined the Princess, shoving her finger into his face. "It is the nastiest hangnail I ever had! It must have happened when I was trying to make this fire."

"A *hangnail*?" gasped Tag, his eyes rolling in exasperation. "That is nothing! Look at this!"

He spread the fingers of his left hand to show the scar on the large knuckle of his middle finger. "This happened with my hunting knife last year."

With animated gestures, he re-enacted the foolish event when, on a dare, he set his opened hand on a block of wood as he rapidly stabbed with the tip of his knife at the gaps between his splayed fingers.

"Got myself real good that time," said Tag, proudly showing off this scar.

"That little *scratch*?" sniffed Rose, completely unimpressed. "That is laughable compared to this!"

Hiking up the hem of her skirt, she displayed her left knee. She still bore the scar of a bad scrape she endured as a child.

"Unfortunately, being a Princess, it means I scar easier than most."

"That is not a scar!" disputed Tag. "*This* is a scar!"

Rolling up his shirtsleeve, Tag showed off a three-inch silvery scar running down his forearm. "Got this falling out of a tree. A sharp branch snagged me. Almost ripped my arm off!"

"I wanna play, too!" exclaimed Cankles. Rather than rolling up a shirtsleeve or hoisting up the leg of his trousers to reveal a scar or two, he whipped off his shirt to show off his back.

Tag and Rose gasped in horror.

Instead of a single scar left by a small scrape or cut, Cankles' back was marred by a multitude of long, linear, silvery white scars that mutilated him from high on his shoulders all the way down to the waist of his trousers. It was obvious he had been whipped or caned.

When his show of one-upmanship did not solicit the *ooohs* and *aaahs* he thought it would, he quickly threw his shirt back on, embarrassed by his comrades stunned response.

"Maybe I should've started with the one on my head..." Cankles said sheepishly as his fingers gingerly traced the large, jagged gash that had healed over and was now hidden by hair. "Or the smaller scars from the stab wounds on my chest."

"Oh my goodness!" gasped Rose, wincing with an equal measure of sympathy and disgust. "What happened to you?"

"Don't rightly know, Princess. I've had these scars for longer than I can, or care to, remember."

"Well, you certainly were not born with them! How can you not know how this happened to you?" questioned Rose, shaking her head in confusion.

"Obviously, he had received a horrific beating," stated Tag, his mind still reeling from the sight. It made his own scars look as minor as Rose's tiny hangnail.

"I know that!" snapped Rose. "But how? And why?"

"Do you remember who did this to you?" questioned Tag, surprised that any man could survive such a brutal assault.

"Can't say I do and I don't think I'd want to," replied Cankles. "If you get my meanin'?"

"Surely, you must remember something? After all, a man is not flogged for no reason, especially to this extreme," noted Rose.

"Like I said before, there isn't much I remember of my life," reminded Cankles. "I'm not even sure of my name, truth be told."

"Did you say you have a scar on your head?" questioned Tag.

"Yep, got cracked on my noggin real good, but you can't see the scar that much anymore with all this hair growin' over it."

"Perhaps that's the reason why you cannot remember the details of this event," said Tag. "My father told me of knights and soldiers, afflicted by serious head traumas, losing their memory. And not just of the events leading up to their injury, but even forgetting their entire lives!"

"Oh, balderdash!" dismissed Rose, scrutinizing the man before her. "This fellow has clearly lost his mind, not his memory!"

"What would you know of this, Princess?" grunted Tag. "My father said it could happen. He has seen it happen after the battle was over when he and his men would undertake the grim task of collecting the wounded and dying."

"Even if that were so, in case you have not noticed, he is the furthest thing from a knight, even more so than you."

"So maybe it didn't happen in battle. Could've been a simple accident," decided Tag.

"No one gets *accidentally* flogged and beaten," disputed Rose.

"Whatever the case, he received a serious injury to his head. It may have been enough to cause memory loss."

"Could be," responded Cankles, rubbing his head. "If that is so, then I consider it blessin', for I really don't think I'd want to remember something like that."

"Well, I am truly curious as to how this could have happened to you. As far as I am concerned, only a criminal would have such a punishment exacted on him," decided Rose.

Cankles' face blanched upon hearing her words.

"If you're insinuatin' I did something evil to someone, then I can't think what it would've been. I know in my heart I'm not one to steal or hurt people."

"Maybe you just can't remember you had?" offered Rose.

"My! You are not one to mince words, are you Princess?" admonished Tag, scowling in resentment at her.

"Well, think on it!" urged the Princess, her eyes narrowing in suspicion as they stared at Cankles. "There was good reason this happened to him."

"There is always a reason, but not necessarily a good one," argued Tag. "It's better not to speculate."

"Speculate?" repeated Cankles. "Whatever happened, it happened to me an' I'd rather not know."

"Are you not even a little curious?" probed Rose.

"I think if I was meant to know, then I'd remember," answered Cankles, speaking with all certainty. "Methinks it's a blessin' I can't."

"But how does one even survive such a beating?" asked the Princess, thinking on the multitude of scars on Cankles' back.

"Wasn't ready to die, I suppose."

"It is the will to survive," decided Tag. "My father once said we all have it in us, but it is stronger in some than others."

"Can't say if it was luck or this will to survive. There's not much I remember at all, so there's really no point in speakin' about it."

"I agree!" said Tag. "Enough talk for now. I'm going to find some rest, but before I do, at the midnight hour, I am going to make sure you wish for those horses before you fall asleep and dream up another pie or who-knows-what."

10

A Sure Cure for the Uglies

"Thank goodness! The horses are still here," said Tag. With a great yawn he stretched his dormant muscles, still sore from pelting rocks at last night's dinner.

"Where did you think they would be? In a jousting competition?" responded Rose, glancing over at the three white horses with braided manes and tails. Tethered to a nearby tree, the animals grazed contentedly in a small clearing.

"After you wished for a worthless horse-drawn carriage to pull us through a forest with not one road, I was worried you were going to wish for something equally useless while we slept."

"Oh, ye of little faith!" sniffed Rose, waving off Tag's concern.

"Little faith, indeed! It was bad enough we had to waste a second wish on riding gear for these horses," reminded Tag.

"Worry not," said Rose. "I would never think of wasting the third wish."

To his relief, Rose still wore her simple frock and apron. She had not wished for a new, jewel-encrusted gown with matching accessories, so there was no need to start the day chastising her."

"No need for concern, Master Yairet," assured Cankles, raising a dainty, porcelain teacup to toast the morning before taking another sip.

Tag rubbed the sleep from his eyes as he stared at the man. There was something not right with this image as he stared at Cankles. He was seated upon one of three beautifully carved chairs at a dining table fitted with a silk damask tablecloth and set with fine porcelain dishes and silver cutlery. Cankles lifted a teapot, pouring fresh, steaming hot tea into another cup. Next to him sat Rose. She was indulging in a bowl of dewy fresh strawberries with sweet, clotted cream that sat between a heaping platter of warm, buttery biscuits slathered in strawberry preserves and a plate of perfectly browned, spicy pork sausages.

"Hey! What's going on here?" gasped Tag, stumbling to his feet.

"Mornin' tea an' breakfast," answered Cankles, waving him over. "Care to join us?"

"You *did* use a wish, *the last wish!*" groaned Tag, his hand smacking his forehead in frustration.

"Yes, but it was *not* wasted," countered Rose, dabbing a succulent strawberry into the cream before stuffing it into her mouth.

"We could have hunted for breakfast," argued Tag, plunking himself down onto the chair Rose had conjured up. For a moment, he was surprised. It fit him perfectly. His back rested against the chair while his feet were flat on the ground.

"True, but after watching you hunt for grouse last evening, I was fearful we would starve to death," teased Rose, unrepentant as she sank her teeth into a warm biscuit.

"How dare you insult me?" Tag fumed.

"It was quite easy, really," admitted Rose.

"No need for angry words, my friends," urged Cankles, cringing as he was caught in the middle of this verbal crossfire. "It's too early for this nastiness!"

"Why must you be so pig-headed? You should just say *thank you* and be grateful you have a hot and hearty breakfast waiting for you!" snapped an agitated Rose, as she ignored Cankles' plea.

"Thank *you*?" snorted Tag. "I think not!"

"I thought it would please you to not sit on the cold ground eating worms for breakfast. Perhaps this is too civilized for you!"

"We could have saved that last wish for when we really needed it! When it was a dire emergency!" retorted Tag.

"This was an emergency! We really needed to eat. So there!" rebuked Rose, stuffing the biscuit into her mouth. "And to think I believed you would be pleased I had used the wish for all our benefit, not just mine!"

"Don't mean to sound like I'm pickin' sides, Master Yairet," interjected Cankles, as he raised his hands in a sign of truce, "but in my humble opinion, the Princess is quite right. She was thinkin' of all of us, you included, when she wished for this meal. She even wished for those fancy sausages she knows you like so much. An' guess what? They're very tasty!"

"She did?"

"Yes, I did!" snapped Rose, glaring at Tag as the shifting breeze sent the tantalizing aroma of fried sausages wafting his way. "But as you said, it was a wish wasted!"

Tag drew a slow, deep breath to gain his composure. He never believed he would begin the first meal of the day by swallowing his pride.

"The deed is done! You might as well stop complaining and eat with us," demanded Rose.

Tag's eyes could barely meet her icy stare as he apologized, "I'm sorry. You meant no harm and you were thinking of us when you conjured up this meal."

"This *scrumptious* meal," added Cankles, as he eagerly filled his plate with another serving of biscuits and sausages.

"Are you apologizing to me because you want to prove you can be the bigger man or because you are truly sorry?" queried Rose.

"Both," admitted Tag, his words contrite. "I just reacted poorly. I was thinking of using the final wish for other things."

"Like what?" asked Rose.

"Suppose we need money to purchase supplies to last us through this trek?" answered Tag, patting his trousers' pocket to remind the Princess of his limited funds.

"Oh... I never thought that far ahead," said Rose.

Before Tag could hit her with another angry exchange, Cankles spoke up, "We can always sell these fine dishes and cutlery when we're done with 'em. It's not like we'll be needin' 'em again."

Tag sat back in his chair as he considered his words, "That's a wonderful idea!"

"It is?" gasped Cankles, the bite of sausage fell from his open mouth to plop onto his plate. "It isn't very often I come up with one."

"It's perfect!" commended Tag, slapping his friend on the back. "This set of porcelain and silverware should fetch us a tidy sum, if not in money, in traded goods."

"So, you are not mad at me anymore," queried Rose.

"Not now. It would be a wasted emotion," decided Tag. "I'm good with this."

"Well, you'll be feeling even better once you get some breakfast into you," insisted Cankles, pushing the plate of sausages toward the famished young man as Rose topped his teacup with cream. "I'm tellin' you, this is the best meal I ever had."

Filling his plate, Tag soon forgot his anger. He busied himself with the business of eating, chasing the biscuit down with a gulp of sweet tea. Sinking his teeth into one of the sausages, he noticed it was identical in texture, but not quite in taste.

"What is wrong now?" questioned Rose, noticing his face as she daintily sipped her tea.

"The sausage…"

"What of it?"

"It is good, but it is somehow different in flavour," commented Tag, taking another mouthful.

"Oh, that! When I conjured up the wish, I had to not only imagine how all this would look, I also had to recreate the taste of each and every item on this table, hence, the perfectly ripe strawberries and extra sweet, clotted cream. As for the sausages, I always found them too salty for my delicate palate. Plus, too much salt bloats me up. Can't have a bloated princess, you know?"

"Of course not," responded Tag, with a chuckle. "Overall, this is very good."

"Oh, I'm enjoyin' this!" exclaimed Cankles, patting his distended belly that seemed to protrude all the more because of his lanky frame. "Even stuffed to the gills, I'm lovin' every bite."

"Then well done, Princess," praised Tag. He surrendered to the fact it was better to enjoy this meal than to gripe over what could not be changed.

Rose sat up, smiling with pride. She never knew such a simple thing as a meal shared with others, for the benefit of others, could prove so satisfying, especially to her soul. It was a feeling quite foreign to her, but nonetheless, it was a good one.

So under the morning sun, this unlikely trio dined on a wonderful breakfast while sharing in many cups of tea served with friendly conversation.

Just as Rose scoffed at Cankles, laughing lightly as he tried to convince her Dimbolt Forest is indeed enchanted because of all the Fairies residing here, a family of black bears foraging for mushrooms on the forest floor ambled into view.

"This is not good," whispered Tag, as he slowly rose from his chair.

"What should we do?" asked Rose. Her heart was racing. She had never seen a wild bear before, only the safely caged ones when the travelling carnival rolled into the neighbouring village.

"We ought to leave! Do so now," urged Cankles, "before they come closer an' spook our horses."

"Good idea," whispered Tag. "Princess, get the horses. Lead them away while Cankles gathers our belongings."

"And what will you be doing?" asked Rose, as she backed away from the table. "Running off in fear?"

"I will keep the bears distracted while you make your escape," replied Tag, tossing the biscuits toward the bears as he armed himself with the remaining sausages.

"Good plan," agreed Rose, as she rushed off in the opposite direction to gather their mounts. "Keep those bears distracted."

Cankles gathered the four corners of the tablecloth, quickly securing the silver and porcelain within as the three bears; a large boar, a smaller sow and a little cub lumbered from the forest. Drawn to the smell of sausages, their snouts were held high as they sniffed the air, homing in on the source of this tantalizing aroma.

"Hurry! Run away!" ordered Tag, throwing the last of the sausages at the furry interlopers. "The last thing we need is to be mauled to death."

Hoisting himself into the saddle, Tag led the others away to safety. As they rode off, the baby bear took advantage of this opportunity. He dashed over to one of the sausages, picking it up in his mouth to devour.

"Drop that piece of meat!" ordered the mother bear. "We are not wild animals. We don't eat food that's been tossed away like refuse."

"Yes," agreed the father bear, sniffing around the table before plopping his big, hairy rump onto the chair vacated by Cankles. "Plus, you never know what those filthy human beings have been touching."

Grunting in disappointment, the cub dropped the sausage as he sulked at the thought of being made to eat a bowl of porridge again.

"I heard that!" snapped the mother bear, making herself comfortable on Tag's chair. "Oh my, these are much better than the ones we have!"

The baby bear scrambled up onto Rose's smaller, daintier chair. He sat with his elbows on the table.

"You know better than that!" scolded the mother bear, poking his offending elbows with her claws. "Where are your manners?"

"Oh, mama!" groaned the cub. He squealed in surprise as the legs of the chair collapsed from his weight, sending the little bear tumbling to the ground as his mother and father laughed.

"Why does that always happen to me!" grumbled the cub, his paws rubbing his bruised posterior that smarted more than his wounded pride.

"Did you hear that?" asked the father bear. His small, round ears pricked up to catch a familiar tune whistled in the distance.

"What?" asked the mother bear.

"Drat! It's that golden-haired girl that keeps getting lost in this forest," warned the father bear, hopping off his chair.

"Oh, not her again!" groaned the baby bear.

"Quick, let's head home! We can secure all the doors and windows before that dreadful child breaks in again," urged the mother bear. She charged off into the forest, the other two following at her heels.

"That was too close!" exclaimed Rose. She had selected the prettiest mare for herself and with a degree of skill, she steered her mount behind Tag's horse.

"Don't think those bears meant us any harm," decided Cankles. "They were probably jus' curious or hungry, smellin' our breakfast from afar."

"Well, we were best to leave," said Tag, bringing his steed to a halt. "There was no point in chancing a bear attack."

"Why are we stopping now?" asked Rose, reining in her mare.

"We must restore these horses to their true and former glory before we encounter other travellers," insisted Tag, dismounting from his stallion.

"What do you mean by that?" queried Rose, patting her mare's neck. "They look absolutely lovely."

"That's the problem. They're looking too lovely," explained Tag, tugging at one of the many pink, satin ribbons and bows woven into his horse's mane and down its tail. "We go no further until we do away with all the frills."

"But why?" asked Rose, bewildered by Tag's strange request.

"Because manly men ride manly steeds. If we wish to be taken seriously and not laughed out of the next town, we must make these horses look like worthy steeds, not pretty little ponies," answered Tag, untying the bows from his stallion's mane.

"Oh, I know all 'bout not being taken seriously an' being laughed out of town," groaned Cankles, dismounting from his horse to remove the adornments. "I quite agree with Master Yairet, no offense to you, Princess."

"Well, I think these bows look wonderful. I refuse to remove them from my horse," defied Rose.

"That's your prerogative," responded Tag, working the braids out of his stallion's mane. "But I will not be caught dead on a horse done up like this."

"It's all right for your mare to look all frilly, being that you're a girlie girl an' all, but us men, we gotta keep our dignity." reasoned Cankles, collecting all the satin ribbons from his mount and Tag's.

"Well, while you two make a big fuss over nothing, I shall water my horse," decided Rose. With a gentle prod of her heels, she urged her mare on to a nearby stream to drink.

When she returned, Tag and Cankles' horses were looking like any other, ordinary white nag this side of Fleetwood. She watched as Cankles collected all the ribbons from the ground, stuffing them into his pack.

"What do you intend to do with them?" queried Rose.

"Don't rightly know jus' yet, but I'm frugal," explained Cankles. "Don't believe in wastin' anything, these fancy ribbons included."

'That explains all the crap you've collected in that shack of a home,' thought Rose. "They are just ordinary ribbons. What other use would they have?"

"I'm jus' thinkin' they might come in handy somewhere along our travels."

"I see…" said Rose, as she thought, *'but not really.'*

"That is much better!" declared Tag, patting his stallion's withers. "Now they look like noble, manly horses, the way horses are meant to look."

"Too bad the same cannot be said of the riders," teased Rose, steering her mare away as Cankles began to laugh aloud.

"Excuse me, but she just insulted you, too!" grunted Tag.

"Suddenly, it doesn't seem so funny," decided Cankles, scratching his head in contemplation.

"It wasn't funny, but who cares?" stated Tag. "At least now, we have achieved a more suitable look for our fine steeds. Let us move on."

"If we keep headin' this way, we'll be out of the forest by late afternoon," assessed Cankles, glancing skyward. "If I remember correctly, there's a town on the outskirts of this forest. We keep headin' eastward 'til nightfall an' we'll get there."

"What is it called?" queried Rose.

"Don't recall, being that there's a few of 'em out that way," replied Cankles. "Jus' remember that it was the closest to this forest an' had an unusual name."

"Then we head to this town," decided Tag. "After all, it is in the general direction of our destination."

"Perhaps we can find a suitable inn for a meal and a place to sleep rather than bedding down with the bugs and slugs?" suggested Rose.

"And just how do you intend to pay?" questioned Tag. "For you didn't wish for a bag of gold along with breakfast, did you?"

"Worry not, I will sell or barter this morning's fine porcelain and silverware for what we need," stated Rose, speaking with utmost confidence, as she glanced over at the silk tablecloth bundled and tied to Cankles' saddle.

"Well, good luck with that," bade Tag, with a doubtful smile. "We shall soon see what kind of bargain you can strike up."

"You sound doubtful I can do this," determined Rose.

"I have no doubt you can strike up a conversation or even strike up a fire now. I just question your negotiating skills as it will take more than a pretty face and a charming smile to deal with the local pawnbroker or any other fellow interested in bargaining with you."

"Oh... so you do think I'm pretty?" probed Rose, smiling inwardly.

"I said it would take more than a pretty face; not that *you have a pretty face*," corrected Tag, his cheeks flushing with embarrassment.

"What do you think?" asked Rose, turning to Cankles for his always candid opinion.

"Oh, you're very pretty, m'lady. An' Master Yairet knows it! He's jus' being shy!"

"Good answer! You may not be smart, but at least you are honest and not blinded by stupidity," praised Rose, giving Cankles a nod of approval.

"I am not shy. I was speaking the truth!" snapped Tag.

"Oh come now, young master. The Princess is beautiful. There's no denying that."

"I will only admit she does not make the average man's eyes bleed, so she is not ugly in the physical sense," said Tag. "The point is, pretty cannot be used as a bargaining tool or to curry a favour in the real world."

"I suppose that's true. At least, it's never worked for me," agreed Cankles. "Most shrewd businessmen can't be swayed by a lady's charm."

"Oh yeah? Well what about this?" said Rose, as her eyes grew large and liquid. The incipient tears magically appeared, brimming her eyes as her quivering lips curled down in the corners to produce the saddest of pouts.

"No! Not that! Not the puppy eyes!" gasped Cankles, turning his head. "Look away, my friend! A face like that can make the hardest of men fall weak to their knees!"

"Yeah, and it can launch a thousand ships and sink them, too," added Tag, in a cynical tone.

"Young master, surely you're moved by this?" asked Cankles, daring to sneak another peek at Rose's pathetic pout.

"Seen it before. Seen it too often," dismissed Tag, with a nonchalant wave of his hand. "You must do better than that, Princess."

"Oh, come now, Master Yairet, you gotta admit, that's pretty cute! Look at those purple eyes."

"*Violet*," corrected Rose, blinking her luxuriant lashes innocently at her comrades.

"Her idea of *cute* has taken on an ugly turn. It no longer works on me," grunted Tag, shrugging his shoulders with indifference.

"Aah! But it used to work!" snipped Rose. "And if men are as gullible in these parts as they are in Cadboll, I suspect I can make good use of this weapon."

"We shall find out soon enough," responded Tag, unleashing a dismal sigh. "Follow me."

"Well…come to T- Toe- Toejam." Cankles struggled to read the sign aloud. "What a strange name."

"*Towgem*," corrected Tag, eyeing the large, wooden sign that pointed the way. "It says: Welcome to Towgem."

"Toe jam, Towgem, either way you say it, I agree with our illiterate friend, here. It is an unusual name no matter how you pronounce it."

"If you remember anything of your history studies, you would remember this town was once a bustling hub for the trade of precious and semi-precious gemstones."

"Bustling?" sniffed Rose, glancing up and down the near-deserted road made all the more desolate under the twilight sky. "I have seen more activity in the palace gardens on a blustery, winter day."

"It is quiet now, but at one time, they say trade in rubies and emeralds was so lucrative, miners carried their gems in wheelbarrows to sell here in town. In turn, the buyers had to tow away their purchases on four-horse wagons, hence the derivative of the name *Towgem*."

"That may be so, but it is hardly the bustling metropolis you made it out to be," stated Rose.

"Over time the mines have been depleted of their treasures, and given that many frequenting this town were transient to begin with, I guess they just headed home," determined Tag, spying several horses tied to a hitching post in front of an inn. Over the doorway, a wooden sign with faded red paint featuring three stylized *R*s read: The Radical Rose Ruby, Public Drinking House & Inn.

"We can spend the night there," said Tag, pointing to the simple, two storey wooden structure.

"Perfect! I like the name, but it can do without the Radical," announced Rose.

"You've yet to see the inside, or the patrons, so the name might be quite fitting," warned Tag.

"I am no longer in my palace, but I still have certain needs. And what I need is to freshen up. I would like to start by washing my dainties."

"You're gonna wash your *unmentionables*?" asked Cankles.

"No! These *dainties*," explained Rose. She waved her digits before his face. Her slender fingers, now smudged with dirt and the palms of her hands grimy with sweat, were the filthiest they had ever been.

"Oh, then go right ahead. You can use the waterin' trough," offered Cankles, pointing to the leaky, wooden container under the hitching post.

"I am not about to wash my hands in water contaminated by animals," protested Rose, her nose wrinkling in disgust.

Cankles gazed into the trough as he noted, "Jus' some dust an' horse slobber floatin' in there. That's all. Other than that, it's fine."

"Maybe for you," grunted Rose, turning her nose up at the offer. "I am going inside. I am in need of a privy chamber. There must be proper facilities inside."

All heads, except for those of the utterly inebriated, gazed up with torpid interest as the trio entered through the gray cloud of pipe smoke. The aromatic haze swirled around them, escaping through the open door to taint the fresh, evening air.

Rose fanned away the smog. Spotting the bar, she marched through the maze of tables and chairs to the innkeeper as he busily catered to his patrons.

"Excuse me, sir. Do you have any rooms available on this night?" asked Rose.

"This night, an' every other, young miss. Are they with you?" questioned the innkeeper, eyeing this peasant girl before glancing over at her male companions.

"Unfortunately, yes."

"Well, there's a house of ill-repute just down the road. You best take your business there, missy. No strumpets an' trollops allowed. I'm tryin' to run a decent, family-type inn."

"How dare you?" gasped Rose, appalled by his insinuation. "I will have you know, I am a – "

Tag's hand slapped over her mouth. "She's a bit confused, that's what! We need two separate rooms, please."

"Oh, I see," said the innkeeper, wiping the counter with a damp rag. "One for your friend, an' one for you an' your missus."

"Now you are the confused one!" rebuked Rose, shuddering in

disgust as her thumb jabbed over her shoulder at Tag. "He is not even my type, let alone in the same class as me."

The innkeeper stopped working to scrutinize the young couple. Beneath his thick walrus moustache, his lips appeared not to move as he commented, "Could be that my eyes deceive me, but I'd say this young fellow is better dressed than you are, missy. If anything, he's more fashionable. No offence, but that frock went out of style years ago."

"Never mind that!" snapped Rose. "I need two rooms, one for me and one for them to share. Preferably, on the opposite sides of this building."

"I've got plenty of rooms," responded the man, filling a mug to overflowing before sliding it down the bar to a thirsty patron. "You can take your pick."

"Wonderful!" stated Rose.

"Are you plannin' to eat an' drink here? Or you jus' needin' a room for the night?" questioned the man.

"Why?" asked Rose.

"If you patronize my fine establishment, usin' all its amenities to its fullest, I can run a tab for you an' maybe even give you a bit of a discount. Plus, you can either pay for everything in one shot prior to departure, or you can pay as you go. Personally, I don't care either way, jus' as long as you pay."

Before Cankles could reveal they had no money, Rose spoke up, "I will pay in the morning, my good man. For now, where are the rooms. I wish to use your facilities before we order some dinner."

"*Facilities?*" repeated the man. He stared at her. His bushy brows that were almost as dense as his moustache furrowed in curiosity.

"You know? The privy, where one can take care of *personal business*," she whispered discreetly.

"Oh, that!" said the innkeeper, as he nodded in understanding. "The *facility* is 'round the back."

"The back of the rooms?" queried Rose.

"No, there's only one an' it's around the back of the inn," answered the man, thrusting his thumb over his shoulder to point at the exit door. "Straight out an' to your left."

"*Outside?* On the street?" gasped Rose, appalled by this news.

"Actually, it's in a back alley an' I'm supposin' there's a good reason why it's called an outhouse to begin with."

"What about a private chamber?" asked Rose.

"Today's your lucky day, young miss! This one's got a door; just put on this afternoon with a latch on the inside, so you can have all the privacy you want. But here, you best take this lamp if you're plannin' to close the door. It can get pretty dark in there an' you wouldn't want to be havin' an accident."

"What do you mean? What kind of accident?"

"Oh, I don't know... Maybe fallin' into a hole or something like that," said the innkeeper, passing her a small lamp.

"Do you need an escort, m'lady?" asked Cankles, offering his arm.

"That will not be necessary," said Rose, heaving a dismal sigh. "I think I can manage."

"I certainly hope so," grunted Tag, sitting on a tall, wooden stool at the bar. "Heaven help us if you can't!"

"Hmph! Still not funny," snapped Rose, as she took the lamp from the innkeeper's hand. Weaving her way through the drunken patrons, she made a concerted effort not to brush up against any of these inebriated, slovenly commoners as she exited through the back door.

Just as the man had said, to her left was the door to the outhouse. It had a small, crescent moon cut into it. Rose was not sure if it was meant to be some kind of adornment to allow light into this dimly lit room or if it was there as a vent for the circulation of air in these stifling confines.

Pulling on the door, it refused to budge, sticking to the frame.

"Stupid thing!" Rose cursed under her breath. Taking a firm hold, she gave it a hard yank, wrenching it free.

She was almost bowled over, but it was not by the force of the door flying open. The stomach-churning, putrid stench of human excrement and urine washed over her like an invisible tidal wave, assaulting her senses as never before. Her eyes watered and she gagged, fighting the urge to vomit. Her hand flew up over her mouth and nose in a futile bid to filter out the malodourous reek pooling inside this privy. It was as though it had been building up, waiting to escape and smother any foolish soul bold enough to venture inside.

Rose held up the lamp, peering inside as the little flame illuminated the tiny room. The buzz of flies winging in and out of the hole cut into a rough, sliver-laden, bench-like seat did nothing to put her at ease.

"I can do this," decided the Princess, as she gathered up her courage. With grim resolve, she untied the apron strings. Wrapping this fabric around her mouth and nose, the lower half of her face looked mummified. She drew in a deep breath to fill her lungs with fresh air before venturing inside. As the door slammed behind her, she prayed this breath would last the duration as she tried not to gaze into the dark, stinking hole.

❁ ❁ ❁

A large, blackened pot filled with lamb stew bubbled as Cankles stared into it. He inhaled the tantalizing aroma as the innkeeper lifted the lid for his consideration.

"Would you gents care to order some dinner?" asked the innkeeper, as a barmaid picked up a tray of bread and stew to deliver to a patron.

"We'll be orderin' food, but we'll wait for our friend first," answered Cankles, his mouth salivating as the enticing scent wafted by him.

"If not food, can I interest you in a drink or two?" he proffered. "I've got stout, ale, wine an' spirits, but I don't have mead, so don't bother askin' for it."

"Ale sounds good," decided Tag.

"Three ales coming up!" announced the innkeeper, doubling as the barkeep. "Jus' give me a chance to roll in a full keg. Don't want to be servin' you the dregs at the bottom of this one."

"You better make it two ales and one glass of wine," decided Tag.

"Ale an' wine it'll be."

Tag and Cankles watched as he lifted the keg, the remaining contents sloshing about as he removed it.

As he disappeared, rolling the empty barrel outside to make room, a patron casually tottered up to the end of the bar. She wavered unsteadily in tight-fitting shoes with dangerously high, stacked heels. Both Tag and Cankles took immediate notice of her, but not because she was a stunning beauty. They caught sight of her from the corners of their eyes as she quaffed down her ale. Slamming the mug onto the bar to let the innkeeper know she was done and ready for another, her gravelly voice croaked, "So, what's a girl gotta do for a drink 'round here?"

This glimpse was more than enough for Tag. By her ghastly, painted face and the vermillion-coloured cream smeared unevenly in a futile bid to make her dried, cracked lips look like tantalizing berries ripe for the picking, there was no mistaking she was a lady of the evening. But for this one, her evening had come and gone a long time ago.

The bright shades of blue and green garishly adorning each baggy eyelid would be the envy of every peacock around. Tag was certain the thick layer of make-up plastered haphazardly over her face only served to accentuate every crease, wrinkle and fold. It either hid her true years or exaggerated them. She had to be well into her sixties, if not older.

Tag averted his eyes, not so much out of politeness, but because they were repulsed by what they saw. The sight of the woman's low-cut, tight-fitting bodice cinched to accentuate her breasts in all their former glory, failed to entice. By what Tag could see, she was far from voluptuous; just very top-heavy like an upside-down pear. He was sure she'd fall over if she didn't have a bar or wall to lean against. Her ample breasts overflowed as though she was trying to hide two bald, twin infants down her top. By the spillage, he was certain it was a major undertaking to stuff those puppies into the bodice of her gown and it was probably just as difficult to keep them contained.

The woman eyed both Tag and Cankles before setting her sights on the youngest of the pair.

"I think she's keen on you," noted Cankles, spying the less-than-desirable patron as she stared hungrily at his comrade.

Tag shuddered, feeling her eyes undress him. "Stop staring at her! That's a sure invitation to join us."

"She looks friendly 'nough," commented Cankles, giving her a courteous nod of his head.

"Too friendly for my liking! Now stop looking her way," ordered Tag, tugging at Cankles' vest. He spied her pulling out a small knife from her handbag. "Bloody hell! Stop looking or she'll use that blade on us."

"Don't think so," countered Cankles. "She's picking her teeth with it, that's all."

"Now there's a lovely sight," groaned Tag.

"She's probably tryin' to make herself look more presentable before she comes over," whispered Cankles.

"I don't want her coming over," stated Tag. He could feel her ravenous eyes eating him up. She was like a beggar at a banquet, and he was about to become her main course. Tag was ready to bolt to his room when the innkeeper returned with a full keg of ale.

"I thought this was a family-type business; *'no strumpets and trollops allowed'* you said," reminded Tag, as he whispered to the innkeeper.

"So I did. What of it?" he grunted, as he hoisted the heavy keg onto the stand, adjusting it so the spigot was at the bottom for easy pouring.

"What is *that* woman doing in here?" asked Tag, pointing at the patron leaning against the bar.

They watched as she tucked her knife away. It disappeared between the quivering, white mounds of her breasts as her slug-like tongue slowly dragged over her cracked, red lips to moisten and plump them up for the benefit of the male patrons.

"This *is* a family business. She's my sister. I make an exception for her. The old girl's a bit long-in-the-tooth an' can do without the competition."

Tag grimaced in revulsion as the woman snorted loudly to clear her throat. The loose, wrinkled skin wobbled as the muscles around her neck contorted, tightening as she worked up what seemed to be an enormous hairball, had she been a cat. With great accuracy and a loud *ping* she spat, lobbing the wad of mucous and saliva into the metal spittoon by her feet.

"Argh!" groaned Tag, averting his eyes, but too late. "That was disgusting!"

"Don't be so hard on her, Master Yairet. She's jus' a diamond in the rough," decided Cankles. He spied her wiping her chin with the back of her liver-spotted hand.

"I don't mean to be rude, but a lump of coal is more like it," whispered Tag. "Let's get out of here, before she decides to make friends with us."

"No need to leave so soon! Drink some of this," offered the innkeeper, sliding two full pints of ale before Tag and his comrade. "It's a sure cure for the uglies!"

"What do you mean?" asked Cankles.

"The more you drink, the less ugly she becomes!" He responded with a wink of his eye. "In no time, she'll be a right bit o' totty, if you get my meanin'?"

"This is your sister you're speaking of," reminded Tag.

"So? Nothing wrong with helpin' the family along," insisted the innkeeper, his broad shoulders shrugging with indifference.

"You are doing her no favour, sir. Perhaps, you'd be better off allowing her to work the bar than the patrons," suggested Tag.

"Already tried that. Believe me, it's better to keep her on that side of the counter. She ended up drinkin' way more than she ever made."

Just as the woman was about to make her move, Rose returned from her outhouse adventure. She was grumbling in discontent over the foul conditions and the potential for slivers when Tag grabbed her, pulling the Princess between them. He was never so glad to see Rose.

"She's with us," explained Tag, using the Princess like she was a shield to ward away unwanted tarts, evil harlots and old women on the prowl.

The Princess eyed this stranger, amazed and disgusted all at once, to see this gaudy display of vanity. It was a desperate attempt at recapturing a level of youthful womanhood that had reached its peak a long time ago, and now, it was downhill all the way.

"Well, little poppet, aren't you the lucky one!" growled the woman, taking a drunken, faltering step back before staggering two steps forward.

"What is she talking about?" asked Rose.

"Who can say? It's obvious she's drunk," whispered Tag, pulling Rose closer.

"Jus' 'cause you're a pretty, young thing now, that don't mean it's gonna last forever," hiccupped the woman, as she shook a balled fist at her competition. "One day, you'll be the one paying for their attention."

"Are you mad? Enough of this crazy talk! Be gone with you!" snapped Rose, turning her nose up at the inebriated patron. "She speaks as though I am a harlot."

"That's because she thinks you are," confirmed Cankles, taking a quick swig of ale.

"*What?*" gasped Rose, as her face was flushed with anger. "Look here you old, painted hussy! I am neither a tart, a trollop, nor am I a strumpet! I am a lady of refined breeding and culture, so bugger off, before this *little poppet* pops you one in that ugly, wrinkled mug!"

"Oooh! That's real ladylike for one of refined breedin'!" snorted the woman. "Well, missy, youth got nothing over experience! An' I got plenty of it!"

"So much so, you're all worn out, you old nag!" snipped Rose. "And you know what they do to horses that have outlived their usefulness, don't you?"

"Now, now! Why can't we all be friends an' jus' get along?" asked Cankles, hoping to ease tensions as Rose and the woman prepared to unleash another verbal volley.

"Fine!" snapped Rose. She shoved Cankles toward her drunken adversary. "You go right ahead. Make friends with that floozie!"

Cankles stumbled, tripping over his feet. He fell forward into the waiting arms of Rose's rival.

To the amazement of all, he landed against the woman's breasts, only to bounce off them like they were cushiony bags of air. Before he could flee, the woman threw her arms around him, thrusting his startled face into the valley between her heaving breasts. The sagging skin and flesh hanging from her upper arms jiggled and slapped against Cankles' face. This excess continued to quiver like flabby chicken wings, even after she stopped moving.

Cankles struggled to pry himself free as this cleavage of doom threatened to smother him.

"Why did you do that?" gasped Tag, staring in disbelief as the woman attempted to drag Cankles off to her lair.

"Why do you ask? Were you hoping I would throw *you* to that beast instead?"

"Of course not! But you didn't have to sacrifice Cankles like that," groaned Tag, dashing to his friend's aid.

"Fine! Then fight her off yourself!" Rose snapped in defiance as she plopped down onto a barstool.

"Can't!" hollered Cankles, gasping for a breath of air. "She's a lady. Can't hit a lady."

"Well, she's not really a lady, but still, we can't fight her," explained Tag, as he yelped in surprise.

As old and inebriated as she was, this woman was unnaturally spry as she set her sight and clutches on Tag.

He winced in pain as her hand wrapped around his head, smooshing his face against her corpulent bosom as he struggled to be free.

"Bloody hell! Don't just stand there watching!" shouted Tag.

"If I help you, you'll owe me!" declared Rose.

"Gladly!" hollered Tag, fighting to pry his head free from this woman's tenacious grasp.

"All right, you old cow!" shouted Rose, as she hopped off the barstool to confront her nemesis. "Unhand them both!"

"You want 'em, come an' get em!" She plastered their flushed faces to her breasts as she issued a challenge.

"Oh, you'll be sorry you ever confronted me!" snapped the Princess.

"If I win, I get to have 'em both!" declared the woman, shoving Tag and Cankles to the floor as she readied for a fight.

"They're not much of a prize, but you're on!" declared Rose, pushing up the sleeves of her frock as she stepped over her male comrades.

"No!" protested Tag, fearful of Rose's defeat. "It's a bad deal!"

"Very bad!" agreed Cankles, scrambling to his feet.

"Bloody hell!" cursed the innkeeper, leaning over the bar to intervene. "Not in here! No fighting allowed!"

His words went ignored as his sister adopted a defensive stance. She hiked up the hem of her gown in preparation for a grand battle, but in doing so, she gave the patrons more to see than they bargained for. The sight of her legs, the lumps of cellulite that protruded like white, blubbery nodules bulging from the holes and tears of her tights and the blue spider-webbing of varicose veins showing through, caused every man, Cankles and Tag included, to avert their eyes as they simultaneously groaned in disgust.

"Eeew! You bloody well better win!" hollered Tag, urging Rose on as she sized up her drunken foe.

"Catfight!" hollered one of the patrons, as he motioned for all to make room.

Every table within body-throwing distance was instantly cleared as customers snatched up their mugs of ale, scurrying off to observe and cheer from a safe distance.

With grim determination, Rose prepared to attack. She bared her talons. Each finger tipped with a manicured nail curled, ready to take a swipe at her adversary as she hissed and meowed.

"What are you doing?" asked Tag, mystified by the Princess' bizarre behaviour.

"You heard the man! He said it's a catfight. Ergo, I am fighting like a cat," responded Rose. A hiss and a guttural growl rumbled forth like she was an enraged feline that had been tossed into a sack, thrown into a tub of ice water, then set free.

In a savage, animalistic display of her own, the old woman displayed her weapons. The chewed-to-the-quick fingernails hardly posed a danger when paired with her teeth. Gnashing, jagged rows of yellowed teeth, some black and chipped, spaced by intermittent gaps on her shrinking gums made her look about as threatening as an old cougar that would be forced to gum its prey to death.

"You're in for it now, you old biddy!" snarled Rose, circling in closer to mount her attack.

"That's what you think, you little trollop!" growled the woman, hobbling in to make her move first.

"Enough!" hollered the innkeeper. He stood on the bar, a bucket of dirty dishwater ready to pitch at his sister. "Enough, Gertie! Why must you go pickin' a fight with every female customer comin' here! You're bad for business, sister or not! Now, you behave or get out!"

"Aww, c'mon!" whined Gertie. "You wouldn't dare!"

"Don't you go testin' me or I will!" vowed her agitated brother. He hoisted the bucket up a little higher to make his intentions clear.

"How can you side with a stranger over your own kin?" she whined in disappointment.

"Easy! She's a paying customer, while you jus' scare my customers away."

"Fine! I'll be leavin' then!" snorted the woman, using her hands to hoist her sagging breasts up to their original, but exaggerated state.

"Right about now, that isn't such a bad thing!" the innkeeper hollered behind his sister as she wobbled out the door.

"And do not think of coming back, not while I am still here!"

shouted Rose, waving an angry fist at her foe.

"Phew! That was a close one!" gasped Tag, breathing a sigh of relief.

"Much too close for my liking," groaned Cankles, rubbing his sore nose where it was mashed up against the woman's blubbery cleavage. "We owe you our lives, m'lady!"

"I wouldn't go as far as that," interjected Tag, scrambling back onto his barstool.

"That is correct! If you be owing me, then I would want something of value. Something that will not depreciate over time," teased Rose.

"Oh, great! Just what will you be wanting from us?" queried Tag, seeing the glint in her eyes.

"I will have to think on it, but for now, let me just say, you owe me *BIG* time!"

"Speakin' of owin'," said the innkeeper. "Your little altercation sent some of my frightened patrons fleein' into the night before paying for their drinks. I'm thinkin' you owe me some kind of compensation, missy."

"Absolutely," agreed Rose. "In fact, why do we not square up now? Drinks, meals *and* rooms!"

"Fine by me!" declared the man. "So, how do you intend to pay? With gems or coins?"

"With this," answered Rose, motioning Cankles to carefully place the silk tablecloth onto the bar. Its contents rattled and clattered as it came to rest on the counter.

Eyeing the big bundle, the innkeeper spoke up, "Don't sound like gemstones or coins."

"What I have in here is better. In fact, it will only serve to elevate the status of your establishment," promised Rose, untying the knot securing the tablecloth.

"What is it?" questioned the man, eager to take a peek.

Rose dropped the four corners of the silk cloth to reveal silver trays and serving platters, silver cutlery and fine porcelain plates and bowls with a matching tea set.

"Behold! Look upon these wondrous treasures!" exclaimed Rose, beaming with pride.

"And what am I supposed to do with this stuff?"

"When we first entered, you were boasting about your fine food and drinks," reminded Rose.

"So?"

"Here is a chance to serve your goods on fine dinnerware that will announce to the world how truly magnificent your establishment is!"

insisted the Princess. "I am sure the competition to lure prospective customers to your inn is stiff at the best of times. Think of how the finest silverware and porcelain can be used to draw the higher echelon of society into your respected establishment."

"This is Towgem we're speaking of," reminded the innkeeper.

"Yes! And no longer will you draw ruffians and scoundrels, the dregs of society, off the streets. Only the upscale merchants coming through this town, those with money to spend, will flock to your inn to indulge in the taste of the high life."

"You think so?"

"Oh, I know so!" confirmed the Princess. "The public is starving for the finer things in life. If you are the only one in town to offer it, of course they will come!"

The innkeeper scrutinized the collection of silver and porcelain. He examined each item with a critical eye as Cankles and Tag gulped down their ale in case Rose's bid at negotiations failed.

"I've got to admit, these are pretty fine pieces, but I'm thinking it's too fine for an inn like this."

"There is no such thing as *too fine*," insisted Rose. "Here is a chance to raise the standards, to make your inn stand out from all the others in this hovel of a town."

"I've always managed to get by," responded the innkeeper, mulling over this deal.

"Who wants to just *get by*? We are talking about exploiting a whole new level of customers who are clamouring for better quality and service! This is your chance to rake in the big money."

"Don't know…" muttered the innkeeper.

"But I do! And you best take advantage of this offer if you are as smart as I think you are," urged Rose.

"I'm smart enough to know when someone's tryin' to push me into a deal I shouldn't be makin', young miss."

"Oh, do not be silly, my good man! See for yourself!" Rose snatched a food tray from a barmaid as she passed by. On this well-worn, wooden tray were two servings of fried sausages and boiled potatoes on plain, earthenware plates. She arranged one meal on a porcelain plate, positioning it on a silver-serving platter while the other grew cold on the cracked plate sitting on the wooden tray. "Now, you tell me: Two identical meals, but which one looks more appetizing to you?"

"I gotta admit, that does look more appealing on the fancy plate, but I don't know…"

"Maybe you should stop. Pay him with money tonight," urged Tag.

"You have money?" questioned the innkeeper, waving the barmaid back to pick up her order for delivery to the hungry customers.

"After midnight we will," admitted Tag.

"But, you are better off accepting these fine pieces of silverware and porcelain," insisted Rose. "I bet there is not one place in this entire town where you can purchase such exquisite pieces no matter how much money you have."

"True…"

"Give it up, Princess," whispered Tag.

"Young Master Yairet is quite right, m'lady," agreed Cankles. "This fellow's a shrewd businessman. He can't be swayed."

"Aaah, but he will be swayed by this!" whispered Rose.

Cankles and Tag knew what was coming next.

"Please kind sir, these are rare and valuable heirlooms I am made to part with. I can think of no better place for them than your fine establishment," insisted Rose, her voice pleading. Her eyes became large and liquid as her lower lip protruded in a sad pout. She peered up at the man, giving him the saddest puppy eyes she could muster.

"Arrgh! I'll take 'em!" snapped the innkeeper. Breaking down after gazing upon her pathetic face, he still attempted to play the part of the clever negotiator. "But only if I get the tablecloth, too!"

"You drive a hard bargain, sir! This is the finest quality silk damask, but I am willing to part with it as a gesture of good will," offered Rose. "Consider it a deal!"

"Deal!" agreed the innkeeper, gathering up his new possessions.

Tag and Cankles sat there, dumbfounded. Rose proved she was indeed able to strike up a bargain, albeit employing methods that men could not and would not use as leverage.

"And as I know the true worth of these fine items, bring us your best meal and finest wine before we retire for the night, my good man!" ordered Rose.

11

My Kingdom for Some Cheese!

Dawn came early as the trio led their horses down the main street. All was quiet. The only sound was the crowing of a rooster at a distant farm as it greeted the morning sun.

"It would have been nice to have rested a little longer," groaned Rose, yawning as the mare's gentle, rolling gait threatened to rock her back to sleep.

"I couldn't agree more, but we're on a mission," reminded Tag, coaxing his mount on. "You can sleep all you want once we break this curse."

"It's best to get an early start," insisted Cankles. "We still have far to travel."

"I suppose you are right," conceded Rose, shaking off her drowsiness. "If it means returning to the palace in time for my birthday gala, it will be worth it."

"Hate to be the bearer of bad tidings, but there's a good chance even if we are unhampered in our travels and have no difficulty in finding that locket of yours, there is a very real possibility we will not return in time," informed Tag.

"Are you saying this because it is true, or because you are mad at me about the gold coins disappearing after I fell asleep?" probed Rose.

"Unfortunately, the distance we're made to travel speaks for itself. As for being mad, what's the point?" responded Tag, with a shrug of his shoulders.

"The point is, the money I had wished for has all but disappeared."

"It was not as though it was deliberate on your part," reasoned Tag. "If anything, it would appear fate, or your conscience, felt you were entitled to only a fraction of what you had originally wished for."

"I'm jus' grateful we still have some coins to speak of," said Cankles, hoping to nip a potential argument in the bud. "Plus, we still have one wish left, should we need it."

"Quite right, my friend," agreed Tag. "As long the Princess doesn't nod off and squander a wish if she dreams again, we should be fine."

"Fear not! I am not about to fall asleep any time soon," promised Rose, her hand lightly slapping her face to prove she was wide-awake. "And we can take advantage of the last wish later so it does not go to waste."

"That's the plan, as long as a situation does not arise forcing us to use it," said Tag.

"Oh, come now! What can happen?" asked the Princess, urging her mare on to follow Tag's steed.

ॐ ॐ ॐ

"Are you positive we are heading in the right direction?" questioned Rose, as she stared at the less-than-welcoming sign posted on the roadside.

"Of course we are," assured Tag. "We've been travelling east since early this morning."

"It does not feel like that," argued the Princess.

"Only because the road we travelled had many twists and turns, but I assure you, we're heading the right way."

"I would feel more confident if you had only stopped to ask for directions," said Rose.

"Real men don't ask for directions," retorted Tag.

"Fine, but what is your excuse?" teased Rose.

"Ha, ha!" grunted Tag, in mock laughter. "If you have to ask for directions, then it only confirms you are truly and surely lost. As far as I'm concerned, we are heading in the correct, *general* direction."

"Yes, so *general*, we are lost," surmised Rose.

"When you think about it, we don't need exact directions until we get to the Land of Big. Once there, we'll be needin' a concise location to find your locket," reminded Cankles.

"I take it, we must cross this country to get there," determined Rose. She gazed at the road sign that had been defaced by vandals.

"I wonder what happened here?" asked Cankles. He noticed the tip of a knife had crudely modified the country's name of Axalon. The letter *T* was added to the beginning of the word while the *n* had been scratched out and replaced by another *t*.

"*Entering the Kingdom of Taxalot*." Tag read aloud. His eyes squinted to read the fine print etched beneath these words that probably went unnoticed by most. "Judging by this sign, the vandals were undoubtedly disgruntled citizens."

"Why? What's it say?" asked Cankles.

"Notice to all: Please report to the nearest Visitors' Center before proceeding any further. Be prepared to report commercial goods for sale or barter to assess Services & Goods Tax. Transportation Tax will be assessed upon filing a destination travel log. Payment of entry toll is applied on a per head basis (expectant women will pay on a sliding scale based on due date and possibility of multiple births). Please pay departure tax upon leaving Axalon. The local tax collector will enforce new taxes, levies and surcharges as they are enacted. Failure to comply will result in a fine payable to the tax collector on behalf of HRH King Maxmillian III."

"Perhaps this too was added by the vandal," said Cankles.

"No simpleton vandal is capable of thinking up a notice like this," disputed Rose. "I recognize the language. It is obviously a decree set forth by the ruler of this nation."

"My goodness!" exclaimed Cankles. "If that's so, it appears this King has taxes for his taxes."

"Sounds like a greedy bugger to me," decided Tag, shaking his head in disgust. "It's no wonder someone renamed the country Taxalot!"

"Do not be so quick to judge King Maxmillian," reprimanded Rose. "You have no idea how costly it can be to administer to the needs of a country."

"I can understand taxing the people within reason, but it can be to the ruin of an entire nation if it is done indiscriminately, and for the sole purpose of allowing the King to live an excessive lifestyle," argued her jester.

"Poor, poor gullible Tag," lamented the Princess, as she gave her head a dismal shake. "There is so much you do not understand. Just because the man is a king, it does not mean his need to tax his subjects is based on avarice."

"Ava- what?" repeated Cankles, frowning in curiosity.

"Avarice. It means to be motivated by greed," explained Tag.

"Whatever the case, we must enter this Axalon or Taxalot or whatever you want to call this kingdom," stated Rose.

"If we are not taxed to death and the gold pieces we have adequately covers our costs, we should be fine," decided Tag.

"Can that truly happen?" asked Cankles, a look of genuine concern contorting his haggard face. "Being taxed to death, that is?"

"Sure it can, especially if you can't come up with the money to pay the taxes immediately," responded Tag. "If you can't pay, off to prison you'll go! Confinement in a dank, dark dungeon would do the average person in, if not physically, then certainly mentally, in a short span of time."

"What a bunch of malarkey!" disputed Rose. "If anything, I am sure King Maxmillian can be reasoned with. Perhaps he is new to the throne and just requires the advice of another royal to provide him with some sound guidance."

"Funny you should say that. I don't see your mother or father anywhere," snorted Tag, glancing about.

"That was not funny!" snapped Rose, scowling at her comrade.

"It was not meant to be," grunted Tag. "As far as I'm concerned, the only advice you can share is a lesson in world domination."

"Perhaps we should venture on," suggested Cankles, hoping to circumvent an argument. "We should go to this Visitors' Center before another tax law is enacted an' we're forced to pay even more."

"Quite right, my friend," agreed Tag, coaxing his steed on down the road. "Follow me."

Less than a half league from the sign posting the way into the heart of Axalon, a small hut marked *Visitors' Center* sat smack-dab in the middle of the road so it could not be ignored, even if one tried. And if one did, two soldiers standing guard on either side of this wooden structure steered all comers inside. On the door hung a small sign: *Always Open for Business.*

Sensing the two men armed with pikes and stationed to this post were in no mood to deal with tax evaders, the trio dismounted. Tying the reins of their horses onto the hitching post, Tag, Cankles and Rose wandered into this small building. Immediately, a wiry, old man in an ill-fitting suit peered up from his ledger.

"Good morning, sir," greeted Tag. "I understand we are to report here if we wish to travel through Taxa – I mean, Axalon."

"That is correct, young man," replied the tax collector, dipping the nib of his quill into the inkwell in preparation to record his calculations.

"Are you citizens of Axalon or visitors?"

"We are just passing through," answered Rose.

"Visitors…" muttered the man, jotting this detail down.

"Does it make a difference?" queried Tag.

"Oh, most definitely! If you're visiting, you're taxed a set amount per person/per night that you intend to be here."

"That can be costly," determined Tag.

"Not really," countered the man. "If you're a citizen, you are only taxed if you are bringing items in for sale or if you've purchased something from a neighbouring country. Depending on what you bought or what you intend to sell, it can cost much more!"

"Then we shall pay this tax and be on our way," said Rose.

"First, do you travel by foot or by horse?"

"Why?" asked Cankles.

"If you travel by foot and you know how far you're going, the tax is far less than to go the same distance on horseback."

"What?" gasped Tag, shaking his head in disbelief. "But the distance to our destination is the same no matter how we get there."

"Transportation taxes, my good man! These roads cost money to maintain. Wagons and carriages, high hoof traffic all takes their toll on our roadways. It's not as though they'll fix themselves."

"Three horses," informed Rose, hoping for nothing more than to be on her way.

"Three, it is! Now, do you have any goods you will be selling while in Axalon?"

"We have nothing we wish to sell," responded Tag.

"Do you intend to buy anything while you're here?"

"Not that we can think of," answered Rose.

"Not even a meal or a drink? A room at the local inn?" queried the tax collector, dabbing the nib into the inkwell once more.

"No. So you cannot tax us for that," replied Tag, hoping to save some money by spending this night under the stars.

"Then I will have to tax you for *not* using our amenities."

"What?" gasped the trio, baffled by this news.

"It's a new tariff just made into law yesterday by King Maxmillian. If you do nothing to support the local economy, we are forced to take appropriate action by imposing the *non-user* tax."

"If you call squeezing blood from a stone taking appropriate action, then you may as well keep squeezing," grunted Tag, shaking his head in dismay.

"That was quite amusing," noted the man, unmoved by Tag's sarcasm. "Just keep in mind it is meant to *encourage* visitors to loosen their purse strings while travelling through Axalon. Share the wealth, so to speak."

"Rob us blind is more like it," Rose muttered beneath her breath.

"The next thing you'll tell us is your King will tax us for the air we breathe!" grumbled Tag.

"He already tried that once, but it didn't go over very well at all. Had people holding their breaths 'til they were blue in the face just to reduce their taxes. A few even died on the first day he decreed it to be law. It was their way of protesting this tax and eventually it worked when the King realized what was happening."

"That his subjects were dying?" asked Rose.

"That... and if they died, ultimately, there'd be less in the way of taxes to collect, not counting the death tax, of course!" admitted the man.

"Good gracious! Let us square up on what taxes we owe before we are subjected to more," suggested Tag.

The tax collector's hunched back straightened upon hearing the delightful jingling of coins in the burgundy, draw-string bag Rose held in her hand.

"Hey! Look at this," called Cankles, pointing up at an etching nailed onto the wall. Above a wooden display rack containing neatly folded parchments featuring some of Axalon's favourite tourist spots, a reward was posted for information leading to the return of Princess Rose-alyn of Fleetwood.

Tag glanced up as Rose paid the man. His eyes opened wide in disbelief as he immediately recognized the drawing of the young lady as being the one in his company. The likeness to Rose, right down to her sour pout was unmistakable.

"This is not good," groaned Tag, scrutinizing her image, and then the smaller one below.

"I'd say it is," contested Cankles, admiring the artwork. "It's a very good likeness of the Princess. An' if I didn't know better, I'd say this young fella looks just like you, Master Yairet."

"I'm not speaking of the quality of the etchings. It says I was the last one to be seen with the Princess and I might somehow be implicated in her disappearance," explained Tag, his hand smacking his forehead in frustration.

"Oh my! I suppose that's not good at all," decided Cankles.

"Never mind that, I look nothing at all like that drawing!" snapped Rose, her brows furrowing in anger. "When I get back, I will see to it that hack of an artist gets the boot!"

"Here's something else to get your knickers in a twist about," noted Tag, reading the print. "Your parents are only offering a *quarter* of your weight in gold for your safe return."

"That is an insult, an outrageous insult! They know I am worth much more than that!"

"Did you not say one of your original wishes was to have the King and Queen basically ignore you?" questioned Tag. "That you even went as far as trading away their love for your deal with the Dream Merchant?"

"Yes... So what?" grumbled the Princess.

"If that is so, it stands to reason why they are willing to pay a minimal reward for your return. It is merely motivated by your father's need to secure the family's place in the monarchy," informed Tag. "If it was motivated by love, he and your mother would spare no expense to secure your safe return. King William would even mount a personal campaign to see you found."

"Well, this stinks..." whimpered Rose. Her eyes welled with tears upon realizing what she had dealt away.

Spying these incipient tears, Tag knew that this time, they were not feigned. His initial feeling was that of spite, for the Princess had brought this upon herself, but feelings of pity tugged at his heart. He knew what it was like to be deprived of a parent's love, having lost both his mother and father at an early age, then again, he never wished for this the way Rose did.

As that first tear tumbled down her cheek, Tag's conscience forced him to swallow his bitterness. "Well, I suppose we'll have to set things right again by breaking this curse to get you back into the palace."

"So you are still willing to help me?" sniffled Rose, blotting away her tears.

"Don't jump to the wrong conclusion, Princess. I'm only doing this because it will mean reclaiming my father's sword."

"I do not care what your motivation is. I just need to get my heart back."

"Then let's be on our way, Princess," suggested Cankles. "Your locket awaits you somewhere to the east."

"Whoa! Hold on here," ordered the tax collector, raising his bony, ink-stained hands. "Did I hear you correctly? Are you the one on that poster?"

"What of it?" questioned Rose, staring suspiciously at the man.

"Well, the reward, of course! If there is money to be had, King Maxmillian will be the one to claim it."

"Oh, no, no, no!" declared the Princess, taking a cautious step away. "We are on an important quest. I am not about to go back now, nor can we be detained in any manner."

"We have paid our taxes so there is no need to hold us here," reminded Tag.

"Oh yes, there is," assured the man, motioning the trio to stop.

"I will give you all my remaining money if you let us go on our way," offered Rose, holding up the bag with its last pieces of gold.

"Are you bribing a government official?" gasped the tax collector.

"Think of it as a business deal," negotiated Rose, giving him a shrewd smile and a wink of her eye.

"Well, I am shocked and appalled!"

"Bloody hell, Princess!" cursed Tag. "Now he'll probably fine you for attempting to bribe a public servant."

"Oh, it's not that! I'd be a poor businessman if I were to accept this *deal.* Any fool can see this puny bag of gold being *offered* is a mere pittance against her weight."

"Are you saying I am fat!" snapped Rose, her voice flared with indignation.

"To the contrary! In my opinion, you can stand to put some meat on those bones, but what I'm saying is, King William's reward is much more than what you offered," explained the tax collector.

"Well, if you refuse to take it, you cannot hold us here," decided Tag, steering Cankles and Rose to the door.

"I will not hold you," agreed the man. Reaching for a brass bell, he sounded the alarm. "However, they will."

Backing into the sharp point of a pike, Tag froze. He glanced over his shoulder to spy upon one soldier as the other turned his weapon on Rose and Cankles.

"On your knees! Bow before the King," ordered the soldier, shoving Tag and Cankles to the floor. They knelt down on a plush wool rug awash in rich colours to match those of the huge, elaborate tapestries adorning the walls.

"They can scrape, grovel *and* bow for all I care," stated Rose, pointing to her companions. "However, I am a princess. I am willing to curtsy before another royal, but that is the extent of it."

"Charming!" snorted the King of Axalon. His fleshy jowls continued to quiver even after he finished speaking. He scrutinized the girl through eyes made all the more beady by the thick, fatty pads of his eyelids.

"Well, thank you," responded Rose, as she stared back at her host. The flames from the many gold candelabras suspended from the high ceiling cast a far-from-flattering light on his porcine features.

"He was being sarcastic," whispered Tag, as he and Cankles remained kneeling.

"I hardly think so," disputed Rose. "Just hold your tongue. I will deal with him, being that we speak the same language."

"Oh great!" grumbled Tag. "Who knew *greed* or *sloth* was a language unto itself."

"Hush!" snapped the Princess. The disapproving scowl disappeared as she stepped toward the throne to address the King.

"Good fortune smiles upon me to deliver you to my fair kingdom, Princess Rose-alyn."

The King's plump, sausage-like fingers snapped, sending one of the servants scurrying off to retrieve a fresh tray of cheese and more wine. As his corpulent form shifted on the throne, this chair seemed to squeal in protest for having to bear so much weight.

It was unlike any throne Rose had ever seen. Instead of the elaborately carved, gilded seat ensconced in velvet, this beast of a chair was overstuffed and upholstered in leather. It was definitely built for comfort, not regal elegance. The wooden, clawed feet looked like they were the amputated paws taken from a huge lion. They appeared to sink into the floor to ascertain its permanence in the throne room. Rose took another cautious step forward, sensing there was something sinister about this piece of furniture. It looked like it would swallow up any person smaller than the King wishing to sit on this throne. Either that, or the clawed feet would lash out with deadly intent, carving up anyone who dare offend the King.

"Good fortune?" repeated the Princess. "How so, Your Highness?"

"Why, the reward your father, King William had posted, of course! However, being his daughter, I had believed he would have been far more generous."

"I fail to understand. What would it matter to you, being that you are so wealthy to begin with?"

"Wealth begets wealth, Princess," explained the King, his ample shoulders rolling in a shrug. "Only a fool would fail to take advantage of an opportunity such as this. And only a bigger fool would not monopolize on it, if there was a chance to do so."

"What are you talking about?"

"Well, the reward is stated to be a quarter of your weight in gold. That being the case, I do believe you are in need of some *plumping up* before you are returned home," revealed the King, snorting with laughter as crumbs from an earlier meal hiding in his thick, salt and pepper beard sprinkled down on his finely embroidered vest. "You shall be well-fed while you are my *guest*."

"It is a thoughtful gesture, but I am really not hungry and I must be on my way."

"I do not think so."

"I am not your prisoner! You cannot hold me against my will," snapped Rose.

"Since when is a prisoner wined and dined in grand style?" reasoned the King.

"The only way you will get me to stay here one second longer than need be is to forcefully detain me."

"Brilliant idea!" With a snap of his fingers, the King's soldiers turned their pikes on Rose and her comrades. "Consider yourself my prisoner!"

"This is outrageous! You cannot do this to me!" declared Rose, her feet stamping the floor in defiance. "To them, yes, but not to me!"

"I am the King of Axalon. I can do whatever I please, when I please!"

"True, but I am a princess! Tell him, Tag! Tell him of the irony of this and how he must set us free."

"The real irony is, he sounds just like you!" grunted Tag.

"Shut it!" snapped Rose, turning to address the King. "Just how long do you intend to keep me prisoner?"

The King scrutinized her, assessing her condition before providing her with an answer.

"You're a thin rake of a girl," decided the King, tenting his pudgy fingers as he deliberated on this matter. "You need lots of feedings to fatten you up."

"How fat?" Rose dared to ask.

"Say… until your waist is as big around as one of my thighs," answered the King. The rolls of fat on his belly wobbled as he laughed heartily, quivering all the more as his sweaty hand slapped his meaty leg.

"What?" gasped Rose.

"You heard me, Princess Rose-alyn. I'll be doing your parents a great favour in undertaking this task. I will make you look more presentable, give you a healthier appearance."

"I look healthy enough!" declared Rose. "What do you intend to do? Force feed me to accomplish this?"

"If I must."

"Mind you, if you offer the Princess all the sweet, sticky desserts she can eat, you won't have to do any kind of force feeding," suggested Tag.

For a fleeting instant the angry scowl on Rose's face dissolved as she thought of dining on a never-ending meal consisting only of decadent desserts. A dreamy sigh escaped her as she recalled her love affair with all things sweet.

"That will only rot her teeth!" disputed the King, wheezing loudly as he shifted about on his throne. "Rather than desserts, I shall offer a special diet of cheese."

"*Cheese!* I detest stinky, old cheese!" retorted Rose, her nose wrinkling in disgust.

"Oh, it is extremely smelly when aged to perfection, but this is no ordinary cheese, my dear Princess. This cheese is not made. It is *crafted* by the skilled hands of artisan Trolls in the Land of Small. They use only the freshest milk produced by the best goats in all the lands," revealed the King. His mouth involuntarily salivated with the mere thought of this sharp, crumbly dairy product as his tongue rolled over his plump lips as though searching for traces of this cheese left over from a previous meal.

"As *tantalizing* as you make it sound, you can think again if you believe I am going to eat that putrid stuff. Unless you find a way to turn grotty, old cheese into a delectable cake, you can forget it!"

"Oh, you say that now, Princess, but one bite and you will soon discover why I indulge in this delicacy."

"Overindulge, perhaps," offered Cankles, deciding one of the King's legs probably weighed as much as his entire, lanky body.

"What did you say?" grunted the King.

"Nothing really, Your Immenseness – I mean, Your Highness," responded Cankles. "Jus' makin' an observation."

"Never mind him!" scolded Rose. "I said it before, I will say it again. You cannot hold me here, nor will I eat that stinking goat cheese."

"Hmph!" grunted the King, waving off her comment. He snapped his fingers, summoning his servant to deliver his mid-morning snack. "What is taking so long? Where is my wine and cheese?"

The man he had initially sent off to retrieve this food reluctantly crept into the throne room. He leaned forward, whispering into the King's ear.

"What do you mean there is no more cheese!" bellowed Maxmillion. His jowls wobbled, trembling with fury.

"I am sorry, Your Highness," apologized the servant, bowing his head in submission. "The cellar is bare. The last wheel of cheese was consumed earlier this morning."

"By whom? Who dare steal from my private stock?" gasped the King, struggling to sit upright on his throne. Wherever his bare, sweaty skin protruded from the straining gaps in his apparel, it made contact against the chair's leather upholstery to squeal and squeak as he shifted about.

"*You* ate the last of the cheese, Your Highness," informed the servant.

"And what of the reserves?"

"That *was* the last of your reserves. The Trolls have not made a delivery since last month."

"Bloody hell! Damn those blasted Trolls!" cursed the King, his hands slamming down against the chair's armrests. "Is it not enough I pay them fair market value for their cheese? Not to mention I had waived the various taxes so they can enter Axalon, unfettered, to make the deliveries."

"It is not that, Your Highness. It is the Elves of the Woodland Glade," informed the servant.

"What of them?"

"The Elf Lord, Rainus Silverthorn is preventing the Trolls from crossing their territory to make the deliveries."

"Why? What has gotten the Elves' tights in a bunch this time?" grumbled the King, his beady eyes rolling in frustration.

"The Elves are angered by the Trolls' farming practices where their goats are concerned."

"What farming practices?"

"That's just it, Your Highness, there are none," answered the servant. "Apparently, these animals roam into the Woodland Glade unchecked and are quite literally eating the Elves out of house and home."

"Good gracious! The Elves are supposed to be nature lovers. You'd think they'd welcome the goats into their forest!" snapped Maxmillian

"They consider goats to be domestic animals, not a natural part of their woodland habitat," explained the servant.

"If that is the case, send an emissary to deal with them," ordered the King. "Bribe them if you must, just do whatever it takes to persuade the Elves to end this cheese embargo."

"The Elves cannot be bribed. They care not for gold and riches, Your Highness. They only care about the well-being of their forest. They feel as you are unsympathetic to their plight, they refuse to meet with you or your royal emissary, if one is sent."

"I must have cheese!" demanded the King. His forehead broke out in beads of sweat as the thought of being deprived overwhelmed him. "I shall declare war on those Elves!"

"You'll go to war over cheese?" gasped Tag, appalled by this declaration.

"The men of Axalon have died for lesser things. They will do so in my name and honour. If those Elves refuse to cooperate, there will indeed be a war, one of unparalleled magnitude!"

"Well then, I guess there is no point in detaining me," said Rose. "No cheese, no way to fatten me up. Too bad! Farewell!"

"Not so fast, Princess," growled the King. "There are other ways to fatten you up. It will just take longer."

"That's what you think!" snapped Rose. "I wish – "

Tag's hand slapped over her mouth as he interjected, "She wishes to have a private word with me! If you please?"

"Will this word help in the movement of cheese back into my kingdom?" questioned Maxmillion.

"Absolutely," vowed Tag, his hand over his heart in solemn promise.

"Then speak, but be quick about it. I shall lapse into a fit if I do not get my daily feed of cheese."

Tag, Rose and Cankles huddled together, speaking in a whisper as the King sipped on a cup of cream and honey discoloured by a little bit of hot tea.

"I refuse to be held prisoner," grumbled Rose. "I can wish us out of here."

"To where? Back to Towgem? Or back to the Visitors' Center?" questioned Tag. "If you are correct, the wish must be precise. That shall mean you can only conjure up an image of where you've been before, not some place you've never seen."

"Then what do you recommend we do?" asked Rose. "We have one wish left on this day. Shall I wish for more gold to bribe the King for our freedom?"

"The opulent surroundings of this castle certainly speak of his financial wealth, however, just by his *portly* appearance, I'd say he is a man who loves his food."

"I'm thinkin' he's more concerned about getting his hands on that cheese," decided Cankles.

He listened as the King wrung his hands in woe as he whined, "My kingdom for some cheese!"

"Precisely," agreed Tag, nodding judiciously. "He is willing to declare war over it."

"Then I shall wish for a cellar stocked full of cheese, enough to appease him," offered Rose.

"Judging by his appetite and ample size, I'm afraid it will not last him for very long," countered Tag. "Plus, it will give him reason to hold you, now that he has a supply of cheese he can use to plump you up."

"Oh, my! I can't have that!" declared Rose.

"There's a way around this, and we may not have to waste a wish," stated Tag.

"How?" asked Rose.

"Run away?" offered Cankles, scratching his head in thought.

"My father said war must always be the last resort. I refuse to be caught up in a war over cheese, of all things," explained Tag. "As we know, the Elves refuse to negotiate with the King. I propose we step in to reason on Maxmillion's behalf as an unbiased third party."

"Good luck in convincing him of this," muttered Rose.

"The man *needs* his cheese. I believe I can persuade him to set us free," insisted Tag.

"And failing this?" questioned the Princess.

"Then, that will be a good time to use the last wish," answered Tag.

"So, have you decided on a plan?" asked the King, his fingers drumming impatiently on the armrest.

"Yes, Your Highness," replied Tag. "I believe we can convince the Elves to allow the Trolls to move their cheese once more."

"What can you offer the Elves that I, the King of Axalon could not, to end this embargo?"

"Diplomacy, Your Highness," offered Tag.

"You impudent, young whelp! Dare you say I am not diplomatic?" grunted the King. "I will have you know, those Elves are not the easiest beings to reason with."

"That may be so, and I mean no offence to you, but did you not say the Elves of the Woodland Glade refuse to negotiate, as they feel you are biased and unsympathetic to them."

"So I did."

"Then would it not stand to reason they will listen to a third party, one promising to be impartial in dealing with their concerns and yours?" added Tag.

"Your words ring true, young man," admitted the King. "However, what do you know of diplomacy, enough to circumvent a war?"

"My father was once the captain of King William's army. He understood that choice words delivered eloquently and sincerely could do much to open the doors to peaceful negotiations. He said, if there was a way to resolve a matter without shedding blood, it was better to take this route. It is a matter of striking a balance, coming up with a solution both parties will be satisfied with."

"And you feel you can accomplish this?"

"I believe I can," answered Tag.

"I like your confidence, young man," praised the King, giving him a nod of approval. "However, if I should release you to do my bidding and you fail, then what?"

"I can only promise to do my utmost to find a peaceful resolution satisfactory for all concerned," vowed Tag. "Should I fail, we will be made to travel through Axalon on our return to Fleetwood. I suspect we shall meet up with one of your many tax collectors and he will turn us in. That being said, you can capitalize on your plan to fatten up the Princess to reap the reward her father had posted. If nothing else, you have much to lose and more to gain in considering my offer."

"Well… why are you still standing here?" questioned the King, waving the trio off. "I want my cheese! Make it so."

"Absolutely, Your Highness," said Tag, bowing politely.

"I shall have my most trusted knight deliver you to the borders of the Woodland Glade. Travel with him and you shall bypass all the Visitors' Centers along the way. I will even wave the departure tax to expedite matters."

12

Real Men Wear Tights

"Continue eastward, but remain on this trail," cautioned the knight; his tone was grave as he pointed the way to the heart of Woodland Glade. "Do not stray from it."

"Or we shall become lost?" asked Rose.

"That, but I'd be more concerned about the strange and wild things in this forest," answered the knight.

"Strange, I've gotten used to," snorted Tag, as he glanced over at the Princess, "but what wild things do you speak of?"

"It is an *enchanted* forest. You'll see for yourself if you last the journey."

"That sounds rather foreboding," said Rose, watching as the knight steered his horse away, abandoning them to venture on without an escort. "I wonder what he meant by that?"

"It was probably nothing, but it'd be prudent to heed his warning nonetheless," decided Tag. "No point in taking unnecessary risks."

"I agree, but you are *so* in trouble if we get eaten by a dragon or skewered on a unicorn's horn," grumbled Rose.

"If you actually took to your studies, you would know dragons prefer the open highlands of the Fire Rim Mountains to the north than the heavily treed forests in this region," informed Tag.

"An' we're not likely to run into any unicorns this time of the day. They're pretty shy, preferin' to come out at night," added Cankles. "If anything, we must be careful of the forest."

"You mean, we must be careful while *in* the forest," corrected Rose.

"Yes, that too, but the forest can kill you, if it really wants to."

"What do you mean?" probed Tag, trying to make sense of Cankles' words of caution. "How can a forest kill?"

"Like that knight said, this is an *enchanted* forest," responded

Cankles. "The trees, particularly those growin' in an' around the Elf haven, can be a bit touchy if you take to disturbin' them."

"Even from you, this sounds too bizarre. How do you know this?" questioned Rose.

"Been this way before."

"You have?" asked Rose and Tag, speaking in unison.

Cankles nodded in confirmation, "It was long ago, so there's not much I remember other than the nasty trees. I hardly think much has changed over time though, so don't do anything to offend them."

Tag and Rose exchanged quizzical glances as they considered their comrade's warning.

"All right then! We won't do anything to anger the trees," promised Tag, but speaking more to humour Cankles. "We won't be burning any wood on this night."

"Wise decision," praised Cankles. "Let's keep ridin' while there's light."

❀ ❀ ❀

Under a milky, twilight sky the trio steered their mounts into a tranquil forest glen. Tag reached over, his finger prodding Rose on the side of her head as the mare's rolling gait lulled her to sleep.

"I'm awake! I'm awake!" yelped Rose. Her lolling head abruptly snapped up as her eyes flashed open.

"You are now and you better stay this way," urged Tag. "The last thing we need is for you to dream away another wish, especially if we need it."

"I was only *resting* my eyes," insisted the Princess, rubbing the sleep from them as she yawned wearily.

"You mustn't sleep, not jus' yet," warned Cankles. "The closer we get to the Elf haven, the more we must keep our wits about us."

"Well, that will be most difficult for you then," grunted Rose.

Cankles' face reddened. He looked momentarily flustered, uncertain if she was speaking in jest.

Tag reached over again, this time flicking Rose's head as he scolded her, "You were only teasing, right Princess?"

"Sure." Her response was non-committal, for she merely wanted to avoid another stinging assault from Tag's finger.

"I take it, we must be aware so we don't miss their tree top abodes?" questioned Tag, searching the forest canopy.

"Yes... an' they say there's old magic that still lingers here," explained Cankles, his eyes probing the growing darkness as the sun settled ever lower on the horizon. "It's strongest where the Elves congregate."

Rose merely yawned in response, shaking off her drowsiness.

"You're not falling asleep again, are you?" queried Tag.

"I will, if we do not stop for a moment," replied the Princess. "I just need to stretch my legs for a bit before my whole body goes numb from sitting in this saddle."

Tag reined in his mount, bringing his stallion to a stop as he hopped down. "I suppose it won't hurt."

As Cankles helped the Princess to dismount from her mare, Tag gathered their water flasks. "While you stretch your legs, I'll replenish these."

"You do that," agreed Rose. "And make sure it is fresh, clear flowing water you fill them with. I refuse to drink if it is from a stagnating pond."

"Yes, yes!" grumbled Tag, waving over his shoulder as he hurried off to the sound of a brook coursing through the forest. "Just don't wander off. I'll return shortly."

As soon as Rose and Cankles were out of sight, Tag darted behind a large willow tree. Glancing around the tree trunk, he checked to make sure his privacy was not about to be interrupted, especially by the Princess.

"Nature calls and I'm gonna answer," muttered Tag, hastily unbuttoning his trousers. With a sigh of relief, he released a torrent of urine to water the base of the grand willow. "Better... much better!"

With a final gush and a shake, Tag buttoned up. Turning about to collect the water flasks, he was surprised to find there were only two where he had left them. The third one had vanished.

A sense of panic and embarrassment washed over him. Perhaps Rose had made off with this flask? And in the process, it would mean she had spied upon him taking care of personal business. This feeling was fleeting as he heard Rose in the distance where he had left her. She was complaining loudly to Cankles about the very real potential of developing saddles sores on her royal bottom if she was made to ride for too long.

"Hmph... I wonder where it went?" grumbled Tag, glancing about the base of the willow in case an animal had made off with the flask. "Now this is odd."

He frowned, crouching down to inspect the dark, loamy earth at his feet. It seemed to shift beneath the leaf litter blanketing the forest floor. As if a giant mole was undertaking a major earth-moving project, the soil churned and surged.

Just as Tag took a cautionary step back, he yelped in fright. The tree's root erupted from the earth, wrapping around one of his ankles as the willow's vine-like branches whipped about to wind around his neck.

As the gnarled root anchored Tag to the ground, the tree's snaky limbs tightened around his throat. These slender, tenacious branches choked him as they pulled, lifting the boy up. Tag's fingers struggled to break this strangling hold, fighting to pry them off. He groaned in pain as the willow tried to pull him in two.

Tag gasped and sputtered. He fought to gulp down a breath of air. In desperation, his one hand reached for his sword, fumbling to extract it from the scabbard. Immediately, this reduced tension to pry off the branches caused the tree to wrap around all the tighter. It trapped the fingers of Tag's other hand against his throat as he struggled to loosen this hold.

In a state of panic, his hand lost its grip, the sword tumbling to the ground. Tag fought against these vines as he felt his head grow lighter even as his heart thundered in his chest. This constricting hold not only cut off his air supply, the flow of blood to his brain was now compromised. As another root burst forth to seize his other ankle to tether him securely to the ground, the tree's limbs fought to pull him higher.

Tag was unable to scream out. He could only manage a stifled groan as the opposing tension caused his muscles to strain to the point of tearing. His joints felt as though they were going to pop from their sockets as the willow attempted to dismember his body with brute force.

Spots of light flashed before his eyes to blur into darkness as his life force ebbed away.

"Drop him!"

These words hummed in Tag's ears, fading as he ceased his struggle to plunge into a black abyss.

The impact of his body hitting the ground jolted Tag's senses. It forced him to gasp, inhaling the life-giving air to fill his aching lungs.

Rose lunged forward. She seized Tag by his shoulders, dragging him away from the vengeful tree as Cankles, having taken up Tag's sword, slashed at the writhing branches once more. As these vines retreated, he attacked the roots, hacking and slashing. The blade bit into the wood to force the tree to release its hold.

As the branches recoiled and the roots sank back, retreating into the earth, Cankles grabbed Tag.

"Quickly, Princess!" hollered Cankles, struggling to help Rose haul their comrade from the reach of this angry willow. "Get him away from here."

Dragging him away from the shadow of the enchanted tree, Cankles and Rose breathed a sigh of relief. Soon, the chirping of crickets and the symphony of chorusing tree frogs smothered the forest in a tranquil calm. They slumped to the ground next to Tag as his eyes flickered open.

All three screamed in terror as the willow suddenly lashed out at them, coming to life once more. Its tenacious branches whipped out, snaking around the trio to hoist them high into its crown. Their horrified cries were replaced by groans of disgust as sap oozed. The willow exacted its revenge, squirting them with a copious quantity of this runny, sticky liquid that promised to become stickier as it dried.

Their frantic struggle came to abrupt end when an angry voice sounded from below.

"All right! Who peed on the tree?"

Like a dejected hound forced to relinquish its favourite bone, the old willow reluctantly unravelled its slender branches. Lowering its captives to the ground, it unceremoniously dumped them onto the forest floor.

"The three of you were lucky we heard you when we did."

The trio glanced up to spy upon nine Elves towering over them.

"This old tree does not take kindly to desecration of *any* form, if you get my meaning?" stated the leader of the Elves.

"Sorry," apologized Tag, his face burning red with embarrassment as he struggled to his feet while Cankles helped Rose to stand. "I wasn't thinking. It never occurred to me that a tree would attack."

"For shame, Master Yairet!" admonished Cankles, shaking his head in disgrace. "Did I not warn you about offendin' the trees in this forest?"

"So you did," admitted Tag, giving his comrade a sheepish smile of acknowledgement. "But it was not as though I *assaulted* the tree. I certainly didn't take an axe to it. I never even plucked a single leaf from it."

"Well, unless you mortals find certain pleasure in a dog lifting its leg on you, believe me, to these old trees, the act of being urinated on is as much an assault as an outright insult," explained the Elf.

"I didn't know. And I assure you, I'll never do that again!" vowed Tag, his hand over his heart in solemn promise.

"Not if you wish to survive in my forest, you won't," responded the Elf.

Rose stared at these pointy-eared beings she had only ever read about. She had vague recollections about the Elves from when the scholars attempted to educate her about the world and people outside the walls of Pepperton Palace.

The Princess was momentarily perplexed by what her eyes beheld. She was pretty certain it was a man's voice coming from this person. However, at first glance it was rather ambiguous when it came to determining whether this person was actually a male Elf or a female. Rose scrutinized her rescuers.

This being, like the eight other Elves standing before her, all possessed flowing, golden hair; lovely tresses even Rose would be envious of. Their perfect features; the symmetrical faces with high, chiselled cheekbones and what Rose could only assume were impeccably plucked brows to frame those piercing, sapphire eyes made her look twice. Tall, lean and toned, but not overly muscular for warriors with such a deadly reputation, each wore green tights topped by a colour-coordinated tunic and cloak of sylvan colours. It allowed them to easily blend into the forest.

Rose concluded these Elves were either masculine looking women or rather feminine looking men. She was strangely attracted to these beings, particularly the leader of this group, but it dawned on her that she could not possibly be drawn to a man more attractive than she was, if indeed this Elf was a male of their species.

"What is *it?*" Rose whispered to Tag.

"I suppose this is what the knight meant by *strange,*" determined Tag, speaking in a hushed voice as he stared at the Elves and their flamboyant ensemble. It was the tights that threw him off.

"Why are they wearing hosiery?" asked Rose, speaking in a whisper. "Only women wear tights."

With such acute hearing, the Elf spoke up, "In your culture, perhaps, but in Elfdom, only real men wear tights. We don this apparel, mantyhoses as we call them-"

"You mean to say panty-hoses," corrected Rose.

"No, I do mean *man*ty-hoses, being that I am a man," explained the Elf. "And we wear them because they are practical. It allows us to move through this forest with ease and in silence. Plus, they are fashionable and slimming, yet defines our muscle tone perfectly."

In a grand flourish, he struck a pose. "Quite flattering, don't you think?"

Rose and Tag were momentarily dumbstruck.

"You gotta admit, only a real man can pull off wearing tights with such style," stated Cankles, giving the Elf a nod of approval. "I know I sure as hell can't."

There was a moment of awkward silence, and then the Elves burst out laughing as they pictured this gangly mortal wearing one of their form-fitting apparels.

"Thank you, good sir," responded the Elf. "Somewhere in there, I am sure there was a compliment."

"Oh, indeed!" declared Cankles, bowing in respect.

"I must say, you look strangely familiar, sir," noted the Elf. His dazzling, blue eyes intensified in colour as he scrutinized Cankles.

"He is just strange, but never mind him," interjected Rose, stepping forward to greet the Elf. "I am Princess Rose-alyn of Fleetwood. This is Tag Yairet – "

"Tagius Yairet," he interjected.

"And this fellow is Cankles Moron," said Rose, concluding introductions.

"Mayron," reminded the village idiot, correcting the Princess for the umpteenth time. "Cankles Mayron."

"Salutations, one and all!" greeted the Elf, bowing his head in polite acknowledgement. "I am Rainus Silverthorn, lord and leader to the Elves of the Woodland Glade."

"It is a pleasure to meet you, my lord," greeted Rose, as she curtsied politely before him.

"Please, call me Rainus."

"Then you must call me Princess."

"You are a long way from home, Princess. What brings you here to our forest?"

"We are on a mission," answered Rose, blotting her face dry on the edge of her apron as the sap released from the vengeful willow continued to drip from her hair.

"Actually, our reason for being here is two-fold, my lord," explained Tag. "We are here on behalf of King Maxmillion of Axalon."

"Say no more, young sir! I do not wish to hear from that despicable mortal," snapped Rainus. He raised his slender, well-manicured hand, motioning for Tag to desist as murmurs of discontent rippled through the men in his company. "That money-grabbing monarch of *Taxalot* is a fool to think I would waste my time listening to his rhetoric, even if it was delivered by a royal emissary."

"Hey! Were you the one to deface the signs?" questioned Cankles, recalling the modified moniker carved into the signpost as they entered Axalon.

"I will neither admit nor deny that specific act of vandalism," responded Rainus, his eyes shifting about nervously. "I will only say whomever took it upon himself to do so, boldly defies that pompous twit of a king. If anything, the fellow should be commended for his actions."

"We understand your sentiments in regards to the monarch's over-zealous actions in handling his country's finances and other sensitive matters of diplomacy," sympathized Tag. "However, we come with word from King Maxmillion."

"Our words, no matter how eloquently or diplomatically delivered to that fool, had fallen on deaf ears in the past," grunted Rainus. "Why should I to listen to him?"

"I am aware of your situation, Lord Silverthorn. However, let me assure you, Princess Rose promises to be an unbiased third party to all of this," promised Tag. "She, or should I say *we*, are here to ensure a peaceful resolution with satisfactory terms for all concerned."

"You claim to be impartial," responded Rainus, his eyes narrowing in skepticism as he scrutinized this young mortal, "but how do I know for sure?"

"We are and we intend to remain so," vowed Tag. "I only ask that you have some faith."

"Where the King of Axalon is concerned, I have lost faith long ago," stated Rainus.

"All is not lost, my lord," responded Tag. "We know what is at stake here. I know what you stand to gain and what the King stands to lose and vice versa, but I also know what will happen to both your nations if a peaceful resolution is not reached."

"Are you threatening me, as well as my people?" questioned Rainus, staring down at the young stranger.

"With all due respect, my lord, I am not. However, King Maxmillion is prepared to declare war," explained Tag. "We are here in hopes of curtailing such an event. He sent us in hopes of negotiating a satisfactory solution for both parties."

"*Negotiate?* That is something new for him," said the Elf. "He must be desperate."

"Desperate for his cheese! That's for sure," said Cankles.

"There is more at stake here than just cheese," stated Rose.

"True, but why should I negotiate with that man when he only cares for himself?" grumbled Rainus.

"The Elves are renowned for being wise. Does wisdom not dictate to find a peaceful resolution than to allow it to escalate to open warfare?" responded Tag. "Especially if there is a way to resolve the matter peacefully."

"True enough," admitted Rainus.

"So, you are willing to hear us out, my lord?" asked Tag.

"I would be a fool not to. But tell me this, young sir, ultimately, what do you stand to gain in all of this?"

"Nothing really," answered Tag.

"Come now! It is rare to find a human being willing to act out of the goodness of his heart. What is in it for you, should you succeed?"

"It's more like what's gonna happen to us, if we should fail," blurted out Cankles.

"Pray tell! Just what do you mean by that, Master Mayron?"

"He means to say, if we fail in persuading you to come to an agreement that ends the embargo you had imposed on King Maxmillion's stinking cheese, we become his prisoners," revealed Rose.

The Elf's perfect brows arched up in surprise.

"She speaks the truth, Lord Silverthorn," confirmed Tag. "Failure is not an option. If we do, none shall come ahead the winner. The King declared he will bring war to your forest if a compromise is not met and the three of us shall be the first casualties."

The Elves fell silent as they pondered this young mortal's warning.

"You are serious," decided Rainus.

"Very much so, my lord," said Tag. "We mean to circumvent a war."

"Perhaps I should seriously consider your words if the King is willing to negotiate a compromise," decided the Elf.

"You are willing to hear us out?" asked Tag.

"A meeting is in order. Let us return to Driven Hill."

"Driven Hill?" repeated Rose.

"Yes," responded Rainus. "It is our secret enclave situated in the heart of Woodland Glade."

"Guess it's not a secret anymore," noted Cankles.

"Actually, it isn't really a secret. Never was. It just sounds more mysterious if you say it is a secret place. It gives Driven Hill an air of mystery," explained Rainus. "It adds to our enigmatic persona, if you get my meaning?"

"I suppose," responded the Princess.

"The point being, we should take the time to discuss this matter at length than to rush to judgment. We shall do so at my residence," stated Rainus. "Now follow me. It is not far from here."

Tag, Rose and Cankles watched in amazement. It was not so much because these beings were reputed to be formidable warriors and they advanced like a cohesive fighting force, marching in synchrony, but because these woodland beings moved with surprising grace. They stood tall and straight, their chests puffed out, their shoulders pulled back. With a toss of their long, luxuriant tresses, the Elves led the way. Their pace and steps seemed choreographed as they sashayed and pranced, but doing so with steps so light, they seemed to float over the forest floor.

"Walk this way," ordered the Elf taking up the rear of this procession. He waved them on, watching with amusement as Cankles attempted to clumsily prance out of time behind him.

"I thought Elves lived in trees," remarked Rose, as she glanced about this settlement. Neat rows of quaint, stone cottages, each with a thatched roof and a window box overflowing with a plethora of brightly coloured flowers that adorned each shuttered window greeted her eyes.

"At one time, but not now," revealed Rainus, escorting the trio to his royal residence as dusk finally surrendered to the coming of night.

"Why not?" asked the Princess. "It goes against tradition?"

"What good is tradition if it gets you killed?" responded Rainus.

"I do not understand," said Rose.

"Even I was under the assumption Elves lived an arboreal lifestyle," added Tag.

"I suppose, from a practical point of view, it makes sense," responded Rainus. "A high vantage point from the tree tops would certainly allow for an unobstructed view of approaching danger and our homes would be less accessible to the enemies, but living up there did present certain risks."

"I guess it can be a bit dangerous way up there," agreed Tag, noticing how many of the trees in this old growth forest towered well over two hundred feet in height.

"You have no idea, especially when the weather is foul," responded the Elf. "Between the lightning strikes and gale force northerly winds that race down from the Fire Rim Mountains during the winter months, it is not easy to maintain one's balance. These trees sway in the wind like stalks of grain in a wheat field on a blustery day."

"That'd be scary," admitted Cankles, for he was not one for heights to begin with.

"Never mind scary! Ever try drinking a cup of tea on a keel-less ship caught in the middle of a raging storm on the open sea?" questioned Rainus.

"Can't say I have," answered Cankles. "Mind you, I could've, but I jus' don't remember."

"Trust me. It is no different. More than one Elf had been burned by spilled tea or boiling hot water! And though we have the ability to heal rapidly from such injuries, it is still bloody painful when that scalding liquid lands on your tenders, if you get my meaning?"

"Not really," said Rose. "What are tenders?"

As though Rainus spoke a universal language understood by all males of every species, Cankles and Tag, as well as each male Elf in her presence, immediately assumed the position. As though someone was taking a red-hot poker to their nether-regions, they flinched, hunching over under a phantom pain as their knees locked together.

"Oh… those *tenders*," said Rose. She nodded in understanding, embarrassed that she asked.

"Say no more," urged Tag. "I believe we understand how dangerous it can be."

"Dealing with spilled beverages was easy enough," continued Rainus. "However, you would be surprised how many of us had fallen from those high walkways over the years."

"From the gusting winds?" asked Tag. He was surprised, considering the Elves' reputation for grace and balance was rivalled only by the most agile of cats.

"Good gracious, no!" exclaimed Rainus. "We like our wine, but when we get tipsy, we are like you mortals. Balance goes right out the window and the swaying walkways only make it worse."

"So this was a recent change to living arrangements?" determined Rose.

"About nine years ago, so by our standards, yes, very recent," informed the long-lived Elf. "We were making merry at the height of the Harvest Moon Festival and a good time was being had by all! The wine was flowing freely when a great windstorm descended upon our forest. The next morning, there was an ugly sight to behold. Inebriated Elves had fallen like nuts shaken from an oak tree, injured bodies were strewn all over the forest floor."

"How terrible!" gasped Cankles.

"It was an absolute disaster, but thankfully, there were no casualties. Being quite intoxicated, most of us were so relaxed when we fell, if we didn't land on shrubs or thick carpets of moss, we pretty much bounced when we hit the earth. Mind you, it did help to have our fall broken by the many boughs on the way down or it would have been a free fall plunge to our demise."

"Then living on the ground makes perfect sense," said Tag. "At least, it is much safer to fall off the stoop of your cottage than to fall from way up there."

"Exactly! That is why we now reside here on Driven Hill," stated Rainus. "Being that this *knoll* is the highest point in Woodland Glade, it offered us a high enough vantage point for whatever comes our way."

"That is an unusual name. Why Driven Hill?" questioned Rose.

"We were forced to *drive out* the resident bears and raccoons – "

"And the skunks," added one of the Elves.

"Oh yes, especially the skunks," continued Rainus. "In fact, we were made to drive all the wild beasts from this place to take over this location, hence the name."

"Don't understand," said Cankles, scratching his head in thought.

"*Driven Hill,*" explained Tag. "They had to *drive away* the wildlife that once resided on this *hill.*"

"I see…" Cankles nodded his head as he finally clued in.

"This is bizarre. I was led to believe the Elves had a love for nature," said Rose.

"Of course we do, but from a respectable distance," revealed one of the Elves in their company.

"We may be one with nature, but that does not stop a rogue bear from eating us if it wants to," explained Rainus. "Nor does a hungry raccoon think twice about raiding our pantries, given the opportunity."

"So these wild creatures have as much respect for your people as they do for us," decided Tag.

"*Respect?*" chuckled Rainus, smiling at this young mortal. "We are speaking of animals. They do what wild animals do in order to survive. In this case, we merely had them *relocate* to other parts of this forest in order to minimize potential deadly encounters."

"Relocate sounds more reasonable than being driven out," decided Cankles, nodding his head in approval.

"Here we go! Step right in," invited the Elf, opening the door to his residence for his guests to enter.

From the exterior, these cottages appeared no bigger than the servants' quarters of her palace. And based on the average height of the Elves she had met so far, all standing over six feet tall, Rose assumed it was exceptionally cramped for such large beings. She entered through the archway only to gasp in surprise.

Instead of a single, small square room, she wandered into a massive, impeccably decorated chamber. A large floor-to-ceiling fireplace constructed of river rocks was the focal point of this room where logs blazed to warm the spacious parlor. Beyond this room, a grand dining hall, a huge library and a long corridor lined on both sides by roomy bedchambers greeted her eyes.

"This is incredible!" marvelled Rose, as she gazed about these grand surroundings. On every wall there were paintings of Rainus Silverthorn in various poses – some cheeky, some dignified, but all artfully capturing the Elf's many moods. "This is a regular palace on the inside!"

"One would never believe it is so spacious in here," agreed Tag, inspecting the exterior once more before following behind the Princess. "How is this possible?"

"I told you, there's old magic at work in this forest," averred Cankles, as he followed Tag inside.

"That may be so, but what kind of magic can do this?" questioned Tag, his eyes surveying their opulent and airy surroundings.

"Actually, we are quite good with our hands when it comes to working with wood. Being so long-lived, we have a great deal of time to devote to our craft."

"That'd be a whole lot of time whittling wood," determined Cankles.

"Yes," agreed Rainus. "And with many years of *whittling* experience behind us, consider this a clever feat of architectural engineering and a wee bit of Elf magic."

"I'd say!" agreed Tag, admiring the craftsmanship of the elaborately carved beams supporting the roof. "It's astonishing on so many levels."

"Thank you, Master Yairet! However, this humble abode is rather modest compared to my winter home in Slothendriel to the south," said Rainus. "At least there is plenty of room on this night for unexpected guests."

"You wish for us to stay this evening?" asked Tag.

"Consider it an invitation. Unlike the King of Axalon, I will not hold you and your comrades against your will. If you wish to stay the night, you are more than welcome to do so."

"It is a kind and generous offer, but we do not mean to be an inconvenience to you and your household," responded Tag.

"Speak for yourself," interjected Rose, willing to accept this invitation than to be subjected to another night in the wild.

"You already had one close call in the forest, young sir. You should keep in mind with the darkness there will be other risks, greater dangers, if you wish to sleep out of doors," warned Rainus, waving at his comrades as the Elves dispersed to their own homes for the night.

"When you put it like that, perhaps one night won't hurt," decided Tag.

"Halen Ironwood!" called out Rainus. He summoned his personal guard and the captain of his army before Halen departed into the night to assign his warriors to sentry duty.

"Yes, my lord," responded the Elf.

"See to it our guests' horses are turned into the stable. Be sure they are watered and fed for the night."

"Of course, my lord," said Halen, with a polite bow of his head before undertaking this task. "I will make sure the horses are safely housed."

"Safely housed from what?" asked Rose, perplexed by these foreboding words.

"It is the height of the rutting season for the unicorns in our forest," explained the Elf, shutting the door behind them. "By nature, they are shy, reclusive creatures. However, the male unicorns can be extremely territorial this time of the year."

"Oooh! You wouldn't want to be gettin' in between a stallion an' his harem," cautioned Cankles, pretending to be impaled upon a spiral horn. "Those male unicorns can be downright dangerous, even more so than an elk stag in its prime when there's a doe in season."

"True enough, however, I'd rather not impose if we can help it. I just sense we'd be fine if we are careful out there," said Tag.

"Well, you be careful then. Just don't go 'watering' any more trees," responded Rose, dismissing Tag with a wave of her hand. "I will be quite happy to take up our host's kind offer of a room for the night."

"I just feel it's rude for us to intrude, disturbing Lord Silverthorn and his people with expectations that they should house us while we are here," explained Tag, not wishing to overstay their welcome.

"Trust me, it is no imposition, young sir," stated Rainus. "If anything, it would put my mind at ease knowing Princess Rose is safe while in this forest. It is bad enough having a gluttonous, self-serving King on one side and irate Trolls on the other. The last thing I need is another enemy. To have the King of Fleetwood up in arms, too, should something terrible befall the Princess and her friends while in my domain is the last thing I am in need of."

"Then we shall accept your invitation," decided Tag. "It would be selfish of us not to heed your concerns for our safety."

"Very good!" exclaimed the Elf, directing his guests into the massive dining hall. "Now, how about some refreshments and a meal before we talk business, my friends?"

"That would be lovely," responded Rose. "However, would it be possible to freshen up first?"

Rainus scrutinized his guests. All three looked pathetically filthy after their harrowing ordeal with the angry willow tree. Leaves, bits of moss and broken twigs adhered wherever the extruded tree sap dried on them.

"Of course, Princess," answered Rainus. Before he could call out, his wife arrived to greet them.

As handsome as the somewhat androgynous male Elves were, there was no mistaking the fairer sex of their species. This woman was of an ethereal beauty that left Tag dumbfounded. His mouth fell open as this vision of loveliness filled his eyes as he stared in awe.

"Good evening," greeted Valara. Her words tinkled like silver bells as she spoke. "I thought I heard voices."

"Valara, allow me to introduce you to Princess Rose of Fleetwood and her friends, Tagius and Cankles."

Rose curtsied and Cankles bowed respectfully while Tag stared, mesmerized by this beauty of legendary proportions.

"Welcome to our home. I am Valara, consort to Lord Silverthorn." The light cast by the many candles glistened off the golden strands of hair cascading down past her waist as her head nodded in polite acknowledgement.

"Good evening," responded Rose. Her elbow poked Tag in his ribs to break his trance. When he continued to stare, mouth agape, the Princess' hand came up, pushing Tag's jaws shut as she scolded him, "It is rude to stare, and ruder still to drool while you stare!"

Her harsh tone and actions were only enough to loosen this hypnotic hold. Tag managed to give the Elf a shy smile as he continued to stare, spellbound by Valara's beauty.

"Please forgive Tag. He does not mean to gawk like an addled-brain dolt," apologized Rose. "I believe he is still traumatized by an earlier mishap."

"Oh, you poor dear!" exclaimed Valara, embracing the young man in a consoling hug. "Perhaps it is something I can heal."

"I believe you are only worsening his condition," determined Rose, prying Tag free of the woman's arms. It annoyed the Princess to no end seeing his shy smile dissolve into a goofy grin. The expression on Tag's face made him look like an adolescent boy besotted by love for the first time as the Elf's sparkling, sapphire eyes held him entranced.

"Good gracious!" exclaimed Valara.

"No need for concern," said Rose. She gave Tag a shake. "Nothing a good slap to the face cannot cure."

"It's a pleasure meetin' you, m'lady," greeted Cankles, bowing low in respect that the hair on the back of his head parted to reveal the scar left by a nasty gash.

For a moment, Valara stared at this reminder of an old wound. "Have we met before, sir?"

"Though I'm quite forgettable on all fronts, a man, not even one as forgetful as me, would not forget meetin' one of such sublime beauty," responded Cankles, as he humbled himself before Valara. "If we had met, not in a hundred years would I forget."

"Such kind words, spoken with such sincerity," praised Valara, flattered by Cankles' compliment.

"I meant every word, m'lady," swore Cankles, staring into her eyes to keep his from wandering down to admire the sheer, luminous gown she wore. This silky material clung to every curve of her perfect body, serving to accentuate her tall, willowy form.

"I used to look just as lovely when I donned my princess finery, but look at me now," lamented Rose, standing before the beautiful Elf. She was embarrassed to appear as a slovenly peasant who had been doused in tree sap and rolled along the forest floor.

"I never assumed this was your normal manner of dress, Princess Rose," said Valara, noticing the clots of drying tree sap tangling her dishevelled head of hair.

"Valara, my dear, please have the servants draw a bath for Princess Rose and deliver a suitable gown for our esteemed guest," requested Rainus.

"Yes, my lord, right away," said Valara. "Please follow me, Princess."

Rose's face reddened, contorting with resentment as she watched Tag stare, mesmerized by this woman as she glided away on light, graceful steps. This trance was only broken as Rose's hand lashed out, swatting Tag sharply on the back of his head to jolt him to his senses.

Rose's abrupt action snapped Tag out of this hypnotic state as he watched her storm off, following Valara out of the room.

"Oh, my!" exclaimed Cankles, startled by Rose's response. "If I didn't know better, I'd say the Princess was jealous."

"The only thing she would be jealous of is knowing there is someone more beautiful than her," grunted Tag, rubbing his smarting head to erase the stinging pain where hand met scalp.

"Oh, Valara, my dear!" called Rainus. "When the Princess is done, ready a bath for her comrades and send a servant to find them some fresh apparel to wear."

Valara gave him a polite nod of understanding as she disappeared down the corridor with Rose.

"But no manty-hoses, please!" pleaded Tag, speaking on Cankles' behalf as well as his own. "We are not permitted to wear tights."

"If you prefer, I can have your attire laundered instead," offered Rainus, glancing at their grubby clothing.

"That would be wonderful, but only if it is not an imposition on your staff," responded Tag.

"You are my guests! It is not an inconvenience at all," stated the

Elf. "I want you to feel at home. And if wearing your usual raiment helps, then by all means, I shall have them cleaned for you."

"Thank you," said Tag.

"We're most grateful," added Cankles, relieved that none would be subjected to seeing his stick legs and knobby knees garbed in the form-fitting tights considered fashionable by the Elf men.

As though one of his keen-eared staff members overheard this exchange, an Elf maiden appeared, robes draped over one arm and a willow laundry hamper in the other.

"If you disrobe now, I can have my servant take care of your raiment immediately," said Rainus. "You are welcome to don one of these robes for the time being."

"Thank you," said Tag. "Where can we get changed?"

"Right here is fine," invited Rainus.

Tag and Cankles exchanged nervous glances, and then peered over at the Elf and the young maiden as they stood there, waiting for them.

"Well, go on!" urged Rainus. "No time like the present. It is not as though your clothes will clean themselves."

"Ah… Do you two mind turning around?" asked Tag. He was ill at ease having the Elves watch as they disrobed.

"Yeah, we're kind of shy," added Cankles. "But if you don't want to turn around, we can."

Rainus frowned in confusion. He considered Cankles' suggestion, and then the Elf chuckled lightheartedly, "Do not be ashamed, good sirs! Just because the human form seems flawed when compared to that of an Elf, there is no reason to be ashamed."

"We're not ashamed," explained Tag, his face blushing with embarrassment. "It is just that we are… modest."

"Modest in what way?" questioned Rainus. "Modestly endowed?"

"Oh, it is nothing like that! I mean to say, we like our privacy," answered Tag, becoming flustered.

"Fair enough," said Rainus. He nodded in understanding as he and the Elf maiden turned their backs to them.

Tag and Cankles quickly shed their clothes and threw the robes on.

"Oooh! I quite like this," exclaimed Cankles, feeling the silky material caress his bare skin. The robe draped his body like a large, loose-fitting kaftan. "It's so light and airy."

"Yes, just watch out for sudden drafts. You don't want to be revealing more than you should," warned Tag, his hands dropping to his sides to make sure the breezy fabric didn't float up on him.

"For now, while we wait for Princess Rose to join us, let us share in a friendly drink," suggested Rainus, holding up a bottle of red wine. "After all, it would be pointless to hold discussions without her."

"I suppose one small glass will do no harm," decided Tag, nodding in agreement.

"This wine is like a magical elixir, full-bodied but mellow. It is an absolute delight to drink; scintillating to the palate with a smooth finish," explained Rainus, his mouth watering as he uncorked the bottle to fill three Elf-size goblets.

"Thank you, m'lord," said Cankles, eagerly accepting the large drinking vessel that held almost a pint of wine.

"Here is to our kind host and to his gracious hospitality," offered Tag, raising the goblet to make a toast to Rainus.

"Here! Here!" cheered Cankles, hoisting his drink to honour the Elf.

"Thank you," said Rainus. "Now drink up. There is plenty more where this came from."

"You are too generous, my lord. We are best to drink in moderation," cautioned Tag, taking a sip of his wine as he savoured this beverage.

"Why? It is not as though you have to ride your horse anywhere on this night," reminded Rainus, topping up their goblets.

"Quite right, m'lord!" agreed Cankles, swallowing down a big gulp with this realization.

"True, there is no fear of reckless riding," agreed Tag. "However, drinking to excess is not recommended for good reason."

"Are you concerned about becoming intoxicated?" questioned Rainus, glancing over at this young mortal.

"Not really, Lord Silverthorn. I'm more concerned about the aftermath, the wretched condition that ravages the mind and body the following morning," explained Tag, rubbing his head as though he had been overcome by a splitting headache.

"You forget, Master Yairet, you are in the land of Elves," assured Rainus. "I have the power to heal what ails you, even the most brutal of hangovers."

"I suppose you are right," conceded Tag, allowing himself a mouthful of wine.

"I have only one word to say," stated Cankles, as he indulged in another generous swig, *"Let's party!"*

"That was *two* words," corrected Tag, frowning in confusion at his comrade.

"Who cares? Bring on the wine!" declared Cankles, polishing off his drink so his goblet can be refilled. "I swear this is the best thing to ever pass these lips!"

"I am pleased you are enjoying this fine vintage, my friend," said Rainus, pouring the aromatic, carmine liquid for his guests. "We shall share in a meal when Princess Rose is done preening and the two of you have had a chance to freshen up."

"Sounds delightful," responded Tag. He could feel his face turning red, warmed by the heat stoked by the alcohol as it insidiously migrated from his empty stomach. It permeated every fibre of his being, numbing his mind and muscles, including his tongue as he started to slur ever so slightly, "We've not eaten since early this afternoon. A meal would definitely do us some good."

"Then I will make it so," said Rainus, taking a sip. "But first, a bit more wine to whet our appetite."

The Elf topped up his guests' crystal goblets, keeping them entertained with tales of Elven folklore as the Princess took her time.

Rose was in no rush to join them. She relaxed, luxuriating in the warm, perfumed water. Lathering up her hair to be rid of the tree sap, she carefully detangled her tresses with an ivory comb as her comrades continued to drink. And as quickly as they consumed the wine, Rainus continued to pour, for it was customary for Elves to play the role of the obliging host to the extreme. By the time the Elf maiden returned with their freshly cleaned apparel, Tag and Cankles could barely stand upright to get dressed.

The wine and conversation had been flowing freely when Rose finally returned to join her comrades. Wandering down the corridor, she followed the bursts of boisterous laughter and friendly banter coming from the parlor where she had last seen Tag and Cankles.

"What is going on here?" gasped Rose. She was appalled to discover the Elf and his guests wallowing in various levels of intoxication.

"Just sharing in a friendly drink," answered Rainus, with a congenial, but drunken smile. "Care to join us, Princess?"

She glared at Cankles as he snored loudly. He lay sprawled out, in a most undignified manner, across one of the comfy loungers. He was immersed in a deep sleep; the empty goblet dangling from his hand while Tag stared in this drunken stupor, gawking at the Princess. Even inebriated, he was stunned by what his eyes beheld.

No longer was Rose donning her frumpy, stained smock and apron. Gone too were the dirt, grime and sticky tree sap. The Princess was fresh, clean and dressed in a simple, flowing gown of understated elegance much like the one Lady Silverthorn wore. There were no heavy embroidery, dainty bows and garish detailing on a tight fitting bodice and full, flouncy skirt. This lovely gown fit her perfectly to show off her feminine form in a way that was not forced or contrived.

"G-good gracious," slurred Tag. His tongue was like a dead, swollen slug as he stared at Rose through bleary, half-closed eyes as he hiccupped, "You look – you look absolutely beau- beauti- *hic!*"

Before he could finish his sentence, Tag's eyes rolled to the back of his head as he keeled over backwards. He collapsed atop Cankles' limp body to join his friend in an alcohol-induced slumber.

Beware the Pooka!

Ba-boom! Ba-boom! Ba-boom!

This steady pounding vibrated through Tag's body, resonating clear through to his head. At first, he thought someone was hammering on the door so hard it could be heard *and* felt, but as soon as Tag forced his eyelids open just enough to see, the dazzling glare of the morning light stabbed at his eyes. It caused his head to throb all the more.

From this first and fleeting glance the world looked like it had tipped over, lying sideways. His eyes squeezed shut as his senses reeled.

It felt like his heart was beating in his ears as his stomach churned, threatening to purge itself of last night's wine. The burn of sour stomach acids rising to scorch the back of Tag's throat forced him to swallow, but his tongue, feeling thick and fuzzy, was stuck to the roof of his mouth. It felt as though he had been chewing on a ball of wool that had absorbed all traces of saliva.

Tag dared not yawn in case it caused him to involuntarily wretch. Instead, he drew in a long, slow breath through his nose, exhaling just as slowly in a bid to clear the fog from his aching head.

How long he'd been asleep, Tag was not sure. The only thing he knew for certain was his entire body was now rebelling against him.

He strained to open his heavy eyelids once more. It was only wide enough to see without letting the fierce brilliance of the morning sun seeping in through the cracks of the window shutters to accost his bleary eyes.

Lifting his head, Tag was vaguely aware of his surroundings from this prone position on the lounger. He used the back of his hand to wipe away the drying crust that was once a rivulet of drool that seeped from the corner of his mouth where it had added to the small pool of saliva staining the upholstery. As he slowly rolled from his stomach onto his side, a gentle sigh sounded in his ears.

Tag froze.

His eyes opened wide in surprise.

Beneath this quilt Rainus had thrown over him as he slept, a warm body snuggled up, spooning against his back as an arm wrapped around his chest.

"Rose!" Tag gasped beneath his breath as the warmth of spent air exhaled against the nape of his neck tickled him.

Panic filled his heart as he fought to remember how the Princess ended up here, sleeping by his side. In that sheer Elven gown she was wearing last night she might as well be naked. Then again, maybe she was and he had been too drunk to notice. Whatever the case, he was too afraid to look.

And just how was he going to explain this situation to her father if the King should ever catch wind of this?

It then dawned on Tag that if he could just slip out from under this counterpane, move with the stealth of an Elf, he could just disappear from this room before the Princess awoke. None, not even Rose, would be the wiser to this.

Just as he eased one foot onto the floor, the body snuggled closer to Tag. The gentle breath of a contented sigh teased the skin on his neck to send a shiver down his spine.

Tag relaxed as he basked in this shared body warmth only to freeze once more. His back straightened and his muscles tensed as a loud snore suddenly rattled in his ears as something hard abruptly poked him low on his back.

Tag tumbled off the lounger, the quilt sliding off the sleeping form as he yelped in surprise. He scrambled to throw this counterpane back over the Princess, but instead, he came face to face with Cankles as the man woke with a start. He and Tag screamed in each other's face, appalled and surprised to find they had been getting cozy with each other.

Jumping to his feet, Tag shuddered in disgust as he realized what part of Cankles' anatomy had been prodding him as he slept.

"What?" asked Cankles, in a confused daze as he fell off the other side of the lounger.

"Bloody hell!" cursed Tag, stammering as he pointed accusingly at his bedmate. "You were touching me with your, with your –"

"Dagger?" finished Cankles, staring through bloodshot eyes at Tag.

"If that's what you want to call it!" snapped Tag. Shuddering once more, he felt utterly violated.

"Actually, it's more of a huntin' knife than a proper dagger," decided Cankles, as he stood up, adjusting the leather sheathe housing the blade on his belt. It had twisted about as he tossed in his drunken slumber. "I suppose I should've taken it off before I fell asleep last night."

Rose burst into the parlor, dashing from her bedchamber upon hearing this great commotion.

"What happened?" asked Rose. "I thought I heard screaming."

"We were *not* screaming," corrected Tag, looking momentarily flustered. "We were shouting in surprise."

Rose stared through narrowed, suspicious eyes at her comrades as she commented, "Am I mistaken, or were you two sharing that lounger?"

"Well, it was quite comfy," admitted Cankles, stretching as he yawned.

"Too comfy for my liking. That's why I slept on the floor," explained Tag. Tossing the quilt onto the lounger, he pretended he had used it to cushion his body against the floor.

"Right…" muttered Rose, her eyes glinting with skepticism.

"Good morning!" greeted Rainus Silverthorn. He breezed into the parlor, throwing the window shutters wide open. "I trust you slept well."

"My bed was absolutely heavenly," said Rose, looking well rested. "I slept like a baby!"

"Wonderful!" exclaimed the Elf.

"We were downright cozy, m'lord! Thank you very much," added Cankles, only to have Tag's elbow discreetly jab him in the ribs.

"Well, I had my concerns. I was not sure how you would fare out here, but all attempts to wake you two failed miserably. Dead to the world, you were," explained Rainus, as he glanced over at Tag and Cankles. "I do believe tying you both behind a horse and having it drag you naked through a stand of nettles would have done nothing to wake either one of you."

"Well, we're wide-awake now," stated Tag, stretching his dormant muscles, "and ready to resume with our meeting this morning."

"In due time, Master Yairet. I do not know about you mortals, but for Elves, we must break this morning fast with a hearty meal."

"Oh, breakfast sounds wonderful," agreed Cankles, his hand rubbing his rumbling belly.

"How can you even think of eating?" gasped Tag, grimacing at the thought.

"Easy! I'm feelin' more than a bit peckish this morn," replied Cankles. "An' I'm bettin' you are too."

"I believe some water is about all my stomach can handle right now," groaned Tag.

"Serves you right!" scolded Rose, feeling no pity for her jester.

"Feeling a bit droopy, are we?" questioned Rainus.

"A bit," admitted Tag, wincing in pain for being on the receiving end of Rose's mincing words and harsh tone.

"I have a cure for that."

"Elven healing magic?" hoped Tag.

"No magic," answered Rainus. "I have some willow tonic. It will effectively dull that throbbing pain in your head."

"Sounds good to me. As long as it works, I'm fine with that," decided Tag, his hands pressing against his temples.

"I promise you, it will," said the Elf.

"An' then you can eat some breakfast," added Cankles, smacking his lips in anticipation of a satisfying meal.

"Absolutely! After all, it is the most important meal of the day; fuels the body and the mind," stated Rainus, directing his guests to the dining room. "Follow me."

Trailing behind Rose, Tag's eyes narrowed in suspicion. A glint of sunlight caught his attention as it sparkled off the Princess' head like a dazzling halo.

"Hey… What's that?" questioned Tag.

"Do you like it?" Rose struck a pose to show off the fine strands of gold, braided and woven to form a simple but stylish tiara to perfectly match the understated elegance of the Elven gown she now wore.

"That would depend."

"On what?" asked Rose.

"Whether that piece of jewellery came with the dress or if it was conjured up in the form of a wish."

"Then it is better not to ask," responded Rose, turning away to escape his scrutiny.

"I knew it! What a waste!"

"You know nothing. If you did, you would know that it was going to be a wish wasted if I did not use it with the approach of the midnight hour."

"You should have consulted with me first before wasting the last wish!"

"I tried, but you were too busy sleeping off the wine!"

"Oh…" was all Tag could manage.

"Is that all you can say?" grumbled Rose, her hands on her hips. "I do believe an apology is in order."

"If I apologize, will you admit it was a waste?"

"That is tantamount to saying that making a fashion statement or being stylish is a waste," protested Rose.

"It is! If being stylish can somehow save our lives or assist us in surviving this quest, then I'll be the first one to admit it wasn't a waste."

"I will have you know, this lovely piece is made of the finest quality gold. I can sell it in a pinch if we are pressed for money."

Tag released a dreary sigh of resignation, "Fine... I suppose if that last wish was not used, it would have gone to waste anyway."

"Exactly!" declared Rose. "And if anything, we still have two more wishes left to use before the end of this day."

"Hold on here!" demanded Tag. "What happened to three?"

"I had to use one of the new wishes to dream up the perfect shoes to match my gown and this tiara, of course," answered Rose. Her words were matter-of-fact as she raised the hem of the dress to reveal her new footwear. "Other than comfort, flat heels do nothing for me. These babies help to make my legs look slender, a bit more statuesque, like an Elf maiden."

"In your dreams," muttered Tag, shaking his head in defeat.

"Say again?"

"Never mind," said Tag, steering Rose to the dining hall.

"Sit, my friends," invited Rainus, as he took his place at the head of the table. "I am sure there is something here to please your discerning palates."

Cankles drooled. His eyes bulged as they stared at the assortment of fruits both dried and freshly picked, warm breads as well as the selection of fresh and lightly steamed vegetables spread across the table.

"This is quite the banquet," said Rose, as she motioned for Cankles to push her chair in closer to the table. "But where's the meat?"

"Excuse me?" responded the Elf.

"Bacon? Sausage? Maybe some ham?" answered Rose, her hungry eyes skimming the table for a platter of hot protein.

"Please forgive the Princess for her ignorance, Lord Silverthorn," said Tag. "As educated as her title implies her to be, it is apparent she is unaware your people do not eat meat."

"They don't?" asked Rose, frowning in confusion.

"That is correct," responded Rainus, passing a crock of freshly churned butter to the ravenous Cankles as the man tore off chunks of bread to bury his plate.

"How can you not eat meat?" questioned Rose.

"We can, but we choose not to. It is difficult to digest and causes bloating. Vegetables and fruits are healthier to consume for both man and Elf."

"I suppose," sighed Rose, eyeing the steam rising from the basket of freshly baked bread. "On this day, I feel a need to indulge on baked goods."

"Here ya go," mumbled Cankles, as he handed her a mangled loaf. He could barely squeeze these muffled words out from a mouth stuffed full of masticated bread.

"This is highly unusual," commented Tag. "I thought, as your appearance was everything to you, that you'd rather eat a healthier diet to maintain your weight?"

"It is very important to me, but it is not *everything*," explained Rose. "Besides, if I get a little plump it is not as though I cannot just wish it away, if I wanted to."

Tag glared at the Princess, giving her the *shut-your-mouth* look of reproach.

"Don't you give me the evil eyes!" snapped Rose, fishing out the crystal suspended on the gold chain. "Or I shall wish you straight into the stable to dine with the horses."

Rainus' back straightened as his keen eyes immediately homed in on the magical stone Rose threatened Tag with.

"Brilliant, Princess!" rebuked Tag, scowling in anger. "Why do you not just announce it to the whole world that you possess the dreamstone?"

Rose's face reddened with embarrassment upon realizing what she had done. She hastily concealed the crystal once more even though it was obvious the Elf was now aware of it.

"The young master is quite correct, Princess. You would be wise to be discreet and discerning as to whom you choose to reveal that crystal to," advised Rainus. "There are those who will risk everything, even kill for it, to claim it as their own."

"Like you?" asked Rose, her voice meek as she nervously glanced over at the Elf.

"Oh, no! Not me! In all honesty, I have no desire to possess that little *trinket*. It has been the cause of more grief and misery for my people than you will ever know," revealed Rainus, dismissing the crystal with a wave of his hand. "When you want for naught and still desire more, it can only lead to trouble."

"You know of this dreamstone?" questioned Tag.

"What Elf does not know of that cursed thing? Though it has been relegated to the memory of most mortals as being nothing more than an article of myth, we know all too well of the Dream Merchant and the magic crystal."

"But this is the crystal imbued with powers to make everything you can dream of into reality," stated Rose, bewildered this Elf showed not even mild interest in claiming this wondrous stone.

"And there's the rub, my dear Princess!" stated Rainus, giving her a judicious nod of his head. "The wise will tell you that getting whatever you wish for does not necessarily lead to happiness, for happiness is a state of mind."

"Gettin' whatever you wish for isn't everything it's cracked up to be," offered Cankles, nodding in agreement. "I'm thinkin' it's kinda like messin' with fate."

"Nonsense!" disputed Rose. "One can control one's fate with the dreamstone."

"What are you talking about? That dreamstone is the cause of all your troubles to begin with," argued Tag.

"I beg to differ! Pancecilia Feldspar is the instigator of my grief," argued the Princess. "As for the dreamstone, it is merely a matter of perfecting my technique and learning to be selective where the wishes are concerned."

"You say that now, but the Elf-kind have existed long enough to know there is intrinsic value in a little honest, hard work to make dreams come true rather than to simply wish, willy-nilly," explained Rainus.

"I will have you know, I have been working hard to make my wishes come true," countered Rose. "No willy-nilly here!"

"You must have worked up a real sweat wishing for those shoes," grunted Tag, rolling his eyes in frustration.

"You have no idea!" Rose snapped as she glared at her jester.

"Are you two married?" asked Rainus.

"Are you insane?" responded Rose and Tag, speaking simultaneously.

"No need to get your hackles up," said Rainus, motioning for calm. "Just an observation."

"Well, you observed wrong, Lord Silverthorn!" stated Tag, grimacing at the thought.

"My mistake," apologized the Elf. "The way you two mortals bicker, I just thought you were a couple."

"There is a matter of class," pointed out the Princess, as she gave Tag a distasteful glance.

"Yes," agreed Tag, giving Rose a snide smile in return. "She has none."

"Still not funny!" pouted Rose.

"Still not trying," grumbled Tag.

"Perhaps we should pay heed to Lord Silverthorn's warning," suggested Cankles, attempting to head off another verbal fisticuff.

"Especially the part where he mentioned 'bout those willin' to kill for the dreamstone."

"Yes. One can never be too careful where that magic crystal is concerned," averred the Elf.

"So we must be watchful of rogues and scoundrels?" asked Cankles.

"Never mind them! There is a greater danger in these parts," cautioned Rainus, his words foreboding. "Beware the Pooka!"

"Beware the *what-a?*" said the trio. They frowned in curiosity, for never had they heard of this word before.

"The Pooka," repeated Rainus. "Come to think of it, be more careful of the Pooka's master. He is the one you should be most fearful of."

"First thing first," said Tag, motioning the Elf to slow down. "What in the world is this *Pooka* thing?"

"Do you know what a Sprite is?" questioned Rainus.

"Of course we do," responded Rose.

"The Pooka is a just that: a rare form of Sprite. However, in this case, I am speaking of an ill-tempered, nasty, *shape-shifting* creature," informed the Elf.

"What do you mean by shape-shiftin'?" asked Cankles. He stopped eating upon hearing this unexpected description.

"I mean exactly that! This particular Sprite has the power to change its appearance at will. It has the ability to take on the form of any animal it wishes. Usually, before mortal man he appears as a beautiful, ebony steed."

"A black horse?" queried Cankles. "If that is so, how will we be able to tell it apart from other dark horses?"

"By its rather sinister looking amber eyes," replied Rainus.

"If that *Poobah* gives me grief, then I shall hope it appears before me as a gnat and I will squash it," warned Rose, her hand slapping down on the tabletop.

"It is a Pooka and he goes by the name of Loken," corrected Rainus. "You would be wise to heed my warning, for not only is this Sprite of a nasty disposition, Loken is Dragonite's minion."

"And this Dragonite fellow is dangerous?" determined Tag.

"This is no ordinary *fellow,*" revealed the Elf. "I am speaking of Parru St. Mime Dragonite. And mark my words, he is very dangerous."

"Still, I cannot say I recognize his name," said Rose.

"If you do not now, then I pray you never will. However, it would be unkind of me not to warn you of him as you travel through these lands."

"And just who is this fellow with the silly name?" asked Rose.

"Dragonite is a rogue Wizard, a Sorcerer if you will. The Pooka does his bidding."

"But we have no grudge with this Sorcerer," stated Tag.

"It matters not," disclosed Rainus. "If he should find out the Princess is in possession of the dreamstone, Dragonite will stop at nothing to claim it as his own."

"Well, as long as she doesn't openly flaunt the thing, we should fine," decided Tag.

"With a minion like the Pooka to aid him, discretion goes right out the window," cautioned Rainus. "Remember, this Sprite can take on the form of a *horse* or a *horsefly*. You can be as careful as you like, but you can never tell if the Pooka is lurking about, listening to your every word."

"We shall heed your warning," said Tag, as he nodded in understanding.

"But what about this rogue Wizard?" asked Cankles. "Why would he be so interested in this dreamstone?"

"That is simple," said Rainus.

"So is he," responded Rose, glancing over at Cankles. "You best explain it to him."

"There is good reason Parru St. Mime Dragonite is now branded a Sorcerer. He held certain beliefs that were viewed as – "

"Evil?" interjected Cankles.

"Perverse is more like it," replied the Elf. "But eventually, the seeds of evil took root in his twisted mind."

"And just what is this perverse evil?" questioned Tag.

"I believe his name says it all," stated Rainus.

"Parru?" asked Cankles.

"No, he means Dragonite," decided Rose.

"I was speaking of *St. Mime*," corrected the Elf. "The demented fellow was, and still is, under the misguided belief that those who perform as mimes should be revered."

"What?" gasped Tag.

"I speak the truth when I say this Sorcerer had taken to the forbidden arts when his bid to garner respect for the *art* of mimicry, and I do use the term loosely, failed miserably."

"This is too bizarre," stated Rose. "Are you speaking of those so-called performers who take to mimicking the actions of others to the point of sheer annoyance?"

"Yes!" Rainus nodded in confirmation. "The Sorcerer believes it is an under appreciated art form. He feels if he does not take certain measures to preserve it, it is doomed to be lost forever."

"As it should be," declared Rose. "The last time a troop of mimes attempted to pass themselves off as entertainers, I had them banned from the palace."

"Well, as most do not share the Sorcerer's same appreciation for this *art*, he has taken up their cause," explained Rainus. "He is the self-proclaimed patron saint of mimes."

"He seems delusional," decided Tag.

"That would be the least of your concerns. Because of the Sorcerer's personal campaign to garner appreciation for this art form, he is venerated by all the mimes of this realm. Dragonite has been elevated to the status of their leader. Of course, this only served to inflate his already bloated ego, fuelling his twisted desire."

"Oh, my! He's quite serious 'bout this," decided Cankles.

"Very much so," warned Rainus. "He is hell-bent on elevating this *art* to an honoured and respected status in society."

"No disrespect to you, Lord Silverthorn, but this is sounding too bizarre to be true," said Tag.

"It is truly bizarre, but Parru St. Mime Dragonite is driven by his own madness," cautioned Rainus. "As much as he is ridiculed and shunned by the Order of Wizards, he is just as respected, even adored, by the mimes. When one walks the fine line between sanity and madness, it is not hard to fall when the scales are already tipped."

"Well, that fool can dream on if his wish is to have a mime in every courtyard and town square," grunted Rose, shaking her head in dismay.

"That is exactly what he wishes for!" exclaimed Rainus. "If Dragonite can claim the dreamstone, he will do this and more, imposing his will and bad taste on all."

"So what if he makes it a respected art form," said Tag. "It can be a hell of a lot worse than that."

"So you say! But you have never been made to endure one of their performances!" snapped Rose, her hands coming up as she pretended to be trapped behind an invisible wall.

"Oh, believe you me, Master Yairet, it will be just that! Dragonite is bitter and vengeful. His heart has turned cold having been made to endure years of ridicule. He has been maligned by mortals, disgraced and scorned by his fellow Wizards, plus, none of us Elves care for him either."

"Serves him right if he thinks he can impose his silly ideas on others," sniffed Rose.

"You should talk, Princess," scolded Tag.

"At least my ideas make absolute sense," argued Rose.

"Getting back to the matter at hand," said Cankles, motioning for his comrades to hold their tongues as he addressed the Elf. "What do you think this Sorcerer will do if he gets his hands on the dreamstone?"

"I can only imagine. Unfortunately, I have a rather fecund imagination," said Rainus, with a disheartened sigh.

"So he is crazy," dismissed Rose.

"He is insane, but make no mistake, Princess, Dragonite is far from stupid. Whatever revenge he will set in motion if he possesses this magic crystal can only promise doom for all he believes wronged him."

"Then I have nothing to fear," stated Rose. "I have never even met the Sorcerer to wrong him in the first place."

"Do you possess an ardent appreciation for the art of mime, Princess?" questioned Rainus.

"Of course not!" exclaimed Rose.'

"Then you have wronged him," stated the Elf.

"As long as he does not intend to unleash his mimes on society, those who truly wronged him, specifically his peers, can deal with his wrath," decided Rose.

"You should know, as far as Dragonite is concerned, he was wronged by society as a whole. You and your kind will not go unscathed should the Sorcerer exact his revenge," cautioned Rainus.

"I propose we take measures to ensure the Sorcerer never finds out that you're in possession of the dreamstone in the first place," suggested Tag.

"If it makes my life easier, then I agree wholeheartedly," said Rose. "I will not speak of the *you-know-what* again, so let us resume with breakfast."

"That will have to wait for now," stated Rainus.

"Why?" asked Cankles.

"We are about to have a visitor."

Tag, Rose and Cankles exchanged quizzical glances, unaware of the rushed footsteps fast approaching the Elf's home.

"By the gait of his steps, I would have to say it is the captain of my army, Halen Ironwood," determined Rainus.

True to his word, the mortals in Rainus' company jumped with a start as the captain burst into the room.

"Lord Silverthorn, we are under attack!"

"Where?" asked Rainus, rising from the table.

"Along the eastern perimeter of our forest bordering the Trolls' territory! If we do not act now, the damage will be devastating and irreversible," warned Halen.

"The Trolls are attacking?" gasped Tag.

"No, but their damned goats are," explained Rainus, throwing his cloak over his shoulders. "Those voracious creatures shall strip the forest bare in no time!"

"But what about our meeting?" questioned Rose.

"Those cursed animals are the reason we have put an embargo on King Maxmillion's cheese supply!" stated Rainus, motioning for Halen to gather his longbow and quiver. "Wait here if you wish, but I must deal with this invasion now!"

"Maybe we can help?" offered Cankles.

"Perhaps we can," decided Tag, nodding in agreement.

"Then follow me," ordered Rainus. "We shall meet those rapacious ungulates head-on and with a vengeance!"

Rainus was an Elf on a mission. With determined steps, he led the others out of the dining hall. Yanking open the cottage door, Cankles and Tag were forced to run just to keep up with him.

"Wait for me!" hollered Rose.

She ducked, her hand slapping out at a large, green moth as it fluttered overhead. It had been drawn to the flame of the porch lantern, resting on the door when it was carried away by the wake of displaced air as the mortals rushed after the Elves.

"Over there, my lord!" shouted Halen. He pointed at the forest invaders that had created a clearing where there was not one before. "Those blasted animals even devoured the barriers of nettle."

"Those mangy beasts!" cursed Rainus, eyeing the herd with contempt. "They are everywhere."

True to his words, a herd of white, grizzled looking, gluttonous goats voraciously munched on grasses, yanking the vegetation from the ground to devour even the roots. Others browsed on shrubs, stripping them of leaves, buds and twigs while the more agile ones managed to climb into the trees. Balanced on branches, they took to nibbling on the foliage and stripping off layers of bark from the young trees.

"I shall be rid of those vermin once and for all," growled Rainus. Taking up his bow, he nocked an arrow. He took aim at a floppy-eared kid bleating noisily as its mother grazed nearby.

"Whoa! Hold on there! You're not thinkin' of killin' that little fella, are you, m'lord?" asked Cankles.

"I intend to kill each an every one of those pesky, eating machines," declared Rainus.

"That's rather extreme," protested Cankles. "They're only goats after all."

"Not only will those goats devour the plants of this forest, they will destroy everything in sight," argued Rainus. "They tear up the earth to encourage soil erosion! And the way they are taking to stripping off bark? It will only be a matter of time before those trees are girdled to expose their inner workings that keep them nourished and alive. Once that happens, these trees will die and fall to decay."

"Have you tried speaking to the Trolls about their wayward herds?" asked Rose. "Did you ask them to keep control of their animals?"

"Many times, but as you can see, it has been an exercise in futility," snapped Rainus. "Not only are the Trolls not particularly intelligent, they are lazy to begin with, too lazy to properly shepherd their animals. And they cannot be bothered to build gates and fences to keep them contained."

"Perhaps they lack the knowledge to build such things?" offered Rose.

"They are a simple lot, but I doubt that. Especially when you consider they are able to build bridges, big and small. We even gave them instructions on how to build simple gates to keep their animals under control, but as you can see, either they ignored our advice completely or did a shoddy job of it," complained Rainus.

"There has got to be a better way to deal with these goats than to kill them," reasoned Tag, as he pondered this dilemma.

"If you are suggesting I herd them back to the Trolls, and then give them a good talking to, forget it! It has not worked before, it will not work now," stated Rainus. "Those Trolls will continue to allow their goats to run loose."

"You have to prevent them from wanting to feed on your forest in the first place," suggested Tag. "Keep them from wanting to come back."

"And how do your propose we do that?" grunted Rainus. "These goats are far from intelligent. They cannot be trained. They tend to follow their stomachs."

"They must be intelligent enough to understand fear," decided Tag. "Like any prey animal, they must be fearful of something."

"If you are speaking of wolves, we have not had wolves in the Woodland Glade for over a century," disclosed Rainus.

"Still, if they can be frightened somehow, that might be enough to drive them off, never to return," said Rose. "If anything, I can *wish* for wolves."

"There is no point in re-introducing those predators now," responded

Rainus. "It might do well for the moment, while there are goats to feed upon, but once this food source is depleted, what do you suppose the wolves will turn their attention to?"

"Elves?" responded Cankles.

"No! The unicorns!" corrected Rainus. "And the unicorns are already a threatened species, no thanks to mankind."

"Good point," responded Tag, as he nodded in understanding.

"Now you know why I have no recourse than to kill these blasted animals," stated Rainus, as he and Halen armed their bows once more.

Just as the Elves raised their weapons to take aim, Cankles burst into the clearing, directly into their line of fire. Like a raving madman, he charged toward the goats, bellowing and frantically waving his hands about.

Instead of running away from danger, the startled goats bleated in surprise, only to fall on their sides. As though their legs stiffened with the sudden onset of paralysis, the animals keeled over, appearing to faint from fright. Some managed to stumble a few steps before collapsing, while the goats in the trees simply dropped like four-legged, hairy fruit falling from the branches.

"This is truly bizarre! I have never seen anything like this before," declared Rose, staring in disbelief at the fainting goats.

"Unfortunately for these animals, they were originally bred to mingle with flocks of sheep," explained Tag. "When wolves attack, these goats would simply drop and become easy prey, allowing for the sheep to escape."

After a few seconds, the goats scrambled back onto their feet. They immediately scurried away, but only until the sense of danger had passed and the urge to eat overtook them. Just as they settled down to devouring the greenery, Cankles made another mad dash, whooping and hollering as he charged at them.

Once again, the goats bleated in surprise before fainting. The entire herd keeled over, their stiffened limbs unable to support their bodies.

"This is your solution? To make these nervous beasts faint with fright?" grumbled Rainus, shaking his head in frustration.

"Did you already try this?" questioned Tag. "Try to just frighten them away?"

"At first, yes. However, as these creatures are predisposed to this condition, it was utterly time consuming to wait for them to come to their senses and then chase them off, only to have them drop again and again. We merely herded them back to the Trolls' territory numerous times, with little results," responded the Elf.

"If you keep this up, they cannot feed. If they cannot feed, it will directly affect milk production," explained Tag. "No milk, no cheese!"

"But it is time consuming," reminded Rainus.

"Yes, but you Elves are long-lived," reasoned Rose. "You have time, and plenty of it to spare. So what if you must allocate a wee bit of your time to frighten off these goats?"

"I suppose the inability to graze will seriously impact milk production," agreed the Elf, watching as Cankles gave chase as soon as the goats recovered enough to stand. Again, their efforts to devour the vegetation were circumvented by their brief fainting spell and the need to avoid this strange human. Each time, the goats scampered off farther, retreating closer to the Trolls' territory.

"Perhaps you are onto something, Master Yairet. This may just work to our benefit," decided Rainus.

"And why waste your time when you can have the children undertake this task? After all, they are predisposed to chasing anything on four legs," suggested Rose. "I am sure they will have great sport in tormenting the goats in this manner."

"I believe it is a better alternative to killing the goats," approved Tag. "After all, if you take such drastic action, you will only aggravate relations with the Trolls."

"What relationship there is, is tenuous at best. The last thing my people need are giant beings with an axe to grind," said Rainus, with a disheartened sigh. "But there will come a day when those goats will realize they are in no real danger. They will return. When they do, they must be killed, for they will refuse to turn back."

"It is too bad those animals find your forest so tasty," said Rose. "As they are driven by their stomachs, you are quite right about them returning to feed."

"Then we must think of a way to make this forest unappealing to them," suggested Tag.

"We have already tried a barrier of nettles, but as you can see, those goats ate their way through it," said Rainus.

"They devoured the tender, young shoots and merely trampled over the mature, tough, bristly ones," added Halen.

"I believe it is better if we made it so the *Trolls* will not want their herds eating in your forest to begin with," determined Tag. "Make it so they will take measures to prevent their animals from wandering into this forest in the first place."

"That would be the ideal thing, however, the only plant that will have the desired results is if those goats grazed on sour-grass," stated

Rainus. "And as you can see, the said plant does not grow in this forest."

"What is sour-grass?" questioned Rose, watching as Cankles disappeared from sight as he continued chasing off the herd.

"You've seen it before, but you've never taken notice of it," said Tag. "It is a type of weed that grows in pastures. Farmers take great pains to eradicate it from their fields where they allow their cows to graze."

"Why?" asked Rose. "I did not think cows were fussy eaters."

"Generally, they are not, however, if cows eat enough of this particular plant, the milk they produce takes on a sour taste, hence the name, sour-grass," explained Tag.

"Oh! I see," said Rose. "That would be the smaller piles of weed picked out from the haystack we were hiding in."

"You remember what it looks like?" asked Tag.

"From its big, glossy leaves, right down to its red-tinged stems," confirmed Rose.

"I have an idea," said Tag.

"What is it?" questioned Rainus.

"I recommend the Princess use one of her wishes to grow a barrier of sour-grass along the eastern perimeter of your forest," suggested Tag.

"You want me to do what?" gasped Rose, alarmed that she'd be asked to waste a wish on growing common weeds.

"You heard me, Princess," responded Tag, a shrewd glint in his eyes.

"You do realize I only have *two* wishes left at my disposal on this day?"

"But it will be a wish that can resolve this goat problem," insisted Rainus. "That is, if you choose to use it as such."

"Perhaps your vermin problem can be permanently resolved with a sharp arrow or two, after all," suggested Rose.

"Think on it, Princess," urged Tag. "To grant this wish will be beneficial for all concerned, you included."

"How so?" questioned Rose, her hand shielding the dreamstone.

"If you conjure up that sour-grass, not only will it dissuade the goats from feeding here, it will prevent Rainus and his people from taking aggressive, and what the Trolls will undoubtedly consider hostile, measures to curtail this invasion."

"And?" said Rose, needing more persuasion.

"It means the goats will be safe to continue producing milk for the making of cheese. In turn, the Trolls can continue doing business with King Maxmillion; the Elves will be happy as the goats will no longer pose a threat to their forest, thereby lifting the embargo; and the King of Axalon will be happy to have access to his cheese supply once more.

"You said I would benefit, too," reminded Rose.

"Give your head a shake, Princess!" scolded Tag. "With his cheese supply flowing once more, we have prevented a war between the King of Axalon and the Elves. King Maxmillion cannot hold us, now that we've resolved this problem on his behalf."

"Oh... I see," said Rose.

"So, you will grant this wish?" asked Rainus. "For if you do, my people will be eternally grateful to you, Princess."

"Grateful is good," decided Rose. "But surely you can do better than that."

Tag scowled at the Princess, scolding her, "There are times when an act of kindness should be just that. You should not expect anything in return, especially since it is to your advantage you do this anyway."

"We will be indebted to you if you'd find it in your heart to rectify this goat problem, Princess Rose. As trivial as it seems to you, this forest is our home," explained Rainus. "If you do not help us to protect it, then we will be forced to do so by the only means available to us."

"And that will mean we, or more specifically *you*, will be trapped in the middle of a war between the Elves, King Maxmillion, and undoubtedly, the Trolls," reminded Tag. "You will never return to Pepperton Palace in time for your birthday gala if you do not intervene."

"Good point," admitted Rose. She clasped the dreamstone in her hand as she closed her eyes, conjuring up the exact image of the sourgrass and the barrier it was to form.

To Journey On

"Master! I come with urgent news!"

Though this voice was tiny, the great walls of stone and earth served to amplify it. These words echoed off the stalagmites and stalactites protruding from the cave floor and hanging down from the ceiling.

In this dreary gloom, a pair of eyes snapped open. Darting about, they gleamed a sinister red, reflecting the light of the torches lining the walls of this chamber.

"Who dare interrupt my meditation?" growled Parru St. Mime Dragonite. The Sorcerer's thin lips drew back into a snarl. His wiry brows furrowed into a scowl as his gnarled hands snatched up his staff.

"One does not snore when mediating," argued the tiny voice, hovering over the Sorcerer's shoulder. "You were fast asleep."

Dragonite glanced up. His suspicious eyes scrutinized a pale green moth as it alighted upon one of the finials crowning this crude throne.

"Pray you be one of my servants or I shall smite you," growled the Sorcerer, "and it will not take magic to do so!"

"Of course it is one of your servants," answered the moth. A small cloud of loose, dust-like scales swirled about as its wings rattled with indignation upon receiving this hostile salutation.

"Loken?" questioned the Sorcerer, staring at the winged insect with tiny, feathery antennae. "Is that you?"

"Just how many moths do you know can speak as I do?" snapped the Pooka.

"None! Mind you, the others never had a chance to speak before I killed them," grunted Dragonite.

In a dull throb of light the insect abruptly transformed back into a Sprite. His tatty attire of tiny chickweed leaves patched together covered his body, all except his gangly little arms and legs. His grimy hands released its grip on the finial.

Instead of dropping down onto his master's shoulder, the puny being pushed off the throne, launching into the damp, musty air. His tattered, translucent wings thrummed in erratic flight, allowing Loken to land lightly upon the armrest of the throne.

When not hunched over, this Sprite stood a good head and shoulders taller than the average Fairy, but Loken was still small in comparison to the Sorcerer's hand that was now balled into a quivering, agitated fist.

"If you value your life, you would be wise to make your presence known in this current form than to constantly appear before me in all manners of beast," warned Dragonite.

"And you would be wise to remember it is my ability to take on these many forms that keeps you one step ahead of danger and living in the lifestyle you've grown accustomed to," reminded Loken, unmoved by the Sorcerer's foul demeanor.

"Oh, hoorah!" grunted Dragonite, rolling his eyes in frustration. "As if anyone can grow accustomed to these dreary surroundings! If I had my way, I would be living in an opulent castle with a huge court-yard. I would be surrounded by nobility whom I'd entertain with the best artists to perform grand shows of pantomime."

"Your wish is but one *dreamstone* away," stated the Pooka.

"Do not mock me!" snapped the Sorcerer. His clenched fist slammed down on the throne's armrest so hard it made Loken bounce with the percussion of the impact. "Silas Agincor no longer wanders these lands to the east; not since I've taken over with my followers."

"True, the Dream Merchant is not about, but that blasted Wizard is not even a consideration. What I speak of is the dreamstone, minus Agincor."

"You speak in riddles! Explain yourself!" demanded the Sorcerer. He snatched up the Sprite, his hand wrapping tightly around Loken's body, attempting to squeeze the news out of him.

"Damn you!" cursed Dragonite, releasing his hold as the tiny being surged with light to morph into a hedgehog. "I will kill you for the blight you are!"

"If you do, you shall never hear my news," warned the Pooka, his coat of sharp spines bristling in annoyance as he dared the Sorcerer to handle him with such disregard again. "Better yet, why don't I become a swift and fly right out of here? I'll never have to bother with you again!"

"No need to get testy! I was just eager to hear from you," responded Dragonite, motioning for the Sprite to calm down as he shook the pain from his hand. "Now, what say you, my little friend?"

"I am *not* your friend! And I need your disrespect as much as you need my impertinence! Yet, as fate would have it, we are forced to rely upon each other for now."

"Yes, we must cooperate for the time being," agreed the Sorcerer. A knotted index finger tapped his chin in pensive thought.

"Just keep that in mind," sniffed Loken. With a snap of his fingers and a throb of light, he adopted his usual form once again.

"So tell me what you know," urged Dragonite, leaning forward to listen to his reluctant minion. "What do you know of the dreamstone?"

"I know it is closer than you think," teased Loken, tempting the Sorcerer with these promising words.

"But you said the Dream Merchant was not close to here."

"So I did, but more importantly, the dreamstone is!" answered the Sprite, his amber eyes gleaming with mischief.

"Where?" asked Dragonite, his voice rose a pitch in excitement. "I need to know!"

"As we speak, it is in the Woodland Glade," revealed Loken, giving his master a knowing smile.

"Rainus Silverthorn has it?" gasped Dragonite. The sharp features of his face became more accentuated as he scowled, angered that his nemesis was now in possession of the magic stone.

"No! That Elf wants nothing to do with the dreamstone. It is in the possession of a mortal girl, Princess Rose-alyn of Fleetwood to be exact."

"Who told you this?" The hard edge to Dragonite's face softened slightly upon hearing this unexpected news.

"No one told me. I heard it with mine own ears. I was there, at Silverthorn's residence, when that girl foolishly blurted out that she possesses the dreamstone."

"Agincor has been known to disguise it in various forms to keep it from falling into the hands of those wishing to abuse its powers. What did it look like this time?" probed the Sorcerer. He crouched before his minion, eager to learn more. "Did you see it?"

"No, I did not. However, I did hear Silverthorn warn the Princess to keep it safe and hidden away from curious eyes. As best as I could tell, she wears it about her neck."

"How clever! Disguised as a bauble on a necklace," determined Dragonite. "It would be easy enough to pass off as a simple trinket of little value."

"I suppose it stands to reason when you consider how many would be in eager pursuit to claim it, if they knew of its existence," responded the Sprite.

"And none saw you at Silverthorn's residence, eavesdropping on his guest?"

"You worry all for naught! I was discreet as usual," assured Loken. "And if anyone did see me, all they saw was an ordinary moth drawn to the flame of the porch lantern. Nothing more."

"Hence your appearance when you returned to my lair," determined Dragonite, nodding in approval.

"Verily! And the dreamstone will be yours once you can steal it away from that Princess."

"And she is in Silverthorn's domain, you say?"

"For now, but she is merely passing through the enchanted forest. And you should know, she does not travel alone," revealed Loken. "The Princess is in the company of two servants."

"Whether it is two or two-hundred, as long as she remains in the Woodland Glade, she is untouchable to me," grunted Dragonite, heaving a disenchanted sigh. "Silverthorn's warriors patrol the borders, keeping their eyes out for my presence. My dark magic, in its present state, will only be repelled by the Elf-kind should I attempt to use it in their cursed forest."

"As I said, she is in the Elf's realm for now, but she ventures east. As I understand it, her ultimate destination is the Land of Big."

For the longest moment, Parru St. Mime Dragonite sat in silence, pondering these words. His eyes gleamed in the most sinister manner as the permanent scowl and drooping corners of his mouth curled up into a most unnatural grin.

"Oh, my! At long last, fortune smiles upon me!" squealed Dragonite, his feet kicking up in the air like an excited child. "That means the Princess, and more importantly, the dreamstone will be passing through my domain and right into my clutches!"

"Indeed!"

"And you say this Princess Rose is in the company of only two knights?" ascertained the Sorcerer, peering over his tented fingers to stare down at the Sprite.

"That is the odd thing. The Princess does not travel with a party of knights to protect her. She is in the company of only two lowly servants. One, a hot-headed young man and the other, a dolt of a simpleton."

"This is too good to be true!" delighted Dragonite, slapping his thigh as he chortled. "This is all part of my plan."

"What plan? You have no plan," argued Loken.

"Ah, but I will," promised the Sorcerer. "I shall come up with a grand plan, for I have no intention of allowing this opportunity to slip by me, especially if that mortal shall be slipping through my lands."

"But are you not curious as to why she ventures this way?" questioned the Sprite. "Does it not give you cause for concern?"

Dragonite's thin, cracked lips pursed together. His eyes narrowed as he mulled over Loken's words.

"I suppose it does beg the question, why does she travel to the east, so far from home? And unescorted by a battalion of knights, to boot?" decided the Sorcerer.

"From what I could discern, she is on some kind of quest."

"That is laughable!" dismissed the Sorcerer. "Since when do princesses go on quests? They are the ones who remain safely locked away in towers playing the role of the damsel-in-distress!"

"Look here, I can only tell you what I know."

"Then it is up to you to find out what she is truly up to," urged Dragonite. "Obviously, she has good reason to be travelling with only two lackeys to keep her safe."

"Are you saying this princess is undertaking a *secret* quest to claim something that is of greater value than the dreamstone she already possesses?" questioned Loken.

"Why else would she leave the comforts of her palace to travel into the wilds? And to travel without a host of knights to keep her safe?" responded the Sorcerer. "She means to move in secret, for a large party will only announce her coming. It would be rather conspicuous. My intuition tells me she is up to something – something *BIG!*"

"Your intuition has forsaken you before," grumbled the Sprite, shaking his head in dismay. "Remember your push to have the *art* of mime elevated from its lowly and despised status?"

"It had nothing to do with intuition and everything to do with taste!" disputed the Sorcerer.

"Or the lack thereof," Loken muttered beneath his breath as his eyes rolled in exasperation.

Ignoring the Sprite's utterance, Dragonite continued, "But never mind my taste in the arts. You must return to the enchanted forest immediately. I sense there is a great secret to be had there! You will find out what the Princess is up to before anyone else does."

"So you can…?" questioned Loken, rolling his tiny shoulders in a bewildered shrug as he failed to guess his master's next move.

"So I can get whatever it is she is after before she can claim it as her own, of course!"

"But what about the dreamstone?"

"I intend to claim that magical stone, too!" declared the Sorcerer, his grubby hands rubbing together as he plotted his next course of action. "There is something of great value at stake here, possibly of greater value than even the coveted dreamstone."

"But you do not know that," reminded Loken.

"I will, once *you* find out."

"And if I do, what's in it for me?" asked the Sprite.

"If we succeed, I shall share the prize, whatever it be, equally with you," promised Dragonite, a shrewd glint gleaming in his eyes.

"Equally?" questioned Loken. His fingers rubbed his chin in thought as he contemplated this deal. "You will do that?"

"Yes, an eighty/twenty split," offered Dragonite, as he clarified, "eighty percent for me, twenty for you."

"How can that be equal?" sputtered the Sprite, his brows furrowing in resentment.

"It is all relative! In accordance to the size of the task and the size of those undertaking the task, it *is* equal," insisted the Sorcerer, standing upright to lend emphasis to his greater height as he stared down at the Sprite. "I believe I am being more than generous where you are concerned."

"I thought I was your partner-in-crime?" groaned Loken, his hand slapping his forehead in frustration.

"No, you are my sidekick – a minion," clarified Dragonite, giving the Sprite a judicious nod.

"A *what?*"

"You heard me! A minion is like a henchman. Actually, on the hierarchal ladder of evilness, a minion stands one rung higher than a henchman or crony," explained the Sorcerer. "But I digress. A partner implies we are equals, and we are obviously not."

"There is no arguing with you, is there?" questioned Loken.

"Not on this matter. Besides, if we are equal, there is no one true leader. Every great undertaking requires one. And since I was nominated for this role, my underling you shall remain."

"Nobody nominated you."

"I did," stated the Sorcerer. "And my vote is all that matters. So there!"

"You are being childish," admonished Loken, his arms crossing his chest in defiance.

"Say that to my staff," grunted Dragonite, lowering the tip adorned by a jagged chunk of obsidian.

"I'd rather not," declined Loken. He stared at the black, glass-like volcanic rock as it glowed with an unnatural light, threatening to unleash the Sorcerer's wrath.

"Just as I thought! So you best be on your way," urged Dragonite, shooing the Sprite off. "Return to the Woodland Glade with speed. Find out what the Princess of Fleetwood is truly up to and where she keeps the dreamstone."

"I will do that," responded Loken, contemplating what form he should adopt to travel unhampered and with haste.

"How about turning back into a moth?" suggested the Sorcerer. "Those wings got you here in a timely manner."

"It was the westerly winds that returned me here with speed," corrected the Pooka. "And these same winds will now work against me."

"Then take to the hoof," coaxed Dragonite. "Become a horse and gallop back to the enchanted forest."

"Then I shall be forced to run the gauntlet of those wishing to capture a stray steed. Instead, allow me to choose the manner of beast to assume that will best accomplish the deed."

"Whatever it be, just make sure you go undetected," urged the Sorcerer, waving off the diminutive being. "Do so with haste!"

"What shall we encounter in these lands?" questioned Tag, as he fastened the sword and its scabbard to his belt.

"Cantankerous Trolls," answered Rainus, his words matter-of-fact.

"And their goats," added Cankles, "more goats than you can shake a stick at."

"So, if we can get these Trolls to cooperate, to keep their mangy beasts from devouring your forest, you will allow the Trolls to pass through Woodland Glade to make their deliveries to King Maxmillion once again?" ascertained Rose.

"Yes, but only if they hold true to their promise that they will learn to control their herds," confirmed the Elf. "I would rather not have to resort to the goats returning and being made to eat sour-grass, but if you can convince them, once and for all, to maintain their animals within their territory, the Trolls can pass through my forest unmolested. They will be free to resume their dealings with the King of Axalon."

"Do you have any sage advice to share with us as to how we are to accomplish this deed?" asked the Princess.

"If I had such advice, I would use it myself to deal with the Trolls," replied Rainus. "Alas, those behemoths are as thick as they are tall. I now lack the patience to deal with them using amenable words."

"Are you saying they cannot be reasoned with?" questioned Tag.

"I did not say that. In fact, I am confident they can be, if one has the patience and skills to diplomatically deal with them in a manner that suits their kind," explained the Elf.

"What do you mean by that?" asked Rose.

"From personal experience, the Trolls are simple folk. The complexities of negotiating an agreement based on directives containing any more than a simple, *'yes, you may do that'* or *'no, you may not'* angers them beyond reason. They like *simple*," explained Rainus.

"Well, we are in luck!" exclaimed Rose, as she glanced over at Cankles. "We have someone who speaks their language."

"Just be warned, they will feel they are being given the run-around or their intelligence is being insulted if you attempt to engage them in dialogue as we do now," cautioned Rainus.

"Are they being insulted?" probed Tag.

"Not deliberately," replied the Elf. "Just keep in mind, though they are large in body, their brain seems disproportionately small. They are undeniably the least intelligent beings in this realm. They prefer monosyllabic words, if you get my meaning?"

"Mono-si-*bollock*?" repeated Cankles; baffled by the pronunciation and meaning of this word he had never heard of before. "I don't get it."

"Lord Silverthorn means to say, the Trolls like simple words arranged in simple sentences," explained Tag.

"Don't we all?" asked Cankles. "Simple is good! It'd put an end to a lot of misunderstandings if we all spoke like this."

"Just keep in mind, they love their goats and hate intruders wandering through their lands," cautioned Rainus. "Especially if those intruders are wishing to tell them how to conduct their business where their animals are concerned."

"Do the Trolls have a leader we should address?" questioned Tag.

"Not one who is formally appointed, but yes, they do, if you can call him that," answered Rainus. "His name is Tiny Goatswain."

"*Tiny?* I thought the Trolls were giants," responded Rose, scratching her head in thought.

"As odd as it sounds, his name is quite fitting and self-explanatory once you see him with your own eyes," said the Elf, as he laid a large parchment mapping out the regions to the east. "And as luck would have it, he will be the first Troll you shall encounter as you enter the Land of Small."

"How do we find this particular Troll?" asked Rose.

"First, you must head east to cross High Creek, and then Low Creek, avoid this patch here, Soggy Swamp," said Rainus, using his index finger to point the way on the map Halen Ironwood held up for them to see. "Once you reach Slow River – "

"What is the meaning of these silly names?" groaned Rose. "I mean no offense, but could you not think of more original names than these?"

"No offense taken," responded Rainus. "This is the Trolls' domain I speak of. I had nothing to do with naming the places in the Land of Small."

"Well, it certainly speaks volumes as to how they like things to be kept simple," decided Tag.

"Yes, well, once you cross Slow River, travel another league eastward and you will come across – "

"Fast River," interjected Cankles.

Tag and Rose stared at him.

"How did you know?" asked Rainus, thinking this man had finally remembered travelling through these lands.

"I just figured if there was a Slow River there had to be a fast one, too," chirped up Cankles, with a shrug of his shoulders. "Just seemed to make sense to me."

"Well, once you reach Fast River, seek out the first, large wooden bridge crossing over this body of water," concluded the Elf. "You should find Tiny Goatswain there, if not in the general vicinity."

"So we journey on," resolved Tag, bowing in gratitude to Rainus and the Elves in his company. "I thank you again for your kind hospitality, Lord Silverthorn."

"No need for thanks. Just find a way to make those Trolls understand that if they fail to control their herds within their territory, the embargo will stand. They will no longer be granted passage through this forest to do business with the King of Axalon. If you can accomplish what I could not, I will be the one to thank you."

"We will find a way," promised Rose.

"Without killing the goats," added Cankles.

"Farewell, my friends," bade Rainus. "May the Gods look kindly upon you and grant you safe passage through these lands. For the sake of all, I wish you luck in dealing with the Trolls."

"Luck will not be necessary, Lord Silverthorn. Being a princess, my diplomatic skills shall easily see us through," stated Rose, speaking with utmost confidence.

"Or get us killed," Tag muttered beneath his breath as he mounted his steed, steering his horse eastward.

"Failing that, I am confident I can still devise a winning plan the Trolls will see fit to adhere to if they wish to resume business with King Maxmillion," said the Princess, giving the Elf a knowing smile as Cankles gave her a leg up into her saddle. "Farewell, until we meet again!"

Rainus watched as Rose coaxed her mare on to catch up to Tag's horse as Cankles took up the rear, his steed trotting along at a leisurely pace.

As their hosts shrank against the backdrop of the forest, Cankles turned about one last time to wave at the Elves as they remained at the edge of the Woodland Glade.

"Am I wrong to assume the mortal, Cankles Mayron, did not recall his first meeting with you?" questioned Valara, raising her hand in parting salutation as she watched the Princess and her comrades disappear over the crest of a distant hill.

"That is so," answered Rainus. "However, I am more surprised he had no recollection of you, considering how much time you spent caring for him when he was at his worst."

"Not that I care to be remembered, but I just cannot help but feel pity for that poor soul," lamented Valara. "I cannot imagine having all memory of my life to be vanquished in such a horrific manner."

"It is not just the passing of time that forces this memory from his mind," decided Rainus, with a worrisome sigh.

"He had suffered through so much," responded Valara, shaking her head in sorrow. "Perhaps it was meant to be."

"I sense if he was meant to remember the events that first brought him to the Woodland Glade and in our care, then he would have memory of this by now."

"So he will never remember what had happened to him?" asked Valara.

"Cankles Mayron has journeyed on in his life, and thus far, there appears not even a glimmer of memory of his earlier life. At this point, I doubt if he will ever remember."

"Perhaps that is for the better then," decided Valara.

"Yes. It might not be such a bad thing," agreed Rainus, taking her by the hand. "Now, let us turn back. Captain Ironwood had mentioned a new unicorn, a stallion never before seen, had been spotted in our forest."

"Potential competition for the resident male?" questioned Valara, thinking back on the last new stallion that had been soundly beaten in its bid to take over the local harem.

"What threat that creature poses is yet to be seen," answered Rainus. "It could be nothing more than a unicorn passing through these parts on its way to the west."

Smaller Than Small

"I can see why the goats prefer to graze in the enchanted forest," commented Tag, glancing about the Trolls' domain. "There is nary a bite to eat here, and that's saying a lot, considering goats are not fussy eaters to begin with."

Dying stubbles of yellowed grasses clipped down to the earth struggled to survive where the roots were not yanked from the ground to be devoured by the voracious herds.

All non-toxic shrubs were browsed upon, denuded of foliage, tender shoots as well as the more manageable, pliable twigs. From the ground right up to the highest point the goats could reach while balanced on their hind-legs, one could easily see where the ungulates had dined, pruning back these bushes in a uniform manner.

"Hungry little buggers, aren't they?" responded Cankles, staring at the devastation left in the wake of the nomadic herds.

"This is looking rather dismal. Lord Silverthorn has every right to keep those animals out of the Woodland Glade," decided Rose. As far as her eyes could see, a landscape marred by uncontrolled, rampant grazing left an indelible mark on the terrain.

"Unfortunately, goats have a gluttonous appetite," stated Tag. "Even when the goats have a full belly, they will continue to eat if there's food about."

"Jus' lookin' at what's left, I can certainly understand the goats wantin' to feed on all that lush greenery in the enchanted forest," sympathized Cankles.

"True enough, but the Trolls need a lesson in responsible farming practices," stated Tag. "They can't allow their animals to run amok as they have been."

"But these beings are cheese-makers, not farmers," disputed Rose.

"Well, if they wish to continue making cheese, they will have to learn to better manage their herds," stated Tag. "That's all there is to it."

"Sounds like a novel idea, but just how do you intend to teach the Trolls about responsible farming practices?" questioned Rose.

"Much shall depend on how receptive they are to new ideas," answered Tag.

"Well, these new ideas better be simple to accommodate their puny brains," warned the Princess.

"The first order of business is to must find the Trolls, or at least their leader," responded Tag.

"This is odd. You'd think being so big, they'd be easy to spot," commented Cankles, glancing about for signs of the local denizens.

"Odd indeed, but what is more odd is the name of this place!" remarked Rose. "Why do they call this the Land of Small when everything we have come across thus far is no smaller or bigger than they are anywhere else? The trees and animals are really no different than the ones we have come across in Dimbolt Forest or in the Woodland Glade."

"Who can say about the origin of the name?" responded Tag, his shoulders arching up in a shrug.

"Perhaps the Trolls are so big, everything that seems normal size to us looks really very small to them?" offered Cankles.

"Maybe you're right," said Tag, nodding in agreement.

"That is too simple and too bizarre to be plausible," responded Rose, dismissing Cankles' words.

"I wouldn't be so quick to discount our friend's explanation," responded Tag. "It makes good sense to me. And remember, Master Silverthorn did say the Trolls are simple folks, preferring to keep things simple."

"It only makes good sense to you because you are both of like mind: simpletons," denounced the Princess, with eyes that glowed of ridicule as she stared at Cankles and Tag.

"Either way, I suppose we shall find out as we venture deeper into Troll country," said Tag.

"Look over there! A bridge," announced Cankles, pointing just up the river. "And a big one at that!"

"That's got to be it," determined Tag, urging his steed on.

As they reached the foot of this large, sturdy bridge spanning the wide, rushing river, all three dismounted. Like all the other bridges they had crossed thus far, by no means was this one an architectural feat of design, it was just very big – wide enough to allow two carriages to easily cross over side-by-side and never touch. It was a simple structure held in place by log pilings driven into the riverbed.

Roughly hewn timber acted as crossbeams upon which planks of wood of varying sizes and shapes, held in place here and there by a rusted nail or two, formed the walkway.

"Do you think this is the bridge Master Silverthorn told us about?" questioned Cankles, staring up and down the length of this coursing waterway for other possibilities.

"It has to be. Comparatively speaking, this river is flowing much faster than the slow one we crossed earlier on. And this is the first big, wooden bridge we've come across," reasoned Tag.

"Master Silverthorn mentioned the Troll would be here at this bridge," noted Cankles. "An' yet, there's not a Troll to be had."

"Hello! Is anybody here?" called Rose, her hands cupping her mouth so her voice would carry above the sounds of the rushing water. "Are there any Trolls about? We come in peace."

"And we might leave in *pieces* if you give them reason to dislike you," warned Tag.

"You are such a dolt!" grunted Rose. "Being a princess, what is there not to like about me?"

"Hush! Do you hear anything?" said Cankles, motioning his young comrades for silence, but more to circumvent a potential verbal scuffle.

For the longest moment, they listened for a response. Other than the persistent splash and gurgle of the turbulent waters, the breeze dancing through the tree canopy and the mellifluous songs of the wren sounding in the distance, there was no answer to the Princess' call.

"Say, look here," said Cankles, pointing to a length of coarse rope tied to the handle of what had to be a battered tin cup, albeit one of great size. It dangled from a post where a gate that should have been blocking access to the bridge swung carelessly to and fro. Instead of guarding the way, it yawned wide open, swaying in the breeze. Displayed over the tin cup was a crude sign nailed onto this post. It had the following message carved into it: *Tollz for the Trollz. Give wat u can.*

"I see what Lord Silverthorn meant when he said they are simple," stated Tag, scrutinizing the misspelled words and the backward '*s*' at the end of *Toll* and *Troll.*

"Hmph!" grunted Cankles, his eyes narrowing as he studied this sign to read aloud. "Tolls for the Trolls. Give what you can."

"You can read that?" asked Rose, staring with wonderment at Cankles.

"This sign? Sure!" he answered proudly. "An' it makes perfect sense to me."

"Figures," grumbled Rose, staring at the cup that was as large as a bucket. Peering inside, this collection cup was devoid of coins.

Tag gave the open gate a push. Instead of closing off the bridge, the rusted hinges squeaked with age and neglect. The gate bounced lightly off the post only to fall victim to wind and gravity as it swung open once more as though to beckon these travellers on to cross the bridge.

"Well, this is kinda useless. Now we know why those goats keep goin' back to the Woodland Glade," determined Cankles. "There's nothing to stop 'em."

"It is not as though the Trolls were ignoring Master Silverthorn's plea to contain their herds," determined Tag, inspecting the simple design and careless slant of the gatepost. "If this gate was at the opposite end of this bridge, I do believe the natural tilt of the terrain and this structure would have prevented all manners of beast from crossing, Trolls included, if they did not have the wits about them to know to pull the gate open."

"You think?" asked Rose, staring skeptically at Tag.

"Oh, I am quite sure," replied Tag, shutting the gate once more to demonstrate how its less-than-straight structure surrendered to the forces of gravity as it slowly yawned open once again. "Even a light breeze can push it open. I sense the builders of this gate just didn't figure out the errors of their design."

"I suppose a herd of goats would have no difficulty crossing this bridge if it is unobstructed," decided Rose, nodding in agreement.

"Yes, and if this gate was situated at the other end, the goats would not be able to cross no matter how hard they pushed against it," added Tag.

"Oh, I don't know 'bout that, young master," disputed Cankles. "Those animals might be clever 'nough to pull it open."

"Nonsense! That means they'd have to have one of these," scoffed Tag, laughing lightly as he waved a thumb in Cankles' face. "I can't think of another animal with opposable thumbs that would allow them to grab something like a gate to pull it open."

"Never mind that, we should move on," urged Rose. "We need to find the leader of the Trolls."

"A toll must be paid to proceed," reminded Tag, pointing to the battered tin.

"I looked into that cup and it is empty, except for the dead fly at the bottom of it. I refuse to pay a toll when others are not," declined Rose, her hand batting defiantly at the container dangling from the rope.

Tag peered in. True to her words he spied upon a bright metallic blue fly lying belly up. Its six legs were bent and pulled tightly against its body; its stiff, crumpled wings folded beneath it.

"See? If others do not pay, why should I?" grumbled Rose. "And if the toll is a disgusting fly, I refuse to waste my time catching one."

"Obviously, the fly died in there, but you should think better on this and loosen your purse strings," suggested Tag.

"Why?"

"Did it ever occur to you, Princess, that the *others* you speak of do not have to negotiate with the Trolls as we are forced to?" responded Tag.

"It's only right," said Cankles, coaxing the Princess to pay up. "Don't want to go offendin' them before we even have a chance to meet them. It's better to put something in that cup, even a token payment."

"I am a princess!" declared Rose, stomping her feet like a spoiled child. "Since when did a princess have to pay tolls to anyone?"

"Just pay up or we shall waste more time and you'll never get back to Fleetwood for your birthday gala," reminded Tag.

"Fine!" snapped Rose. She shoved her mare's reins into Cankles' hand. "Take my horse. You two go on ahead while I pay."

"Very good, Princess," praised Cankles, urging the horses on to follow behind Tag's mount.

With the dull thud of hooves resonating through the wooden bridge as Tag led the way, Rose glanced up to see if her comrades were watching her. With their eyes momentarily turned away, she quickly crouched down, snatching up three sizeable pebbles from the ground. Taking another furtive glance, just as Tag gazed back at her, Rose pretended to take coins from her purse, noisily dropping in the three pebbles instead.

Rattling the huge tin cup for the others to hear, she announced, "There! Happy now? The toll is paid."

"Good! Now catch up, will you?" ordered Tag, waving her on to follow.

Stepping through the already opened gate, Rose took a tentative step onto the bridge. Though it was large, its simple design made her question its stability. She could feel the vibration of water pounding against the pilings and resonating through the planks of wood beneath her feet. Staring down through the narrow gaps between the boards, she could see the rocky riverbank gradually give way to water.

For a fleeting instant, Rose was sure she saw a shadow of movement. Crouching down, she peeked between the boards, uncertain if it was nothing more than the reflection of sunlight dancing off the river. She gasped as a huge eyeball suddenly peered up at her.

Rose shrieked in fright, falling backward as a long, sharp wooden stick abruptly stabbed through the slat, narrowly missing her face.

"What the?" gasped Tag, turning with a start upon hearing her scream. Thrusting his stallion's reins into Cankles' hands, he barked his orders, "Take the horses! Go!"

Tag sprinted to Rose as she rolled to her side to escape the assault just as the pointed stick was thrust through the gap in the boards to almost jab her rump. Grabbing her by the hands, he yanked the Princess to her feet as he hollered, *"Run!"*

The pair was forced to dodge and weave, darting to and fro, to avoid this simple, but effective weapon attempting to impale them.

"Quickly!" shouted Cankles. He hopped about, frantically waving as he urged them on. "Get over here!"

"We're trying!" hollered Tag, pulling the Princess along behind him as they twisted about to avoid the point of the stick angrily stabbing through another gap.

Before they could reach safety on the other side, Rose screamed in fright. The rusted nails securing one of the boards squealed in protest as the wood plank forcefully popped open before them.

"Bloody hell!" gasped Tag.

He stared in disbelief as towering wisps of ginger hair appeared through the floor of the bridge. A massive, round face with a lumpy, flattened nose and dark eyes whose whites stood out against skin of blue followed this great pile of hair.

"What blue demon is this?" gasped Rose, ducking behind Tag to use him as a human shield as he drew his sword.

"I'm no demon!" Each word was delivered with a low, resonating boom, spoken slowly as though this being had to deliberate on each one. "I'm a Troll!"

"She meant no offense, good sir," apologized Tag, cautiously lowering his sword, but not yet ready to put it away altogether. "We mean to cross this bridge, nothing more."

"No one crosses without first payin' the toll!" snapped the giant whose head poked out from the hole in the bridge. Even angry, the Troll's words were delivered slowly. Only his inflection gave true indication of his ire.

"But we did pay," insisted Tag, pointing to the collection tin that dangled from the gatepost. "Right, Princess?"

Rose said nothing, only nodding her head in confirmation.

"I know coins when I hears 'em!" bellowed the Troll. Scowling in resentment, the whites of his eyes disappeared as they narrowed in suspicion. "An' that weren't no coins you dropped in the cup, missy!"

"Princess?" growled Tag, glaring at Rose as he waited for a response.

"I did pay!" declared Rose, stomping back to the end of the bridge. Before Tag or the Troll could join her to see what she was doing, the Princess discreetly dumped the three pebbles out. "Obviously, it was not enough!"

Yanking open the drawstring on her purse, Rose thrust her hand in. Extracting some coins, she promptly deposited six pieces of copper into the container, pretending she was adding to the toll she had already paid.

The Troll waded back to the other side. Lumbering along with slow, deliberate steps he marched up the riverbank. Wandering around the gaping gate that refused to remain closed, he cursed beneath his breath, "Stupid thing!"

Rose backed away as the Troll's disproportionately large, blue hands armed with huge sausage fingers snatched up what now appeared to be a small, tin cup. Holding it up to his big cauliflower ear, he first shook it, listening to the coins rattling about.

"Aah, music ta my ears!" delighted the Troll.

And then, he peered inside. His thick lips pulled into a broad grin that stretched across his face.

"So, we are good to cross your bridge?" questioned Rose.

"You're free ta do so now, but don't you go pullin' no funnies again," warned the Troll, dumping the tiny coins into his hand to tuck into the pocket of his tatty, old trousers for safekeeping.

"No funnies intended," gulped Rose, darting behind Tag for cover. "It was just a little misunderstanding."

"Well, don't you go makin' this mistake again! Us Trolls gotta make a livin' somehow if we can't sell no more cheese."

"Speaking of cheese, would you happen to know where we can find a Troll by the name of Tiny Goatswain?" queried Tag, as he sheathed his sword.

"Sure, I know," responded the Troll, staring down his nose to gaze upon the diminutive human beings. "But first, why are ya lookin' for him? He ain't in some kinda trouble, is he?"

"That shall depend on the manner Master Goatswain receives the emissaries sent forth by the King of Axalon," disclosed Tag.

"The *emissaries*?" questioned the Troll, scratching his head in thought, if indeed his fingers could even reach through the great, tangled mess of hair to itch his scalp.

"You know? Royal messengers," explained Rose.

"Oh, yeah!" nodded the Troll, pretending he knew what this word meant. "So what's the King wantin' with Tiny Goatswain?"

"Not that it is any of your business, but King Maxmillion would like the delivery of cheese to resume immediately," answered Rose.

"Same here, but that ain't gonna happen any time soon if those bloody Elves have their way," grumbled the Troll, heaving a disheartened sigh as he gazed to the west.

"That's why we are here," disclosed Tag. "We wish to resolve this matter in a diplomatic manner so a satisfactory solution may be adopted to resume trade and encourage commerce once more."

"What're ya sayin'? Speak without usin' 'em fancy words," demanded the Troll. He absentmindedly wiped his runny nose with the back of his hand as he stared at the mortals cowering before him.

"The young master means to say, we're here to help find a peaceful answer to this problem that the Trolls, the Elves *and* King Maxmillion will be happy with," explained Cankles, bowing before the great being in respectful greeting.

"I see," responded the Troll, giving this mortal a nod of understanding.

"So, do you know where we can find this Tiny fellow?" asked Rose. "We were told he loiters about this bridge."

"Well, I don't know 'bout *loiterin'* 'round bridges, but we've been known to hang around, usually underneath, these things."

"Then surely you must know of this particular Troll we seek?" determined Tag.

"I sure do!" declared the Troll. The haystack of hair swayed to and fro as he eagerly nodded.

"May we speak to him?" asked Rose.

"Ya sure can!" His large, potato head loaded down with bland features nodded in confirmation again.

"Well? Go on then," urged the Princess, shooing him on to take them to his leader.

"Go where? I thought ya said you'd be wantin' ta speak?" responded the Troll, wiping the drool hanging from the corner of his thick, drooping lips.

"We do, but where is Tiny Goatswain?" probed Rose. "We need to speak to him immediately and in person."

"Well, you go right ahead then, young miss. Get ta speakin' an' I'll listen," invited the Troll. "I'm all ears an' then sum. So, what do ya gotta say?"

"Are you Tiny Goatswain?" questioned Tag, staring at the blue behemoth standing before him.

"Didn't I already tell ya?"

"No, you did not," grunted Rose, her hands on her hips.

"Well then, I'm Tiny."

"No, you are not," argued Rose, looking the great Troll up and down. "You are bigger than big."

"But I *am* tiny an' my name's Tiny," insisted the Troll.

"Do you take me for a fool? I know tiny when I see tiny. And you are not tiny," disputed the Princess. "You are scary big!"

"Don't rightly know ya 'nough ta say if you're a fool, or not, but Tiny's short for Tintinus. Plus, I'm pretty small for a Troll. Or at least, I was tiny when I was a baby, but even all grownup, I'm still puny as far as Trolls go."

"I hardly think so," scoffed Rose, her voice tainted by sarcasm. "If *you* are small, then *I* am an Elf maiden."

The Troll's eyes narrowed in suspicion as he stared at the mortal. "I'd say you're a smidgen short to be an Elf, but ya look ta be dressed like one of 'em woodland folks an' I suppose you're pretty 'nough ta be an Elf maiden."

"Thank you for the compliment, but stop wasting our time," snapped Rose, the toe of her shoe tapping impatiently on the bridge deck. "We must speak to Tiny Goatswain, immediately!"

"I say again, I'm Tiny Goatswain. If ya don't believe me, then you're free ta ask 'em."

Tag, Rose and Cankles turned with a start to see three gargantuan, blue Trolls standing at the other end of the bridge, surrounding their steeds. They watched in stunned silence as the biggest of the Trolls easily picked up Rose's mare in his hand. He sniffed the frightened horse's back end as a generous dollop of manure was either squeezed out or involuntarily evacuated by the animal.

"Good gracious!" gasped Rose, staring skyward.

"Relatively speaking, you *are* small for a Troll!" agreed Tag, staring at Tiny, and then the three standing a good head and shoulder taller than him. "Now I understand what Lord Silverthorn meant when he said your name is self-explanatory."

"I feel smaller than small," squeaked Rose, in a timid voice as she sized up the trio of Trolls now blocking their way.

"Told ya so," snorted Tiny. A deep, guttural rumble shook the air like thunder rolling across a stormy sky as he laughed heartily at their response.

"Please, don't hurt our horses," pleaded Cankles, dashing over to boldly confront Tiny's comrades. He watched helplessly as the mare's hooves flailed about in the air. "Put the poor beast down, I say!"

"We don't hurt horsies," promised the largest of the Trolls, gently placing the mare back onto the ground. His word came out just as deep and paced as Tiny's as he spoke. "Me jus' lookin' at her."

"You're welcome to look, but the horses don't like being picked up like that," warned Cankles, approaching the trio to claim their mounts.

"Sorry," apologized the Troll. Patting the mare on her head with the tip of his finger only to smudge more blue onto the horse to match the handprint he left behind on its body when he handled the mare.

"No harm done," insisted Tiny. "My lil' brother was jus' curious. We don't see horses in these parts very often, mostly jus' goats."

"Me thought it was *big* goat," grumbled Tiny's sibling. Like an overgrown child sulking after being reprimanded, his monstrous hands tucked behind his back while his large, bare feet pushed about a large rock like it was a small pebble.

"He is your *little* brother?" gasped Rose, staring at Tiny, and then the house of a Troll now looking guilty after handling her mare.

"Yep, by a good fourteen years or so," responded Tiny. He watched as his brother nodded in agreement, holding up all his fingers and thumbs in confirmation.

"Something is not right here. How is it that you are the leader?" questioned Rose.

"I may be the runt of the litter, but I'm the smartest," insisted Tiny, puffing out his chest in pride so it extended beyond his great belly. "Don't take size ta be a leader, jus' takes some smarts. An' I don't mean ta sound like I'm boastin', but I've got more smarts than all my brothers combined."

"Take no offense to her words, Master Goatswain," urged Tag. "She is not as smart as most human beings so she understands."

Rose was speechless. Her mouth fell agape as she glared at Tag.

"No offense taken, lil' man," said Tiny. "We rarely have puny folks like you in these parts. So jus' who might you be?"

"I am Tagius Yairet. This is my friend Cankles Mayron and she," said Tag, jabbing his thumb over his shoulder in Rose's general direction, "is Princess Rose-alyn of Fleetwood."

"Well, mighty pleased ta meet you three," greeted Tiny, bowing in acknowledgement.

"The pleasure is ours!" said Cankles, reciprocating with a bow of his own.

"If I recall, you were sayin' ya wanted ta find a way that'll let my people move through the Elves' forest ta sell our cheese ta King Max again," said Tiny.

"Indeed," responded Tag, nodding in confirmation.

"A safe passage through the enchanted forest would be great. Though the Elves are wee folks next ta us Trolls, they're bloody good with their arrows. Stings something fierce, if ya get my meanin'?"

"I believe we do," said Tag.

"An' though we're great in size, we find the Elves ta be pretty scary when they get mad an' start scurryin' 'bout real fast like squirrelly mice you can't even stomp on."

"You should not have to stomp on them, nor should the Elves be given a reason to raise their arms to you," said Tag. "I believe we can help you secure safe passage through the Woodland Glade if your people are willing to listen to us."

"I'm willin' ta hear you out, lil' master," offered Tiny. "But we should head ta safety before darkness comes."

"Is there some kind of danger that comes with the night?" questioned Tag, perplexed by Tiny's ominous words.

"Indeed, lil' master," claimed the Troll, nodding his great head.

"What is it?" asked Rose.

"Can't rightly say, Princess. Being an unseen danger an' all, when the darkness comes, you can't see it."

"So, you've never actually seen this so-called *danger*," queried Tag, trying to get a better grasp of the Troll's anxiety.

"Jus' cause you can't see it, it don't mean it ain't out there," responded Tiny, his comrades nodding in agreement.

"Are you saying that Trolls are afraid of the dark?" probed Tag.

"No," replied Tiny. "We're afraid of what *lurks* in the dark. We don't like being snuck up on by something that might be hidin' in the night."

"So, they *are* afraid of the dark," decided Rose. "Interesting…"

"It's more scary than interesting," insisted Tiny. "We should be on our way, before the sun sets. A warm fire awaits you an' so, too, is a great wheel of goat cheese."

"Sounds delightful," said Tag, as the Troll herded them to the other end of the bridge.

"Shall we follow you?" questioned Rose, tottering about. She fought to keep her balance as the Troll's great footfalls caused the bridge to shake, rattle and squeak with each lumbering step he took.

"Oh, you won't be able to keep up with us, even if we walked slowly," stated Tiny. "An' being so puny, you might get underfoot. There's nothing worse than feelin' a tiny human getting squashed between yer toes."

Tiny's comrades shuddered in horror, their blue faces grimacing in disgust.

"We certainly do not want that to happen," gasped Rose, mortified by the thought of this horrific demise.

"We can ride our horses," suggested Tag, pointing to their mounts. "I'm sure our steeds can keep pace with you."

"I'm sure they can, lil' master," agreed Tiny. "But they'll be slowed by the great brambles an' the wide rivers to get to my home."

"Well, there must be another way," said Rose.

"There sure is, Princess," responded Tiny.

"Then make it so," ordered Rose.

She squealed in fright as Tiny suddenly plucked her up, tucking her under his arm to carry her. His younger sibling followed suit, scooping up Tag and Cankles into his massive, sweaty blue hands.

"Whoa! Easy big guy!" grunted Tag, pushing against the Troll's thumb to loosen his grip.

"What about our steeds?" asked Cankles, pointing down to the ground where the three horses nervously skittered about.

"Don't ya worry 'bout them," said Tiny's comrade, as he and the last Troll easily picked up the horses to ensure they arrived with their masters.

ॐ ॐ ॐ

"That was utterly disgusting," complained Rose. "It was bad enough being handled like a doll tucked in the crook of his arm, but being so close to his armpit? He reeked of rancid mutton stew. The stench almost killed me!"

"Too bad it was an *almost*," grumbled Tag. "If it had, I wouldn't have to listen to you whine."

"Just for that, I shall air more of my grievances!" snapped Rose, using the palms of her hands to smooth out the creases and brush away the blue residue left on her Elven dress. "Look what that Troll did to my gown."

"No need for concern, Princess. You can always wish for a new one," responded Cankles.

Tag and Rose shot an angry glance in his direction.

"What?" asked Cankles, frowning in bewilderment. "You still have one more wish to use before the midnight hour, don't you?"

"Shut it!" growled Rose, as Tag slapped his hand over Cankles' mouth.

"Others must not know of the *you-know-what*," reminded Tag, speaking in a whisper. "Remember, Master Silverthorn said to be discreet."

"Right," responded Cankles, as he nodded in understanding. "Sorry 'bout that. Almost let it slip!"

"Let what slip?" asked a slow, booming voice.

The trio turned to see their host had returned with an armload of firewood. Some pieces were whole trees that had fallen over in the last great windstorm.

"Oh, no need for concern, Master Goatswain," answered Tag. "My friend said he almost slipped when your brother put him back on the ground. Just took a minute to get the feeling back in his legs, that's all."

"I'll be speakin' ta Umber 'bout that," said Tiny. "My lil' brother meant no harm. He jus' gets a tad bit 'xcited about seein' wee folks, but I thought he already learned his lesson with what happened the last time."

"What did happen?" asked Cankles.

"I don't rightly know," confessed Tiny. "He picked the man up in his hand jus' like he picked you up, but when he put him back down, the lil' gaffer wasn't breathin' no more."

"He squeezed the life out him?" gasped Rose, her eyes wide in horror.

"Didn't see anything get squeezed out either end of the man. So I'm thinkin' he jus' stopped breathin' or died of fright, maybe."

"That is terrible!" exclaimed Rose.

"Terrible indeed," agreed Tiny. "Umber was so ashamed of what happened, I was sure he'd be more careful this time 'round."

"Worry not," assured Tag. "We're both fine."

"That's a good thing, lil' master. Now, let's head to my home."

Turning in the direction the Troll had pointed, Tag, Cankles and Rose all gasped in surprise to see, rising over the tree line, a billowing column of smoke swirling into the deepening sky as a great amber glow pushed back against the impending darkness.

"Good gracious!" shrieked Rose, turning away from danger. "Forest fire! Run before we burn to death!"

Tiny and the other Trolls began to laugh so hard and so loud, this raucous display caused the Trolls' bellies to wobble and quiver in an unsightly manner as the earth beneath the mortals' feet quivered as much.

"Oh no, Princess Rose," chortled Tiny, slapping his thigh in laughter. "That ain't a forest fire! That's our campfire. Come see for yourself!"

Ducking between the rows of shrub the Trolls easily stepped over, Rose and her comrades were astonished to find a half dozen Trolls gathered around an inviting fire. In this vast clearing, a cluster of simple huts, each as grand in size as all of Pepperton Palace filled this space. What Rose mistook for a huge forest fire was indeed a campfire. Though an adequate size for the Trolls to cook by and keep warm, this was a raging inferno by human standards.

She watched in awe as one of the Trolls snatched a round disk of unleavened bread cooking on the heat of a flat, round rock sitting in the center of this campfire. He tossed it onto a stack of freshly cooked breads cooling in a huge, wicker basket on a table.

"A humble meal awaits you," announced Tiny, picking up each mortal one at a time to place onto the tabletop. They looked like Troll-sized dolls placed upon the table for a Troll-child's tea party. "You best stay up here though. Don't want to see any of you gettin' trampled underfoot."

"Good idea," agreed Tag, knowing how less than graceful the Trolls could be. He took his place next to Rose, his legs dangling over the edge of the table, while Cankles wandered over to the wicker basket. He stood up on his toes to peer into the basket, drooling over the golden brown stack of bread waiting to be consumed. Each one was as big as the old, wool rug in his shack.

"Help yourself," offered Tiny. "There's plenty."

"Smells delicious," responded Cankles. "But I'm thinkin' one of those breads weigh more than I do. It'll be too much to handle."

"Don't you fret, lil' sir. I'll go wash up first, then I'll serve some up ta ya," offered Tiny. The tabletop shook beneath their feet as the Troll lumbered over to a large, hollowed out stump filled with water. Here, Tiny washed up, removing all traces of grime and blue colouring from his face and hands.

"That's better," sighed Tiny, plunking his hulking frame down onto a stool.

"Oh my! You are no longer blue," noted Rose, staring up at the Troll.

"It's dark now. The sun's set so I don't need ta wear no blue mudsie," explained Tiny.

"So that blue was not some kind of fashion statement?" queried the Princess.

"What do ya mean?" responded Tiny, staring down at the tiny mortal.

"The Princess means to say that you don't wear the blue skin colouring as part of your accessory, like a belt or a scarf to complement or accent your manner of dress," explained Tag.

"Still not sure what ya mean, but ya don't want to be standing out in the sun, 'specially in the middle of the day, with no blue mudsie on if you're a Troll," responded Tiny.

"It shields you from the sun so you won't turn to stone?" queried Rose.

"Don't know who started that silly story 'bout the sun's light turnin' us ta stone, but it's a lie," stated Tiny, his paced words matter-of-fact. "We jus' take ta burnin' if the sun's really strong. It gets real red an' painful. Can even blister if it's bad 'nough."

"Oh... I see," responded Tag, his head nodded in understanding. "The blue mud prevents sunburn."

"Sunburn nasty," muttered Umber, plopping down on the stool next to Tiny. "Sun bad fer Trolls."

"And that's why you were under the bridge," determined Tag. "You were trying to remain in the shade."

"You're pretty smart for such a puny being," praised Tiny. "That's why we need ta move through the Woodland Glade ta deliver King Max's cheese. The shade of the forest protects us from the sun."

"Then why don't you travel around Lord Silverthorn's domain or through it during the night?" asked Rose.

"Oh, no! No travel in dark," gasped Umber, the threads of drool hanging from the corners of his mouth splattering in all directions as he shook his head.

"Oh, that's right," recalled the Princess, ducking to miss the globule of spit flying at her. "They have an illogical fear of the dark."

"That may be so, but to them, the fear is quite real," stated Tag. "But to skirt the enchanted forest still does not resolve the problem of wayward goats."

"Quite right, Master Yairet," said Cankles. "We did make a promise to Lord Silverthorn that we'd find a way to rectify this little problem."

"Hey, I thought ya said you're here for King Max?" questioned Tiny, his eyes narrowing in suspicion.

"We are here on behalf of all those wishing to come up with a peaceful solution that will allow you to move your cheese through Lord Silverthorn's domain. However, that will only happen if you make certain your goats no longer invade the Woodland Glade," explained Tag.

"We tried ta stop our goats from wanderin', but those gates the Elves told us how ta build don't work," grumbled Tiny. "They keep openin' by themselves. An' even when we tried ta tie them shut with rope, the goats would chew on it an' get free."

"So you really did try to keep your animals in?" asked Rose.

"Sure, we tried," insisted Tiny, his mountainous shoulders rolling in a shrug of defeat. "We tried as best we could."

"Come now, if you truly made an effort, why do we see no sign of fences anywhere?" argued Rose.

"Fence too much work to make," grunted Umber.

"So, you were being lazy?" decided Rose.

"Not so," disputed Tiny, denying this claim. "We're real hard workers when we want ta be."

"Not according to your little brother," argued Rose.

"It's better ta say it's hard as in *fussy*," explained Tiny, holding up his cumbersome, sausage fingers that were not designed for fine, detailed work. "Our hands are too big ta make rows an' rows of fences small 'nough ta keep the goats in. We figured that since we can't go an' put up a great fence 'round our entire domain, we'd use the rivers as natural barriers an' the goats could only move from place to place where there's a bridge as they don't take ta water at all."

"And yet, they continue to roam unabated, devouring everything in sight, including the Woodland Glade," admonished Rose, her tone accusing.

"We tried ta build a gate on the main bridge ta keep our herds from runnin' amok, but as ya saw with yer own, beady lil' eyes, the gate the Elves told us how ta build don't work."

"What if we can fix the gate so your goats can no longer roam free so you can control their movements?" offered Tag.

"But what goats eat then?" blurted out Umber, as Tiny flashed an angry stare at him.

"Aah, so the truth comes out!" said Rose. "You really don't mind your animals wandering into the enchanted forest to devour the Elves' domain."

Even under the light of the great campfire, the flames did nothing to diminish the red glow of embarrassment from Tiny's face.

"The goats gotta eat something," confided Tiny. "They're always eatin' an' they eat 'til there's nothing left."

"If we can get your gate working properly, you'll be able to move your herds from place to place before they can do such damage," explained Tag. "You allow them to graze in one pasture. Before they've eaten the grasses down to the roots, you move them into another area, allowing these grasses sufficient time to grow back. Control where they graze and how much, and there will be no need to let them roam into the Woodland Glade to find food."

"I see," said Tiny, giving Tag a nod of understanding. "That'd certainly please the Elves."

"Most definitely," responded Rose. "They promised a safe passage if you are willing to keep your goats from ravaging their forest."

"Well, if you're sayin' you can fix our gate problem an' we're able ta do what ya said 'bout movin' our herds from field ta field before they eat every plant ta the point of killin' 'em, I suppose it's doable."

"I promise you, it is," averred Tag.

"But what's in it for you an' your friends, lil' master?" queried Tiny. "I may be a simple Troll, but even I know ya human types rarely do something for nothing."

"Truth be told, if we are able to fix this problem, not only will we prevent a war between the King of Axalon and the Elves, but King Maxmillion promised we will not be held prisoners should we return home to Fleetwood via his country," explained Tag. "Not to mention the fact we also require safe passage through the Land of Small as we journey eastward."

"Well, if you can truly help us, I'd be most grateful. I'll promise a safe passage all right," vowed Tiny. "But why'd ya ever want ta go that a-way? Us Trolls don't even venture through the Sorcerer's land unless we got no choice but ta do bizness with the Dwarves."

"Are you speakin' of Parru St. Mime Dragonite?" questioned Tag.

"There's only one Sorcerer I know of in these parts an' that'll be his name," replied Tiny, with a nod of his head. His face grimaced as he growled, "Hey, you ain't in cahoots with Dragonite, are ya? 'Cause if you are with that Sorcerer, it'll be better that I squash ya now!"

"Oh no, my good Troll!" assured Rose. "Never met the demented soul, nor do we have any intentions of doing so."

"We plan to move through his land in secret as we venture on to the Land of Big," added Cankles.

"So... you're on yer way ta see the Dwarves," determined Tiny, breaking off a chunk of bread to tear into manageable pieces for his guests. "An' what's yer bizness with 'em wee, ground folk?"

Before Cankles or Rose could respond, Tag answered, "It's a very long, complicated story of which there is no short, simple version. I can try to explain it to you, but it shall take several steps to make this most difficult story understandable."

"Us Trolls like simple stories. No point in tellin' it if it needs a great deal of explainin' ta understand it," responded Tiny, as his comrades nodded in agreement. "As long as you an' yer lil' friends aren't up ta no-good an' don't do the Sorcerer's biddin', then I'll have ta trust ya on this."

"I assure you, Master Goatswain, we can be trusted," vowed Tag. "There is nothing to gain in lying to you and much to lose if we did."

"Well, ya look like you're worth trustin', lil' master," acknowledged the Troll, with a nod of approval. "Why don't we drink on our newfound friendship?"

"That'll be a fine idea, but we have no wine to share with you," said Tag, apologetically.

"Who needs the juice of grapes when we have this!" declared Tiny, grabbing a huge ceramic jug from a passing Troll.

"What is it?" asked Rose, wobbling about as the jug slammed down on the table to rattle her senses and compromise her balance.

"It's a special brew we make from 'taters," explained Tiny, searching about the table for a container small enough to serve this beverage to his tiny guests.

"What are taters?" questioned Rose, her delicate brows furrowing in curiosity.

"You know, Princess? Spuds," said Cankles, as he nodded in understanding to the Troll.

"Good heavens! You are as bad as the Troll! What are you talking about," asked Rose.

"They mean to say *potato*," explained Tag.

"How can a drink be made from potatoes?" scoffed the Princess, baffled by this claim. "This is sounding all very strange."

"Oh, it can be done," assured Tiny, as he ordered his little brother to get their mother's thimble. "Jus' need ta know what ta do. Mind you, jus' as we're best at makin' cheese, the Dwarves are best at makin' 'tater juice."

"They are?" asked Rose.

"Well, sure," stated Tiny. "Those Dwarves do love their root veggies, being ground-dwellers an' all."

"I suppose that makes sense, but still, how can one make a drink from a hard vegetable like a potato?" queried the Princess.

"Probably not that different than making ale by fermenting wheat and barley in hot water," offered Tag.

"Sounds disgusting," grumbled Rose, her face contorting in repulsion. "I think I shall stick to wine, but as I have none, water will suffice."

"We got water a-plenty, but first, let's take care of this," said Tiny, the Troll-sized thimble disappearing in his massive hand as he carefully attempted to pour a serving of this spirit for his guests to share.

Full to overflowing, Tiny carefully set this drinking vessel down between Cankles and Tag. As small as it was in the Troll's hand, to his guests, this thimble was still as large as a mug capable of holding a pint of ale.

"Thank you," said Cankles, as Tag gazed into the thimble. This liquid was the consistency of water, but it looked murky, like overused dishwater that should have been tossed out long ago.

"It looks… appetizing," gulped Tag, selecting his words prudently as he scrutinized the potato-based beverage.

"No need ta be so kind, lil' master. I know it don't look like much, but believe you me," warned Tiny, "it's got more of a kick than any ale you'll ever drink in your wee life. In fact, you don't want ta be smokin' pipeweed or sittin' too close to fire drinkin' this stuff."

"We'll be sure not to guzzle it down in one swallow," assured Tag, reluctant to deliberately assault his taste buds. "We'll take our time to savour its full flavour."

"Don't think you'll be wantin' it ta linger on your tongue for too long," cautioned Tiny. "If you've never had this before, it'll make your toes curl an' put hairs on your chest. Melt it off too, should ya spill some down your front."

"Better drink up, Tag," urged Rose, teasing her jester. "I am sure you can add to the strand or two you already have."

"And maybe you should spill some down your front? Take advantage of its hair removing properties to do away with the liberal growth on yours," grunted Tag, giving the Princess a snide smile as he offered her the thimble of fermented potato juice.

"Coming from you, that was almost funny," sniffed Rose, her hands coming up to decline the offer. "And knowing how well you two handled Lord Silverthorn's wine, I highly recommend you imbibe with care. If look and stench is a determining factor, not only will you become severely intoxicated in a short time, it will probably kill you if you consume enough of it."

Glancing over at Cankles, Tag thought back on their night of drinking with the Elf Lord. The aftermath, the pounding headache and queasy stomach, not to forget waking up in Cankles' arms was something he had no intention of reliving.

Tag shuddered, nodding in agreement, "The Princess is quite right, Cankles. We need to keep our wits about us. It's best to indulge in moderation."

"No harm in that," agreed Cankles. Recoiling from the invisible fumes of alcohol wafting from the modified drinking vessel to assault his olfactory senses, his eyes watered. "It smells potent."

"Don't know 'bout potent, but I'm sure it'll knock the boots off yer little feet if you never tried this before," cautioned Tiny. "Probably best sipped, if ya get my meanin'?"

"Age before beauty. You go first," offered Tag, pushing the thimble to Cankles.

"Oh no, you go right ahead, Master Yairet."

"Don't want to go offending our host," said Tag, offering it to his comrade. "Go on, drink."

"I suppose a little sip won't hurt." Cankles hoisted the thimble to his lips as he held his breath and closed his eyes to spare him the burn of the alcohol vapours that continued to rise from this drink.

Tag watched as Cankles swished the liquid about his mouth like he was sampling a full-bodied wine. Little did Tag realize, Cankles was desperately trying to dilute the vile drink with his saliva. Before the true potency of this evil tasting spirit could fully brutalize Cankles' senses, he shoved the thimble into Tag's hand.

The full burn of alcohol evaporating on his tongue and escaping from his nostrils prevented Cankles from warning Tag. His young comrade followed suit. Holding his breath and closing his eyes, he allowed himself the smallest of sips.

If ever a drink had teeth, this was one of them. Before Tag could swallow, the liquid felt like fire, burning his tongue. The little he managed to swallow burned all the way down from his throat to his belly.

"Oh my!" squeaked Tag. These high-pitched words were carried on the light vapour of alcohol evaporating in his throat.

"I swear I'm gonna die," gasped Cankles, clutching his throat as these words wheezed out on notes higher than any girl could reach.

"Thought they sounded funny before," chortled Tiny, as he and the other Trolls burst out in laughter. "They sound like ants, if ants could talk!"

Rose shook her head in disgust as she watched Tag and Cankles shudder and gag.

"I suppose I could have warned you both, but I did not think it'd take a fool to see how truly potent this drink is. It's troubling to think just how foolish you two really are."

"Unlike you, we were just trying to show a bit of gratitude to our host for his kind hospitality," protested Tag, his face flushing red from the alcohol fuelled beverage.

"You can do that without killing yourself," grunted Rose.

"Have something ta eat," urged Tiny. "It'll help ta ease the burnin'. Give your stomach something ta work on an' it'll help ta sop up what ya swallowed."

"Yes, please," agreed Tag. "Before it burns a hole straight through my belly."

The Troll reached across the great table for a small piece of cheese large enough for the trio to share.

"Here ya go," said Tiny. "The bread's bland, but it'll be tasty with this cheese."

"It smells as bad as that fermented potato juice," Rose gagged as she whispered to Tag.

"We already expressed our gratitude by having a drink. Now it's your turn," insisted Tag. "Eat! You look hungry."

"Right now, we've got a lot of cheese on hand since the sales ta King Max were put ta a stop," said Tiny, stuffing into his mouth a wad of unleavened bread wrapped around a chunk of cheese as big as Cankles' head. "Go on! Eat."

Famished, Rose decided to dine. She was certain it could be nowhere near as hideous as the vile drink Cankles and Tag had sampled. She tore off dainty piece of bread so small the Troll could barely see it. Cankles used his knife to slice a piece of cheese from the generous helping Tiny served up, placing it on the Princess' chunk of bread.

Holding her breath, Rose shoved the food into her mouth, hoping to swallow without chewing. Instead, the combination of dry bread and crumbly cheese forced her to chew, lest she choked on this mouthful.

The distasteful grimace on Rose's face dissolved as the bread and cheese meshed and mingled. The initial sharp smell of aged goat cheese was deceptive, as it gave way to a mild, almost nutty sweetness.

"Oh my! This cheese is delicious!" declared Rose, her eyes wide in wonder. She tore off another, bigger helping of bread, motioning to Cankles to serve up another helping of cheese. "You really must try this."

Cankles shaved off some more cheese, placing it on Rose's bread. He then made an offering to Tag before helping himself.

"She's quite right! This cheese is delicious," agreed Tag, nodding in approval as he took a second bite.

"For a commoner with no taste, you finally have some," decided Rose. "At least where cheese is concerned."

"Now I can understand why the King of Axalon craves this cheese," stated Cankles. "It is truly delicious!"

"Well, thank you," said Tiny. "We take great pride in the makin' of it."

"I can see, or should I say, I can taste that," responded Tag, foregoing the alcohol-fuelled beverage for another helping of bread and cheese.

"It's made from only the freshest milk from our best goats," explained Tiny, breaking off another piece of cheese.

"I am curious. How are you even able to milk the goats when your hands are so big?" wondered Rose. She was perplexed upon seeing the true size of the Trolls and how even the largest goats looked very small next to one of these beings.

"Oh, we get our young ones to do the milkin', but even at that, it's fussy bizness being that the goats' teats are so puny," explained Tiny, using the tips of his thumb and index finger of each hand to demonstrate the delicate, pull and squeeze procedure needed to undertake this task without injuring the nanny goats.

"I see," said Tag, knowing that his entire hand would be needed to milk a goat.

"Enough talk of goat teats. It's *udderly* disgusting," quipped Cankles, slapping his thigh as he burst out in laughter. "Get it?"

"Can't rightly say I do," admitted Tiny, scratching his head in thought.

"Speaking of goats, there's one of your animals now," said Tag, pointing to a billy goat peering at them from between a stand of shrubs.

"Hmph," grunted Tiny, as he scrutinized the goat. "As it's not useful for makin' milk, why don't we butcher it? We can roast him up for you, being that you're our special guests."

Before they could decline this offer, the goat abruptly bolted away.

"Come back here, ya lil' bugger!" hollered Umber, as he jumped to his feet.

The earth trembled under the Troll's steps as he lumbered after the fleet-footed ungulate. He came to an abrupt stop where the light of the campfire pushed against the blackness of the night, watching in disappointment as the goat scurried off to become one with the darkness. Umber suddenly squealed in surprise as a little brown bat fluttered past his head. Easily startled by all things tiny that move quickly, the Troll's large hand swatted at the air. With this slow, ungainly movement, the bat easily dodged this obstacle. It flew off toward the trees overhanging the table to disappear into the deep shadows.

"So that old goat got away from you," teased Tiny, seeing his brother return empty handed.

"Yeah," admitted Umber, with a sullen nod. "Too fast."

"Not to worry," assured Tag. "This cheese and bread is more than adequate."

"Yes, no need to sacrifice a goat on our behalf," assured Rose, cringing inwardly at the thought of having to dine on tough, stringy meat.

"Well, like I said, there's plenty of cheese, so eat up," urged Tiny.

"Once that gate is fixed, you'll have more control over your wandering herds," promised Tag.

"But jus' how you plannin' ta do that?" asked Tiny. "I can't figure how it'll be fixed."

"Anything is possible, once you set your mind to it," stated Tag. "The problem is not that difficult to resolve in the first place."

"So, will you be startin' tomorrow morn?" asked Tiny.

"I think we should start this very night," answered Tag.

"We should?" Cankles and Rose responded simultaneously.

"Yes," replied Tag. "If we do, we'll be able to journey on as soon as we're done."

"But it's dark out there!" gasped Tiny, as he reminded his tiny guests of the potential danger lurking about. "Remember the *unseen danger*?"

"I remember," acknowledged Tag, "but I have a way to remedy this fear. When we're done, I will share it with you."

"You're a noble man, Master Yairet! So noble, if I didn't know better I'd say you were a knight," praised Tiny, his fellow Trolls nodding in agreement.

"Only in my dreams," Tag muttered beneath his breath he shot a baleful glance at Rose.

"If you can truly rid us of this fear, we'd be most grateful to ya," said the Troll.

"One thing at a time," responded Tag. "First, we must fix the problem gate."

"Oh no, my lil' friend! First, we finish feastin' an' drinkin', then you can tend to that gate," corrected Tiny, passing the jug of potato juice to his brother.

"I suppose we have time," decided Tag, for he knew they'd be forced to wait until the midnight hour for the next cycle of wishes to put their plan into motion.

The Bad Lands

"Are ya sure 'bout walkin' in the dark?" asked Tiny. His words were foreboding, even as he spoke in a whisper so as not to wake his fellow Trolls. Fast asleep in an alcohol-induced slumber, they were now snoring away around the embers of the dying campfire. "If ya wait 'til mornin', it'll be much safer then."

"True, it's dark, but speaking for Cankles and myself, there is nothing to fear," assured Tag.

"I am not afraid of the dark either," added Rose, putting on a brave face before the Troll. "Valuable time is wasting away. The sooner we fix your gate problem, the sooner we can be on our way."

"I'm supposin' you're right, Princess," admitted Tiny. "But should something happen to ya while you're out there, it's not like I haven't warned ya. Even if we wanted, it's not like any of us Trolls will be rushin' ta the rescue, if you're in danger."

"No need for concern," responded Tag. "I have my sword should a situation arise, but I hardly think that will happen."

"For such tiny folks, you're sure brave," praised Tiny, wringing his hands in woe. "If I was brave, I'd be goin' along with ya. But I'm not, so I won't."

Rose stared with raised eyebrows as she scrutinized him. As far as she was concerned, any creature, man or beast foolish enough to be lurking about in the dark in Troll country had every right to be fearful of this behemoth. Even if Tiny did not launch a hostile attack, there was a very real possibility of becoming a sorry smear on the forest floor with one misplaced step.

"For now, remain here with the others," ordered Tag. "We'll be fine. When we are done, we'll meet back here."

"If ya say so. I won't be goin' anywhere," agreed Tiny, through a great yawn. He rested his head on folded arms as he leaned against the tabletop to sleep.

Taking the torch fashioned from rags wound tightly around a stick and then set ablaze, Tag led the way. When the cacophony of Troll snores became nothing more than a distant drone, the trio came to a stop in a small clearing.

"This should do," decided Tag. He rammed the end of the torch into the earth to hold it steady as he glanced about to make sure there was no one spying on them.

"Are you sure, Master Yairet?" questioned Cankles, his eyes scrutinizing the deep shadows smothering the lands beyond the glow of the torch's light.

"We're safely hidden away," assured Tag. "The only things close to here are the goat herds grazing down yonder."

"I hardly think a bunch of goats would give us cause for concern," agreed Cankles.

"Precisely! So, Princess, do you recall what that gate looked like?" queried Tag.

"Do you take me for some kind of fool? Of course I do!" snapped Rose.

"Just making sure," responded Tag. "After all, you're not one for details. Unless, of course, they're pertaining to clothing or jewellery."

"It is called *having an eye for fashion*. A quality you are sorely lacking in, by the way," argued Rose. "Besides, how hard could it be to correct the problem?"

"All you must do is picture that very gate on the opposite end of the bridge so it must be pulled open and the goats can't push against it to access the bridge."

"I know what I must do. But first, I must clear my mind," said Rose, drawing in a deep, cleansing breath.

"That shouldn't be hard to do," smirked Tag, with a shake of his head.

Rose's eyes were like daggers as she glared at him.

"Hush! I must concentrate," grunted the Princess.

"Now that will definitely take more effort," teased Tag.

"Look here! Do you want this to work, or not?" snapped Rose, her arms crossing her chest in defiance.

"No need to get your knickers in a twist, Princess," replied Tag. "Just trying to be the jester you always wanted me to be."

"Well, you are doing a poor job of it," retorted Rose. "And there is nothing humorous about sarcasm, especially when it is coming from you and directed at me!"

"Now, now my young friends! This isn't the time to exchange barbed words. We have work to do," reminded Cankles, speaking up to bring this verbal sniping to an end.

"Quite right," agreed Tag. "By all means, Princess, go to it. Concentrate!"

"I will, once you hold steady that flippant tongue of yours," snipped Rose.

Tag pressed his lips shut, taking a cautionary step back to allow the Princess breathing room to focus on the task at hand.

Cankles sat quietly, squatting low to the ground by the torch. He waited patiently for Rose to call upon the powers of the dreamstone now that it was after midnight.

"Silence is good," noted Rose. With a nod of approval, she clasped the magic crystal in her hand. Closing her eyes so she could better concentrate, with a deep breath she felt the cool night air swirling through her lungs. As she slowly exhaled, her diaphragm expanding to squeeze out every bit of spent air from her lungs, she calmly inhaled once again, feeling a bit more relaxed as she entered the proper mindset to dream while wide awake.

Just as she pictured the gate that wouldn't stay shut, her concentration was suddenly broken. Her eyes opened as she snapped at Tag, "Will you stop it?"

"Stop what?"

"Making that annoying sound!" grumbled Rose, as she glared at Tag.

"I didn't say a thing."

"I did not say you were speaking, but you were making noise."

"I was not!" insisted Tag.

"Not meanin' to point the finger at anyone, but it certainly wasn't me," said Cankles, glancing about to spot the culprit.

"There it is again," announced Rose. She spun about to look behind, only to squeal in fright.

A bat's leathery wings slapped against the air. It hovered just above the Princess' head like it was preparing to swoop down.

"It's just a harmless, little bat," dismissed Tag. "It's probably drawn to the moths attracted to the light of the torch."

"There is no such thing as a harmless bat," protested Rose. "It means to become tangled in my hair!"

"What makes you think that?" questioned Tag, watching as the bat fluttered about before diving at a large, green moth hovering near to the flames of the torch.

"It's what bats do," answered Rose, staring in disgust as the moth pushed off into the darkness to avoid the sharp incisors of this winged predator.

"Never heard of a bat doin' such a thing," said Cankles, watching as the nocturnal creature spun about, executing a haphazard aerial loop as it pursued the moth. "Believe it's nothing more than an old wives' tale to tell you the truth."

"You've never had this happen because bats only like to become tangled in long, beautiful tresses. They avoid oily mops of hair from which they would only slide out of."

"I hardly think so!" disputed Tag.

"The point is, I cannot concentrate with that little beast flying about, waiting to attack. It is much too unnerving and distracting!"

"What do you want me to do?" grunted Tag. "Kill it?"

"That would work for me," replied Rose, nodding in approval.

"No need to kill the poor thing. I'll jus' chase it away," offered Cankles, freeing the torch from the earth. Waving the flame about, he attempted to drive the bat off. "Shoo, ya little bugger!"

Instead of winging away into the darkness, the bat circled about, as though drawn to this light. It abruptly swerved, dodging the torch thrust in its direction as Cankles gave chase.

"Happy now?" grumbled Tag. He watched as his friend rushed off, waving the torch about like a madman dashing off into the night.

"What would make me happier is to not have to waste a wish fixing the Trolls' incompetence," grumbled Rose, thinking back on the poorly positioned gate.

"Suppose if you do this, and do it right, you can do what you want with the last two remaining wishes?" bribed Tag.

"Oooh, that would make me very happy!" announced Rose, her hands clapping together in glee.

"Go to it then," ordered Tag. "The night is wasting away. I'd still like to steal away with a few hours of sleep before we move on."

"Wake up, lil' master!"

These words, though spoken in a whisper, rumbled through the air like the low roll of thunder as a huge fingertip prodded Tag on his back. He woke with a start, wiping his bleary eyes to spy upon Tiny. The Troll peered beneath the table where Tag, Cankles and Rose took refuge late in the night to keep from being trod upon by these giants.

"What is it?" asked Tag, throwing off his bedroll as he yawned.

"The gate, of course!" exclaimed Tiny. His thick lips drew back into a tremendous smile. "Ya fixed it!"

"You already checked?" questioned Tag. He glanced over to see Rose stirring from her slumber as Cankles wheezed, and then snorted, only to nod off again.

"At first light," answered Tiny. "The gate's workin' jus' fine now. So Umber an' the others gone ta gather all the goats. We're movin' them ta a pasture ta the north. Lockin' 'em in 'til we're ready ta move 'em ta the next pasture like ya said."

"Good job!" praised Tag, stretching as he yawned once more.

"Good job, indeed! You an' yer friends are the ones ta be doin' the good job," corrected Tiny. "Don't know how ya teeny folks did all that work last night, but ya did it! An' we're right grateful ta ya. How're we ever gonna repay ya fer helpin' us?"

"By letting us sleep for a little longer," grumbled Rose, prying her eyes open, only to squeeze them shut again upon seeing the gleeful Troll kneeling on the ground before them.

"But I thought ya said you're in a hurry ta move on?" responded Tiny.

"So I did," replied Rose, through a great yawn. She struggled to sit up, prodding Cankles with her foot to wake him.

"Never mind the Princess," urged Tag, compressing his bedroll into a tight bundle. "She's not used to sleeping like regular people."

"Regular people do not need beauty sleep," snipped Rose. "People of royal blood do."

"So you're sayin' that folks of royalty need more sleep 'cause if they don't, they'll end up lookin' ugly?" questioned Tiny, perplexed by her claim.

"Some more ugly than others," interjected Tag, with a smug grin.

Ignoring Tag's words, Rose explained to the Troll, "I do not do ugly. It cannot happen to someone like me."

"Oh... so you're jus' lazy?" surmised Tiny, nodding his head in understanding. "Ya like ta sleep in 'cause it's better than wakin' up early ta work."

Tag burst out laughing, chortling loudly at the Troll's observation.

"That is far from the truth. I am not lazy!" exclaimed Rose. "I will have you know a restful night's sleep helps to *enhance* my beauty."

"Did -- did I miss something?" mumbled Cankles, struggling to sit upright as he wiped the sleep from his eyes.

"You certainly did, my friend," chortled Tag. "Master Goatswain spoke the truth while the Princess exaggerated it."

"And the jester here is just plain exaggerating," scoffed Rose, dismissing Tag's comment.

"I'm confused," said Cankles, through a great yawn.

"It is a normal state for you, but believe me, it is not worth repeating," said Rose, bundling up her bedroll.

"What is worth saying again is that the Trolls are pleased the problem gate had been fixed to their satisfaction," stated Tag.

"You don't say!" exclaimed Cankles, rising up to meet the morning.

"Oh, I certainly do!" declared Tiny. "Even as we speak, the others are workin' ta move the goat herds ta a field afar."

"Splendid!" responded Cankles; pleased the Trolls were accepting Tag's advice so eagerly.

"Well, now that everyone is happy, I suppose we shall be on our way," announced Rose.

"What 'bout a wee bit of brekkie?" asked Tiny. "Can't have ya leavin' without havin' something ta eat first."

"Breakfast sounds like a wonderful idea," said Cankles.

"No disrespect to our kind host, but I'd rather not. I have had my fair share of cheese and potato juice to last a lifetime," declined Rose. "Besides, we are in a hurry."

"Perhaps we should take up Master Goatswain's offer," suggested Tag. "It may be a while before we eat again."

"Just because your hunting prowess leaves much to be desired, it does not mean we will go hungry," argued Rose, her hand discreetly coming to a rest over the dreamstone hidden beneath her gown.

"Oh, yes!" agreed Tag, as he nodded in understanding. "I suppose we should head out, take advantage of the light of day while we can."

"But Master Yairet, remember our failed attempts at catchin' those grouse?" reminded Cankles. He rolled his bony shoulder as though it was still menaced by phantom pains from over extending his throwing arm.

"Fear not, my friend," assured Tag, giving Cankles a wink of his eye. "I'm sure the Princess can come up with something to feed us along the way. If you get my meaning?"

"Can't say I do, but if you say we must go, then go we must," decided Cankles. "I'll ready the horses."

"Before ya leave though, ya promised ta tell me yer secret," reminded Tiny.

"What secret?" asked Tag, as he frowned in curiosity at the Troll towering before him.

"You know the one," responded Tiny, speaking in a whisper as he leaned down to the little human. "Yer secret fer not being 'fraid of the dark."

"Oh, that one!" recalled Tag.

"Yep, that'd be the one I'm speakin' of."

"Do you really want to know?" questioned Tag, staring Tiny in his eyes.

"I sure do! Don't like being scared of the darkness. None of us do."

"If I told you what to do, it'll only work if you truly believe, with all your heart, in what I say. If there's even a smidgen of doubt, it's not going to work for you."

"Well, after you an' yer friends fixed the gate jus' as ya promised, there's no reason not ta believe anything ya say, wee master," assured Tiny, placing his hand over his heart in solemn promise. "You tell me what I gotta do an' I'll believe with all my heart it's gonna work."

"Very well then, but first, tell me what it is you fear the most about the dark?" probed Tag.

"That's easy," answered Tiny. "It's the unseen evil, that danger I've been tellin' you folks about."

"And you've never actually seen this evil. Is that so?"

"That's right. It's out there though, lurkin' about in the night."

"Tag, get to the point before you confuse the Troll," urged Rose, eager to be on her way.

"Just close your eyes as tight as you can and cover them so the light of day cannot get through," ordered Tag.

Tiny did exactly as he was instructed, squeezing his eyes shut and hiding them in the crook of his elbow.

"Now what?" asked the Troll, staring into this enforced darkness.

"Tell me, what do you see?" asked Tag.

"Nothing… I see nothing at all."

"And it's dark?"

"Yep, it's even darker than the night an' I see nothing," admitted Tiny.

"And you are not scared?" ascertained Tag.

"No. Can't say I am."

"There you go then!" exclaimed Tag. "You, Master Goatswain, are cured!"

"I am?" asked Tiny. His bushy brows furrowed in bewilderment as he peered over his arm to gaze down at the human.

"Of course you are! You said yourself you saw nothing and being such a clever Troll, you know as well as I do, only a fool would be scared of *nothing*."

"Well, I'll be! I *am* cured!" declared Tiny, gasping in absolute amazement.

"And that is it?" grumbled Rose, staring at Tag in disbelief.

"That's it and that's all he needs. He is cured as long as he believes this to be true," responded Tag.

"Works for me," confided Cankles, as he opened his eyes after following Tag's instructions. "Mind you, I'm not really scared of the dark, but it makes perfect sense to me. If there's nothing there to be afraid of, then there's no need to be scared."

"*Woohoo!*" whooped the Troll, gleefully skipping about. The earth trembled beneath them as Tiny's footfalls landed lightly, as lightly as far a Troll was concerned, upon the ground. "Can't wait ta share this secret with the others."

Tiny's exuberant display came to an abrupt halt as he gazed down at Tag to ask for permission. "It's all right fer me ta share this secret, ain't it?"

"You go right ahead," urged Tag. "And now that you have nothing to fear, should you be made to check on your herds through the night, anything lurking about in the dark will be forced to flee in fear from you."

"You think so?" asked Tiny, sounding hopeful.

"I *know* so," assured Tag. "Where before you were too afraid to venture into the night, now, all will know you are the one to be feared should they cross paths with you in the darkness!"

"By golly! You're right, wee master!" declared Tiny, puffing out his chest in pride.

"Good! Gate fixed, fear gone, let's move on," suggested Rose. "Just tell us the fastest route to get to the Land of Big."

"First, you'll be needin' ta cross the Bad Lands ta get ta Dwarf country," said Tiny, his words shadowed by a sense of foreboding.

"Are you speakin' of the Sorcerer's domain?" questioned Cankles, casting his gaze eastward.

"Yep, an' it's called the Bad Lands fer good reason," responded Tiny.

"Because it is a dark, desolate place full of vile magic, crawling with dangerous rogues and scoundrels?" assumed Rose.

"If the Sorcerer's about he'll be sure ta unleash his dark magic, but we call it the Bad Lands 'cause it's easier than always sayin' the Land of Real Bad Actin'," explained Tiny.

"You're speaking of Dragonite's followers," determined Tag, "the mimes."

"Don't know 'bout no *mines*, but the Sorcerer's got an army of followers who act, an' they're real bad at it. An' they don't speak 'cause they keep forgettin' their lines," revealed the Troll. "They even pretend ta be doing things 'cause they don't even bother with props an' such. That's how bad their actin' is."

"They are called mimes," responded Rose, rolling her eyes in exasperation. "They *mimic* actions and use it, rather than words, to tell a story as a form of entertainment."

"Oh… I jus' thought they were all actin' the fool," said Tiny, scratching his head in thought. "Always found them folks ta be kinda irritatin' in a strange way. Didn't know they were tryin' to be entertainin'."

"Whether they are, or not, is up for debate," said Tag.

"Well, accordin' ta the Dwarves they captured an' forced ta watch a performance, it was not entertainin' at all. They said it was downright hellish, truth be told!" exclaimed Tiny.

"Hellish, indeed!" stated Rose. "And who would have thought Dwarves have a sense of taste when it comes to culture and the arts?"

"If being forced to endure a performance by mimes is the worst that can happen to us if we should confront the Sorcerer, then it will be the least of our worries," decided Tag.

"Here, here!" agreed Cankles.

"Then let us be on our way," urged Rose, staring up at the Troll. "Now, the fastest route? Can you tell us the way?"

"I can do better than that, Princess," responded Tiny.

As Rose sat high on Tiny's shoulder, Tag and Cankles were perched on Umber's. The trio held on for dear life, clenching the collar of the shirts the Trolls wore as their slow, rolling gait became all the more obvious from this high vantage point.

Behind them, two more Trolls followed, carrying their horses to the border of their territory.

"Well, here ya go," announced Tiny, his big, sausage finger pointing the way. "Beyond this bridge is the Sorcerer's domain."

Tiny placed the Princess on the ground at the foot of the bridge next to Cankles and Tag as his comrades placed the horses before them.

"So this is it," said Tag, staring eastward. "We must now part ways."

"Indeed, lil' master," acknowledged Tiny. "But before we do, I've gotta ask a favour of you."

"What is it?" asked Tag.

"I'd appreciate it if you'd kindly deliver this wheel of cheese ta the leader of the Dwarves, Giblet Barscowl," said Tiny.

"They like cheese?" asked Tag.

"Who doesn't?" responded Cankles, staring at the large wheel protected in a wax coating.

"And just how are we to deliver this huge helping of cheese?" questioned Rose. "It is not as though we have a large cart to carry it in."

"Well, they don't call it a *wheel of cheese* fer nothing, Princess," replied Tiny, pushing a stick through the center. "Ya wheel it along."

Tag stared at the disc of cheese. It was almost as tall as he stood and had to measure at least two handspans in width.

"If you an' Master Mayron stood on either side an' jus' rolled it along, it can be done," assured Tiny.

"I'm sure it can," agreed Tag. "However, time is of the essence. We must get to the Land of Big with speed."

"What's the point of goin' all the way there, only ta be turned back?" questioned the Troll.

"Why would we be turned back?" asked Rose.

"Have ya ever been to Dwarf country?" probed Tiny.

"Never," answered Tag.

"Well, there ya go then!" exclaimed Tiny. "Dwarves are nervous types, an' rightfully so. They don't take ta trustin' jus' anyone, but if ya come bearing gifts, it opens the doors an' they can be downright hospitable folks. Mind you, if ya anger 'em, they'll have no qualms 'bout puttin' their halberds ta yer little heads."

"We can do without having our heads cleaved," decided Tag, giving the Troll's warning some thought.

"Hence, the cheese," explained Tiny. "You tell 'em you're our friends an' prove it by deliverin' this wheel of cheese. Those crazy, lil' dwarves will be welcomin' yous with hairy, open arms."

"An' that's jus' the women-folk," added Umber.

"Lovely…" groaned Rose, shuddering inwardly.

"So, if we deliver this cheese, we are more likely to be welcomed, even helped, by the Dwarves?" determined Tag.

"Look at it this way, Master Yairet. To them folks, it's downright rude ta show up empty-handed," responded Tiny. "Plus, we'd be owin' them this cheese, for all their trouble."

"What trouble?" asked Cankles.

"The last time they delivered the blue powder they get from their mines that we mix inta our mudsie, that crazy Sorcerer an' his underlings captured 'em. Forced those poor Dwarves ta sit through one of their goofy shows."

"Sounds dreadful!" exclaimed Rose.

"Was dreadful," confirmed Tiny. "Those teeny folk haven't made a delivery since then. An' with the comin' of summer, we'll be needin' more of that blue stuff. I'm jus' hopin' this bit of cheese will tempt them inta doin' business with us again. An' if it don't, at least it'll kinda make up fer their sufferin' at the Sorcerer's hands."

"Well, it sounds like the neighbourly thing to do, however, you really cannot expect us to deliver this huge wheel of cheese, do you?" asked Rose.

"Why not?" asked Tiny. "I thought if you fixed the gate like you did, you'd be able ta handle a simple task like deliverin' some cheese."

"This is not a small morsel! This is a monstrous wheel of cheese. It can mow a person down if it should get away from you on a hill," protested Rose.

"But surely ya can see the reasonin' why it'd be good fer ya ta be deliverin' this fer us?"

"Of course we can," responded Tag.

"We can?" asked Rose, her words glib.

"I know enough about the Dwarves' demeanor that even though they're small in size compared to us, if provoked, it can lead to a hostile encounter," warned Tag.

"Surely, they can be reasoned with," argued Rose.

"They tend to throw their axe first, ask questions later," explained Tag. "Better to make allies of them, especially if we need their help to find your locket."

"Fine then," grunted Rose, with a sigh of resignation. "But know this, I am not about to roll a stinking, big wheel of cheese through the country."

"That does not surprise me," responded Tag, with a shrug of his shoulders. "You deal with the horses. Cankles and I will deal with the cheese."

"So, you'll do it?" asked Tiny, staring down at the little humans.

"One kind turn begets another," replied Tag. "We shall do this for you, and in turn, you shall meet with Lord Silverthorn. You will tell him that you and your people promise to abide by his request to control your herds. With reassurance the Woodland Glade not be ravaged by goats, he will allow you safe passage through his domain so you can resume trade with the King of Axalon once more."

"I'll get right to it," promised Tiny. "You jus' be careful crossin' through these Bad Lands ta get ta where you're goin', my lil' friends."

"Ooh! Now there's a plump one!" Dragonite made his selection through the flurry of wings as the bats returned to roost. After their nocturnal foray, they were ready to retreat into the deepest, darkest chamber of this network of caves.

With unerring precision and surprising speed for one looking so decrepit, the Sorcerer jabbed the end of his staff into this swirling cyclone of black wings to down his prey.

"Gotcha!"

Dragonite scampered across the cave to where the bat he had accosted fell to the ground. He eagerly snatched up the dazed creature before it could take to the air again. Picking it up by a limp wing, the Sorcerer prepared to end its misery by slamming his dinner against the cave wall.

He gasped in disgust, releasing his hold as the bat's wing abruptly morphed into the Pooka's.

Loken groaned in pain as he fell onto the cave floor again.

"Ugh! It's you," grumbled Dragonite.

"Why must you always assault me when I return to your lair?" moaned Loken. Staggering to his feet, he shook the fog from his throbbing head.

"It is not as though you make your presence obvious now, do you?" muttered Dragonite, made all the more irate as he stomach growled and his dinner took on its true, unappetizing form.

"You insisted I be discreet!" snapped Loken, his wings rattled as he pushed off the ground to hover before Dragonite's face. "Can't be any more discreet than a bat returning to roost in this cave with other bats."

"Still, you should be more careful. I could have eaten you."

"You would have choked, had you tried," grunted Loken, following behind the Sorcerer as he retreated to his throne.

"Never mind that, you're here now. So, have you learned anymore of the dreamstone and it's whereabouts?"

"Why don't you show some concern first? Ask me how I fare?" demanded Loken, thoroughly agitated by the Sorcerer's total disregard for his well-being, especially after the bashing he received.

"Fine!" snapped Dragonite, as he glared back at the Pooka. "How do you fare?"

"Terrible! You were going to eat me, you fool!" rebuked Loken, his wings trembling with indignation.

"It was an honest mistake! You looked like all the other bats, only tastier."

"I stood out from the others! How many bats have amber eyes?"

"And just how am I expected to take notice of that when, as a bat, your eyes were so bloody small and beady?" argued the Sorcerer, attempting to justify his actions.

"Fine! This time, I will give you that, but what person in his right mind eats bats to begin with?"

"I *am* in my right mind. And with the proper spices, bats make for a scrumptious snack."

"Your state of mind is up for debate, but where is your sense of taste? Why do you not dine on pheasant, even a nice trout, like most people do than to eat less tantalizing fare such as bats, eels and other lowly creatures? It is as though you have been reduced to some kind of scavenging beast!"

"I am not like most people, nor do I strive to be!" grunted the Sorcerer, staring down at the Pooka as he paced along the armrest. "And consider this, who presents more of a threat: A fool partaking in afternoon tea while snacking on dainty wedges of crust-less sandwiches or a monster that willingly devours what others would not see fit to eat?"

"Your choice of food items does not make you threatening at all. It only confirms you have no taste!"

"This is coming from one who regularly snacks on fly maggots and thinks nothing of drinking pond scum!" retorted Dragonite, shaking his head in disgust. "It is no wonder the Queen of the Tooth Fairies is repulsed by you. Even I am repulsed!"

"Leave Pancecilia Feldspar out of this!" snapped Loken, his amber eyes flashing in resentment. "Besides, I am not the one trying to create a threatening image, you are! And you are doing a poor job of it, for one who claims to be an all-powerful Sorcerer."

Dragonite's hand balled into an angry, quivering fist. Before it could slam down to crush the Pooka, in a swell of eerie green light, Loken gave the Sorcerer a good reason to refrain from taking violent action.

With his stinger poised to strike, Loken's fierce-looking pincers were held agape in a threatening gesture. As a black emperor scorpion, his venom-filled stinger would easily pierce Dragonite's hand before it had a chance to pound him into a permanent fixture on this throne.

The Sorcerer's hand recoiled as he gasped in surprise, "Why must our conversations be so adversarial?"

"Because, in many ways, we *are* adversaries," reminded Loken, admiring his new sleek, black exoskeleton. The articulated joints allowed the stinger tipped tail the flexibility to strike from a number of angles.

"True, but a common enemy makes friends of us all," responded Dragonite, unclenching his fist as a gesture of calm.

"We will never be friends," snorted Loken. His tail curled over his back in threat. "Not with the way you treat me."

"Suppose I promise to never make a meal of you?" offered the Sorcerer, hoping to pacify the shape-shifting Sprite.

"Nor will you swipe, hit, strike, swat, and in general, attack any creature that wanders into your lair should it be me!" warned Loken, as he set the protocol to ensure his survival.

"Perhaps you should enter my abode as a great beast I would have reason to respect than a measly vermin I would see fit to mistreat," proposed Dragonite. "Or even appearing in your true form will prevent such a mishap from happening again."

"Perhaps I will."

"Good! Now it is settled. So what news have you regarding my dreamstone?" queried the Sorcerer, his eyes gleaming with lust.

"It is not yours yet," reminded Loken, assuming his usual form once more. "And you will be pleased to hear it journeys ever closer."

"Splendid!" exclaimed Dragonite, his grubby hands rubbing together in eager anticipation. "So it has left Silverthorn's domain?"

"Indeed it has. The mortals, most notably the Princess in possession of the stone, had left the Woodland Glade to venture on."

"Where are they now?" questioned the Sorcerer.

"As of late last night, the trio had wandered into the heart of the Land of Small. And lucky for them, they were not stepped on. It would appear they had made friends with the blue behemoths."

"What were they doing in Troll country?"

"My first two efforts to eavesdrop when they were amongst the Trolls almost ended in disaster," confided Loken. "The best I can tell, they were attempting to negotiate some kind of truce between the Trolls and the Elves."

"This is disturbing... Peace between those two races undermines my efforts to cultivate a sense of instability and fear across the lands. Did the mortals succeed?"

"How would I know? I was chased off by one of the Trolls hoping to serve me up for dinner."

"You are utterly useless!" snapped Dragonite.

"Look here, I thought I was sent forth to gather information that will allow you to get your hands on the dreamstone, not to gauge the political atmosphere of those you despise," protested Loken.

"So I digress. Tell me of the dreamstone! Were you able to steal away with it?"

"That was never part of the deal," grunted Loken. "Mine was to keep you informed of comings and goings in this realm."

"True," admitted Dragonite, nodding in confirmation. "In all likelihood, you would fail at this task anyway. Better for me to undertake this little mission if I am to guarantee success."

"Thanks for the vote of confidence," grumbled the Pooka.

"The stone?" reminded the Sorcerer.

"As I was saying, the Princess is still in possession of it."

"So you saw it? What form did Silas Agincor disguise it in this time? A lowly agate or a precious diamond?" questioned Dragonite, eager to learn all he can.

"I never said I saw it. What I do know is the Princess bears the stone disguised as a jewel she wears about her neck. She keeps it shielded from unwanted eyes by hiding it down the bodice of her gown."

"Not exactly clever, but I suppose it works."

"Of course it works! Why do you think I've yet to see it with mine own eyes," snapped Loken.

"And…?"

"And she was about to use it last night."

"For what purpose?"

"As best as I could tell, she was attempting to wish for a gate to be repaired," answered Loken.

"That is an odd use of a wish. What more can you tell me?"

"Sadly, that is all."

"What do you mean by that? You were supposed to spy on them to glean information for me."

"I did my best, however, one of the Princess' bodyguards, if you can call him that, took off after me at the most crucial and telling moment. I was singed by his torch, and then a bloody, big owl gave chase."

"Why did you not present yourself as a huge, terrifying dragon? That would have taught those mortals to chase you off like you were nothing more than a despised vermin."

"That would hardly be conspicuous. If I did that, they would either attempt to kill me than drive me away or they'd all head off in different directions screaming at the top of their lungs. What would have that accomplished?"

"It would give me reason to laugh," snorted Dragonite.

"The important thing is, I know where they are heading."

"Go on!" urged the Sorcerer, leaning in close to learn more.

"They plan to venture across your territory on their way to the Land of Big," revealed Loken.

"So I shall cross paths with these fools in the comfort of my own domain," gasped Dragonite, kicking his feet in the air with delight. "This is too good to be true!"

"You are a fool to celebrate prematurely. When you consider the allies they have made during their travels and how many enemies you have cultivated in your dealings beyond this domain, you could be getting in well over your head."

"You are ever the pessimist, Loken!" denounced Dragonite, dismissing the Pooka's warning.

"And you are ever the delusional, optimistic fool, choosing to wallow in an imagined life of magnificence."

"So you say, but keep this in mind, little Sprite, if you think I will hand over that potion you wish to use on the Tooth Fairy when you are proving to be a less than effective and obedient minion to me, then think again!"

For a moment, Loken's eyes narrowed as he glared at the Sorcerer. Their relationship was strained at the best of times, but to jeopardize his own personal agenda now, after all he had endured in carrying out demented orders that rarely seemed logical? He heaved a weary sigh of resignation as he caved in to Dragonite's will.

"I suppose it does no harm to remain positive," conceded Loken. "But how do you plan to hold the enemy at bay should they choose to rally around those mortals."

"And why would they do that?"

"You are a creature of habit," grunted Loken. "When it comes to getting what you want, there is no such thing as reaching a mutually satisfying agreement. You tend to take things by force, and the more force, the better."

"Look here! I have a reputation to uphold!" snapped Dragonite; incensed he was made to explain his actions to the Pooka. "What is the point of being an evil Sorcerer if I willingly partake in peaceful negotiations with those who see fit to ridicule me?"

"They ridicule you because you give them good reason to!"

"My passion for mime and to elevate it to the grand art form it truly is cannot be used against me as a source of ridicule. It comes down to a matter of taste and those who do not appreciate this art have no taste at all."

"This is all very subjective," warned Loken. "And it is not so much they ridicule you for championing this *art form*. You cultivate your enemies by forcing everyone else in the world to agree with your belief that mimes are artists."

"And they are."

"The point being, if you take hostile action to claim the dreamstone, and whatever else it is they are after, you stand to raise the ire of mortal man, Elves and Trolls. You stand a good chance of facing hostile retaliation from your enemies."

"Fret not, my odd, little friend," responded Dragonite. His thin lips curled into a cruel smile as his grubby fingers fondled the grizzled whiskers of his beard. "My men will be ready for such an attack."

"Your men are roving bands of *entertainers*, and I use the word loosely! How can an army of mimes be prepared to face the enemy? Especially if they be Elves and Trolls?"

"Should my hand be forced and I am made to unleash my wrath to smite my foes, my men will be ready! Even as we speak, they undertake military exercises to insure my victory."

"Oh... so that's what those cretins were doing in Pleno'Gore Fields," responded Loken. "Looked more like an exercise in futility."

Loken recalled the bizarre spectacle he had witnessed while winging his way back to Dragonite's lair; a multitude of mimes engaged in mock combat against invisible adversaries.

"All it will take is strategy, leadership and a wee bit of magic to encourage those mimes to do my will," explained Dragonite.

"So that is how you *convinced* the mimes to pretend they are now soldiers."

"They are *actors*. With proper motivation, they can take on any role they are asked to perform," responded the Sorcerer.

"Did you tell them they could die?" questioned Loken.

"A minor detail! Sure they cowered at the mere thought, but it was easily remedied with one of my spells."

"That was underhanded and devious," rebuked the Pooka, shaking his head in disgust.

"Why, thank you! It is not often I receive such a flattering compliment from you, or anybody for that matter."

Loken pushed off against the armrest, his translucent wings beating against the damp air as he hovered before the Sorcerer's face.

"As you are so confident your army is ready to do battle, do you intend to capture the Princess to steal away with the dreamstone as she enters your domain?"

"As tempting as it is, I believe it to be prudent to exercise patience where the object of my desire is concerned," responded Dragonite, a shrewd glint sparkling in his eyes. "It would be easy enough to capture the Princess so I can claim the coveted stone, however, if I do so, I shall be making extra work for myself."

"How so?"

"If I am patient, that lowly human will complete her quest, securing the prize she seeks. When that is done, then I will make my move, stealing away with this prize as well as the dreamstone."

"For once, you make sense," agreed Loken.

"Which brings us back to the quest and this prize. Have you discovered what it is Princess Rose seeks?"

"She and her cohorts have been extremely secretive," confided Loken. "I have yet to uncover the nature of their mission and the object of this quest."

"Then you know what you must do."

"Yes, yes…" groaned Loken.

"Good! And this time, use your cunning. Instead of being discreet, take on a form that will encourage those mortals to invite your presence, rather than to drive you off," recommended the Sorcerer.

"If you are suggesting I take the form of a cuddly, little creature, forget it. I do not do cute!"

"All I am saying is to adopt a form that is *non-threatening* so they will not chase you off and unappealing so they will not want to make a meal of you. Take on a form that will invite your close proximity to allow you to eavesdrop so you may glean information."

"Easier said than done," sighed Loken.

"Are you saying you cannot do it?"

"I can do whatever I set my mind to. I just need to give this a great deal of thought."

"So you did not do so during your earlier attempts?" grumbled Dragonite.

"Never you mind!" snapped Loken, his wings trembling with indignation. "Just leave it to me. I will find a way to gather the information you need."

"Good! For I will be devoting my time to training and organizing my military forces, should I be made to deploy my men into battle."

"Why do you not use your magic to annihilate your foes? Just be done with them?"

"You are an idiot!" declared Dragonite. "You know my powers have been stilted by my brother Wizards! I am like a gelded stallion -- impotent! Impotent, I tell you!"

"Do you really think this is something you should be announcing at the top of your lungs for the whole world to hear?" questioned Loken, backing away from the Sorcerer's snarling face.

"The point is, my powers are such that I will leave nothing to chance. If I must rely on my army of mimes to repel and defeat my enemies, then so be it! Until I can get my hands on the dreamstone, I cannot hope to restore my magic to its full powers."

"And you are confident the dreamstone will do this?" queried Loken.

"It is not called a dreamstone for no reason! Of course it can. I can dream of being even more powerful than before. That will teach Silas and the others who did this to me!"

"You did this to yourself," countered Loken.

"Shall I kill you now?" growled Dragonite, aiming the black crystal at the Pooka.

"I am in no hurry to die, at least, not by your hands," replied Loken, maintaining a safe distance with a flutter of his wings. "And remember, you need me!"

"For now," said Dragonite, acknowledging this uneasy alliance as he lowered his staff. "So you best be on your way."

"Say no more," responded Loken. "Consider me gone!"

Parru St. Mime Dragonite watched in silence as the Pooka made haste, winging his way to the mouth of the cave to commence his search for the trio.

Heart of the Matter

"Even for me, that was too bizarre," whispered Cankles. He shook his head to vanquish this strange memory from his usually forgetful mind as he helped Tag maneuver the massive wheel of cheese along a narrow trail.

"Now you know why I had my parents ban all mimes from the palace," responded Rose, her words hushed as she led the horses on through the dimming forest. "There is nothing entertaining about their silly shenanigans."

"What do you suppose they were doin' back there?" questioned Cankles, still baffled by the odd performance they had witnessed as they skirted Pleno'Gore Fields to remain undetected.

"If I did not know better, I'd say they were rehearsing a battle scene," responded Tag, giving the cheese a hard shove as it came to rest in a rut in the middle of the trail.

"They could have been pretending to hang laundry, for all you know," dismissed Rose.

"Since when does anyone hang laundry in formation?" countered Tag. "As crude as their lines were, a person in the know would see they were pretending to throw spears and fire arrows."

"So what if they were? Mimes do that – pretend that is! They hardly pose a threat to us," insisted Rose.

"But if Master Yairet was right, suppose those mimes are preparin' to do battle?" asked Cankles.

"Against what? An imaginary army of invisible rabble-rousers bearing pretend weapons of war?" grunted Rose.

"Just the same, we'd be wise to give them a wide berth," suggested Tag. "After all, Lord Silverthorn did warn us they are the Sorcerer's loyal followers."

"Oh, quite right, Master Yairet," agreed Cankles. "We don't need to get in a tangle with them if it means avoidin' that Dragonite fella."

"Can you imagine being forced to watch a performance by those buffoons?" asked Rose, with a shudder.

"All the more reason to keep moving. The farther away we are from them, the less likely a chance of that happening," said Tag.

"We'd travel faster an' farther if we didn't have to wheel this cheese along with us," grunted Cankles, pressing his shoulder against the sturdy pole the Troll had driven through its center. "But as we promised to deliver it to the Dwarves, then deliver we must."

"There's an easier way of getting this cheese to its final destination," offered Tag, glancing over at the Princess.

Gazing over her shoulder at Tag, Rose's eyes narrowed in suspicion. "After using the second wish to conjure up a meal fit for a queen, of which I shared with you both, I only have one left to last us to the end of the day. If you think I am going to waste it to magically transport us to the Dwarves' settlement, think again! It cannot be done."

"I'm no fool!" retorted Tag, stopping to wipe the sweat from his forehead with the back of his hand. "You've never been to this settlement, so of course you cannot conjure up a precise image in your mind."

"Then what were you thinking?" questioned Rose, bringing the horses to a halt so she could consider Tag's words.

"I was thinking of using the last wish to transform this humongous wheel of cheese into a more manageable size -- preferably small enough to fit into my vest pocket so it will be easy to transport," suggested Tag.

"That is doable, but I hardly think it will work," countered Rose.

"Why not?" asked Cankles. "Sounds like a grand idea to me."

"It is, except for the fact that even though the Dwarves are small, I hardly think they are so diminutive a palm-sized disk of cheese will go very far shared amongst them."

"We won't be giving them a tiny round of cheese. Once we arrive at our destination, we'll use another wish to return the cheese to it former size," explained Tag.

"I knew you were going to say that!" grumbled Rose. "That is why I must say *no* to your request."

"But it's a good, practical use of a wish," argued Tag.

"*Two* wishes," reminded Rose. "And what good is a wish if it is not used for my benefit?"

"If you do this, we will be able to ride our horses and be far removed from the Sorcerer's territory before he catches wind that we are here," reasoned Tag. "And remember, the sooner we are done with this quest, the sooner you will be able to return to Fleetwood. You might even return in time for your birthday celebration."

"An' it's not as if you won't have more wishes comin' your way," reminded Cankles.

"True, but I think we are already making wonderful progress," responded Rose.

"It'd be better if you took a turn helping to roll this wheel of cheese, since you refuse to use that last wish," suggested Tag, glancing eastward to the foothills leading to the Stony Mountains. "It'll only get harder as we near Dwarf country."

"Are you saying you want *me*, a princess, to undertake a physically intensive task?" gasped Rose. "To subject myself to menial labour?"

"As far as I'm concerned, you are only a princess in Fleetwood. At this moment, you are far from home. Surely, in all fairness, you don't expect us to do all the work?"

"I was hoping."

"Well then, you can keep on hoping. I can just as soon abandon you and this damned quest to head home," decided Tag.

"You wouldn't!" gasped Rose.

"What do I have to gain in being subjected to such misery?" responded Tag, with a shrug of indifference. "Especially when you are the instigator of it and yet, you refuse to share equally in the drudgery of this quest."

"But you promised to undertake this mission! You said you would do this so I may return your father's sword to you once we are done."

"I've been doing some thinking, Princess. I have no way of knowing if you truly do have my father's sword to begin with. For all I know, you've been lying to me all along to make me undertake this burden for you."

"Are you calling me a liar?"

"Let me just say you have a tendency to stretch the truth if it is to your benefit," replied Tag.

"The truth is not being stretched!" protested Rose. "Not at all!"

"And I am to take your word for it?" questioned Tag, giving her a doubtful glance.

"You used to trust me. Why would you change now?"

"That was when we were children. That was before *you* changed," argued Tag.

"But you were the one to change first!" countered Rose, digging her heels in.

"Not so! There was a time when you were not a deceitful, manipulative snip of a girl. That was the princess I befriended, not the one you've become now. And to think you would stoop so low, you'd lie to me about my father's sword, withholding it from me all this time, if indeed you do have it."

"Withholding information is not really lying, and if it was, then I had good reason!" declared Rose.

"If the reason was self-serving, then I don't want to hear about it!" snapped Tag, his nerves bristling with resentment.

Rose was silent as she struggled to come up with an explanation that would present her actions as being selfless.

"Well? Were they?" interrogated Tag.

Her mouth fell open, but no words came out, for there was none that would explain away her past action as being anything but self-serving.

"Thought not!" snapped Tag, thoroughly angered and frustrated by the Princess. "Your silence betrays you. I've had enough!"

Rose watched in stunned disbelief as her jester stormed off, abandoning her and Cankles to deal with the cheese. Before she could give chase, Cankles stopped her.

"Allow cooler heads to prevail, Princess. It'll do him good to have some time for himself," recommended Cankles, watching as his young friend came to a stop at the top of a small rise. Tag plopped down on a large rock, staring across the twilight landscape. "Perhaps now's a good time to set up camp before it gets real dark."

"If this is your way to keep me from speaking my mind where he is concerned, it is not as though I was going to pick a fight with him," explained Rose.

"I didn't say you were, Princess," responded Cankles, maneuvering the wheel of cheese off the trail and into a protected thicket. "It's jus' that the young master's quite upset. I hardly think justifyin' your past actions will put his mind at ease."

"I do not have to justify anything to him," sniffed Rose, as she tethered the horses to a tree. "After all, he started it! Tag was the one who was going to change. He was going to change everything."

Cankles glanced up from the small pile of tinder he had gathered. "I must've heard him wrong, Princess. I thought he said you were the one to change first."

"What difference does it make? The only thing that really mattered was that Tag was going to change if I did not try to stop him."

"Call me a fool, but I fail to understand," said Cankles, striking the flint to send a small shower of golden sparks onto the dried leaves and moss. "Don't we all change as we grow up, or am I missin' something?"

"You would not understand," sulked Rose. She sat down next to Cankles as the twilight sky dissolved into the coming night. Her arms wrapped around her legs as she rested her forehead on bended knees.

"I know I'm a simple man, but I'd like to try," responded Cankles. He nursed the tiny flame, feeding it broken twigs.

"I would not know where to start," whispered Rose, not even peering up to address Cankles.

"I do believe the beginnin' is always the best place to start. You were sayin' you were tryin' to stop him from changin'. Changin' what, pray tell?"

"From the time I was a small child, I have always known Tag. His father, being the captain of my father's army, was a constant presence around the palace and so, too, was Tag. We practically grew up together and as we got older, I got wise to those who wished to be my friend because they liked the prestige that comes with socializing with a princess. None of those snooty, high society children actually liked me, but they certainly enjoyed my title and the privileges it afforded them in dropping my name. They were like leeches, clinging to me for no other reason."

"And the young master was one of these leeches?"

"Oh, no!" explained Rose, a small smile appeared as she remembered better days. "Tag was a true friend. At least, I thought he was. He used to stand up to all these uppity, class-conscious snobs who were polite to my face, but thought nothing of teasing me behind my back, as I was far from being the perfect princess I am now."

"You look fine to me."

"I always look fine. Even on the rare, bad day, I still look lovely, but I am not talking about my appearance. I used to have a speech impediment."

"A what?"

"I spoke with a lisp and a bit of a stutter," revealed Rose, her cheeks burning red with embarrassment. "It was worse when I was nervous, but eventually, I outgrew this condition. Singing lessons helped, but I was so self-conscious at first, I did not even want to try singing, until Tag encouraged me. Somehow, it worked, but I would never have tried if it were not for him."

"So the young sir was being noble in defendin' you an' a true friend in givin' you courage. It sounds like he had the makings of a great knight, like his father."

"That is just it. Tag is very much like his father. He was bound to follow in his footsteps. When Tag was seven, he was ready to serve as his father's page. He was intent on becoming a squire and learning all he could of the knighthood. That is all he ever dreamed of; becoming a knight."

"There's nothing wrong with followin' one's dreams."

"You do not understand. If I did not stop him, if he became a knight, he would no longer have time for me. He would eventually go off with his father to prepare him for battle and to go to war himself one day. Tag would be gone, and then who would be my..."

Rose's voice trailed off as silver tears spilled from her eyes.

"Your friend?" concluded Cankles, peering into her sad eyes.

"And why would he be? After all, I crushed whatever dreams he had."

"I'm not the smartest person in the world, but I'm pretty sure those qualities you admired in him from the start would've remained true, even strengthened. He'd likely continue being your champion; defendin' your name an' honour, had he been able to pursue his dreams."

"Do you think so?" queried Rose, blotting away the trail of tears from her cheeks onto the sleeve of her gown.

"I'm pretty sure those enterin' the knighthood must uphold a higher standard than the common man," answered Cankles, throwing another piece of wood into the campfire. "I suspect, somewhere beneath his crushed dream, there still lingers some of the qualities you once admired. Perhaps, given the chance, the young master can be all that an' more."

Rose glanced over at the Village Idiot of Cadboll, wondering if it was compassion, wisdom or merely random thoughts behind these words and if he even understood how profound they were. Either way, she had to marvel at the fact that as simple as he was, Cankles Mayron had become the voice of reason in their trio. It was a cause for real elation or genuine concern.

"And he would still be my friend? I think not!"

"I'd say he'd be even truer a friend had you supported, than hindered him. After all, what good is a knight if he does not stand for all that is good an' true?"

"I hardly believe he thinks of me as either," said Rose, unleashing a disheartened sigh. "At least, not anymore."

"Maybe, jus' as you hoped he'd stay the same if you kept him close, he clings to the hope that behind your grand title you're still the girl he had reason to care for, enough to stand up to the others when he didn't have to."

"You think?"

"Sometimes I do think, but being that the young master is like me, in that we both don't have a family to speak of, gettin' to the heart of the matter, I'd say true friendship would be worth fightin' for. Maybe that's why he's still here?"

"He's here because I promised to give him his father's sword if he helped me," stated Rose.

"So he says," responded Cankles, with a thoughtful nod. "But I sense he has other reasons for undertakin' this task."

"You are just trying to make me feel better."

"If I did an' you do, no harm in that," reasoned Cankles.

Rose smiled as he gave her a reassuring pat on the shoulder.

"Even if I tried to apologize to Tag, I hardly think he will accept," lamented Rose.

"I wouldn't be so sure of that. Those three, tiny words, *I am sorry*, are pretty powerful when said with utmost sincerity. Of course, it'd mean more if delivered first an' with no other intention than to make amends."

"So you are saying, it must begin with me?" questioned Rose, glancing up to the rise where Tag sat alone, silhouetted against the night sky as he continued to brood in silence.

"It'd be a good start, Princess."

❀ ❀ ❀

"Tag?"

From the meek tone he knew it was Princess Rose traipsing up the trail to verbally accost him again.

"If you're here for an apology, forget it," grumbled Tag, standing up to put some distance between them as Rose sat down on the rock he had been resting on.

"I know you are mad at me."

"Well, aren't you brilliant to come to this deduction all on your own," muttered Tag.

"You won't be making this easy for me, will you?"

"Make what easy?' questioned Tag.

"I am trying to apologize."

For the longest moment, Tag was silent, mulling over her words. Gazing down at the Princess, she sat there, crestfallen. Her chin drooped, resting on her chest. Her eyes were cast to the ground, unable to meet his unforgiving stare.

"Why? Because you think you can trick me into resuming this damned quest just to help you?" grunted Tag.

"I am trying to apologize to you because I was w- wro- wrong!"

Rose's declaration was met with utter silence once more.

"There! I said it! I was wrong. You were right," acknowledged Rose, her words tinged with sincerity. "I was being thoughtless and selfish."

Tag could not believe his ears.

"I am the one to blame. It was my fault, so I am here to apologize," continued Rose, humbling herself before her jester.

"Whoa! This is all too much. I can handle you apologizing, even admitting to a flaw in your personality, but to accept blame, too? That's more than I can deal with in one turn," responded Tag, raising his hands for Rose to stop talking.

"So not only must I swallow my pride in admitting this, you insist on making me choke on it, too?"

"All I am saying is one sincere apology will suffice."

"It would?"

"I've known you all my life, Princess. I know how hard it was for you to do this. So of course it would be adequate, if you truly meant it."

"Then I will say it again, I am *truly* sorry." Rose sounded as contrite as she looked.

"Apology accepted."

"And that is it?" questioned Rose, bewildered by this easily accepted truce.

"My father always said only a small-minded man would spit on a hand extended in peace, and only a fool would discount the power of forgiveness," explained Tag. "I'm not a knight, but I intend to honour my father's memory by living by a code he instilled in me. And heaven forbid should I ever require your forgiveness!"

"You were never going to quit, were you? You had no intention of abandoning me to this quest on my own," determined Rose.

Tag gave her a knowing smile as he responded: "A promise is a promise. This is one I made, and one I intend to keep. I spouted off in anger, but I believe one's actions have more bearing than what is said."

"You are your father's son, Tagius Oliver Yairet," conceded Rose.

"I shall take that as a compliment."

"As you should," said Rose, giving him a nod of approval.

For a moment, Tag was taken aback. The only time she called him by his full name was when she was seething mad, verbally slamming him by modifying his middle name to reflect her opinion of him. This time, there was no '*Oddball*' thrown in for good measure, nor was there bitterness in her tone.

"Just know that I have given your idea serious thought. You were right. The last wish is better spent on making our trek to the Land of Big as easy as possible."

"So you agree to use the last wish to shrink that wheel of cheese into a more manageable size?"

"I will make it whatever size you want," vowed Rose, her hand over her heart and the concealed dreamstone in solemn promise.

"But what about another fabulous meal or a new gown?" queried Tag.

"We still have leftovers from this morning. I am sure they will be fine. And so what if I must wear this gown for another day? It is not as though I need to impress anyone out here."

"Well, I'm more than just a little impressed."

"You are?" gasped Rose, her face blushing with embarrassment.

"Yes! I've never known you to willingly wear the same dress two days in a row," teased Tag.

"I did not say I was not going to use one tomorrow to conjure up a new outfit," responded Rose, with a giggle.

"If our luck holds, there will be no need to use all three wishes to help survive this quest for another day. There may be a chance for you to be frivolous yet."

"You are teasing me!" scolded Rose.

"That's what friends do."

"Thank goodness!" gasped Rose, leaping up from the rock to embrace Tag in an exuberant hug. "We're friends again!"

Tag momentarily froze, feeling the Princess' arms wrap tightly around him as she squeezed him against her body in a grateful hug as his arms hung awkwardly, not knowing what to do.

The last time she ever hugged him was when they were children and royal protocol had little relevance to either of them. Tag had boldly told off a much bigger boy who felt it was his moral right and obligation as a future, potential suitor, that Rose be told he was disturbed by her purple eyes.

It was Tag who set him straight, explaining to this young noble that Rose's eyes were not purple, but in fact violet, like the finest cut amethyst. And if his undiscerning eyes took such offence to them, he'd be glad to poke them out so they would not have to see Rose's eyes again.

Of course, for insulting a nobleman's son, Tag was punished by his father. However, under these extenuating circumstances, King William saw fit to request a very lenient form of punishment to be doled out. After all, it was his daughter's feelings that had been spared by Tag's selfless actions.

When Rose finally came to the realization Tag was not reciprocating with a hug of his own, she jumped back, her hands dropping to her side as she muttered beneath her breath, "That was awkward."

"I won't speak about it, if you don't," offered Tag, not knowing how else to respond to this unexpected contact.

"Deal!" agreed Rose, shuddering to make it clear to him that she did not enjoy this fleeting moment of physical impropriety. Still embarrassed, she chose to quickly change the subject. "As I was saying, I shall use the last wish to shrink the cheese down to a manageable size."

"We'll be able to travel much faster," said Tag, nodding in approval. "Thank you for allowing this."

"If it helps me to reclaim my heart, then that is all that really matters."

"There is no other way," reminded Tag. "And besides, there is always a chance if we meet up with the Dwarves, they'll have a good idea where to find that locket."

"Do you think they will help us?"

"Time will tell. At least we'll have a hefty serving of cheese we can use as a bargaining tool, if we must."

"I know it seems trivial to you, but that locket is the only thing the Tooth Fairy will accept. It is the only thing that will break the hold of the power those in the palace are under. Until it is broken, I shall remain vanquished."

"We'll find it and Pancecilia Feldspar will have no choice but to undo the curse, I'll promise you that," vowed Tag.

"Knight's honour?" asked Rose.

"It's wrong to tease me like that. Just accept it as my promise to see it done," responded Tag.

"Who said I was teasing?" said Rose.

Tag spun about, unsheathing his sword just as quickly. Poised to strike, he motioned for Rose to stay behind him as the rustlings of leaves caught his attention.

"What is it?" whispered Rose, peering around Tag as he crept toward a shrub.

"Quiet! I heard something coming from behind this bush." Tag pointed with the tip of his sword.

Again, the faintest of rustling caught his ears. Tag inched forward. Brandishing his weapon in one hand, he used the other to thrust aside the branches. Just as he lunged forward to strike, Rose shouted, *"Stop!"*

She seized Tag by his arm, hampering the blow he was about to deliver to a small, shivering baby rabbit cowering beneath this shrub.

"The poor little thing! And to think, you were about to skewer this bunny," scolded Rose. "For shame!"

Tag drew a deep breath, sighing with relief as he lowered his sword. "For a moment, I thought it was one of Dragonite's followers here to menace us."

"A bunny is hardly a menace," stated Rose, kneeling down before the trembling ball of fur with the cutest cottonball tail. "Look how tiny and adorable it is!"

Instead of bounding away in fear to become one with the shadows, the animal limped toward the Princess. With half-closed eyes, and ears that flopped pathetically, it hobbled along, favouring its front paw.

"Oh, you poor thing," whispered Rose, carefully scooping the animal into her hands. She could feel its tiny heart pounding in its frail chest as she cradled it in her arm. "I think it's hurt."

"You should put it back."

"I do not see the mother rabbit around and I hardly think she'd care, otherwise, she would be here, protecting her young."

"Of course she wouldn't care," confirmed Tag. "She'd only invest her time and energy in caring for the offspring she knows will survive. Nature is cruel that way."

"Well, all the more reason not to abandon the pitiful creature," countered Rose, wrapping the bunny in her cloak to keep it warm.

"What are you doing?"

"I am bringing it back to our camp. It will be safer by our fire than left to fend for itself. There may be wolves lurking about."

"Even wolves must eat," reasoned Tag.

"I cannot believe you just said that!" scolded Rose, holding the shivering ball of fur to her chest as though to shield it from Tag's words. "The bunny is coming with me. I will take care of it."

"You can hardly take care of yourself," muttered Tag, following as Rose headed back to camp.

"I heard that!" snapped Rose, leading the way to the thicket where Cankles waited by the campfire for their return.

"You were meant to," responded Tag, watching as she sat on the log next to Cankles. "Aren't you worried you'll get fleas or something being so close?"

"Oh, I don't have fleas," insisted Cankles, absentmindedly scratching his head. "The odd nit, but no fleas, I assure you."

"Tag was talking about this bunny," explained Rose, raising the edge of her cloak to reveal the soft bundle of fur. Its ears continued to droop and its eyes remained closed as a tiny nose twitched rhythmically with each rapid breath it drew. "And I will have you know, it's way too cute to have fleas or any such parasites."

"Cuteness is not the determining factor in whether something picks up parasites," argued Tag.

"Then how come I have no fleas?" countered Rose.

"They just haven't found you yet," answered Tag. "If anything, I think you're more likely to attract deer ticks."

"You are disgusting!" snapped Rose, scowling in repulsion.

"Lovely! I see things are back to normal," stated Cankles, pleased to see Tag had returned to their camp and both were bickering as usual.

"Where he is concerned, there is no normal," snipped Rose, glaring at Tag as he gave her a smug smile.

"Got yourself a rabbit, did ya?" said Cankles, staring at the pathetic creature. "Won't be much if we're gonna eat it for dinner."

"How dare you say such a terrible thing!" gasped Rose, her hands cupping the animal's ears to shield it from these words. "This poor animal is hurt. I want to help it."

"If it's hurt, you should help it by puttin' it out of its misery as quickly as you can," suggested Cankles.

"That's what I've been trying to tell her. A wolf or a fox would make quick work of it and it won't go to waste," said Tag.

"Enough with this wicked talk!" snapped Rose. "If anything, I thought you'd both be pleased I was not thinking of myself in wanting to help this innocent creature."

"I suppose we should give you credit for that," conceded Tag. "But how do you intend to help it? *Wish* it better?"

"That is a brilliant idea!" exclaimed Rose. "I can use the last wish of the day to heal this bunny."

"Oh no, you won't!" argued Tag. "You promised to use the wish to shrink the cheese."

"In a few hours, it will be midnight," stated Rose. "I shall use one of those wishes to do so. For now, I can use this last one to fix my furry, little friend."

"I don't want to say it'll be a waste of a wish, but it will be," insisted Tag, with a dismal sigh. "I know it sounds cruel, but so is nature."

"I've taken care of a rabbit or two. Why don't I have a look?" offered Cankles. "Maybe I can fix it if it's not too bad."

"Promise you will do nothing to hurt him," urged Rose, as Cankles knelt before her to inspect the baby rabbit.

"Not on purpose," vowed Cankles, using his fingertip to gently stroke the animal's silky-soft fur between its ears. Whether the creature had been trembling in fear or pain, the shivering had now stopped as it found a safe refuge on a warm lap. "It might raise a bit of a fuss when I handle its foot, but it'll be fine."

"It was the right, front paw being favoured," disclosed Rose, slowly peeling back the edge of the cloak so Cankles could better assess the damage. "Just be careful."

"I'll do my utmost," promised Cankles, using the tip of his index finger to gently feel through the soft fur to trace muscles and bones down to the animal's paw. His finger stopped its tactile inspection when it came to rest on a tiny protrusion under the skin just above the animal's wrist, if it were a human and had hands instead of paws.

"What's wrong with it?" questioned Tag, tossing another piece of wood onto the fire to create greater light for his friend to work by. "Is it a thorn stuck in its paw?"

"It feels to be a bone out of place," answered Cankles. "An' it may've been like this for a while 'cause this critter seems unfazed with me handlin' it. It hasn't even opened its eyes once."

"How can you tell it is broken?" asked Rose, her voice filled with dread.

"I've broken practically every bone in my body, includin' my noggin," replied Cankles. "I know a break when I feel one, but it's nothing that can't be fixed."

"Without magic?" queried Tag.

"Don't need magic for this. Jus' a skilled hand to reset it an' a wee splint to keep it healin' right."

"Are you sure about this?" asked Rose, reluctant to subject this wounded creature to more pain.

"Don't you worry, Princess, this bunny will be as good as new when I'm done workin' on it," vowed Cankles. "With jus' a bit of skillful manipulation, it'll be done."

"Be very gentle," urged Rose, holding the creature steady as Cankles used one hand to brace its leg and the other to hold the paw so he could set it with one quick pull.

"Ready?" asked Cankles.

"It's not as if the animal is going to answer you," said Tag. "While it's still asleep, just do the deed. Get it over with."

Just as Cankles tightened his grip, the bunny unleashed the most eerie, bloodcurdling scream. Cankles' hand recoiled in surprised. And then he, too, screamed but this time in pain as the creature deliberately sank its razor-sharp incisors into his fingertip.

Rose shrieked, bowling Tag over as she jumped in fright to see the bunny attack Cankles, savaging his finger with a vengeance driven by the taste of warm human blood.

"Bloody hell!" cursed Tag, alarmed by this strange turn of events. Seizing a stick from the campfire to knock off the maniacal rabbit dangling from Cankles' fingertip, he swung with all his might. Rose dropped to the ground, ducking beneath this wild swing that narrowly missed striking Cankles and came nowhere near to dislodging his attacker.

In a sheer panic, Cankles frantically danced about, his arm flapping madly as he attempted to shake off the snarling bunny that continued to hang by its teeth from his finger.

"Keep still!" hollered Tag, taking up the burning stick again to take another swat at the deranged animal.

Just as the stick swung out to strike the creature, it pulled its body up, curling away from this weapon as it latched on even tighter to Cankles' bloodied finger. It unleashed another snarl as its eyes flashed open in anger.

"*Aaawww!* It's a bunny possessed!" declared Cankles, frantically shaking off his furry assailant as its eyes glowed amber.

"It's rabid, I tell you!" shouted Rose. "It's a rabid rabbit!"

With another mighty swing, the stick made hard contact. The bunny's body folded with the impact, releasing its grip on Cankles' mangled digit. Spinning through the air like a fur-covered ball, the airborne bunny struck Rose in her chest just as she stood up to peer from behind the log she was crouched behind.

Bowled over by the force, for a terrifying moment Rose lay there, the animal sitting on her chest. Its blood-soaked lips curled back in a fierce snarl as sinister, golden-yellow eyes stared into hers. Pushing off with powerful hind legs, the rampaging beast lunged for her neck.

Rose screamed.

Her hands flew up to shield her face just as Tag's smoldering piece of firewood swung down. Before the bunny could snatch up the chain hanging from about Rose's neck, the blow sent the creature tumbling through the air.

"When it comes down, kill it!" ordered Tag, gripping his weapon in preparation for another swing.

The bunny tumbled through the air, but instead of dropping back to earth, the light of the stars were dimmed as a sickly green glow erupted from the creature. With a loud rattling of wings, Loken dove at Tag's head, abruptly turning away to avoid the tip of the stick he wielded.

"It's that thing!" yelped Rose, jumping to her feet to hide behind Tag. "That Poo-poo thing!"

"The Pooka!" hollered Tag, dropping the smoldering weapon to unsheathe his sword from its scabbard. "It's called a Pooka!"

"Who cares what it's called! Just kill it!" shouted Rose, urging Cankles to join Tag in taking more action than just nursing his injury.

Swooping down in another bid to steal away with the dreamstone, Loken was forced to take evasive action, veering away as Tag's sword sliced through the air. The very tip of the sword clipped the edge of Loken's wing.

"Curse you!" snarled Loken, darting into the shadows of the forest. "You'll pay for this!"

"Should we go after him?" asked Rose, staring off into the night as she searched for the shape-shifting Sprite.

"What's the point? I hardly think we'll catch up to it now," determined Tag, watching as the pale aura cast by the Pooka dissolved into the darkness.

"I don't know about you two, but I sure as hell wasn't expectin' that," groaned Cankles, squeezing his bloodied finger that pulsed, throbbing in pain with every beat of his heart.

Tag turned to Rose, glaring at her as he issued an order: "No more adopting bunnies, birds or any other stray creatures you deem cute. Cute could have got us killed tonight!"

"How was I to know it was that evil Sprite?" responded Rose. "Neither of you knew!"

"Quite right, Princess Rose," admitted Cankles. "I certainly believed it was nothing more than a harmless rabbit."

"One thing is for certain, it will only be a matter of time before the Sorcerer becomes aware of our presence and the fact the Princess has the magic crystal," said Tag.

"If he doesn't already know," added Cankles.

"All the more reason to tread through these lands in secret," decided Tag. "Let's take nothing for chance. Put out this fire. We cannot stay here tonight."

18

Think Big

"Can we rest now?" asked Rose, through a great yawn. "I think we should. If anything, our horses are more tired than we are."

Under the predawn sky, with the impending sun leaching away the darkness, the land was quiet. It was strangely serene after their bizarre encounter with the shape-shifting Sprite.

Tag glanced about, cocking his head to and fro as he looked and listened. The only sounds to be heard were the shrill songs of the male wood thrush as they established their territories, vocalizing to attract a mate. He knew they had nothing to fear, as long as these animals were actually birds, and not the Pooka in disguise. Unfortunately, from where Tag and his comrades stood, there was no way to tell for sure.

"What say you, young master?" asked Cankles. "Hidin' in the shadows of the Stony Mountains, we're well into Dwarf country now. Surely we can sleep for a while."

"I'm concerned that wretched Sprite might be lurking about," admitted Tag. "There's no telling what form he'll take next."

"Suppose one of us stands guard while the others sleep?" offered Cankles.

"Even I will do a turn, if it means we can stop for a while," volunteered Rose.

"You must be desperate," decided Tag, glancing over at the Princess.

"Very much so, but I also know I should help carry the burden of this quest," explained Rose, hoping Tag would see she was attempting to turn a new leaf to better herself in his eyes.

"I suppose if we take precautions we should be fine," determined Tag, reining in his steed.

"I'm sure we left those mimes far behind," assured Rose, eager to dismount before she fell asleep on her mare. "And I will be watchful of any animals acting strangely around us."

"Especially if they're cute lookin' an' have amber eyes," added Cankles, shaking off his drowsiness.

"Well, we've travelled a good distance thanks to the Princess using the last wish as she had promised," said Tag, patting the small disk of cheese now tucked away in his pack.

"I would say our friend is more to thank," stated Rose, nodding to Cankles. "He was the one to insist I use that last wish to transform the humongous wheel of cheese than to use it to heal his finger right away."

"It bloody well hurt, but I've endured worse in my life," assured Cankles. "Besides, it was only a few hours before you were allotted your next three wishes. It jus' made sense so we could leave that place as fast as we could."

"Well, it was considerate of you to wait," said Tag, giving Cankles a nod of approval as he turned to address Rose. "And kind of you to use one of your wishes to aid him."

Rose smiled, but oddly, she felt as though she was smiling from the inside. It was obvious Tag appreciated this gesture, even recognizing the fact she had offered to heal Cankles without being cajoled or even asked in the first place.

"Is that your way of sayin' we can rest?" questioned Cankles. "For even if we did sleep for a few hours, we'd still arrive at the Dwarf settlement by early evening if Master Troll was correct in his directions."

"As Rose made it possible for us to travel this far, I suppose it would do us all some good to get some sleep while we can," replied Tag, dismounting from his stallion.

"When I take my turn to stand guard, may I borrow your sword, Tag?" questioned Rose.

"And just what do you plan to do with it?"

"I will not be fooled again. The next cute bunny limping my way will get it!" threatened Rose.

"Do you think we slept for too long?" asked Rose, coaxing her mare to keep pace with Tag's mount. Venturing on, the twilight landscape was made all the more claustrophobic by the shadows of the mountains leaning in all around them. "We should have arrived by now."

"Perhaps, but I don't believe we are lost," replied Tag. "We've remained on the course as prescribed by the Troll."

"Could it be Tiny Goatswain was off with his estimation?" queried

Cankles. "His strides are much greater than ours, after all."

"That's a very real possibility," responded Tag. "At this point, the only thing I can recommend is to stay the course until it's too dark to travel and hope that tomorrow morning will find us at the Dwarves' settlement."

"Suppose we jus' head as far as the base of the next mountain," suggested Cankles, glancing ahead. "It'll take us that much closer, an' who knows, if we're lucky, it might even be our final destination."

"We can certainly use some luck, but I would not count on it," said Rose. "Either way, to go that distance will bring us closer to where we want to be."

"So you are willing to ride on to the next mountain?" asked Tag, seeking confirmation, for up until now, it was rare for the Princess to willingly put in the extra effort even if it was for her own good.

"It is not that much further," Rose attempted to convince herself. "And I am sure we can be there well before darkness comes so we will still have time to set up camp if need be."

"Then on we go," said Tag, spurring his stallion on.

Rose and Cankles urged their steeds on to follow as Tag led them on a winding trail snaking between the mountains.

As dusk surrendered to the night, the trio dismounted as the trail came to an abrupt end. Instead of meandering up the sloping side of a mountain or going around it, the trail came to a stop where a sheer wall of granite towered before them. Overgrown ivy draped this edifice with a tangle of vines.

"This is odd. Tiny Goatswain told us to follow this trail and it would lead us straight to the heart of the Dwarf community," commented Tag.

"You must admit, that Troll was not the brightest being we have encountered to date," reminded Rose. "I suspect he made a mistake."

"I suggest we set up camp now. In the morning, we'll have the light we need to see what's happened to this trail or if we've taken a wrong turn somewhere," recommended Cankles.

"Good plan," agreed Tag. "We'll rest for the night."

"Sounds good to me," said Rose. "I still have two wishes to use before midnight. Why don't I use one to set up camp?"

"Camp?" asked Tag, gazing over at the Princess.

"You know? A ready-made campfire, a scrumptious roast of venison dinner with pan-fried veggies and baby potatoes; served up with rich, creamy gravy and freshly baked bread," explained Rose.

"Sounds tempting, but I thought you only like desserts," said Tag.

"You did not let me finish. I was going to top off the meal with custard cream-filled cakes glazed with honey and dusted with powdered sugar."

"I'm surprised. I was sure dessert was going to be the main course," responded Tag.

"As much as I love my sweets, I have come to the conclusion that dessert is no longer dessert if it is consumed as the main meal. Somehow, it would lose its appeal if it were not regarded as a tantalizing, little treat. Of course, I would also be a fool to compromise my figure, being a princess and all."

Tag stared at Rose, stunned to hear there was finally some logic in her words.

"What brought this on? Did you use one of the wishes to grant you some common sense?" queried a mystified Tag.

"If you must know, I had a chance to speak to Cankles last night. He spoke some sense to me. It gave me a chance to rethink my choices and actions."

Tag scratched his head in thought, glancing at the Princess, and then over to the man she held in low regard, thinking of Cankles as nothing more than a simpleton of an idiot.

"*You* talked sense into *her*?" asked Tag, scrutinizing Cankles as he gathered their horses to tether to a tree for the night.

"Sure, I talked to the Princess, but I can't say how much sense I made," admitted Cankles, rolling his shoulders in a shrug.

"What is the big deal?" asked Rose. "I am a Princess. It is my perogative to change my mind if, and when, I see fit."

"Better late than never, I suppose," decided Tag, inwardly pleased their altercation of last night was the catalyst to bring about this change. As minor as it seemed, knowing the Princess as he did, it was no small feat.

"Then what say you to a hot, delicious meal by a roaring campfire?" offered Rose. "Or should I save the last two wishes until we truly need them?"

"I like the sounds of that," said Cankles. "A hot meal, that is."

"The people have spoken! Two against one," exclaimed Rose, glancing over at Tag to see if he was going to dispute this.

An ardent supporter of all things democratic, Tag was not about to raise a fuss. This late in the day, and with no apparent emergency to force them to use their remaining wishes, there was also no reason to allow them to go to waste either with the coming of the midnight hour.

"Go on then," urged Tag. "And while you're at it, can you please conjure up some ale to accompany our meal?"

"I am still not keen on that nasty beverage," admitted Rose, cringing as the memory of the foul taste reminiscent of stagnant swamp water continued to linger on her tongue, if only in her mind. "I shall wish up two pints of ale and a glass of fine, red wine for me."

"An excellent idea!" praised Tag. "Get to it, Princess!"

"And just remember, I will not be conjuring up seconds when it comes to drinks," warned Rose. "We need to keep our wits about us in these strange lands, especially if that creepy, little Sprite is lurking about."

"Sounds reasonable to me," agreed Cankles.

"Any other requests?" asked Rose.

"A ready-made fire, a hot meal and a pint! What more can we wish for?" responded Tag.

"Very well then," said Rose. Closing her eyes and drawing in a slow, deep breath, the Princess focused on the task at hand. As she slowly exhaled, she cleared her mind. A precise picture of the sumptuous meal she craved, along with a delectable beverage served up on the finest china and crystal with the silverware to match formed in her mind's eye. From the fine silk damask tablecloth and candelabra on the center of this table to the high-backed chairs seated around it with the warmth of a campfire to add to the ambience, Rose could see each perfect portion of food. Once she imagined how each morsel would taste in her mouth and smell to her nose, she knew she was ready to make this wish become reality as her hand firmly clasped the dreamstone.

"Brilliant!" exclaimed Tag, jumping back as a round dining table in all its formal elegance appeared before him. Set for a party of three, Rose and her companions were ready to dine in style.

Cankles seated Rose at the table first, before taking his place. As the stars dotted the velvety night sky, the trio enjoyed a hot, delicious meal by candlelight.

With their appetites well sated, Tag stretched and yawned. As satisfying as the meal was, he now felt lethargic. Shaking off his drowsiness, he took up his sword in preparation for the first watch.

"You are more tired than I am. I will take the first watch," offered Rose, rising up from the table.

"Are you sure?" asked Tag.

"Of course."

Though Rose did not admit it, she knew she'd be struggling to stay awake if she were made to take the later shift or she'd be fighting to wake up before dawn to take the final watch.

"Fine by me," said Tag, rubbing his full belly in contentment. "I'd be a fool to refuse."

"And I'd be a fool if I didn't take advantage of this chance to get some sleep while I can. I'll fetch the bedrolls," offered Cankles.

"Let's not feed this fire; allow it to die out so the light of the flames and the crackling as it burns will not keep us awake," suggested Tag, catching the bedroll Cankles tossed to him.

"Good plan," agreed Cankles, stifling a yawn as he unfurled his bedroll by the campfire across from Tag's.

"Hey! What about me?" asked Rose.

"I thought you said you wanted to take the first watch?" responded Tag.

"I did! And I will, but in the dark?" replied the Princess, glancing over at the fire Tag had recommended to burn out.

"When the campfire is no more, you'll still have the candles," said Tag, pointing to the candelabra glowing brightly on the table.

"And when the candles burn out, then what?"

"Then the stars will continue to glow long after," answered Tag, crawling into his bedroll.

"So I am to sit in the dark?"

"If you need light so badly, I suggest you only use one or two candles at a time," replied Tag, resting his head on his pack that now doubled as a pillow. "Make them last."

"I suppose that will have to do," decided Rose.

"Of course it will," said Tag, rolling over so the dying flames of the campfire were to his back. "And the fewer lights, the better we'll sleep."

"Wake me in four hours, Princess. I'll take the next watch," offered Cankles, nestling down into his bedroll.

"How will I know when has come to pass?" queried Rose.

"When the moon travels across the sky to come over that mountain top, that'll be about four hours," estimated Cankles, pointing to the celestial orb peeking low over the trees.

"That is easy enough," said Rose.

Not surprisingly, Tag and Cankles were fast asleep within minutes of laying their heads down. No doubt for them, they were immersed in a wonderful dream. For Rose, these were the longest minutes she had ever endured. Sitting alone with nothing more than the light of a single candle to ward of the darkness threatening to swallow her whole, Rose had nothing to do to ease the tedium.

She sat on the chair, staring into the shadows of the night as her imagination wandered, straying to places she really did not want it to go. It was only a matter of time before every owl that flew overhead was potentially a shape-shifting Sprite and every shadow in the trees was some kind of monster waiting to attack.

"I really must stop this," she muttered beneath her breath as her eyes nervously darted about.

Shaking her head to dispel these troubling thoughts, the combination of boredom and an overactive imagination forced Rose to take action. And never being one to enjoy tedious work that comes with cross-stitching or embroidery, Rose chose to indulge in an activity more to her liking.

Clasping the dreamstone in her hand, she proceeded to clear her mind to conjure up an image of her desired object. When Rose opened her eyes, there was her favourite book. It lay on the table before her, the bookmark still embedded between the pages where she last read.

This was not one of those textbooks considered mandatory reading by the scholars tutoring her. Instead, it was a work of fiction about a fantastical world of the future where human beings were the only race and Elves, Fairies, Wizards and Troll were relegated to lore and myth. It was a world of supposedly enlightened beings using religion and race as a reason to war, and yet, inspite of all this chaos, human compassion struggled to rise above adversity.

"Brilliant," Rose said in a whisper, smiling as though reunited with a familiar friend. With the campfire reduced to nothing more than glowing embers and the candle's flame barely exuding enough light to read with some eye strain, Rose decided to light two more candles.

Taking up the candelabra, Rose crept over to the granite face of the mountain. Here, the additional candles would not disturb Tag and Cankles as they slept.

In secluded comfort, the Princess sat on the ground, cracking open her book to delve into the next chapter. Leaning into the candlelight, Rose relished this moment to reacquaint herself with the hero of the story. Squinting to see under the glow of the wavering flames, she read the calligraphy.

"I need better light," whispered Rose. Lifting the candelabra onto a small boulder, it rested against the rock wall. With the flames of the candles shining down on the pages, she was ready to resume reading.

Immersed in this imaginary world, Rose followed the exploits of the star-crossed lovers fighting against an intolerant world that refused to acknowledge their relationship because the hero and his ladylove were of differing cultures.

Rose sniffled, dabbing away a teardrop.

She came to the abrupt realization her runny nose and tearing eyes were not the symptoms of reading a sad excerpt from this tale, but was the result of the smoke swirling around her. Rose glanced up as the candles' light suddenly paled. The vines hanging from the granite wall erupted into great flames. Like a fiery curtain rising up on this sheer mountain face, leaves already dried by the lack of rain crackled, burning intensely.

With this great burst of light, Rose, in a state of panic momentarily froze. She stared dumbfounded at this disaster in the making. When the initial shock wore off, the only thing the Princess could think of doing was to blow out the flames of the candles lest they exacerbated the situation.

"Oh my!" gasped Cankles. He woke to the loud snapping and crackling of rapacious flames racing up the rock wall to devour all manner of vegetation.

"What have you done?" cried Tag, squinting under the glare as he stumbled from his bedroll. He searched for something, anything, to extinguish the fire.

"I haven't done a thing," insisted Rose, in her own defense. "At least, not on purpose."

"It's not as though those vines set themselves on fire," countered Tag, watching helplessly as the flames rushed up the rock face until there was nothing left to burn.

As quickly as it started, the fire burned out as it reached a bare expanse of granite.

"Thank goodness it didn't spread much further," said Tag, sighing with relief as he stared at the blackened wall before them.

"Say, look here!" exclaimed Cankles, his fingertips running lightly over the stone surface.

"What is it?" asked Rose.

As the moon crested the mountaintop, its silvery light shone down to illuminate the rock wall. Burned ivy left black soot over the surface of the granite. It was everywhere, except in the recesses riddling the rock face. Standing back, Tag studied the indentations that stood out in the moonlight against the black soot.

"These were created by chisel and hammer," noted Tag.

"They could mean something," said Cankles, noting the uniform size and spacing of the characters.

"Perhaps it is an antiquated language no longer used by man?" suggested Rose.

"Right on both counts," confirmed Tag, as he scrutinized the ancient runes.

"We are?" asked Rose.

"I'd say it's an old dialect once used by the Dwarves," said Tag.

"How do you know?" questioned Rose.

"You certainly don't pay attention to your language studies, but I do," explained Tag. "This is definitely Dwarvish."

"What does it say?" asked Cankles.

"As best as I can make out, it roughly translates into this," responded Tag.

> *"All who stand before this den,*
> *Must bring a gift, if you want in.*
> *If your hand is empty and hat is doffed,*
> *Then think again, just bugger off."*

"If you are correct, then that was rather rude!" gasped Rose.

"The Dwarves are not exactly the most social of beings," explained Tag. "Tiny did warn us they must have reason to extend any form of hospitality to you."

"Just because they might know where the Tooth Fairy hid my locket, that does not mean I wish to be invited into their fold," said Rose. "If we are forced to interact with them, I prefer to do so from a respectable distance."

"And if they do know where your heart is, wouldn't it be better to appeal to their senses so there is some level of cooperation from them?" reasoned Tag.

"Well, if it's a gift they be wantin', they're welcome to the Troll cheese," announced Cankles, returning with a torch lit by the last embers of the campfire.

"First, we have to find the Dwarves," responded Tag, his hands running over the surface of the rock face as his fingertips traced what felt to be an outline of a doorway.

"Are you saying this is the concealed entrance to the Dwarf settlement?" questioned Rose. "They live *in* this mountain?"

"It *was* concealed until someone set fire to the foliage," stated Tag, pressing his shoulder to the massive slab of granite. "And it makes sense to me, after all, Dwarves are miners."

"If you have a need to accuse someone, it was not me who did this," insisted Rose. "It was the evening breeze and the flames of the candles. They conspired against me to make it look like I was responsible for this mishap."

"The point being, this welcome sign, if you can call it that, is here for a reason," explained Tag, pushing against the entrance.

Standing back, Cankles' eyes took in the double doors that were so tall, a Troll need not stoop to enter.

"Methinks it odd the Dwarves would take the time to built such a large doorway when they're so small in size," commented Cankles, as he admired the interwoven, geometric designs chiselled around the arching doorway.

"Perhaps they are compensating for something," offered Rose, refusing to get her hands dirty by helping Tag push his way in.

"Like what?" questioned Cankles.

"Their lack of stature, perhaps," replied the Princess.

"Well, whatever the case, it's mighty impressive," stated Cankles.

"If this is the way in, then I suggest we use a wish to transform the cheese back to its original size now," recommended Tag.

"Why?" asked Rose, glancing to the moon to determine if it was midnight yet.

"Because you don't want to be giving the Dwarves that small sampling of cheese if they happen to be waiting on the other side of this door, nor do you want to be seen using the dreamstone."

"Oh, you're quite right," agreed Cankles, dashing over to the pack where Tag stowed away the cheese. He returned with it, placing the food on the ground before the entranceway.

Rose stared at the cheese for a moment.

"Well, go on," urged Tag. "Make it big again."

Glancing up to the moon once more, Rose estimated it had to be midnight, but if she was off by even a second, Tag and Cankles would know she had used the last wish to conjure up her book. To buy some time so she would have access to the next allotment of wishes, Rose lollygagged, circling the cheese as though assessing its potential size.

"What are you waiting for?" asked Tag.

"Magic cannot be hurried. I am attempting to recall the exact size and dimension of the wheel, not to forget all its stinky, tasty qualities if you want the cheese to be everything it was."

"Sorry," muttered Tag.

Rose drew several slow, deep breaths, holding each longer than usual as she bided her time. Each spent breath was expelled just as slowly as she cleared her mind and set to work.

In her mind's eyes, Rose conjured up the monster wheel of cheese. She was meticulous as she envisioned unnecessary details such as the small pebbles and twigs embedded in the wax coating, gathered when Tag and Cankles rolled it on their travels.

Knowing that she had taken less time to conjure up fancy gowns and elaborate meals, Tag fought to be patient. He knew that coaxing her to hurry would only break Rose's concentration, forcing her to start over again.

When he was close to gnawing off his tongue to keep from speaking, he was bowled over as the behemoth dairy product erupted back to its original size.

"Brilliant!" exclaimed Cankles, pleased to see the goat cheese in all its smelly glory.

"I'd say!" agreed Tag.

Rose was just relieved to see her efforts were not wasted, nor would she have to explain the use of the last wish that inadvertently led to the fire.

"Now to find our way in and be rid of this cheese once and for all," said Tag, putting his shoulder to the granite doors. "Give me a hand with this."

"Of course," said Rose, as she directed Cankles over. "You heard Tag, give him a hand."

With shoulders pressed to the double doors, Tag and Cankles pushed with all their might, but it wouldn't budge, not even a crack.

"Again," ordered Tag. "One! Two! Three! *PUSH!*"

Plying every ounce of strength they had, Tag and Cankles succeeded in raising a small cloud of dust that had settled along the seams of the doors as it came loose.

"If we were as thin as a strand of hair, we might fit," teased Rose.

"Just be patient," grumbled Tag, wiping the sweat from his brows he glanced over at the Princess. "We can use a little help here."

"I am helping," she insisted.

"How can standing there gawking at us, be helping?" questioned Tag, rubbing his sore shoulder.

"I am looking for a door knocker or chime," answered Rose.

"A *what?*" gasped Tag.

"You heard me."

Rose searched through the ornate carvings chiselled around the entrance. "Did it ever occur to you this door must be opened from the inside and you have been pushing when you should have been pulling?"

"The Princess could be right," determined Cankles. "Maybe that's why there's no door latch on this side."

"Maybe, but I say we give it one more try," suggested Tag. "This time, we take a running start."

"You do that," said Rose, with a dismissive nod as she knelt down to examine the designs. "I shall keep looking for a door chime."

Cankles and Tag backed up, creating adequate space to build up enough momentum to charge at the double doors and ram them open. Drawing a deep breath as they steeled their nerves for the task at hand, the pair sized up their seemingly immovable foe.

"Ready?" asked Tag, as he leaned forward.

"Yep!" responded Cankles, rolling the shoulder he intended to ply to the granite.

"*NOW!*" hollered Tag.

Charging full tilt, they raced to the doors.

"What is this?" wondered Rose.

Pressing her hand against a circular pattern carved into the doorway, it suddenly sank into the granite with a loud *clunk* just as Tag and Cankles launched themselves into the air. They threw their bodies against the double doors. Instead of miraculously swinging open, muscles and bones collided against solid rock.

"I thought it'd open," groaned Rose, her hand slapping against the circular depression as Tag and Cankles lay writhing on the ground, groaning in pain.

All three screamed in fright as the ground suddenly opened beneath them, plunging the trio into darkness.

Tumbling, sliding and crashing off each other and the walls of the tunnel, they landed in a crumpled heap.

"Get off, Tag!" groaned Rose, pushing off the body that had landed on top of her. "You're crushing me!"

"What are you talking about?" snapped Tag, his eyes straining to see.

"Sorry, Princess," apologized Cankles, struggling to stand. "Didn't mean for you to break my fall."

"I can't see a thing," muttered Tag.

"I wish we had some light," said Rose, her hands blindly reaching out before her.

"Now there's a good wish," stated Cankles.

The trio turned with a start as an orange spark ignited, producing a ribbon of light that followed a narrow trough lining this subterranean chamber.

"Did you do that?" asked Tag, glancing over at the Princess.

"I had nothing to do with this," answered Rose, staring at the walls of the cave. "I was thinking more of candles or torches!"

"Oh, my! Look at all these symbols," noted Cankles. The flames illuminated the chamber to reveal unfamiliar runes carved from floor to ceiling. "Do you think it's another warning to all who enter, or perhaps it tells of a glorious myth of old?"

Tag scrutinized the haphazard chiselling. "If I'm correct, you'll not want to know what these characters mean."

"Why not?" questioned Cankles, marvelling at this mystery.

"Dwarvish profanity," explained Tag.

"Say no more," responded Cankles.

"Hush! I hear noises," whispered Rose, motioning for silence. They froze as the clanging of metal and rushed footfalls echoing from a long, dark tunnel drew closer.

As the light of a torch glowed in this passageway, a huge shadow stretched along the walls of the tunnel to herald the coming of a multi-armed creature with many heads.

"Something's coming," warned Tag.

"Mon– monster!" stuttered Cankles, staring at the shadow as it grew larger.

"There is no way out!" yelped Rose; staring up to the high chute they fell from.

"Get behind me!" ordered Tag, drawing his sword in preparation for a great clash.

Rose needed no prompting. Already hiding behind Tag, she used Cankles as a human shield.

"Come no further!" hollered Tag, weapon poised in his hands.

Instead of retreating in fear, the shadow neared, growing in size.

"Get back! We're armed to the teeth and we know how to fight!" hollered Tag, hoping his one sword would be enough to slay the beast.

As though inviting this challenge, an angry snarl rumbled from the tunnel to reverberate through the chamber. Heavy footfalls thundered through the musty air as the lights cast a gargantuan shadow towering before them.

"We're gonna die!" squeaked Cankles, his eyes squeezing shut.

With a fierce roar, angry dwarves burst into the chamber. Armed with picks and shovels, seven short but stout beings made a defiant stand. As small as they were, it was evident they were quite prepared to use their mining tools on the intruders.

For a moment, Tag, Rose and Cankles stared back at the beings standing no taller than a child.

"Well, hello!" greeted Rose, donning a forced smile as she did her utmost to sound congenial.

Instead of laying down the tools they now brandished as weapons, the Dwarves said nothing as they scrutinized these strangers.

"Don't be bashful. I am Princess Rose-alyn. Who might you be?"

"Bloody hell!" grumbled the Dwarf leading this procession. "That's all we need, another princess in our midst!"

"Last one almost ate us out of house an' home," added another Dwarf, yawning as he wiped the sleep from his eyes.

"My! Aren't you grumpy!" exclaimed Rose.

"I'm not grumpy! I'm downright irked!" snapped the diminutive being.

"Irked is an odd name for a Dwarf, or anyone else for that matter," commented Cankles.

"I believe he's angry, as in not happy to see us here," corrected Tag.

"Is that so?" queried Rose, staring down at the disgruntled Dwarf.

"Do I look happy to you?" The blade of his shovel bit into the earth. "What business have you here?"

"We're here to see a great Dwarf by the name of Giblet Barscowl," responded Tag.

"Great in esteem, not in stature," explained Cankles, to make sure there was no misunderstanding.

"I think they know that," said Tag.

"I'm no dolt! Of course I do, but jus' what would you be wantin' with Barscowl?" questioned the grumpy one.

"We're here on behalf of the Trolls," answered Tag. "We come with a gift. Master Goatswain said you'd be more inclined to help us if we brought this to you."

"If it's a stinkin' old goat, forget it!" grumbled a sniffling Dwarf, sneezing as the dust settled around him.

"It's a stinkin', huge wheel of goat *cheese*," responded Cankles.

"Well, now! Can't say no to cheese," declared the grumpy one. "Where is it?"

"Up there," said Rose, pointing above. "We fell through a trapdoor. That is how we came to be here."

"Yes, yes! But where's the cheese?" asked the Dwarf leader.

"It was too big to fit through," explained Tag. "It's stuck above ground and good thing, too. It probably would've crushed us had it come down when we did."

"The cheese! Rescue the cheese!" ordered the grumpy Dwarf, turning to instruct his comrades. "Slappy, open the doors to the mine. Droolie, gather the men to wheel the cheese in before the critters start feedin' on it."

Slappy's hands lashed out. He smacked the other Dwarves to get out of his way as Droolie, wiping the thread of saliva from his watering mouth as he dreamed of cheese, scampered off to recruit helpers.

"Hey! What about us?" asked Tag.

"What about you?" The grumpy Dwarf shot a glance over his shoulder at the mortal.

"That cheese was meant to be delivered to Giblet Barscowl, the leader of the Dwarves," explained Tag.

"That'd be me!" announced the grumpiest of the Dwarves, as he headed back down the tunnel. "I'm Barscowl, but you can jus' call me Gibby."

"Well, don't jus' stand there!" snapped Shortie, the smallest of the Dwarves in their presence. He waved his torch for the trio to follow. "Come along."

"You heard him," said Tag, as he sheathed his sword. "Let's follow."

With Giblet Barscowl leading the way, Cankles was forced to duck to avoid bumping or scraping his head on the ceiling of the tunnel as they traipsed behind the Dwarves. As the tunnel terminated, Giblet raised his hand, motioning for Shortie to step forward and light the way.

Lowering the torch, the flame lapped at the oily sheen reflecting from a narrow trough. The liquid erupted into fire, a trail of orange flames blazing along the perimeter to reveal a massive chamber.

"Behold! Welcome to the Mines of Euphoria!" announced Giblet.

"Oh my! You Dwarves like to do things in grand style!" marvelled Cankles, staring with wide-eyed fascination.

"It is called overcompensating," whispered Rose, staring at the massive pillars supporting the dome-like ceiling that bore the brunt of the mountain's weight.

"Though we're small in stature, we like to think big," explained the Dwarf. "Do things in a big way, if you get my meanin'? Plus, being underground, it can get claustrophobic if it weren't for these vast, open chambers."

"So this is why it's called the Land of Big. Your people take to excavating structures on a grand scale," decided Tag, admiring the craftsmanship and skill needed to create a chamber of such mammoth proportions.

"Naw," grunted Giblet, shaking his head to send a small cloud of dust from his beard. "It's called the Land of Big 'cause everything's so bloody huge compared to us. Didn't you see the size of the squirrels an' raccoons out there?"

"Not to mention the bears an' eagles that'll make an easy meal of us if we're not careful," added Shortie.

"I knew it!" exclaimed Cankles.

"That may be so, but look at the size of this chamber. It's huge!" gasped Tag. "Even a Troll would be impressed by its size."

"Well, don't know 'bout you human-types, but we'd be sleepin' 'bout now if you hadn't dropped in when you did," explained Giblet. "As you were so kind to bring us a gift, I'd like to extend the hospitality

Dwarves are famous for."

"By putting us to work with a pick-axe in one of your dreary mines?" questioned Rose.

"Only if you want. I was speakin' of a safe, warm bed for the remainder of the night an' a hearty breakfast in the morning."

"It is kind of you to offer, Master Barscowl, but suppose we just got right down to business, and then we will be on our merry way?" suggested Rose.

"Being that you're in my domain, I'm thinkin' that you'd do right by abidin' by our customs," countered Giblet. His bushy brows furrowed into a scowl as he stared up at the Princess; the blade of his shovel biting into the earth as he made his stand. "Especially if you're thinkin' of doin' any kinda business with us."

"Master Dwarf is quite right, Princess Rose," stated Cankles.

"Besides, what's a few hours?" asked Tag, jumping with a start as Slappy returned, his short, stout legs pumping as fast as they could as he rushed into the chamber. "Would you rather be above ground, standing watch or sleeping in a cozy bed?"

"When you put it that way, Dwarf hospitality is starting to sound rather appealing," decided Rose.

"Master Barscowl!" called Slappy, swatting at Tag to move aside to deliver word to Giblet. " We've rolled the cheese in, an' it's a grand wheel of cheese, indeed!"

"Excellent!" exclaimed Giblet, his pudgy hands rubbing together in eager anticipation.

"We've also taken the liberty of bringin' in these folks' belongings," added Slappy. "Their horses were fine, but the raccoons were rummagin' through their packs, so we thought we'd better bring 'em in, too."

"That was right decent of you," praised Cankles, bowing in gratitude.

"Think nothin' of it," grunted Slappy. "Better than cleanin' up the mess those critters were goin' to make."

"Well, thank you nonetheless," said Tag.

"It's settled then! You'll be spendin' the night," stated Giblet. "The cheese is now safely inside, as are your personal belongings an' there's no business I know of that can't wait 'til the morning. We'll talk after we've all had some rest."

"There is no arguing with you, is there?" determined Rose.

"I'm a Dwarf, Princess. What I lack in stature, I make up for in will. I am renowned for my stubbornness."

"Very well, sleep it is," conceded Rose.

"Jus' follow Slappy. He'll show you to the guest chambers," ordered Giblet, as he stifled a great yawn. "Sleep well! We'll meet over some breakfast in the morn."

Bang! Bang! Bang!

Rose's eyes snapped open. A moment of dazed confusion vanished as she glanced about these gloomy surroundings, her mind and body struggling to determine if it was still night.

"M'lady, we're here to ready you for breakfast," a female voice called through the door.

"Just a moment," responded Rose. She struggled to be free of the holes in the footboard of her bed that allowed her to sleep flat on her back, albeit with her feet protruding over the edge. She could only guess Tag and Cankles had suffered all the more, being taller and provided with the same *king-size* beds, at least, king-size by Dwarf standards.

Wrapping the sheet around her body, Rose hurried to the door. Kneeling down, she slid the small wooden panel open to spy upon a pair of dark brown eyes peering back at her.

"Mornin', m'lady! I've got your gown an' cloak here. All freshly cleaned after your little tumble last night."

"Come in," invited Rose, throwing the door open.

As the three Dwarves marched in with her laundered apparel, Rose shrieked in surprise, clutching the sheet tightly around her body as she hollered, "Get out! I thought you were women!"

The diminutive beings stopped in their tracks. They began to giggle at the Princess.

"We are," explained the oldest of the trio.

Rose's eyes narrowed in suspicion as she scrutinized the beings before her. Wearing less-than-feminine apparel that was far from form flattering, their clothes were the same drab, earth tone colours as those worn by the male Dwarves. Distinctly masculine overtones, in particular, the hairy knuckles, bushy brows and wisps of facial hair added to the illusion of manliness.

Though not as robust and slightly less hirsute than their male counterparts, these Dwarves, at first glance, could easily be mistaken for men.

"Oh, my mistake!" apologized Rose. "I had never met a Dwarf, male or female, until last night."

"No need for apology, m'lady, especially when our own men mistake us for one of 'em from time to time," responded the oldest female Dwarf.

"That is terrible!" exclaimed Rose, accepting her cleaned clothes.

"Terrible, indeed!" she grumbled as her companions muttered in agreement. "At the best of times, we can't even get them to notice us. Even my husband would rather spend his days minin' an' his nights carousin' than to spend time with me."

"You are married?" asked Rose, surprised that even one of their own would find her attractive enough to wed.

"Gibby Barscowl's his name. An' it's bad enough when these fine, young ladies can't find a mate, but when a woman can't even get her husband to look at her, then our whole race is doomed for extinction!"

"Perhaps if you tried to make yourselves look more appealing to the men-folk?" offered Rose.

"Like how?" asked Barscowl's wife. "We're open to suggestions."

"Maybe shave off those whiskers for starters."

"Oh, we can't be doin' that!" gasped the Dwarf. "It goes against our teachings."

"Someone taught you that it is wrong to shave?" questioned Rose.

"Men and women-folk alike don't shave. It's a sign of respect to one of our foundin' fathers," she explained.

"Well, there must be other things you can do to make yourselves look more attractive to the men."

"You're a pretty thing. If you can come up with other ideas, we'd love to hear 'em," Barscowl's wife responded with a disheartened sigh. "In the meantime, get dressed an' we'll deliver you to the grand dinin' hall for breakfast."

"Oh my! This *is* a grand dining hall, even more so than the one in my palace!" declared Rose, as the double doors opened to reveal a long, tall cavernous chamber. At the far end of the room was a massive fireplace that provided both heat and light while rows of torches lined both walls to illuminate the tall, ornately carved ceiling. Down the center of this room was a huge dining table chiselled from a single block of granite and lined on both sides with bench seats of stone.

"About time you joined us," greeted Tag, glancing up from where he sat at the table next to Giblet Barscowl. "Take your seat. Be quick about it and be careful. Don't bang your knees on the underside of this table. It's a tight fit."

Rose took her place across the table from Giblet, as his wife took the empty seat directly across from Cankles.

"Cut the Princess some slack," urged their host. "After all, it's my understandin' you human girlie types like to preen an' fuss to look pretty."

Knowing now that Giblet was making a slight at his homely wife, Rose spoke up, "There is an art to it, but it is all in vain if it goes unnoticed."

"If our women looked more like you, we'd notice," grunted insensitive Slappy. He smacked Droolie on his shoulder, chortling as he gave the Princess a lewd wink of his eye.

"Thank goodness! Here comes the food!" announced Cankles. The timing couldn't have been better as he felt uncomfortable with the topic of conversation and more so, that the Princess was the center of it.

"Smells delicious!" declared Tag, watching a small army of Dwarves delivered bowls, platters and soup tureens. "What's for breakfast?"

"Our favourites, of course," said Giblet, tying a napkin around his stout neck. "Root vegetables!"

"As in carrots?" asked Rose.

"As well as parsnips, beets, radishes, an' turnips," answered the Dwarf. "We love 'em all. Boiled, baked, roasted, steamed, mashed, in soups and stews, if it grows in the earth; we'll eat 'em!"

"Oh my! That's basically every root vegetable 'cept for spuds," said Cankles.

"Oh, there's spuds all right, my friend," assured Giblet, as he reached for a ceramic jug. "Mashed an' fermented, it's right in here!"

"Potato juice," groaned Rose, grimacing in disgust.

"You can call it that! But it's nothing like the swill those Trolls concoct. They're better off makin' cheese," answered Giblet. "Want some?"

"Thank you, but no," responded Rose, placing her hand over the goblet to prevent him serving it to her.

"Say, what's that round, ugly thing?" asked Cankles, pointing across the table in the general direction of a small plate before Giblet Barscowl's wife.

"That'd be my missus," replied Giblet, his words matter-of-fact.

An awkward silence seized all those sharing the table as they stared at the small, squat female Dwarf with almost as much facial hair as her husband.

"I was speakin' of the small, moldy-looking food on that platter before her," gulped Cankles, his face red with embarrassment as the male Dwarves burst out in laughter. "If indeed it is food."

"Oh, that'd be the last of the old cheese we had. Jus' wanted to use it up before we serve the new one you brought last night," explained Giblet. "Don't believe in wastin' anything. Jus' try it. It looks disgustin', but it's got a sharp bite that'll bite ya back, an' then some!"

"I think I'll pass," responded Cankles, as he slid the platter closer to Giblet's wife. "But you go ahead though."

"I do not mean to sound ungrateful," said Rose. "But we are here for good reason."

"So, what did bring you here, my friends?" asked Giblet, using the back of his hand to wipe away the potato spirits dribbling into his bristling beard. "Are you lookin' for a special gem?"

"Silver," replied Rose.

"You've come to the wrong mine, Princess. We delve into these mountains for its wealth of precious gems, not precious metals," responded the Dwarf.

"We do not seek silver ore," explained Tag. "We are looking for a silver locket."

"A heart-shaped locket?" questioned Giblet, his wiry brows arching up.

"Yes!" Tag, Cankles and Rose answered simultaneously.

"On a fine, silver chain?" continued the Dwarf.

"That's the one!" exclaimed Rose.

"I've seen a heart-shaped locket," ascertained Giblet. "It was brought here by the Queen of the Tooth Fairies for safekeeping."

"Brilliant!" exclaimed Tag; relieved the quest was now at its end.

"So where is it?" asked Rose.

"Hell if I know," responded the Dwarf, his round shoulders rolling in a shrug.

"Bollocks!" cursed Cankles, with a deflated sigh.

"But you said it was here," said Rose.

"*Was* being the key word," explained Giblet. "Pancecilia Feldspar saw fit to take it back."

"Back to where?" asked Cankles.

"And why?" added Tag.

"I demand to know!" snapped Rose. Banging her knees against the table as she confronted the Dwarf, she was more annoyed he continued to stuff his face instead of addressing this matter.

"Don't get your knickers in a twist, Princess," responded Giblet, speaking between mouthfuls of food. "It was jus' a necklace, an' silver at that. It's not as though it was studded with rare stones."

"But you do not understand! It was my necklace! I need it back."

"Well, it ain't here," grunted Giblet. "The Fairy took it back. Said it wasn't safe here anymore."

"But where?" asked Rose.

A loud clanging of a brass bell suddenly erupted from deep within the main shaft. Its urgent call echoed through the dining hall to summon all able hands.

"What's that?" asked Cankles, watching as the Dwarves scrambled from the table to rushed off and gather their tools.

"There's been a cave-in," replied Giblet's wife.

"Let's go, Cankles!" ordered Tag, racing after the Dwarves. "Maybe we can help."

"What about me?" Rose asked as she watched her comrades dash away.

"We may need your help yet!" hollered Tag, as he disappeared down the tunnel.

"But who is going to help me?" whimpered Rose, plopping down onto the seat.

"I can," answered Giblet's wife.

"You?"

"Sure! In fact, we can help each other."

"How so?" questioned the Princess.

"I believe knowledge is meant to be shared. Come with me, m'lady."

"Princess!" hollered Tag, shaking the loose dirt from his hair. "Where are you?"

"Couldn't have gone far, being that we're underground an' all," determined Cankles, as he brushed the dust and grime from his clothing.

"Over here!" A familiar voice echoed from down a long corridor.

"The guests' quarters," announced Giblet, pointing the way.

"I wonder what she's been up to?" grumbled Tag, staring down the passage to see the Princess suddenly appear from one of the chambers.

"Is everyone safe?" asked Rose.

"Thankfully, yes," answered Tag. "The next shift hadn't started yet, so luckily, no one was trapped or hurt."

"An' thanks to your friends, they made sure of it," praised Giblet. "Masters Mayron an' Yairet helped us move the rocks an' debris. Then they helped us shore up the walls to make sure it didn't happen again."

"It was nothing, Master Barscowl," insisted Tag. "I'm just relieved no one was hurt."

"Please, call me Gibby! Only true friends would have stepped up as you two had."

"It was the least we could do," said Cankles.

"Which brings to mind, what have you been up to, Princess?" queried Tag.

"I have been on a personal mission to better the lives of others," replied Rose.

"*You?*" asked Tag.

There was something ominous about these words. His eyes narrowed in suspicion as he stared at the Princess. He had never known her to volunteer to better anyone's life but her own.

"Ladies!" called Rose, waving the female Dwarves to step from the chamber.

"Whoa!" gasped Giblet, rubbing his eyes in disbelief. "Ladies, indeed!"

Cankles and Tag looked twice as the hairy, little women sashayed before them. Now donning frocks of feminine pink, blue or yellow that were embellished with lace and adorned with jewellery studded with the rubies and emeralds taken from these very mines, there was a Dwarvish elegance about them.

They held their whiskered heads high as they showed off their tamed hair. Once wild and frizzy, Rose had brushed, combed and curled their tresses. She even used the pink ribbons Cankles had salvaged when he and Tag took to stripping them off the horses.

"I knew they'd come in useful!" exclaimed Cankles, pleased the ribbons finally found a practical use, than to be buried and forgotten at the bottom of his pack.

"You like?" asked Giblet's wife, giving him a coy smile. With this makeover complete, her poise and confidence received a substantial boost.

"Oooh! I like indeed!" declared the Dwarf, his beady eyes gleaming with desire. "You're as beautiful as any jewel in this mine!"

"Well, I'm flattered," responded his wife, smiling as Rose gave her a nod of approval.

"My work is done! It is time for us to move on," stated the Princess, brushing off her hands now that her personal mission was met with success.

"But what about your necklace?" questioned Tag.

"As Master Dwarf said before, it is not here," responded Rose, with a shrug of her shoulders.

19

Mime Your Manners

"I knew you wouldn't leave without first learning about your locket," said Tag.

"Contrary to what you might believe, I am no fool," responded Rose, urging her mare to keep up with Tag's mount.

"I take it, you bribed those women for this information, hence the reason for making over their appearance," guessed Tag.

"Bribe them? I did not have to resort to such underhanded tactics to garner their cooperation."

"How did you do it then?"

"I hardly think you would understand, but when women get together to primp and preen, a special bond is forged. Small talk is sure to follow, not to mention the sharing of news on the latest goings-on, gossip and whatnot."

"Sounds like typical girlie stuff to me," agreed Cankles. "Not that I'd know."

"I'll give you that," conceded Tag. "But exactly what did Gibby's wife mean when she told you the Tooth Fairy decided it was unsafe to keep your locket in the Mines of Euphoria any longer?"

"And exactly what did she mean by '*home is where the heart is*'?" questioned Cankles.

"I do not know. She merely repeated what she heard the Fairy muttering. I could only ascertain that my locket was taken from there," replied Rose.

"But taken where?" queried Cankles.

"That is just it," explained Rose. "Master Barscowl's wife claimed Pance was in a tizzy; a bit of panic to be gone with my locket before danger followed."

"I hardly think we're the dangerous type," stated Cankles.

"I don't think she meant us," said Tag. "I believe she meant Parru

St. Mime Dragonite."

"You think?" asked Rose.

"It makes sense. After our encounter with the Pooka, I have no doubt that ghastly, little Sprite returned to his master with word of our quest," determined Tag. "No doubt the Tooth Fairy did not want to endanger the Dwarves. Pance removed the locket, securing it in a place the Sorcerer would have difficulty accessing."

"So the question remains, where is it?" Rose wondered aloud. "All the Dwarf could suggest was to retrace our steps."

"Perhaps that's what Pance meant by home and heart," suggested Cankles. "Maybe she returned the locket to Pepperton Palace."

"Now why in the world would she do that? Send me trekking clear across this country only to have me turn around and go home again?" grumbled Rose. "Not only would it be extraordinarily cruel, it would be much too simple."

"Simple is good," responded Cankles. "What's wrong with simple?"

"In your case, it isn't," snorted Rose. "I am sure that demented little Tooth Fairy means to test my will. She would not make it so easy."

"We don't know that for sure. Suppose she feels you've endured enough?" replied Tag. "Perhaps it was to send us back, for she has hidden the locket somewhere along the way. That could be why Barscowl's wife said that we should retrace our steps."

"If she means all the way back home, then why do I not wish for us to be back at the palace?" asked Rose.

"And what happens if it's not there? Suppose it is hidden somewhere between here and there?" countered Tag.

"Then it would've been a waste of a wish and time 'cause we'd be made to come back here to start lookin' all over again," decided Cankles.

"Exactly!" agreed Tag, hoping that if this man could see the logic, so too, would the Princess.

"So, I will not be wishing us back home?" queried Rose.

"Not right now," answered Tag, his words emphatic. "It'd be prudent for us to search out possible clues starting from here."

"I suppose you are right," conceded Rose. "After all, if I do not already possess my locket, then I shall only be chased out of the palace again in my bid to search it out."

"All the more reason to be thorough rather than hasty," responded Tag. "Besides, as it is clear we must cross the Sorcerer's domain, we might still have a need for the last two wishes of the day."

"The last wish of the day," corrected Rose.

"All right, what did you waste the second one on?" groaned Tag, staring in disbelief at Rose.

"I used it to wish for the colourful fabric, elegant lace and lovely buttons that were used to make the Dwarves' frocks."

"What?" asked Tag.

" Believe me, I needed all the help I could conjure to fancy up those female Dwarves."

"Well, I suppose you were doing them a favour," decided Tag.

"And they were grateful for my help," assured Rose.

"We still have one wish left 'til midnight," reminded Cankles. "If we're lucky, we won't even have to use it."

"Let's hope," said Tag.

"So what are we looking for?" questioned Rose.

"Can't rightly say," responded Tag, pondering the type of clues Pance could have left in her wake.

"Something shiny like a silver, heart-shaped locket," suggested Cankles.

"Especially that, but be mindful of the Pooka lurking about. We don't need him alerting Dragonite of our presence," warned Tag. "Now, let's move."

The stifling, musty air swirled through the tunnel. The wavering torch flames illuminating the mouth of the lair alerted Parru St. Mime Dragonite that he was not alone.

Snatching up his staff, the Sorcerer crept from his throne. He watched in silence as a man's shadow, contorted and dancing in the flame's unsteady light, advanced. With his weapon poised, Dragonite darted to the far wall, clinging to the deep shadows as he edged his way to the entrance of this chamber.

"Where are you? I know you're about!" hollered an oddly familiar voice.

Just as the mysterious figure draped in an ebony cloak stepped into the lair, the Sorcerer unleashed his powers. A blast of light erupted from the obsidian crystal to send the stranger hurdling across the chamber. With a loud *thud,* his body slammed against the cave wall. A loud moan of pain wheezed from the dazed stranger as the tremors coursing through his body began to subside.

"Who are you? How dare you trespass?" growled Dragonite.

"Why do I even bother?" muttered an angry voice. He tossed back the cloak's hood to reveal his face.

"Bloody hell!" gasped the Sorcerer, stumbling back in astonishment. "It's me!"

"I only look like you, you fool!" With a snap of his fingers, Loken morphed into his usual form. "I thought I'd be safe taking on your form."

"You gave me a fright," admonished Dragonite, clutching his thundering heart as he justified his actions.

"How could seeing your likeness frighten you?" snapped Loken.

"What can I say? I am a scary fellow! Even I find my very presence frightening at times!"

"You are mad! That's what you are," growled Loken, his hair still smoldering from the assault.

"You are the one who has taken leave of his senses!" countered Dragonite. "How dare you appear before me as *me* when there is room in this world for only one great Sorcerer?"

"I'd say the Dream Merchant is greater."

"Aah, he is but a lowly Wizard," corrected Dragonite, "not a powerful Sorcerer."

"So you delve into the forbidden arts? Big deal! The point is, you need to kill your brother Wizard to be greater than him, but to do so, you'd have to resort to deceit as your powers are left wanting," rebuked Loken, his wings trembling with rage as he launched off the ground. "And if I did not know better, I'd say you want nothing more than to kill me!"

"I'd kill you both if I could, but not just yet. Later perhaps," grunted the Sorcerer, resisting the urge to swat at Loken as he buzzed about his head. "I suspect you come with news of my dreamstone, as well as the Princess and her quest."

"If you assault me with that blasted crystal one more time, you'll learn nothing," vowed Loken.

"No need to get testy! So I was a little premature in unleashing my powers. You did take me by surprise after all. I wasn't expecting you back so soon."

"Enough with the feeble excuses!" snorted Loken.

"There is nothing feeble about them! And remember, cooperation is paramount. If you do not fulfill your end of our agreement, neither will you get the magic potion you desire."

"Fine!"

"So, what say you, Loken? What do you know?"

"I know plenty!" replied the Pooka, alighting upon the Sorcerer's shoulder. "The Princess and her two cohorts had sought out the Dwarves to aid in their search."

"Their search for what?"

"A silver, heart-shaped locket."

"They come all this way for a tawdry piece of jewellery?"

"This is no ordinary locket," assured Loken. "She claims it has the power to break curses."

"I knew it!" exclaimed Dragonite, slapping his knee in delight. "I knew there had to be good reason for that girl to venture all this way! Do you have any idea what I can do with both this locket *and* the dreamstone in my hands?"

"Conjure up a new lair, perhaps? Preferably, something above ground with windows?"

"Alas, a small idea hatched from a puny mind! I am speaking of world domination, Loken!" gloated Dragonite, his gnarled hands rubbing together as he plotted his next move.

"I thought revenge was your primary objective."

"I never said it wasn't," confided the Sorcerer. "If I plan it just so, revenge on the road to world domination can go hand in hand."

"Of course! What was I thinking?" said Loken, rolling his eyes in exasperation.

"You don't! Hence the reason I am the mastermind behind any grand scheme," snorted Dragonite, "and why I send you forth, scurrying about to gather information that I put to practical, strategic use, being the great mime that I am."

"Did you say *mime*?" queried Loken, staring suspiciously at the Sorcerer.

"*Mind!* I meant to say mind," corrected Dragonite. It was a slip of the tongue, for he could only dream of mastering this art to fully appreciate all its subtle nuances. He also knew that with the dreamstone, even this long desired wish could be fulfilled.

"And just what does your great *mind* think on now?" questioned Loken. "A plan to acquire both the dreamstone and locket, I presume?"

"Naturally," muttered Dragonite. His eyes narrowed and his thin, drawn lips pursed together in pensive thought as he wondered aloud, "The question is, how best to execute this plan?"

"As you plot, here's some information sure to affect your strategy," revealed Loken. "I followed the three mortals to the Mines of Euphoria. There, I learned that Pancecilia Feldspar had indeed left the locket with the Dwarves. As I understand it, she felt the locket was in danger of being found by the Princess, so she moved it to another location."

"Damn it all!" cursed Dragonite. "Where? Did you find out?"

"I was able to create a diversion -- a cave-in of one of the mine shafts," replied Loken. "All able-bodied Dwarves, as well as the two mortals in the Princess' company, hurried off to search for casualties and to shore up the walls of the tunnel. While they were distracted, as a centipede, I was able to move unnoticed through the tunnels and chambers."

"And?"

"And, as the Dwarves told the Princess, the locket was no longer there," confirmed Loken. "Its current location, unknown."

"*Arrrgh!* You are bloody useless to me!" snarled the Sorcerer, snatching the Pooka from mid-air.

Loken gasped in pain, his eyes bugging from his head as Dragonite trembled with rage, squeezing the Pooka in his clenched fist.

Loken's eyes popped right out, protruding from flexible stalks as his body transmogrified into a greenish-yellow, mottled slug. Large and fleshy, he secreted a copious quantity of slimy mucous the tighter the Sorcerer squeezed.

"*Ewww!*" groaned Dragonite, unleashing his hold as the slime oozed between his fingers. Instead of falling from his grip, the slug adhered to the palm of his hand. "You are utterly disgusting!"

Just as the Sorcerer was about to scrape off this undulating gastropod, smearing it against the cave wall, Loken morphed back into his original form. He took to the air, hovering a respectable distance above the Sorcerer.

"You touch me again and I shall become an ill-tempered viper with the speed to strike before you can call upon any kind of magic to save your life!" vowed Loken, his wings fluttering with indignation. "You will be so dead! No powers of the dark arts will bring you back."

"Yes, yes!" muttered Dragonite, wiping the slime on his cloak. "Just tell me where that locket is!"

"Your guess is as good as mine," grunted Loken. "If it's of any consolation, neither does the Princess know."

"Are you positive?"

"Absolutely! As a little cave cricket, I heard it through the ears on my knees and they worked very well," explained Loken. "The Dwarves have sent the trio off. Even as I speak, the Princess retraces her steps, searching for the locket."

"And the dreamstone? Does she still possess it?"

"She most certainly does."

"Then not for long!" exclaimed Dragonite. "We shall move while they are within striking distance! Go muster my men -- all of them."

"And what will you be doing?" asked Loken.

"I will make ready the machines of war."

"All that, just to capture three mortals? That is rather extreme!"

"How soon you forget! Once I claim the dreamstone, we shall be in a position to wage war against my enemies. Now, be off! Let us hunt them down so I can claim what is rightfully mine."

"It has been strangely quiet," noted Tag, glancing about the twilight landscape as the sky deepened.

"We are smack-dab in the heart of the Bad Lands. I find it odd we have yet to see one mime skulking about," added Rose, urging her mare on to follow Tag's steed up a rise.

"As mimes don't usually speak, doesn't it make sense that the lands would be quiet?" questioned Cankles.

"I mean unnaturally so," explained Tag. "It's as though the woodland creatures have taken to hiding; like it is the calm before a great storm."

"Yet, there's nary a cloud in the sky and the winds have been fair," responded Cankles.

"Instead of worrying about how quiet it is, we should take advantage of it to look for my locket," suggested Rose.

"That's why we're heading up this bluff," responded Tag. "It'll give us a chance to survey the lands from a higher vantage point. From up there, not only can we potentially spot a clue as to the location of your locket, we should be able to see if the Sorcerer's followers are in the vicinity so we can steer clear of them."

"Good plan!" praised Cankles. "If we can avoid those mimes, all the better I say!"

"And that is why we are going to take our rest tonight up there," added Tag, dismounting from his stallion. "We'll spot the Sorcerer and his minions if they're about before they know we're here."

"But what about my locket?" asked Rose. As tired as she was, she was prepared to venture on to find it.

"It would be folly to search for it in the blackness of night," answered Tag. "I fear there's a chance we'll pass right on by, unawares."

"Suppose I use the last wish to give us the eyes of a cat, so we can see well in the dark?" offered Rose.

"Look here, Princess, I am not keen on spending the night in the Sorcerer's domain and neither do I care to be hampered by the darkness, but to wish for cat's eyes? Now that is too bizarre!" argued Tag.

"Especially if you couldn't undo the wish," added Cankles. "That'd be pretty creepy, if you ask me."

"Besides, if ever we need to call on a wish, it'll be available," reminded Tag, removing his pack from the saddle. "There's a chance we'll need the miracle of magic to battle magic should the Sorcerer confront us."

"But we do not even know if the Sorcerer is after us," countered Rose.

"Why take the chance? Knowing the shape-shifting Sprite had been in our company, listening to our every word, I'd say we best be careful passing through Dragonite's domain."

"I suppose you are right," conceded Rose.

"Of course I am," responded Tag. "Now, let us ready for the night. And on this eve, no fire."

"Do you think I will accidentally set something ablaze?" questioned Rose.

"Perhaps…" teased Tag, "but we do not want to draw the enemy's attention."

"I see," acknowledged Rose.

"And as you have the extra energy to continue the hunt for your locket, you can expend it on taking the first watch," decided Tag.

Rose thought better of arguing with him. It was bad enough standing guard, waiting alone in the dark until she was relieved of duty, but worse if she was made to take the second or third watch as the night wore on. For some reason, time seemed to crawl by torturously slow in the wee hours of the morning when waiting for the sun to show its face again.

After sharing a meal, Rose took up Tag's weapon. As he and Cankles curled up in their bedrolls to sleep, she cozied up to the sword. Clutching it close to her chest, she waited and watched.

With the tedium of sentry duty, boredom soon took hold. Hefting the sword, she carefully unsheathed it. Freed of the scabbard, Rose still found the weapon to be weighty and cumbersome. How a knight or a person like Tag was able to fight using this sword for anything more than a few minutes was beyond her. In the most ideal situation, she decided she might get in one, maybe two, good swipes before it became too heavy in her hands to remain effective.

"There must be something better, something that is lightweight and deadly in skilled hands. But I am not trained to fight, nor would I ever want to get so close to the enemy to be made to deal with him hands-on. In fact, the only thing I excel at is throwing things," Rose muttered to herself as she recalled the last shoe she had hurled at her attendants and not to forget the game birds she downed when Tag and Cankles could not. "Yes, I do have a bloody good aim…"

She contemplated this dilemma, palming a smooth, round stone she picked up from the ground. Eyeing the stand of oak trees across from her, Rose aimed for a hollow. Pitching the projectile, the stone was swallowed up in the dark cavity to send a family of startled squirrels scattering from their nest.

"An excellent aim, if I do say so myself," boasted Rose, admiring her marksmanship. "Say... That's it! I can wish for a long-range weapon designed for one with my skills."

With the midnight hour advancing and the chance to use the last wish of the day soon to expire, Rose set to work. When she was done wishing, she opened her eyes to find a leather sling and a butter-soft suede pouch in her hands.

This innocuous looking length of leather was tanned a rich, chestnut brown and the end pieces to be held in one's hand were made of the same supple suede to match the pouch. Not only was it fashionable, the soft suede promised to be gentle on her hands.

Pulling open the drawstring, she peered inside the pouch to spy six steel balls, each measuring one inch in diameter. And these were no ordinary metal balls. These beauties were of highly polished steel. Each one was etched with an image of a rose and a dagger; a warning to the unfortunate recipient of this weapon that not only is the bearer of this sling beautiful, but she also poses a real danger. Removing two, Rose checked inside the pouch to make sure her wish was complete. Sure enough, the two balls she removed were magically replaced by two more. She was guaranteed a never-ending supply and at the same time, she would not be encumbered by the weight of a sizeable arsenal. In this case, having six steel balls was truly as good as having sixty!

"Perfect!" exclaimed Rose, as she tied the pouch onto the sash of her gown. "This will do nicely. If I am forced to confront my enemies, I shall now lay waste to them without even having to touch a single person."

The sudden rustling of leaves high above drew Rose's attention, forcing her eyes to search the shadows of the treetop. Between the high boughs a pair of round, amber eyes reflected the light of the moon. They stared down at her, unblinking.

"An owl," whispered Rose, peering up at the bird as she pondered its presence. "Or is it?"

Rising to her feet, the Princess waved off the raptor, "Shoo! Go away!"

Instead of flying off into the night, the owl ruffled it feathers, rotating its head from front to back as it ignored her.

"Curse you! I command you to leave!" growled Rose, shaking a fist at the bird.

"*Whoo-who-whoo!*" The owl hooted mournfully.

"*Who?* I am Princess Rose of Fleetwood, that's who! And I order you to leave. Now, scat!"

The bird merely gazed down, its stare unyielding.

"This is not right," muttered Rose, and it was not so much that the bird refused to bend to her will. "I do believe a little test is in order."

Taking up her new weapon, she wrapped one end around her hand as the opposite end was held in place by her thumb and secured in the palm as her fingers rolled into a fist. Taking a single steel ball from the pouch, she placed it in the cradle of the sling. Rotating the it from her wrist than her shoulder, the ball spun in ever-faster circles as Rose set her sights on the intended target.

As though to mock this audacious display, the owl merely fluffed up its feathers once more, closing its eyes as it settled down to sleep.

With a flick of her wrist, Rose released the end of the sling gripped in her hand. The steel ball whistled through the night in unerring flight to hit its target. In a small cloud of mottled feathers, the owl toppled from its perch to land on a layer of dried leaves.

"Serves you right, stupid bird!" muttered Rose, as she took up a stick to prod her victim to see if it was still alive. Pushing aside the leaf litter, she was shocked to see the downed owl transform before her very eyes.

"I knew it! I knew you were that evil Poo-doo thing!" exclaimed Rose, poking Loken with the stick. "Even I know an owl would be hunting, not sleeping, at night!"

"What's going on?" asked Tag, stumbling from his bedroll upon hearing the commotion.

"See for yourself," responded Rose. "I killed the Poo-doo."

"The what?"

"That shape-shifting vermin," explained Rose, giving the Sprite another prod of her stick. "He was spying on us."

This time, a pained breath wheezed from Loken's parted lips as his face grimaced in agony.

"He's still alive!" corrected Tag, picking up the Pooka by its wings. Loken's limp body dangled before him, emitting a sickly aura.

"I can remedy that," offered Rose, searching for a large rock.

"I have a better idea," said Tag. "Gather some twigs and I'll need some twine, too."

"Don't know what you did to the little bugger, but he's still unconscious," commented Cankles. He raised the small, twig cage to inspect the prisoner sprawled out on the floor.

"That creature found us last night. He had assumed the form of an owl to spy on us," explained Rose. "However, I was not fooled. I downed him with this."

She proudly displayed the offending weapon.

"A sling?" said Cankles. "Where did that come from?"

"I wished for it."

Cankles glanced over at Tag, anticipating a verbal altercation.

"It would've been a wish wasted had she not used it before midnight," assured Tag. "As luck would have it, this sling and her aim worked in tandem to down the pesky Sprite."

"What are you gonna to do with him?" questioned Cankles, watching the slow rise and fall of Loken's chest.

"Not sure yet," answered Tag. "But as he's in alliance with the Sorcerer, there's a chance he'll be a worthy bargaining tool."

"I see," said Cankles. "But suppose he wakes up? What then?"

"Haven't thought that far ahead yet," admitted Tag.

"We can't just leave him here, trapped like this," stated Cankles.

"Neither can we set him free," countered Tag.

"Kill him, I say!" suggested Rose.

"Don't be so hasty, Princess!" urged Cankles, as Rose snatched the cage from his hand. "Perhaps the young master is right. He may come in handy."

"Cannot think how, but we certainly cannot free him," responded Rose.

"For now, we'll just keep him detained," recommended Tag.

"Hey! Did you hear that?" asked Cankles, glancing about.

"Move, you fools!" An voice bellowed through the air.

"This way," whispered Tag, motioning his comrades to follow him to the crest of the rise. Crawling on their bellies, Tag and Cankles kept close to the ground to remain undetected. They peered over the edge of the bluff.

"Come away from there! It's too dangerous," whispered Rose, urging them to watch from a safe place, but more so because she didn't want to crawl about on the ground next to them.

She gasped in horror, watching as the earth beneath Cankles and Tag suddenly crumbled, taking the pair down in a small landslide.

"Idiots!" grunted Rose. "What were they thinking to stand so close to the edge?"

Rose yelped in surprised as the earth disintegrated, collapsing beneath her feet to send her sliding down behind them.

"Were you speaking of yourself?" grumbled Tag, brushing the dirt and dust from his raiment.

"Obviously, you two loosened the earth for this to happen to me," snapped Rose, wondering how she managed to keep hold of the Sprite's prison on her downward slide.

"Hush!" scolded Cankles. "They'll hear us!"

"Too late!" snarled the voice. A dark, tattered cloak swirled about as the Sorcerer turned to confront the three trespassers. "You were just as well to have sounded a horn to announce your arrival."

"Who are you?" asked Tag, his hand poised on the hilt of his sword as he brazenly stepped forward.

"I need no introduction," he gloated as he drew back the hood to reveal a sneering smile on his gaunt face. "Everyone knows who I am."

For a moment, they stared at the man as he straightened his hunched back to puff out his bony chest so they could admire him in all his glory.

"Can't say we do," decided Tag, shaking his head.

"Step closer!" The man waved them forward as he struck a menacing pose. "Look again."

"You definitely have an ill-favoured look about you, but no… you do not look familiar," responded Rose.

"Do not raise my ire! If you do not know me now, I will give you reason to remember me for all eternity!" The crystal atop his staff crackled with energy.

"Parru St. Mime Dragonite!" Cankles yelped in recognition.

"Aha! So you do know me!" exclaimed the Sorcerer.

"Only because of them," responded Tag. He pointed to the army of mimes silently appearing from the forest to assemble behind their leader.

They marched along using the most exaggerated gestures, falling into neat rows just as they had practiced.

Tag, Rose and Cankles chuckled aloud as the mimes proceeded to adopt the Sorcerer's stance. They imitated his every move, right down to the nervous twitch of his face and that lopsided, sinister grin.

Dragonite spun about, facing his army to bark his command, "Stop it! Stop, I say!"

Instead of complying with this order, the mimes continued with this impromptu performance. The more agitated the Sorcerer became and the more the trio laughed, the more animated the mimes became, shaking a balled fist into the air as they mouthed the words: *Stop it! Stop, I say!*

"I do not care for mimes, but these ones are quite humorous," commented Rose, as she giggled at their impromptu impersonation of their master.

"Cease this silliness!" growled Dragonite, the end of his staff hammered the earth as he issued this order.

Again, his army mimicked his every angry gesture, each driving the end of an imaginary staff into the ground.

"Your army hardly poses a threat to us," mocked Tag.

"Then what about this?" snarled the Sorcerer, discharging a bolt of energy from his crystal at the mime nearest to him.

Overcome by violent convulsions, the man fell over dead. He smoldered from the intensity of the power that coursed through his body as his fellow mimes abruptly stood at attention. The fear of being the Sorcerer's next victim forced to them to finally comply with his order.

"What say you now?" growled Dragonite, levelling the black crystal toward the trio.

"Bloody hell!" gulped Cankles.

"We did not mean to intrude on you and your party, Master Sorcerer," apologized the Princess. "Just pretend we were never here. We shall be on our way."

"Why the hurry, Princess Rose-alyn?"

"You know me?"

"I so rarely get royalty in these parts," responded Dragonite. "I was told of your coming."

"And now, we'll be going," said Tag, grabbing Rose's hand to pull her away.

"Stop!" commanded the Sorcerer. "Give me the dreamstone, Princess!"

"How did you know?" asked Tag.

"How can I not? I am omnipotent! Now, give it to me!"

"Never!" snapped Rose.

"You dare challenge me and my forces?" growled Dragonite.

"Look at the pathetic forces you speak of," grunted the Princess. "They are not men! They are mimes!"

"And you will mime your manners!"

"You just said *mime*," teased Tag.

"I meant *mind*! And I will not stand for such audacity and neither will they!" cursed Dragonite. Raising his staff on high, he stoked the flames of war in his men's hearts. The mimes clenched their fists in defiance as they unleashed a great battle cry, albeit a silent one.

Tag, Cankles and Rose stared in disbelief at the agitated, animated mob as they pretended to howl a bloodcurdling challenge.

"My! That was scary," mocked Rose, her tone sarcastic as she feigned her fright as only the mimes could appreciate.

"They are silent, but deadly!" warned Dragonite. "They will smite you!"

"Speak up!" hollered Tag, joining Rose in ridiculing the strangest military force they've ever encountered. "I can't hear you. My ears are still ringing from that war cry!"

"Do not scorn me! These mimes have been trained for battle. They are prepared to unleash their wrath! If you do not hand over the dream-stone, they will dispense a quick and bloody death!"

"So, are we to pretend we're dying when you unleash your mute mob?" quipped Rose, unmoved by the Sorcerer's threat.

"Attack!" bellowed Dragonite, motioning the battalion closest to the trio to commence the assault. "Fire at will!"

As they unleashed another silent battle cry the mimes immediately launched into action. With deliberate, exaggerated movements, they released a great volley of arrows.

Instead of falling over dead, skewered by many arrows, Rose and her companions were doubled over in laughter as the Sorcerer's men continued to dispense make-believe arrows from invisible bows. In a bizarre performance strangely reminiscent of the one they had witnessed in their travels eastward, some of the mimes dropped to the ground, writhing in death-throes as they pretended to be the recipients of an invisible counterattack.

"You idiots!" swore Dragonite, as he sputtered in rage. "For bloody sake, put down those damned ropes and arm yourselves with real weapons!"

At the edge of the battlefield, six huge catapults abandoned from a previous war had been dusted off and refurbished for the Sorcerer's use. The mimes struggling with imaginary lengths of ropes they pretended were attached to these machines of war sheepishly dropped their invisible prop to arm themselves with swords and spears.

"Bollocks!" swore Cankles, watching as the mimes regrouped. "Those weapons are real!"

With only one sword to fend off an entire army, Tag shouted to Rose and Cankles, "Run! Back to our horses!"

Seizing Rose by her hand, he pulled her along as he raced back to the base of the bluff.

"We cannot hope to climb this!" gasped Rose, watching as loose substrate trickled down the incline as the earth felt the tremors of the many footfalls marching in synchrony as the mimes advanced.

"Hide!" ordered Tag, shoving Rose behind a massive boulder.

"What good is this?" snapped the Princess, her hand slapping in frustration against the granite. "They know we are behind it!"

"This is what they must mean when they say between a rock and a hard place," decided Cankles, glancing over this protective barrier to spy upon the encroaching hordes.

"Hush! Let me think," ordered Tag, staring over the boulder to assess the situation.

"So what is the worst case scenario?" asked Rose, peering over Tag's shoulder.

"We die," decided Tag.

"Let me rephrase the question. What is the best that can happen?" asked Rose.

"We die quickly," gulped Cankles.

As the army stood poised to attack, Dragonite revelled in glory, "Loken! Where the hell are you? Damn that good-for-nothing Sprite! Why must he always miss my moments of triumph?"

"I have an idea!" whispered Rose, glancing around the boulder to see the Sorcerer searching about for the Pooka's presence.

"It better be good!" responded Tag, hefting his sword in preparation for a confrontation.

"It is nothing short of brilliant," assured Rose. "Wait here!"

The Princess cautiously reappeared from behind the boulder as she called out, "Do not attack!"

"Why? Do you wish to surrender, Princess?" questioned the Sorcerer.

"I wish to negotiate. My life, and the lives and freedom of my comrades, for something you have been searching for."

"The dreamstone?" queried Dragonite, his eyes gleaming in anticipation.

"This!" announced Rose. From the folds of her cloak she revealed the twig cage. Inside, the dazed Sprite finally stirred. "You can have your Poobah in exchange."

"Pooka!" corrected Tag and Cankles, hollering simultaneously from behind the boulder.

"Surely you jest?" snorted the Sorcerer, insulted by the offer.

"I am serious! It is a fair trade."

"If I had a sense of humour, I would laugh!" growled Dragonite. "So what do you deem fair?"

"Grant us our freedom and I shall return your friend to you," insisted Rose. "That is more than fair!"

"And just what do you think I will do with that shape-shifting miscreant?"

"He is your friend," reasoned Rose. She held forth the cage as Loken staggered to his feet, pressing his face between the bars to appeal to his master.

"This is what I think of friendship!" snarled Dragonite.

Without hesitation, the Sorcerer discharged a bolt of energy at the Princess and the Pooka. She froze in terror, but just as the charge was about to strike them down, Loken was aglow with magical light.

Rose screamed as the Sprite suddenly morphed.

The sides of the prison burst open as massive, leathery wings and the gargantuan, scaly body of a dragon erupted through the bars. The blast of power simply deflected from Loken's armoured rump to strike down the frontline of mimes. Panic ensued as these men unleashed a silent cry of fear. They madly dashed about, retreating from the battle-field as Dragonite ordered them to regroup.

With a mighty roar, Loken's dragon form snatched up Rose in his talons, his powerful haunches launching him into the air. With huge wings billowing like the sails of a tall ship, Loken took to the sky with his quarry.

"Put her down!" hollered Tag. Brandishing his sword, he leaped out from behind the boulder. "Fight, you coward!"

Loken snorted in disgust. Filling his lungs with air, he exhaled to unleash a torrent of fire at the boy.

"Look out!" hollered Cankles. He seized Tag by the shoulders, yanking him behind the boulder, away from the fiery blast.

"Put me down!" shrieked Rose, her fists pummelling the dragon's chest to no avail as he ascended into the sky.

"After everything you've done to me? I think not!" These angry words rumbled forth from the beast.

"Unhand me! I demand it!"

"As you wish!" snapped Loken, his scaly shoulders rolling in a shrug of indifference.

Rose screamed as the dragon released his grip. His wings beat rapidly as he hovered, watching as the Princess clawed helplessly at the air as she plunged down to earth.

Tag and Cankles were as speechless as the mimes. They watched in horror, unable to aid Rose as she tumbled through the air in a free fall.

"Look away!" shouted Cankles, averting his eyes just as she was about to slam into the ground.

Tag could not bear to look, but his eyes snapped open as a great *whoosh* of air bowled him over and a loud scream sounded in his ears as the dragon swooped down to snatch the Princess from certain death. All were forced low to the ground as Loken's wings skimmed over their heads.

"How dare you?" shrieked Rose, more outraged than terrified by this treatment as she squirmed in Loken's suffocating grip.

"You make it so very easy!" grunted Loken, his wings pumping madly to thrust him high into the sky.

"Two can play this game!" snapped Rose. Closing her eyes and gripping the dreamstone in her hand, she set to work.

Loken bellowed in surprise. His talons were wrenched open, unable to grip his prisoner. Glancing down, his head recoiled as a blast of heat and flames shot his way. More surprising than this unexpected inferno was its source. He roared in agony as a large, rosy pink dragon donning a gold necklace with a crystal pendant soared past him, lashing his snout with the tip of her heavily armoured tail.

"Brilliant!" cheered Tag, his fist pumping the air as he watched Rose's adopted form attack Loken. She was even bigger than the Pooka and twice as mad.

Careering through the sky, the pink behemoth dodged a fiery blast as Loken closed the distance. Veering to the left, and then the right, she flew straight to the cover of a thick, grey cloud to disappear into the mist.

"I know where you are!" snarled Loken, his wings driving him on to follow. Just as he rushed into the swirling, vapourous threads of moisture, Rose dove down, only to circle back up and behind Loken.

A bellow of pain thundered through the air as Rose's snout rammed her adversary just as he burst above the cloud cover. Taken by surprise, he tumbled head over tail from the powerful blow.

"Take that, you belligerent beast!" snapped Rose, as she headed back down to earth. "That will teach you to attack a princess!"

"Watch out!" hollered Tag.

"Behind you!" cried Cankles, his finger pointing for Rose to look back.

Unable to hear their frantic cries above the beating of her wings and the wind rushing around her, Loken attacked, his jaws snapping down on the end of her tail.

With wings flapping to remain airborne, her hind legs kicked out while her tail whipped about, trying to shake off her nemesis. Her fight for freedom was in vain. Loken was too powerful.

With a hard yank, he pulled her down to within striking distance. Just as his hind legs kicked out to deliver a terrible blow to Rose's midriff, she lashed out to block this attack, only to have their talons lock together.

They plummeted to earth like two eagles engaged in a death spiral.

"This will not end well!" yelped Cankles, ducking behind the boulder to shield him from the impact should the winged leviathans crash down.

As the earth rushed toward them, within a few feet of impacting the ground, the dragons broke free of each other, winging skyward once again.

Never had Rose exerted this much energy as a human and now as a dragon, her lack of stamina was becoming evident as each beat of her wings slowed. Loken was swifter, stronger and it was obvious he possessed far greater endurance. He was in deadly pursuit and quickly gaining on her. Each time they swooped low to the ground, the mimes scattered in fear, only to be threatened by Dragonite to regroup.

All Rose could do was dive, dodge and pivot away from the searing heat and flames Loken belched at her, but these daring, aerial acrobatics were wearing her down. With her wings fully extended, Rose hitched a ride on a thermal. The bank of warm, rising air allowed her to glide effortlessly into the sky.

"Any higher and she'll be touching the sun!" marvelled Cankles, watching her rise above the clouds.

"Oh, no!" groaned Tag. "Here comes the Pooka again!"

Loken took advantage of the thermals, too. Being smaller and lighter than Rose, this rising draft delivered him right up to her in no time.

Unable to maneuver away fast enough, Rose bellowed in pain as Loken came up from beneath her. With thrusts of his wings, he pushed past her, allowing one of the spiny protrusions adorning his head to clip her on the lower jaw as he flew by.

Stunned by the blow, Rose tumbled through the air, falling back to earth.

She shook off the pain, opening her wings wide to catch the wind and stop this free fall. Glancing up, she spied Loken screaming toward her. Folding her wings close to her sides, Rose dove down to avoid a collision.

All were forced to the ground as Rose's massive form skimmed low over the battlefield with Loken in hot pursuit.

"He's too fast! Think small, Princess! Become smaller and faster so he can't catch you!" hollered Tag, shouting at Rose as she winged by him to elude her foe.

Rose knew Tag was right. Her only hope of surviving this encounter was to take extreme, evasive action while adopting a new form. She swooped down low, heading straight to a stand of trees at the edge of the battlefield.

Loken bellowed in triumph as he gained speed, flying straight behind her. With his pink target within striking distance, Loken's wings thrust him through the air. Just as his jaws opened to snap down on her tail, Rose veered upward.

Waiting until the very last second, she avoided colliding with a towering pine tree. She was so close the ventral scales on her belly scraped against the tree's trunk as her wings snapped off branches as they grazed by them.

So intent on catching her, Loken was surprised by this evasive maneuver. Veering to the right, narrowly missing this tree, he was forced to duck between the pines if he were to avoid crashing or clipping a wing.

Rose glanced down and behind. Just as she had hoped, Loken was busy dodging vegetation to save his life. Now was her chance to transform into something that would allow her to move with greater agility without sacrificing speed.

Infuriated that she was clever enough to elude him, Loken burst through the canopy, destroying the treetops as he resumed the chase.

"He's gaining on you!" Tag hollered in warning, watching Rose all the while, using his peripheral vision to keep stock of the Sorcerer as he continued to rally his forces.

As Loken closed in, winging toward his rival, his eyes narrowed, squinting from the intense glare of brilliant light engulfing Rose.

For a moment, all on the ground thought the Princess had disappeared completely. It was only when Loken hovered about, snapping at the air around his head did they realize what became of Rose.

Instead of wishing to become a winged raptor like the swift moving falcon, Rose took to the air, but this time, as a little wasp.

"What was she thinking?" gasped Tag, his hand slapping his forehead in frustration. "He'll only swat her down!"

"Or worse!" yelped Cankles, grimacing in horror as Loken's talons slashed at the agitated insect buzzing around him.

"Don't say that!"

"It's not like she can sting him through those scales," explained Cankles.

"That's it!" shouted Tag. "Rose, sting him! Sting him in the eyes! Blind the Pooka!"

With wings a-blur she darted, hovered and dove at her foe.

Setting her sights and stinger on Loken's amber eye; she dove at her target. The Pooka pivoted, opening his massive jaws. Even without snapping in her direction, the vacuum created by this yawning gape sucked her into his awaiting mouth. Clamping down, Rose disappears from sight.

"Good God!" gasped Tag, staring in disbelief.

"Didn't see that comin'!" added Cankles, now fearing the worst.

"He killed her!" shouted Tag.

Before the dragon could swallow, he bellowed in pain. Coughing and gagging, he sent the wasp spewing from his mouth. The back of his throat immediately swelled, narrowing the airway as the venom took hold. A severe reaction caused his neck and face to swell like an air filled bladder, the scales protruding grotesquely like the spines of an inflated puffer fish.

As dragon and wasp fell to earth, before the venom could completely paralyze him, Loken used his powers to transform back into a Sprite. Caught in the wake of his powers, Rose assumed her human form.

"Got you!" exclaimed Tag, catching Rose in his arms. Both tumbled to the ground as Cankles stepped forward, kicking the now bloated Sprite. He punted the Pooka from the battlefield.

"Take that, you scoundrel!" cursed Cankles, shaking an angry fist behind Loken as he bounced over the tree line. "We won't be seeing you any more!"

"But now you must face me!" snarled Dragonite, as his army of mimes closed their ranks to encircle the unconscious Princess and her comrades. "Give me the dreamstone!"

Easing Rose's head onto the ground, Tag motioned for Cankles to watch over her.

"I shall die first before that happens!" declared Tag, as he brandished his sword.

"That is the plan," smirked Dragonite, the crystal atop his staff crackled with energy as he took aim at the boy.

The Sorcerer suddenly gasped in surprise as the whine of arrows filled the air. Dozens of projectiles rained down from the sky, impaling the earth at the feet of his frontline of defense.

The mimes took a tentative step back only to be ordered by Dragonite to stand their ground as Rainus Silverthorn and a small battalion of Elves appeared at the top of the bluff.

"You missed!" taunted Dragonite, mocking the Elves and the perfect row of evenly spaced arrows landing at the feet of the mimes. "You downed not one of us!"

"The arrows fell precisely where we had intended," countered Rainus, motioning the captain of his army, Halen Ironwood to have his men arm their bows once more. "You cross that line of arrows and there will be good reason to kill your minions."

"Such audacious words! I hardly think you and your measly clan of Elves can stand up to my numbers!" mocked Dragonite, undaunted by this show of marksmanship.

"I was not speaking of us," responded Rainus, glancing to the western edge of the battlefield. "I was referring to them!"

The Sorcerer turned with a start as the trumpeting of horns announced the coming of a great army. King Maxmillion emerged from the shadows of the surrounding forest with mounted knights at the vanguard while Tiny Goatswain and his fellow Trolls took up the rear. They hoisted massive boulders onto their shoulders, a demonstration they were more than capable of ending this battle quickly.

Undeterred by this military show of force, the Sorcerer was not about to surrender, nor was he intent on giving up on the dreamstone when it was within his grasp after all these years.

"To war!" bellowed Dragonite, urging his men on. "Fight to the death! I shall deal with the boy myself!"

Though they outnumbered their foes, the mimes visibly trembled with fear. Before them, armoured knights presented a cohesive, disciplined force while a dozen Trolls were prepared to take offensive action. Behind the rows of mimes, the Sorcerer raged, threatening them with certain death if they chose to defy him at this crucial moment.

"Fight, I say!" snarled Dragonite. A great bolt of energy erupted from the crystal atop his staff to destroy the earth behind them. "Kill them or I will kill you all myself!"

Intimidated into action, the mimes surged forward only to stop dead in their tracks as the Trolls grunted, heaving boulders high over the mimes. Before the catapults could be deployed, the boulders came crashing down to demolish the machines.

"Stand your ground," ordered the Sorcerer. "Fight!"

"Charge!" hollered Maxmillion, ordering his mounted knights to lower their pikes so they could plow through to break the ranks. With weapons poised, the knights raced into battle.

The mimes that did not fleeing instantly did only enough to deflect the deadly blows, as though only pretending to fight. The many not killed from this assault simply collapsed to the ground, feigning their death.

"Attack, my minions!" ordered Dragonite, angered by this performance. "Stand your ground and fight!"

Instead, a good number of his men scattered, while only the most foolhardy pretended to be soldiers. Seizing one of the deserters as he dashed past him, the Sorcerer shook the mime as he snarled his demand, "Fight! Fight for your master!"

Rather than silently complying, the mime snapped back, "Are you mad? You're on your own, mate!"

He wrenched free of the Sorcerer's grip to flee with his fellow mimes than to do battle.

"Curse you! Come back and fight!" raged Dragonite. "The enemy can still be defeated!"

"By you and whose army?" mocked Tag. He now stood between the Sorcerer and the Princess, sword poised in his hands.

"You insolent whelp!" snarled Dragonite, spinning the staff in his hand as he prepared to square off against the boy. "It will not take magic to kill you."

"I do not fear you!" growled Tag, his grip tightening on the hilt of his sword.

"You're as good as dead. There'll be no time for fear!" promised Dragonite. With astonishing speed, he brought the staff down on Tag's head.

The boy angled away, his sword intercepting the blow. Using the blade in a sweeping, downward stroke, Tag redirected the end of the staff. Stepping forward, he lunged at the Sorcerer. The tip of the sword pierced through Dragonite's flowing robe, but being so gaunt, the blade failed to connect with flesh, merely skimming by his bony ribcage.

"You missed!" mocked the Sorcerer, spinning his staff about to knock the sword away from his body before the boy could take another swipe at him.

Tag was stunned. This decrepit looking being was much faster and stronger than he anticipated. Before he could recover from Dragonite's deflective blow, the Sorcerer attacked. The end of the staff flew straight for the side of Tag's head. From the corner of his eye, the boy detected a blur of movement as the obsidian crystal flew toward him. He veered away, ducking as the staff grazed his scalp.

So certain this strike would connect, Dragonite had swung with all his might. With no resistance to meet this blow, the Sorcerer stumbled past the boy, propelled by his own momentum.

Tag recovered, levelling his sword as the Sorcerer turned to face him once more. This time, he did not wait for Dragonite to attack first. Tag's sword sliced through the air; the repercussion of the impact as the blade collided with the Sorcerer's magical staff rattled him to his bones. It was as though this wooden staff was made of steel, not even denting under the blade's keen edge.

Dragonite parried each blow with unexpected ease, countering each of Tag's strikes with one of his own.

Having only tested his skills against the scarecrows from farmers' fields, the Sorcerer was proving to be a genuine challenge for Tag. He struggled to remain composed as he guided his sword, slicing and thrusting the blade in hopes he would meet his mark.

Just as Tag lunged forward to impale Dragonite, the Sorcerer angled away ever so slightly. It was just enough for the boy to miss, and for him to strike Tag in his midriff with the end of his staff. Doubling over in pain, as Tag's body lurched forward, folding with the impact, Dragonite's staff swung upward, striking the boy under his chin.

Tag reeled from the blow, staggering back as his adversary continued the assault. With a flick of his wrist, Dragonite's staff spun about to knock the sword from Tag's hand. The weapon tumbled to the ground as the Sorcerer continued his attack.

Dragonite swung the end of his staff down, striking the boy low on the back of his legs to sweep him off his feet. Falling hard on his back, the wind was knocked out of Tag. He groaned in pain. Rolling to his side, he strained to reach the hilt of his sword. The tips of his fingers pulled the weapon to within his grasp, but just as Tag was about to take it into his hand, he bellowed in pain as a foot slammed down. Trapped between the sword handle and the earth, his fingers were mashed into the ground. Only the cross-guard biting into the soil spared Tag's bones from being shattered.

Kicking the sword away, Dragonite turned the end of the staff down, pressing the dark crystal against Tag's right temple.

"Now you die," snarled the Sorcerer. The crystal throbbed with light that seemed to feed off his anger.

"You first!" A voice growled into Dragonite's ear. The cold bite of a sword's blade pressed against the Sorcerer's throat as Cankles vowed, "I will cut your throat if you do him harm!"

"No need for such hostility, I merely speak in jest," explained Dragonite. Feeling the keen edge of the blade against his skin, he removed the crystal he pressed against Tag's head as the light glowing within dimmed.

"Back off," ordered Cankles, using the tip of the blade to guide the Sorcerer away. "Get away from the boy!"

"No harm done!" grumbled Dragonite, as he took a cautious step back. "At least to him!"

Cankles raised his sword to deflect the blow as the Sorcerer's staff came down to strike him. Being so wiry and lacking in brute strength, Cankles angled away, repelling each strike rather than remaining planted and receiving the powerful blows. Tag watched through bleary eyes, shaking the fog from his head as he observed his friend engage in battle. Cankles' footwork seemed timed and deliberate, delivering him away from danger, but at the same time, keeping him within range to effectively counter each of Dragonite's moves.

"I grow weary of this!" snapped the Sorcerer.

"You wish to call a truce?" asked Cankles, dropping his guard as he lowered the tip of the sword.

"I wish to see you dead!" Dragonite unleashed a bolt to strike Cankles down.

The debilitating energy coursed through Cankles' body. The sword tumbled from his grip as he collapsed to the ground, writhing in agony.

"The next time, I will have the power to kill you with one blow," vowed the Sorcerer. He stepped over Cankles' convulsing form, triumphantly marching up to where Rose lay on the ground, stirring from her unnatural sleep.

"Victory is mine!" declared Dragonite, even as his ill-prepared army waged a losing battle. Spying the gold chain around the Princess' neck, his eyes gleamed with lust, for he knew on the end of this necklace was the dreamstone. As he knelt down to claim his prize, his hand recoiled in surprise as a swarm of arrows rained down, piercing the ground to form a physical barrier between him and the object of his desire. He glanced up to see Rainus Silverthorn lead his men down the bluff to confront him.

"So much for your legendary marksmanship!" snapped Dragonite, glaring at his foes as they readied their bows. "You will never kill me at this rate."

"It is not for us to deal in your death, if that is to be your destiny," responded Rainus.

"That is because you cannot stop me!" mocked Dragonite.

"I do not intend to," said the Elf, nodding in agreement as he pointed behind the Sorcerer. "But he will."

Dragonite turned to peer over his shoulder.

"Hello, brother!"

The Sorcerer yelped in pain as Silas Agincourt gave him a sharp jab of the staff to his forehead.

"*You!*" growled Dragonite. Reeling from the blow, he sneered in contempt. "You are no brother of mine!"

"We are of the same brotherhood," responded Silas, his staff's crystal poised to strike. "Mind you, as you delve into the black arts, I suppose you are no longer one of us."

"What I do is my own business. What brings you here?"

"Pancecilia Feldspar had warned me that you were up to mischief," replied Silas. "In fact, that is how we all came to be here."

"Curse that wretched Fairy! And I will have you know, I do not deal in mischief. I only dispense full-scale death and carnage!"

"With an army composed of mimes?" queried Silas, glances about at those still remaining to fight. "They are not trained soldiers. They are performers and they are doing a poor job of it! Now, put a stop to this madness."

"Or what?" growled the Sorcerer. "You will kill me?"

"If I must."

"That will never happen," said Dragonite, lowering his staff as he stood at ease.

"So, you will surrender?"

"Only after you're dead!" snarled the Sorcerer, his staff swinging out to strike Silas down.

"Why must you always be so difficult?" cursed Silas, deflecting this blow with the end of his staff as he countered this attack. "I know your powers are limited in the daylight. You have already squandered your magic threatening your minions into action."

"You are a fool to underestimate my abilities!" The Sorcerer attacked with a vengeance, battling staff to staff against the Wizard.

"And you are more the fool to test mine!" grunted Silas, knocking Dragonite's weapon from his face as the Sorcerer took aim with his orb.

Dragonite backed away, his crystal still poised to strike his nemesis down. Braced to unleash his magic, the Sorcerer willed the orb to discharge a great bolt of light.

Anticipating this attack, Silas used his magic to shield him from this assault. As the frenetic energy discharged by their orbs collided, a brilliant swell of white light erupted with a thunderous explosion as Silas' powers overwhelmed Dragonite. The force of the impact sent the Sorcerer hurling through the air into the thick of the forest.

"Quickly!" shouted Silas, waving Rainus on to follow him. "We must contain Dragonite before he disappears once more!"

"Should he flee to the east, the Dwarves have set up defensive lines along their borders," informed Rainus, motioning his men to join in the search. "He will not get far, should he try."

The percussive force of this explosion jolted the dazed Princess awake. Her eyes opened in time to see a handsome, young man with exquisite taste in apparel leading the pursuit.

"He came," marvelled Rose, easing herself up onto her elbow.

"Who was that?" asked Tag, watching as the old man wearing a garish cloak embellished with moons and stars took off after the Sorcerer.

"That dashing young man was the Dream Merchant," disclosed the Princess, as Tag helped her back onto her feet.

"You must have taken a knock to your head," decided Tag. "I assure you, that was a wizened, old man dashing off after the Sorcerer."

"I see him as I wish him to appear," explained Rose. "Hence, the princely good looks."

"Say no more, that explains everything," said Tag, watching as the Elves joined the Wizard in his bid to hunt the Sorcerer down.

"What happened?" asked Rose, glancing about in confusion to see dead mimes scattered about. Among them, there were those only feigning their demise. They only moved when King Maxmillion's soldiers went from man to man, rounding up the survivors.

"Dragonite's army was overwhelmed. It appears the Tooth Fairy sent word to the Elves."

"She did?" asked Rose.

"Our alliance with those we met along the way came in handy on this day," disclosed Tag, pulling Cankles back onto his wobbling legs. He propped his friend up as Cankles collapsed onto his knees, still trembling from the effects of Dragonite's magic.

"But what happened to that ghastly Sprite?" questioned Rose, her eyes searching about for the dragon.

"You defeated the creature," informed Tag.

"No!" gasped Rose, shaking her head in doubt.

"He speaks the truth, Princess," confirmed Cankles. "In a move that was nothing short of brilliant, you became a wasp. Just when we thought all was lost an' that dragon had swallowed you alive, you stung him in his throat!"

"I did?"

"Most certainly," confirmed Tag. "He swelled up like a bloated puffer fish!"

"Coughed you up 'cause he couldn't even swallow his own spit!" added Cankles.

"Where is he?" asked Rose.

"Don't rightly know, Princess," answered Cankles. "Last we saw, he was sailing above the trees after I gave him a hard boot to the backside."

"So he will be back for his revenge?" queried Rose, her eyes shadowed in dread.

"He was in a sorry state," responded Tag, as he sheathed his sword. "If we're lucky, he is either dead or dying."

"Let us hope," prayed Rose.

20

Between the Cracks

"And just where did you learn to fight?" questioned Tag, glancing over at Cankles as he brushed the dust and dirt from his cloak. "You handled the sword with surprising skill."

"Thank you, but I merely did what any man would've done," replied Cankles. "Was a natural response, I suppose."

"No need for such modesty," said Tag. "A natural response is to wildly hack and slash. I've seen knights in training. You handled this weapon as though you had trained all your life."

Rose frowned in confusion as she stared at the man. "How can that be? He is the village id-- "

"Idol!" interjected Tag. "He'd be idolized by villagers far and wide had they been witness to his great feat of today. He battled the demented Sorcerer with skill and incredible courage."

"Such kind words," responded Cankles, blushing with embarrassment.

Rose muttered in doubt, "I suppose I would believe it had I seen it with mine own eyes."

"Just know I was duly impressed," praised Tag, giving his friend a nod of approval.

"Well, I'll tell you now, you'll never see me handle a sword again," vowed Cankles. "Unless it's to save a life, I can't say it was a pleasant experience at all."

"I hate to be the one to cast a shadow on his abilities, but if his skills with the sword were as good as you claim, then why did the Sorcerer escape?" questioned Rose, looking to Tag for an explanation.

"He was holding his own until Dragonite used the powers of the forbidden arts. Cankles fought valiantly, but the Sorcerer overpowered him with magic when he feared defeat. Even the Dream Merchant was challenged in battling Dragonite."

"I will give you that, but where is the Wizard?" asked Rose, glancing over as Rainus Silverthorn emerged from the forest alone.

"As we speak, Master Agincor continues to search with my men for the Sorcerer," informed Rainus. "He is determined to hunt Dragonite down and bring him to justice."

"I was so hoping to have a word with the Wizard," said Rose, unleashing a dismal sigh. "If anyone could have told me where I'd find my locket, it would have been him."

"A silver locket? One in the shape of a heart?" queried Rainus.

"You have seen it?"

"A mere four days ago, if that, Princess."

"Where?" asked Tag.

"It was in the possession of Pancecilia Feldspar," explained Rainus. "When she delivered news of Dragonite rallying his forces in a bid to capture you to steal away with the dreamstone, I recall seeing it then."

"Did she say what she intended to do with the locket?" queried Rose.

"I remember she said she had underestimated your will to find this trinket and she had unintentionally endangered your life and the lives of others when you chose to undertake this quest to retrieve it," answered Rainus.

"But where did she take it?" questioned Tag. "Surely she told you something."

"I only recall her muttering something about hiding it where it rightfully belongs," responded the Elf. "I suspect she meant to deliver the locket back to where she got it from."

"The palace!" exclaimed Tag.

"Miracle of miracles! I was right," marvelled Cankles.

"Miracle indeed," responded Rose. "And speaking of miracles, I have one wish left before day's end."

"I have an idea," said Tag. "We need to go home."

"Back to my palace?" queried Rose.

"No. We are going to Cankles' cottage."

"Is your mind cracked?" asked Rose, staring suspiciously at Tag. "My *heart* would not be there!"

"Just trust me," urged Tag.

"Oh, my!" gasped Cankles, glancing about in confusion. "I thought we were going back to my place."

"We are," stated Rose.

"It is?" questioned Cankles, as he admired the transformation. "This charming, little cottage is my home?"

Instead of the clutter he was accustomed to, his humble abode was spotlessly clean. A fine oak table and a set of four matching chairs replaced the rickety one with the carved stumps used as seating.

All the cracked earthenware cups and dishes had vanished and in its place, the finest porcelain ware graced the table and cupboards. Even the once grime-covered windows were cleaned and adorned with lace curtains as the fading sun shone through to reveal all dust bunnies had been vanquished and the floor was free of hairballs and pools of dog drool, as Honk and Puke waited outside, hoping to be let in.

"I hope you do not take offense, but I thought I would take full advantage of the wish to make this stay in your home as bearable as possible."

"No offense taken, Princess," responded Cankles, sliding a chair from the table to seat Rose first. "I can get used to this."

"Don't get too cozy," advised Tag. "We shall bide our time until the midnight hour passes, and then we'll ride to the palace."

"Can we not rest for the night and be off at first light?" asked Rose, feeling more at ease in these hospitable surroundings she created. "It is not as though we have far to go now."

"I thought you were in a hurry to get this quest done?" responded Tag.

"I am," admitted Rose. "However, after last night's encounter with the evil Sprite while you two slept, and then doing battle with that deranged being as a dragon, I am now utterly exhausted."

"What say you, young master?" asked Cankles. "It's not like the palace will be goin' anywhere. What's one more night?"

"Please," begged Rose. She stared with doleful, puppy eyes at Tag.

"I'll allow it. But don't believe for a moment it's because of those eyes, Princess."

As darkness settled, inside this quaint cottage the trio shared in a well-deserved meal that did not consist of the stale dregs from the bottom of an ale cask and freshly roasted water rats. And as the night wore on, they settled down for a restful night of sleep, undisturbed by the shape-shifting Sprite or other potential dangers.

In the morning when Rose awoke, the sun was barely peering over the horizon, but Tag and Cankles were already preparing the horses for the ride to Pepperton Palace.

She wiped the sleep from her eyes as she stumbled to the door.

"We are leaving now?" asked Rose.

"As soon as you eat, we'll go," answered Tag, brushing his stallion's coat before placing the saddle blanket on. "Breakfast is on the table. It's nothing fancy, but it'll do."

A simple meal consisting of a cup of milk, a slice of buttered bread, one soft boiled egg and a dish of stewed prunes awaited her.

Her delicate features screwed up in disgust as she glared at the bowl of wrinkled fruit.

"I hate – "

Rose immediately bit her tongue. The last time she said she hated prunes, in the eyes of all in the palace, she became as wrinkled as one of these overgrown raisins. Sitting down at the table, she took up a spoon. Rose devoured each prune as this one thought entered her mind: *Mother would be proud of me.*

The ride to the palace was thankfully uneventful. This early in the morning, only those tending to their crops or milking their cows and goats were up and about. They acknowledged the trio's passing with a friendly wave, unaware the young maiden in the company of Tag and Cankles was the Princess of Fleetwood.

As they approached the moat surrounding the palace grounds, Tag issued a warning to his comrades, "Don't say a word. I'll do the talking."

The loud plodding of hooves against the wooden planks of the drawbridge caused the two drowsy soldiers guarding the gateway to abruptly stand at attention as their pikes lowered, crossing over to block their way.

"Halt!" called one of the soldiers. "What business have you here?"

"It's me, Tagius Yairet."

"Tag? Where have you been all this time? You've been gone for as long as Princess Rose has been missing," noted the soldier.

"We've been on an adventure of sorts."

"*We?*" probed the soldier, glancing over at the two strangers in his company.

It was apparent these men were still affected by the curse Rose had set into motion. Before Tag could explain, the other soldier chirped up, "Say... That's the old hag we chased from the palace when the Princess first disappeared."

"You are mistaken, sir," lied Rose. "I have never been here before."

The first soldier stared at the old peasant on the white mare. With critical eyes, he scrutinized her. "Come to think of it, you do look familiar."

Before the soldier could sound his horn to alert the captain, Tag's foot came up, kicking the man in his chest. His horse spun about, its rump knocking against the second soldier. With a loud *sploosh* the men landed in the moat, floundering about in the stagnating water.

"Quickly!" ordered Tag, the heels of his boots urging the stallion on. Before the guard manning the gate could drop the portcullis, they charged through. Cankles was forced to duck, coaxing his mount to a full gallop as the iron grate crashed down to snag strands of the horse's tail as it bolted through.

As soldiers dashed to the stairs of the keep to form a physical barrier, Tag spurred his steed on as Rose and Cankles' mounts followed close behind, their hooves clattering up the stone steps.

Knights and soldiers scattered, forced from the path of the on-coming horses as Tag led the charge.

"Guard the King and Queen!" hollered the captain, waving his soldiers on to pursue the intruders. "After them!"

Once inside, Tag dismounted, as did Rose and Cankles. With a slap on his stallion's rump, he sent the three horses bolting from the keep and down the stairs to send the men scattering once again.

"Follow me!" ordered Tag, dashing to the stairs leading to the palace kitchen.

"But my bedchamber is that way!" exclaimed Rose, pointing in the opposite direction.

"So is the throne room," responded Tag, bounding down the steps three at a time. In the distance, the thunder of footfalls echoed as soldiers charged off to protect the monarchs from the intruders. "We need to hide!"

Peering into the kitchen, the only sounds were the crackling of wood in the fireplace. Outside, they could hear Mildred with the domestic staff as they took care of the daily laundry chores.

"In here, quickly!" ordered Tag, yanking open the door to the broom closet.

The old, grey tomcat that roamed the palace grounds hunting for pesky rodents peered up at them. Napping on a cushioned chair by the fireplace, the cat meowed loudly as the trio scrambled to hide in the closet. Cankles closed the door behind them as the captain shouted orders for several of the knights to check the kitchen for the intruders.

Rose and Cankles pressed their backs to the wall. Their hands held steady the broom and mop handles to prevent them from falling over while Tag crouched, peering through the keyhole.

For what felt like an eternity, they dared not move, not even breathing as they waited for the knights to move on.

Spying through the hole, Tag watched as one knight pulled open the trapdoor situated in the floor to inspect the root cellar as another ducked outside to check with Mildred if she had seen any unsavoury characters lurking about. Tag's heart jumped to his throat. He watched as the third knight slowly turned in the direction of the broom closet.

"No!" Tag whispered under his breath. He braced the door latch so it would seem locked.

Just as the man's hand reached out to test the door, his comrade returned from outside as the other dropped the trapdoor, frustrated with his search.

"The ladies said no one has come by this way since breakfast," announced the knight who had spoken to Mildred.

"They must be hiding on the main floor," decided the third knight, instructing his comrades to head back up.

The trio breathed a collective sigh of relief as the knights' footsteps faded away in the distance.

"The palace is crawling with men by now," groaned Rose. "They will be sure to see us no matter what route we take to get to my bedchamber."

"If that's indeed where the locket is," reminded Cankles.

"Where else would it be?" argued Rose. "One thing is for certain, with the knights on high alert, it will only be a matter of time before we are captured."

"Then we must take appropriate action," decided Tag, staring through the keyhole to ascertain the room was abandoned. "You must make it so we can move through the keep unnoticed."

"How am I to do that?" asked Rose.

"The dreamstone," reminded Tag, motioning for her and Cankles to follow him out of the broom closet. "Now quickly, make it so."

"Do not even ask me to wish for us to be invisible," grumbled the Princess. "I do not even know how I would begin imagining something like that."

"Then make us small," ordered Tag, quietly closing the closet door, "so small we'll slip by undetected."

"As small as a mouse?" questioned Rose, clasping the magic crystal in her hand.

Recalling how the Princess had easily spotted Squeakers his pet mouse when they were last in the kitchen, Tag made his request. "Much smaller! As small as a ladybug."

"Oh, I do like ladybugs!" exclaimed Cankles.

"I can manage that," responded Rose, closing her eyes to focus on the task.

"Do so quickly," demanded Tag; hearing Mildred's voice just outside the kitchen as she explained to Evelyn the evils of beating a dusty rug too close to freshly hung laundry. "Wish before we are found out!"

It was at this very moment the cat resting by the fireplace decided to hop down to greet the Princess. It was as though the old feline knew Rose despised it when he'd rub up against her legs, shedding enough fur to knit a sweater to dress another cat. Just as the crystal worked it's magic to shrink the trio in size, the animal was caught in the wake of its powers. With a startled meow, the cat shrank down, too. For a bewildering moment, its amber eyes just stared at Rose, Tag and Cankles. Although the cat was now the size of a humongous beetle, the humans were no bigger than the smallest of ladybugs, making them the perfect sized meal.

"Good gracious!" squeaked Cankles, staring up at the huge cat.

"Run!" hollered Tag.

In a mad sprint back to the closet, they did not even duck to fit beneath the closed door as the cat gave chase, easily fitting through the gap between the floor and the door.

The race to the hole in the wall Squeakers used to evade this cat was out of the question. They watched in horror as the feline scampered ahead, blocking their escape.

"Over here!" shouted Rose, pointing to the gaps between the flagstone floor where bits of mortar had broken off and had long since been swept away. They dove down, falling between the cracks as the cat's moist nose pressed against the flat stones to sniff out its intended meal.

"Get down!" ordered Tag, squeezing Rose into a crevice as the needle-sharp tips of curved claws probed about, hoping to snag a meal.

Rose screamed in fright as one of the claws managed to catch Cankles by the hood of his cloak as he crouched down to protect his head. Tag used his sword, stabbing at one of the toe pads in hopes that it would be enough to make the cat sheathe its claws and drop his friend. Instead, Tag jabbed at the fur between the toe pads as the cat fished Cankles out from the crack.

"Stay here!" shouted Tag.

He jumped, pulling himself up onto the flagstone to confront the beast. Brandishing his sword, he charged after the cat as it sauntered off to dine while Cankles dangled from its mouth, frantically struggling to be free.

The cat hissed, spinning about to face Tag. Instead of retreating, he jabbed at the animal, stabbing its front paw. Instead of dropping its prey, the cat shook off the prick of the sword. Tag attacked once more, shouting at the beast, "Unhand him, you monster!"

Just as he slashed at its paw again, the cat was physically yanked back. A pained caterwauling rumbled from the animal's throat as it dropped Cankles. It spun about to face a new foe.

To Tag's astonishment, there was Squeakers, his pet mouse. As big as a draft horse, the rodent now towered above the startled tomcat.

Tag had no intention of waiting to see what was about to happen with this strange encounter between cat and mouse. He grabbed Cankles by the shoulders of his raiment, dragging him back to the safety of the crack in the flooring where he left Rose.

They both tumbled into this recess as a loud hiss and bloodcurdling *meow* filled the air. An eerie silence followed, but it was abruptly broken by a loud crunch and the unmistakable sounds of munching.

Tag reluctantly peered up to see a macabre sight. The mouse was snacking on a feline morsel, the cat's tail dangling limply from the corner of its mouth!

"Bloody hell! Rose, you've got to see this!" gasped Tag, watching as the rodent scampered away to finish its meal in the privacy of its nest. "Squeakers just ate the cat!"

"That is strangely disturbing!" said Rose, frowning in disgust. "I have no desire to watch."

"Didn't I tell you my mouse would save your life one day," reminded Tag, revelling in the irony of the cat's fate.

"Never mind my life!" gasped Rose. She knelt by Cankles as he groaned in pain, a hand pressing against his chest to staunch the flow of blood.

"Oh, no!" gasped Tag.

"The cat bit me hard. I'm gonna die," moaned Cankles.

"Don't move! You'll be fine," promised Tag. "We can fix this! Right, Princess?"

"I'm dyin'! Don't waste a wish on me," urged Cankles, grimacing in agony. "You'll need 'em to finish the quest."

"You don't know that," said Tag, cradling his friend's head on his lap.

"Neither do you," countered Cankles, his face taking on a sickly pallor as his life drained away.

"But suppose he is right?" asked Rose.

"Why are we arguing about this?" snapped Tag. "Do the right and decent thing, for pity's sake!"

"I'm a lost cause," groaned Cankles. "If there's a chance you'll be needin' the last wish to save yourself -- to break this curse, then go."

"No time for foolish sacrifices," argued Tag. "Please, Rose, you've got to do this."

"But to sacrifice for a friend... is no... sacrifice at all," countered

Cankles, his words faltering. He fought to breathe as blood filled his punctured lung. "Now, go. If you're... my friend, you'll... do this."

Rose was torn, glancing at Tag, and then as Cankles as his life force continued to slip away.

"Make him whole again! I beg of you! If you do, I swear, I'll never speak of being a knight again!" pleaded Tag, as Cankles fell unconscious in his arms. "I promise to be your jester forever!"

A hard lump caught in the back of Rose's throat as Tag's sadness overwhelmed her. It was the same devastated look that filled his eyes the day he received news from the King that his father had been killed in battle. Clutching the pendant to her heart, she immediately set to work.

Please! Please, let this wish come true! Rose prayed as memories of this dying man flashed through her mind; vivid images of Cankles standing by their side, valiantly coming to her rescue throughout their adventure or being the voice of reason when she and Tag were at odds. *From the bottom of my heart, I wish for him to be healed – to be whole again. Please, I will change my ways – I promise to be a better person if his life is spared.*

Rose opened her eyes, confident the dreamstone had worked its magic. She frowned in bewilderment as she gazed down at Cankles' lifeless form.

"Why didn't you use a wish?" gasped Tag, staring in disbelief.

"I -- I did!" she stammered.

"Then why this? Why didn't it work?" Tag's frustration boiled over as he gave Cankles a desperate shake.

"I tried! I really did!" insisted Rose, her eyes brimming with tears as grief seized her heart.

"Not hard enough!" rebuked Tag, dumping his friend's body onto the ground as he confronted her.

"*Ouch!*"

Tag and Rose glanced down to see Cankles' eyes flutter open as he propped himself up on his elbows.

"Cankles?" said Tag, unsure if he was hallucinating from grief.

"What happened?" Cankles moaned, shaking the fog from his head as he gazed over at his friends.

"You don't remember?" asked Tag, noticing that all traces of the injury and blood had miraculously disappeared.

"I remember the Pooka pluckin' me out of here..."

"Pooka?" repeated Rose. "Did you take a knock to your head? That was a cat!"

"Had amber eyes," explained Cankles, rubbing his noggin. "Just assumed it was the Pooka."

"Could've been, but we'll never know now," responded Tag. "There's nothing else you remember?"

"I recall you yellin' an' runnin' after the beast. After that, everything's a blur."

"The important thing is, you're alive," said Rose.

"You saved my life!" exclaimed Cankles, clasping Tag's hand in gratitude.

"Princess Rose did," responded Tag.

"You sacrificed one of your wishes to save me?" gasped Cankles, staring into Rose's eyes.

"For a friend? It was no sacrifice at all," answered Rose, as she hugged Cankles.

"Are you fit to move on?" questioned Tag.

"Never felt better!"

"What do we do now?" asked Rose, peering at the light shining from the gap between the floor and the closed door.

"We head to the most obvious place first," replied Tag, "your bedchamber."

"To claim my necklace?"

"If it's even in there," reminded Cankles.

"That is why we are going to begin our search there," explained Tag. "Failing that, we will go from room to room, working our way down until we find it."

"But suppose my heart is not in the palace?" questioned Rose.

"At this moment, there's no reason to believe it isn't," responded Tag.

"Correct me if I'm wrong, but isn't it a long way from this closet to your bedchamber? Especially being so puny?" asked Cankles.

"In my way of thinking, I believe we stand to face more danger back in our original size. The knights and soldiers have probably been instructed to kill us on sight now, so it poses more of a threat than to run into another cat in our present form," replied Tag.

"You do realize that to make the trek as we are now all the way to my bedchamber will be tantamount to journeying clear across Fleetwood?" questioned Rose, wondering how they were going to ascend the stairs.

"That is why you are going to use the last wish of the day to deliver us directly to the room in question," responded Tag.

"If I do this, we shall have to wait until midnight to use a wish to make us big again," reminded Rose.

"Being this small, we can easily hide until then," explained Tag.

"I am not big on long or arduous treks," admitted Rose. "Nor do I wish to encounter the captain and his knights."

"There you go then!" exclaimed Tag. "Wish us up there."

The tiny puff of golden light was barely noticeable in the sun drenched room as the trio materialized in Rose's bedchamber. It was exactly the way she had left it on the night she first made the ill-fated deal with the Tooth Fairy.

For a moment, they stared in awe at the immense size of this room Rose had often complained about as being too small.

"Over there," said Rose, pointing to the dresser near the open window. "If that locket is anywhere, it will be in my jewellery box."

"Let's hope you're right, Princess," responded Cankles, staring up at the sheer wall of oak to be conquered. "But how do we get up there?"

Tag glanced about, searching for a way to scale the furniture.

"Follow me," instructed Tag. He proceeded to climb the bed-skirt, using the holes in the eyelet embroidery as hand and footholds to scale the four-poster bed.

"You do know this is nowhere near the dresser?" asked Rose. She struggled to keep up, losing sight of Cankles and Tag as they disappeared each time their bouncing gait landed them in one of the billowy pockets making up the goose down counterpane.

"I know," responded Tag, sizing up the distance he must clear to land atop the nightstand. "But it's the only way to get over there."

Rose gasped, fearing for Tag's life as he took a running leap to clear the narrow gap between the bed and the nightstand. The edge of the pillow sham protruding over the edge of the bed was a mere inch from the side of this nightstand, but the distance to overcome was much more daunting when one is no bigger than a ladybug. Sailing over this yawning chasm, Tag landed hard, his ribs folding against the sharp edge as he fell short of his landing.

"Hold on, Master Yairet!" shouted Cankles. "I'm comin'!"

"I'm fine!" hollered Tag. "Stay where you are."

Using all his strength, Tag pulled his body up over the edge to safety. Taking a moment to catch his breath, he then scampered across the nightstand to the drawer that was left ajar when Pance tumbled off after being captured. Tag lowered himself down, disappearing from sight.

"Here we go!" announced Tag. A gold strand of embroidery thread poked out from the drawer.

"This is no time for needlework," scolded Rose, frowning as she watched Tag drag out a length of thread that was as big as a rope.

"We are going to use this," explained Tag, holding up the end of the thread as he pointed to the dresser, "to get from here to there."

"Brilliant!" praised Cankles.

"Yes, but just how do you intend to accomplish that?" asked Rose.

"*You* are going to do this," replied Tag, taking another running leap to land and tumble onto the sham.

"And *you* are crazy," countered the Princess.

"Do you still have your sling?" queried Tag. "Or more precisely, those steel balls?"

"Yes," responded Rose, removing the suede pouch from her sash. "How many do you need?"

"All of them," said Tag.

Taking the pouch from her hand, he wound the thread around it, before tying it off.

"This should do nicely," said Tag, feeling the weight.

"And what am I supposed to do with this?" asked Rose, as Tag passed it on to her.

"Do what you do best! Throw it," explained Tag. "Aim for one of the legs of your jewellery box."

"Are you mad?" grumbled Rose.

"You can do this. Just spin it like you're using the sling. Employ the same focus you use when you're aiming a shoe at one of your attendants."

"How did you know?" asked Rose, staring suspiciously at Tag as she blushed with embarrassment.

"Believe me, word gets around about your aim. Now, use it to get this rope to the other side. You throw, Cankles and I will handle the line to make sure it doesn't tangle."

"I suppose it is doable," decided Rose, testing the weight of the rope as it spun about. "It might take a few tries."

"Try as often as necessary," urged Cankles, setting the carefully coiled length of rope at her feet.

With focused determination, Rose's eyes remained fixed on her target. The weighted end whirred, spinning by her ear and getting louder with each revolution until, just as she aimed and exhaled on release, it flew from her hand.

"Yes!" exclaimed Cankles, his fists pumping the air in triumph as he watched the end of the rope wrap several times around the leg of the jewellery box.

"*No!*" hollered Tag. He dove forward, snatching up the end of the rope just before it disappeared over the edge of the bed.

"That was lucky!" gasped Cankles, yanking Tag away from the

sheer drop to the floor below. "I thought you had it."

"I thought *you* did," responded Tag, his heart still thundering in his chest.

"Well, it's obvious neither of you were holding the rope," scolded Rose, snatching the thread from Tag's hand to lash it around the bedpost.

"No harm done, Princess," assured Cankles. "We have it now."

"We'll go nice and easy. If your hands tire, to give them a rest just slip your arm – the crook of your elbow over the rope until you can move on," said Tag, testing the line with a hard jerk. "I'll go first."

"Good idea," agreed Rose.

At first tentative, and then moving with confidence as the rope held up to his weight, Tag shouted for his comrades to follow as he advanced, hand over fist.

"Ladies first," offered Cankles. "I'll be right behind you, Princess."

"Are you positive it is safe?" questioned Rose.

Tag threw his legs over the line, wrapping his ankles together as his hands let go so he could dangle upside down for her to see. "Do you think I'd be doing this if it wasn't?"

"Could be the famous last words of a show-off," grumbled Rose. Her knuckles whitening as she gripped the rope, easing her body off the quilt to dangle over the dowry chest at the foot of her bed.

She glanced down, only to gasp as she squeezed her eyes shut.

"Don't look down!" ordered Tag, hanging by his hands again as he moved on. "Just keep going. Be quick about it! The faster you move, the easier it'll be on your hands."

"He's right, Princess. Go on! One hand at a time," urged Cankles.

Rose's eyes snapped open as the rope grew taut, seeming to drop slightly as Cankles added his weight to the line.

"I'm going! I'm going!" yelped Rose. Instead of inching along, she threw one hand over the other to catch up to Tag.

"Take it easy!" hollered Tag, holding tight as he felt the rope vibrate under Rose's frantic movements.

Rose struggled to distance the gap. She fought to hold on as the rope quivered in her grip from Tag and Cankle's combined movements.

"Careful now!" called Cankles, coming up behind her. "You're almost there."

With the palm of her hands growing slick with sweat, her only consolation was that Tag was nearing the end of this treacherous trek and she was right behind him.

"Just a little more," said Tag. His fingertips trembled as they strained to reach solid ground on the dresser's surface. Just as he gripped the edge, he yelped in surprise. Rose screamed in fright as the rope they clung to suddenly dropped, and then jerked to a stop.

"Bloody hell!" cursed Cankles, glancing about nervously. "What the heck was that?"

"The knot's coming apart!" cried Tag, seeing how it was loosened by their movements to slip down the bedpost. His hand lunged up to grab the edge of the dresser as he hollered, *"Move!"*

All three screamed as the knot unravelled. The rope they clung to abruptly fell limp. They were slammed against the top drawer, the impact jarring Rose so hard she lost her grip. Cankles reached down, seizing her by the wrist before she fell beyond his grasp.

"I won't let you fall, Princess!" vowed Cankles. He felt her fingernails sink into his flesh as her hand wrap around his wrist. "Jus' hold on a little longer."

He waited for Tag to pull himself to safety before instructing Rose to use her free hand to grab a hold of the rope so she could climb. As soon as Cankles reached the top, clambering onto the dresser, he and Tag took up the rope, quickly pulling Rose up the rest of the way.

Back on solid ground, they collapsed, flopping onto their backs in utter exhaustion.

"I thought you tied the rope off, Princess," said Tag, wiping the sweat from his brows.

"I did, but now I remember why I was never any good at needlework," responded Rose, recalling some of her works unravelling because she did not listen to her mother's instructions about properly tying off the loose threads.

"That could've been the death of us," admonished Tag.

"I am truly sorry," apologized Rose.

"Can't go blamin' the Princess, Master Yairet. After all, that knot jiggled free from all three of us climbin' about," reasoned Cankles.

"I suppose you're right," admitted Tag, his racing heart slowing a beat as he composed himself. "At least we're still alive."

"An' able to complete this quest," added Cankles.

Rose hopped onto her feet. Using the designs etched into the wooden jewellery box inlaid with iridescent tiles of mother-of-pearl, she clambered inside, disappearing amidst the precious stones and pieces of gold.

Tag and Cankles followed, wading through the glittering sea made up of a regular treasure trove of necklaces, bracelets and other pieces of jewellery.

"Oh my! With all this gold, it shouldn't be hard to spot a silver chain and pendant," decided Cankles, climbing over a massive ring studded with a perfect pear-shaped ruby.

"Here it is!" announced Rose, digging through the jewels to uncover the heart-shaped locket.

Tag and Cankles picked up the silver chain, pulling it free as Rose struggled to push jewellery out of the way. It was like digging for buried treasure within a heap of treasures.

"A little more!" grunted Tag, tugging on the chain that was tangled around a gold bracelet.

Just as they uncovered the locket, the trio gasped in surprise. The items filling the jewellery box abruptly lost their sparkle as a dark shadow was cast down upon them.

Rose screamed in terror as a huge goldfinch fluttered into the room to perch upon the edge of the jewellery box. It's head cocked from side to side as it stared down at this dazzling display of decadence.

"Shoo! Go away!" shouted Cankles, waving the bird off.

Instead, the bird's beak slammed down, narrowly missing Cankles as Tag pulled him out of the way. Aborting a second attack, the finch hopped into the jewellery box to seize the silver chain Tag and Cankles had been pulling on.

"No!" shouted Rose, staring in disbelief as the bird took flight with the locket in its clawed feet.

Tag dove forward, grabbing the links of the bracelet that had snagged onto the locket, becoming more entangled as the finch attempted to fly away. Being larger and stronger than this tiny version of Tag, the bird took off, only to be hampered as Rose leapt up, throwing her arms around Tag's legs.

She screamed in surprise as the finch's wings fluttered wildly, lifting both she and Tag off until Cankles seized her by the ankle with both hands. He braced his feet against the corner of the jewellery box, using it as an anchor as he held onto the Princess for dear life.

"Let go, Tag!" ordered Rose. "Just let it go!"

"But you'll never get it back!" argued Tag, clinging to the tangled bracelet that prevented the bird from flying away with her locket.

"You'll die!" said Rose, knowing that Tag would never survive a fall whether it was from the top of this dresser or the palace window.

"I -- I can't hold -- hold on for much longer," grunted Cankles, grimacing in pain as he struggled to maintain his grip on the Princess as the bird continued to tug at the locket.

"Let go, Tag!"

"But this is your only chance to break the curse!" The hard edge of the precious metal cut into Tag's hands as he fought to hang on.

"I don't care!" snapped Rose.

Realizing he was not about to let this bird make off with her locket, even if it killed him, she did the first and only thing that came to mind. Rose's teeth sank into the fleshy bit of muscle just above his ankle.

"Owww!" wailed Tag. Instinctively, his hands released their hold on the chain to nurse the sharp pain she inflicted on him.

Just as Tag let go, the sudden lack of resistance caused the struggling goldfinch to tumble through the air. It struck the sill to bounce off through the open window as the silver necklace fell from its grasp. The locket hit the floor, its two halves popped open as a loud boom sounded, sending a resonating shockwave rippling through the air.

Cankles crashed onto the floor. He groaned in pain as Rose fell by him, her head landing on his midriff to knock the wind out of him as Tag tumbled off the dresser. He landed on top of her, lying nose-to-nose with the Princess as they stared into each other's startled eyes. For a moment, there was only silence as they felt their racing hearts beating against each other.

"Oh, my! This is awkward!" groaned Cankles, breaking this strange hush as he glanced at the pair.

"What just happened?" gasped Rose, pushing Tag off her body.

"You bit me, that's what!" sputtered Tag, as he rubbed his smarting ankle. "I can't believe you did that!"

"Nor can I!" groaned Rose, wiping her mouth with the back of her hand. "But look at us!"

"Hey! We're back to our normal size!" marvelled Cankles. He sprawled out on the floor next to the locket. Picking it up, he held it forth for all to admire.

"The curse is broken!" announced Tag, staring back into Rose's confused eyes.

"But how?" asked Rose, scrutinizing the locket that had popped open as it hit the floor, bending at its hinge from the force so it would no longer close properly.

"Don't you get it?" asked Tag, pulling Rose onto her feet. "The Fairy was using the heart-shaped locket as a metaphor for your heart."

"A meta-what?" questioned Cankles, as he frowned in bewilderment.

"But I don't understand. Pance said the curse would remain until I find my heart and until I know what it is like when nobody loves me."

"You did!" explained Tag. "Pance meant that to *find* your heart, you were to have a *change* of heart. You found it in your heart to use a wish to save Cankles' life first. And then, by biting me, as strange as it sounds, you saved my life, too. You gave up that necklace for something you placed above your own personal wants and needs."

"Sounds reasonable to me, but who is Toy?" questioned Cankles, picking up the silver locket for her to see.

"Toy?" repeated Rose, staring at the letters engraved inside the locket.

A tiny message read: *Friends forever... Love T.O.Y.*

"Tagius Oliver Yairet..." whispered Rose, as her fingertip touched this inscription. "You gave this to me."

"So I did," admitted Tag. His face flushed with embarrassment as he recalled how she hugged him so hard when she first received this gift, the other young boys who loathed this kind of close contact with any girl teased him for days on end.

"Maybe that's it, Princess," decided Cankles. "You always said Tag was a *nobody* and it states right here, as clear as day, that he loves you."

"That was another time," dismissed Tag, his face still burning red.

"Perhaps that was all it took," said Rose.

"Or maybe it was a combination of these things," offered Cankles. "For you did show your true heart when you bit the young master."

"I hardly think a vicious assault on Tag's person would reflect well on me in the Fairy's eyes," countered Rose.

"But in your heart, why did you do it?" asked Tag.

"Because I cared more if you were to die than I cared about that silly locket."

"You do?" asked Tag.

"You are an idiot!" snapped the Princess, her cheeks glowing as fiercely as his. "Of course I do."

"Then that must be it! Your true character shone through in that one, nasty bite!" determined Tag.

"Perhaps I should have bit you harder," teased Rose.

They turned with a start as the door flew open.

"I thought I heard voices," said King William, as he peered into the room. "And just what are you doing with these two in your bedchamber, Princess Rose-alyn? Do you mean to start the people's tongues wagging?"

"It's not what you think, Your Highness," explained Tag.

"Silence, young man! You have no idea what I am thinking at this moment!"

"But, father," pleaded Rose, "I can vouch for his good character."

"And who will vouch for yours, child?" snapped the King, scowling in disapproval. "Ever since you acquired the dreamstone, you have been less than prudent in your use of it. That crystal has brought nothing but grief! Give it to me. I shall do away with it. And as further punishment, give me that cursed locket, too!"

"But it's broken," said Rose, her finger fondling the bent hinge. "It is worthless now!"

"Well, I suppose that is punishment enough if it can no longer be used. Now, give me the dreamstone," ordered the King, extending his hand expectantly.

Rose stared at her father, for never were his words to her so harsh.

"How did you know?" probed Rose. "I said nothing to you about the magic crystal."

"Never you mind! As your father, it is my business to know. Now give me the dreamstone."

"Though I no longer want it, it is not for me to give," responded Rose, her hand coming to rest over the crystal.

"But I do want it, so give it to me!" bellowed the King, his hand trembling in anticipation. "Or there will be great trouble in store for you, young lady."

Never before had her father seemed so eager to dispense punishment. This was no veiled threat. It was a promise of harsh retribution for failing to comply with his demand.

Rose undid the clasp of this necklace, holding the gold chain and its crystal before him.

The King gasped in delight. His hand reached out to seize it, only to meet up against the broad edge of Tag's sword.

"Your Highness, you in all your wisdom, a man who wants for naught knows there can be grave consequences in manipulating the powers of the dreamstone," warned Tag.

"I care not for the advice of a jester!" With a defiant roar, he shoved Tag into Cankles as he snatched the dreamstone from Rose.

"What is all the commotion in here?" asked King William, as he and Queen Beatrice rushed into the room.

"Father?" asked Rose, staring at the man standing at the doorway, and then glancing over to the one now coveting the dreamstone.

"Rose? Is that you?" gasped the Queen. She rushed in, hugging her daughter; grateful that she was still alive.

"You know me?" asked Rose, staring up into her mother's familiar eyes.

"What kind of question is that? Of course I know my own daughter!" exclaimed the Queen.

"Imposter!" shouted the King, pointing at his doppelganger clutching the magic crystal. "Guards! Seize him!"

Armed soldiers stormed the bedchamber just as Tag and Cankles scrambled to their feet. They lunged at the man to detain him, but all were forced to shield their eyes as a burst of light flooded the room.

"It's the Pooka!" hollered Tag, his sword slicing through the air as the shape-shifting Sprite morphed into a crow. In a flurry of ebony wings, Loken took evasive action; fluttering and darting about the room as the dreamstone dangled from his claws.

Before Cankles could race over to close the shutters, Loken flew straight out the window. Guards armed with bows attempted to strike the Sprite down with their arrows, but Loken's anxious caws launched into the air a great flock of crows perched in the courtyard trees. In a matter of seconds, not only did Loken dodge all the projectiles coming his way, he quickly became just one of the many raucous birds circling over the palace. Together, they winged over the battlement, flying off to become nothing more than specks against the northern sky.

"Bloody hell!" cursed Cankles. "He got away with the crystal!"

"What if he plans to deliver it to the Sorcerer?" asked Rose, dreading the worst outcome. "What are we going to do?"

"There's only one thing to do," responded Tag. He opened up the oak dowry chest at the foot of her bed to reclaim his father's sword. "Are you up for another quest?"

"I'm always up for a rousing adventure," chirped Cankles.

"Do I have a choice?" groaned Rose.

"Think of it as doing the right thing, Princess" encouraged Tag, flashing her a knowing smile as he unsheathed his cherished sword.

"Not so fast, young lady!" demanded Queen Beatrice.

"What do you mean?" asked Rose. Her nerves prickled under her mother's scathing tone.

"Before you go dashing off to who-knows-where to do who-knows-what, you have much to explain, my dear," answered the Queen. She braced herself for one of her daughter's rebellious tirades, only to see the scowl on Rose's face dissolve before her eyes.

"Of course, mother." She responded with an obedient nod as she lovingly clasped the Queen's hands into hers. "I wouldn't have it any other way. Now, where to begin?"

"Better make it quick, Princess," urged Tag, as he glanced out the window. "I sense something evil in the wind."

YA Fantasy Series
(in reading order)

The Dream Merchant Saga:
Book One, The Magic Crystal

The Dream Merchant Saga:
Book Two, The Silver Sword
(Publication date: 2011)

Adult Fantasy Series
(in reading order)

Imago Chronicles: Book One, A Warrior's Tale
Imago Chronicles: Book Two, Tales from the West
Imago Chronicles: Book Three, Tales from the East
Imago Chronicles: Book Four, The Tears of God
Imago Chronicles: Book Five, Destiny's End
Imago Chronicles: Book Six, The Spell Binder
Imago Chronicles: Book Seven, The Broken Covenant
Imago Prophecy (Prequel to Imago Chronicles series)
Imago Legacy (Sequel to Imago Prophecy)

About the Author

L.T. Suzuki is a fantasy novelist, script-writer and
a practitioner and instructor of the martial arts system,
Bujinkan Budo Taijutsu; a system incorporating
six traditional samurai schools and
three schools of ninjutsu.

For more information, please check out L.T. Suzuki's
*official website at: **http://web.me.com/imagobooks***

LaVergne, TN USA
15 September 2010
197033LV00004B/3/P